Unraveling the Truth About Love

Sweet with Heat: Weston Bradens

Addison Cole

ISBN-13: 978-1-948004-91-6
ISBN-10: 1-948004-91-7

UNRAVELING THE TRUTH ABOUT LOVE

Cover Design: Elizabeth Mackey Designs

WORLD LITERARY PRESS
PRINTED IN THE UNITED STATES OF AMERICA

A Note to Readers

Josh Braden has a lot on his shoulders, and when he finally finds the woman he wants to share it all with, their love is put to the test. Prepare yourself for an emotional ride. I hope you love Josh and Riley's story as much as I do.

Sign up for the Sweet with Heat newsletter to be notified of the next release, sales, and special events.
www.AddisonCole.com/Newsletter

About Sweet with Heat Novels

The Bradens are just one of the family series in the Sweet with Heat romance collection. All Sweet with Heat books may be enjoyed as stand-alone novels or as part of the larger series. There are no cliffhangers or unresolved issues, and characters from each series make appearances in future books, so you never miss an engagement, wedding, or birth. A list of Sweet with Heat titles is included at the end of this book.

Sweet with Heat novels are the sweet editions of the award-winning, steamy romance collection Love in Bloom written by *New York Times* bestselling author Melissa Foster. Addison Cole is Melissa's sweet-romance pen name. These emotional romances portray all the passion two people in love convey without any graphic love scenes and little or no harsh language (with the exception of an occasional "damn" or "hell"). For more explicit romance, please pick up Melissa's Love in Bloom series.
www.MelissaFoster.com

For more information on Sweet with Heat titles visit
www.AddisonCole.com

For Les

Chapter One

RILEY BANKS HURRIED down Thirty-Seventh Street in her red Catherine Malandrino dress and Giuseppe Zanotti leopard-print, calf-hair pumps. It was the week after Thanksgiving, and Manhattan was buzzing with the feverish zeal of the holidays. Riley slowed her pace to catch her breath. *Tomorrow I'll find the courage to take the subway. Maybe.* She tugged her coat tighter across her chest to ward off the chilly air and silently hoped that nobody would figure out that she'd purchased her outfit on Outnet.com, an online designer outlet store. She felt like such a hypocrite, heading to her first day at her new job as one of world-renowned designer Josh Braden's assistants wearing discounted clothing. The thought turned her stomach—but not as much as showing up in her hometown jeans and cowgirl boots would have. She was a long way from Weston, Colorado, and she'd spent the last few weeks gathering discount designer clothes and practicing omitting "y'all" from her vocabulary.

She stood before the thick glass door of Josh Braden Designs and took a deep breath. The sign above the door read, JBD. *This is it.* She closed her eyes for a split second to repeat the mantra she'd been playing in her mind like a broken record for weeks: *I'm educated, knowledgeable, and eager. I can do this.*

A warm hand on her lower back pulled her from her thoughts.

"Have any trouble finding us?" Josh Braden stood beside her with a friendly smile and perfectly shorn, thick dark hair. His black Armani suit fit his lean, muscular frame perfectly. A few years earlier, he'd been named one of America's Most Eligible Bachelors. Back then she hadn't given the magazine cover a second thought. He was in New York, and she was back in Colorado, so far removed from him that she'd still thought of him as Josh Braden, the boy she'd had a crush on for too many years to count. Now, standing on the streets of New York City beside the man whose name rivaled Vera Wang, she felt the air sucked from her lungs.

His deep voice sent a shiver right through her. Not only had she had the good fortune to be reconnected with Josh when he was back home visiting his family, but during his visit, the two of them had also spent a few days getting reacquainted. Riley hadn't been sure if it was her crush going haywire or if there was something more real blossoming between them, but those few days had each felt a little more intimate than the last. And while their lips never touched and their bodies remained apart, she'd felt like they were always one breath away from falling into each other's arms.

"Uh...ye...no." *Oh, please kill me now.*

Josh smiled, lighting up his brown eyes. "Nervous?"

At five foot eight, she was a full seven inches shorter than him. She wondered what it might be like to stand on her tiptoes and kiss him on those luscious lips of his. *Stop it!* The way he held her gaze brought goose bumps to her arms. *Stopitstopitstopit.* She envisioned him at seventeen; he'd reached his full height by then, thin but well muscled, with testosterone

2

practically oozing from his pores. She'd wanted him then, but those schoolgirl feelings didn't come close to the desire that begged to be set free now. She cast her eyes away and took a deep breath, trying to ignore her thundering heart. The last thing she needed was to become one of those girls who swooned every time her boss appeared. She was here to build a career, not a reputation.

"A little," she answered honestly.

He pulled the heavy door open and waited for her to walk through before placing his hand on the small of her back once again. Josh spoke softly, his mouth close to her ear as he guided her through the expansive lobby.

"Think of this as Macy's back home. There's the customer service area." He nodded toward the elegant mahogany and granite reception desk.

Her heels clacked across the marble tile as they passed the desk.

"Good morning, Chantal." Josh smiled at the blond woman behind the desk, who looked like she'd come straight from an eight-hour session at a local salon. Her hair glistened, and her green eyes were perfectly shadowed to match her emerald-green blouse.

Riley reached up and touched her shoulder-length brown hair, feeling the little confidence she'd mustered being whittled away. *If the receptionist is that perfect, what are the other employees like?*

"Good morning, Mr. Braden," Chantal said with a practiced smile. "Good morning, Riley."

You know my name? Riley pushed past her rattled nerves, forcing her mouth to obey her thoughts, and felt the grace of a smile. "Good morning...Chantal." She pulled her shoulders back, reclaiming a bit of her lost confidence. *She knows my name!*

"Chantal is an assistant in the design studio. She fills in for our receptionist when she steps away from her desk. I'm sure you'll see her in the design studio later," Josh explained.

Riley felt like she was in a dream as she walked beside Josh through the elegant offices. She'd spent years dreaming of what it might feel like to work in New York City, and more specifically, in a design studio. After graduating with a degree in fashion design with a 3.8 GPA and winning two design awards, she'd longed to move to New York City and land a job in the design field. After several months of applying for positions and receiving enough rejection letters to wallpaper her bedroom, Riley had given up and settled into her life in Weston, working at Macy's and designing clothes no one would ever see. Riley had come to accept that working in the fashion industry had more to do with connections than skills. She'd given up that dream until Jade had begun dating Rex, one of Josh's older brothers, and she'd worn one of Riley's dresses on their first date. One recommendation from Rex, and a few days later Riley was having lunch at his father's ranch, Josh eagerly reviewed her portfolio, and the next thing she knew, she had a job offer and was packing to move to New York City. Now, as she walked beside Josh, Riley wondered if he was thinking about the time they'd spent together as much as she was.

They rounded a hall and Riley stifled a gasp. Racks of designer clothing lined the walls; dozens of fabric samples were strewn across long drawing tables, and sketches littered an entire wall. The combination sent her pulse soaring. Men and women milled about, talking quietly and fingering through the samples. A woman wearing jeans, her jet-black hair cut short, pulled a rolling cart filled with clothes across the floor. A man scurried around her with a notebook in hand, talking into an headset.

Without thinking, Riley grabbed Josh's arm—as if they were back in Weston at a farm show and he were Jade. "Oh my goodness. This is amazing!" she exclaimed.

He laughed, and several eyes turned in their direction.

Riley cringed. She must have looked like an excited child seeing Santa for the first time.

"I'm sorry," she said, frantically patting down Josh's suit sleeve. "I just…I'm so sorry." *Ugh, I'm an idiot.*

"That's the kind of reaction I'd hoped for," he said.

She let out a relieved sigh as a tall, auburn-haired woman appeared at Josh's side and locked her green eyes on Riley, then drew them down her dress, over her curvy figure, all the way to her heels.

"This must be Riley Banks?" She extended a pencil-thin arm in Riley's direction. "Claudia Raven, head design assistant."

Claudia's forced smile and threatening gaze reminded Riley of Cruella De Vil. There was no mistaking the way she pressed her right shoulder into Josh's back. Riley thought she saw him flinch, but his eyes never wavered from her, his smile never faltered, and she realized that she must have been projecting her own bodily response onto him. Every ounce of Riley's cognitive thought screamed, *Run! Run far and fast.* She wanted to flee from the awful woman who, by the look in her evil eyes, already hated her. The woman who silently staked claim to Josh. Instead, Riley forced a smile and took her hand in a firm grip.

"I'm honored to be working with you," she said, and tucked away any lingering thoughts about Josh. She needed a career, not a *Fatal Attraction* situation.

JOSH STIFLED A flinch at the feel of Claudia against him. She'd made no bones about being open to sleeping her way to the top, and while at first he'd found her innuendos comical, recently he'd begun to loathe them. But she was a dedicated worker and had been with JBD for five years, the last two as the head design assistant. She hadn't slept her way to that position. Josh had better scruples than that, even if to an outsider Claudia might appear to be the "right" kind of woman for him. He couldn't deny that she was attractive, intelligent, and she knew the design business inside and out. But Josh had seen the other side of Claudia—the manipulative, competitive-to-the-point-of-nasty side—and those were qualities that Josh was not looking for in a lover. As the niece of one of his oldest supporters, Josh felt trapped by loyalty to keep her on staff.

He was impressed by Riley's steely, though professional, reserve. He doubted that Claudia or anyone else could tell that her smile was forced. They couldn't know that the way her lips pulled tightly at the corners was different from the casual, natural smile Riley usually possessed. And they wouldn't notice the underlying discomfort in her hazel eyes, the discomfort that Josh recognized and longed to soothe.

He couldn't seem to remove his hand from her back. The feel of her curves beneath his palm were refreshing. The women he'd dated were usually pencil thin. Going out to dinner equated to watching skeletons graze on leafy greens, with fake smiles plastered on their artificially plumped lips and dollar signs in their eyes. Then again, Josh's dates had primarily been setups from business colleagues who believed he needed to date the "right" women for his social status. Over the past year or so, he'd become disenchanted with those expectations, and he'd taken to dating fewer and fewer of them, but that was a thought for another time.

"I can take her from here," Claudia said, pushing between them.

Josh reluctantly removed his hand. He looked into Riley's eyes again, remembering how he'd been drawn to her when they were teens. The way her eyes had always been like windows to her emotions. Even back then he'd known when she was happy or sad, angry or bored. He had an urge to put his arm around her and soothe away the worry that lay there, but just behind that worry, he saw excitement mounting, and he knew she'd fare just fine—at least he hoped she would.

"Riley, I'm glad you're here." Josh ignored the narrowing of Claudia's eyes and the iciness that surrounded her like a cloak. "If you need anything, just let Claudia know. She'll take good care of you. Right, Claudia?" He took pleasure in nudging Claudia out of her villainous stare.

"Thanks, Josh. I appreciate everything. I won't let you down," Riley said.

"Shall we?" Claudia grabbed her arm and dragged her away.

Josh headed for his office, thinking about Riley. Her designs were really good—fresh and stylistic in a way that was different from the typical New York trends. He'd have brought her on as a junior designer if he hadn't believed that she needed to first learn the down-and-dirty side of the business. Claudia's designs, on the other hand, left much to be desired, as did her people skills, but as head design assistant, he knew she was the cream of the crop. Organized, efficient, dedicated, and never missed a deadline. Claudia kept the staff in line, even if a little heavy-handedly. He hoped she'd put away her claws long enough to teach Riley the ins and outs of the fashion world.

If not, he thought, *I just might have to do it myself.*

Chapter Two

"THIS IS THE design studio," Claudia said. She waved a hand at the tables as they passed. "Everything happens here as far as design is concerned, but it'll be a while before you sit at one of those tables."

"Yes, of course," Riley agreed, taking note of how the other employees put their heads down as Claudia passed. She wanted to run up and greet each of them. *Hi. I'm Riley Banks. I can't wait to work with you!* But she already knew better than to irk Cruella. She wondered how a cold fish like Claudia got the job working for someone as warm as Josh in the first place. *Is there another side of Josh that I'm not seeing?* Riley made a mental note to watch how other employees reacted to Josh. Maybe he was one of those guys who knew how to charm women but sometimes forgot to hide their wolfhound ways. She didn't want to believe that the Josh she'd spent time with would have that side to him, but Riley was a realist. *Anything is possible.*

"Fashion design is not for the faint of heart. There are few pats on the back but plenty of harsh stares, head shakes, and starting over." Claudia led Riley into a cubicle at the far end of the open studio. "This is where you'll work."

Riley felt her smile falter. She tried to right her frown but feared she'd failed. The dingy metal desk tucked into the tiny cubicle looked more like something that belonged in a ware-house than a design studio. She eyed the computer and the cloth rolling chair with distaste. *You're here. That's all that matters.* She couldn't help but feel that this was Claudia's way of showing her who was the superior design assistant. She wouldn't be taken down by her—or anyone else, for that matter. She was there to make a career, and Josh must have believed in her design skills to have hired her. She smiled, meeting Claudia's one-upping, cold eyes.

"This is perfect. Nice and private." Riley set her purse in the desk drawer. "Where do I start?"

BY SEVEN O'CLOCK, Riley's feet ached. She wasn't used to wearing four-inch heels all day, but then again, she was used to working at Macy's in her hometown, where "heels" meant fancy cowgirl boots and people greeted her like she mattered. She'd had time to chat with customers, other employees, and even her friends, when they'd swing by on their shopping trips. She'd laughed; she'd nearly cried when friends were having trouble— even at work, she'd let her emotions come through. At JBD, people worked as if they were on speed, and with Claudia watching her every move, she dared not be overly friendly with the other staff members just yet. She needed Claudia to like her, or at least to tolerate her.

"Still here?" Claudia peered into her cubicle, a Valentino bag hanging from her forearm.

"I'm just studying up on line sheets and tech packs, making organizational charts for myself to be sure I don't miss anything." *And maybe I'll run into Josh.* "I really appreciate all of the guidance you've given me today. There's so much to learn."

Claudia tilted her chin up. She spun around and said, "We'll see if you can keep up." Her voice trailed behind her as she left the office.

"I'll not only keep up. I'll shine," Riley whispered angrily. She waited until the click-clack of Claudia's heels disappeared before venturing out of her cubicle and was surprised to see almost everyone was gone for the evening. She eyed the design tables, taking one tentative step after another, her eyes darting around the empty room as if she were a jewel thief. She stood at the edge of the long table and dug her fingers into the silken fabrics. A smile crept across her lips, and she closed her eyes, savoring the feel of the rich fabric between her fingers. She brought it to her nose and inhaled the smell of the finishing chemicals and dyes that others might find severe but that she drew inspiration from.

"Some people might think you had a real problem, smelling fabric like that," Josh teased.

Riley's eyes flew open. She dropped the fabric and stepped back from the table. "I'm sorry. I know I'm not supposed to be touching things. I just couldn't help myself." She felt heat rush up her cheeks. Josh carried his suit coat over his forearm, his shirt still perfectly pressed. The word *dashing* ran through Riley's mind. *Stopitstopitstopit.*

He laughed, just as he had earlier that morning. "Riley, it's fine. How was your first day? Does Claudia have you working late?"

"Good. Fine. Exciting." *I sound like a babbling idiot.* "I really enjoyed it." Riley had stayed late, hoping to see him in addition to trying to catch up on her work, but she wasn't going to tell him that. "I just wanted to be sure I had everything in order before I left."

"Were you treated well?" He leaned against the table and folded his arms, his attention focused solely on her.

Riley pressed her lips together, mulling over the potential answers: *Claudia hates me. I didn't talk to anyone. I hate my cubicle. I need to be around people.*

"Yes. Fine. Claudia filled me in on everything I'll be doing, and I'm really excited." Despite the awful cubicle and Claudia's weird need to make clear that she had an advantage over her, Riley was excited to actually be working in a real design studio, and Claudia had filled her in, so technically, she wasn't lying.

"Good." He smiled.

He looked at her for a beat too long. Butterflies nested in her stomach, and Riley dropped her eyes before she blushed again. *Don't misread his looks. He's being polite. He's well mannered, nothing more. Then why is my heart racing?*

Josh looked at his watch and pursed his lips. "I have to run to a meeting, but Mia is still here. She can lock up when you're ready."

She didn't know what she wanted from Josh, but she was relieved that the electricity that had filled the space between them was now draped in a conversation. "Mia?"

"You didn't meet her today?" Josh pushed away from the table and stood so close to her that she could smell toothpaste on his breath.

You brushed your teeth for a meeting? Just what kind of meeting *is this?* She tucked away the curiosity—and a pang of something that felt a lot like jealousy—and focused on answering his question. "Nope, not yet. Truthfully, I haven't really met many people yet, but it's only my first day. I figured

Claudia would get around to introductions when she was ready."

Josh offered Riley his arm. "Come with me."

She wrapped her arm in his, and a thrill rushed through her. She swallowed hard, trying not to let the stirring in her belly sidetrack her from remembering that she was in a professional New York design office, walking down a hallway with her *boss*.

At the end of the wide hallway, he unwrapped his arm from hers.

"Excuse me," he said, then pulled the doors open, revealing the largest "closet" Riley had ever seen. The walls were lined with designer heels, boots, flats—every shoe imaginable from floor to ceiling. Accessories hung from hooks and hangers, and row after row of clothing racks filled the remaining space.

Riley felt her jaw go slack. She followed Josh into the room, wide eyed, full of awe and powerless to hide it.

"Mia is my assistant, but she spends a lot of time in the closet," Josh said.

"I'd love to have a closet like this," Riley said.

Josh turned to face her. "Our closet is your closet." He flashed a warm smile again, and Riley felt the butterflies squirreling around again.

"Hey, boss." A short, thin, dark-haired woman moving in spiked heels like they were sneakers appeared beside Josh.

Riley looked down at her own heels. *How does she make it look so easy?*

"Busy day today. Need an outfit?" The woman smiled at Riley and extended her hand. "I'm Mia."

Relieved at finally meeting a nice person, Riley smiled back and shook her hand. "I'm Riley, and I have to say, you have the greatest job ever!"

"I know, right?" Mia turned and opened her arms toward the clothes. "I dress everyone." She eyed Riley from head to toe.

"Oh, I won't fit in any of this stuff. I'm not here to be dressed." Riley felt her cheeks warm and sucked in her stomach. She wasn't under any misguided impressions about her size, and while she had been confident about her curves in Weston, New York City was a whole different ball game. She'd been in town for only a few days, but from what she'd witnessed so far, there were the tourists and then there were the New Yorkers, and you could tell them apart by the clothes they wore, the shoes on their feet, and the food, or lack thereof, in their grocery bags. It was as if resident New Yorkers survived on air alone to maintain their super-skinny figures.

"Riley, our new design assistant, of course. Sorry. I should have known that. Welcome to JBD." Mia tucked her straight black hair behind her ear, arched a brow, and asked, "Did you survive Claudia?"

Riley shot a look at Josh.

He shrugged, like he'd expected trouble with her mentor.

"Yes. She's..." Riley didn't want to overstep her bounds, even if Mia seemed like the type of person she could easily be friends with. She was wearing skinny jeans, a designer belt, and a low-cut blouse—an outfit similar to what Riley might have been comfortable in, minus the spiky heels. In Weston she wore skinny jeans proudly, even with her curves. Now she contemplated shying away from them. At least when she was in New York. "Professional. I think she'll be a good mentor."

"Honey, you don't have to lie to me," Mia said with a wave of her hand.

"Careful, Mia," Josh warned, but his eyes were light, playful even.

Mia looked at Josh and crossed her arms. "She's a shark, and she's competitive. You know she is. I'm just giving the girl a chance."

Riley drank in the conversation, feeling a bit like she should come to someone's defense—either Mia's or Claudia's; she wasn't sure which.

Josh shook his head. "Riley's working late tonight and she'll need you to lock up for her."

Mia checked her watch. "You have to leave before you're late," she said to Josh. "And don't forget, tomorrow morning at seven we have a conference call with the Stafford Agency about dressing the girls for their spring show."

The Stafford Agency was one of the top modeling agencies in New York. Riley tried to repress the shock at how casually the name of the agency was tossed about. Witnessing the natural ease of conversation between Josh and Mia made Riley feel guilty for wondering if there was some other side to Josh. He was clearly easy to work with.

"I'll be here for the call," he said.

"We'll ring them at six fifty, so I'll get espresso instead of your typical latte."

Josh touched her shoulder. "You're the best, Mia." He turned toward Riley. "Be sure Claudia introduces you around tomorrow. We're like a big family here. You need to meet the staff. You're one of us now."

Riley couldn't help but smile. *One of us. Part of the JBD team. Maybe dreams really can come true.*

Chapter Three

RILEY SAT ON the edge of her bed in the guest bedroom of Savannah Braden's apartment, where she was staying until she found an apartment of her own to rent. Savannah worked as an entertainment attorney in the city, but she traveled often, and for the next two weeks, Riley had the apartment to herself. The apartment wasn't enormous. In fact, it was quite cozy, with two bedrooms and two bathrooms, a moderately-sized kitchen, and a living room dining room combination. It was just a few blocks from Central Park. She couldn't have asked for more comfortable surroundings.

Riley changed into sweatpants and a T-shirt. It was eight o'clock, and if she worked this late every night, she'd have to put off her apartment search until the weekend. Exhaustion and excitement coalesced, bringing with it an ounce of homesickness. Riley reached for her cell and called Jade.

She tucked her cell phone against her chin.

"I'm stuck with Cruella De Vil as my mentor—or boss, I guess. I can't even imagine how Josh works with her, or how I'll survive her," she said when Jade answered the phone.

"Cruella De Vil?" Jade laughed.

"Yeah, and don't laugh. She's awful." Before Jade could

respond, she added, "And I met Josh's assistant, Mia, who's just the opposite. She's really nice and down-to-earth. I wish *she* was my mentor." Riley sighed.

"You can handle Cruella. You told me yourself that it was a cutthroat industry, remember? Don't let her get you down," Jade said. "She's probably just feeling threatened because you're such an awesome designer."

Riley smiled. She pictured Jade in her jeans and cowgirl boots, her long black hair flowing to her waist, sitting on her front porch. "I miss you," Riley said.

"Of course you do." Jade laughed. "But you'll survive, and you'll thrive. This is your big break. It's all you've ever wanted, remember?"

"Yes, of course, and I'm thankful, but I miss you. I miss the smell of the farms and driving. It's only been a week, but I miss driving already." Riley realized how whiny she sounded and she took a deep breath and blew it out slowly. "I do love it here, even if it smells a little like dirty feet, wilted food, and car exhaust. I swear, it's almost eight at night and the entire city is still outside walking around. It's so different from home."

"I know, but Weston can't offer you a career," Jade reminded her.

And Weston can't offer me Josh, either. "I know. I want New York. I want this. I just wish you were here with me. I could use a friend and a drink right now." Riley walked to the kitchen and opened a bottle of water, making a mental note to buy some alcohol for times like this. "Bottled water doesn't cut it. I want to celebrate my new job with you, and I want you to hug me and tell me that Cruella sucks and that I'm ten times better than her."

"Cruella does suck, and you are ten times better than her."

Jade grew quiet, then said with mischief in her voice, "Tell me what it's like to work with Josh."

Riley took a gulp of water, then plopped onto the leather couch. "I never realized how sweet he was. All those years in school...I mean, he was cute. All the Bradens are. But Josh is..." She remembered the way he'd looked at her, the feel of his hand on her back. "He's just really nice."

"Riley, it's me, remember? You never describe guys as *really nice*. And it's Josh Braden, for goodness sake. Spill it already."

She laughed. "It's not like there's anything between us. He's just...he's different. You know how Rex is all take-me-to-bed sexy and his brother Treat is more refined?"

"Yeah? And by the way, thanks for noticing Rex is take-me-to-bed sexy." Jade laughed. Jade's and Rex's fathers had been feuding since before Jade was born, and when she'd moved back home after the end of a bad relationship, a chance meeting with Rex unleashed years of forbidden passion. Not only were Jade and Rex madly in love, but they were also in the midst of designing a house together. If Jade and Rex hadn't eased the feud between the families, Riley, being Jade's best friend, would never have had a chance to get closer to Josh.

"You know what I mean. I'm happy for you." Riley curled her legs up on the couch and rubbed her aching feet. "Anyway, you know how their brother Hugh is kind of self-centered and Dane is so smooth that you just know he's got to be a player?" She didn't wait for Jade to concur. "Well, Josh is like a mixture of all of them. He's smooth, but I don't see him as a player. He's refined, but not snooty; he's not self-centered, but one look at how meticulous he is about his clothing and hair, and you know there's a bit of self-centeredness in him. He's just...different."

"You're all breathy. This is the guy you lusted over for all those years, and your answer is that he's *different?*" Jade accused her.

She and Jade had been best friends since they learned to talk, and she knew Jade would see through any false impressions she tried to give, so instead she told her the truth. "I'm here for a career, not a relationship. I'm trying not to let myself think of him in that way."

"Um, Ri, you just did," Jade teased.

"You know what I mean. I know he exists, and I am a woman, after all, but I'm not going there. Not with him." She remembered Claudia leaning in to Josh's back when they were introduced. "Besides, I'm not so sure Cruella isn't sleeping with him."

"What about all that, 'I swear I wanted to kiss him' stuff that you said when you guys were meeting to talk about you working for him, and yes, I'm using air quotes around 'working for him,'" Jade said.

"Ugh! Jade. It's hard enough seeing his handsome face and feeling those things. Do I really have to acknowledge them, too? I'm here for a career, like I said. Not for Josh." She wasn't sure if she was trying to convince herself or Jade.

"Well, I'm glad to hear you're keeping your eye on what matters," Jade said. "But even if you weren't, I'd be right there, cheering you on."

"That's because you're the best friend ever. On the upside, I stayed late tonight and sketched a bit."

"Really? Will you make me something wonderful to wear for Christmas?"

The excitement in Jade's voice inspired Riley. "Yes, of course. I tossed the ones I drew tonight. I was too tired to do anything worthwhile, but I'll work on it. And you know what? You're right. I'm not gonna let Cruella get to me. She'll zap me of all my creativity." She felt a burst of renewed focus. "Tell me something fun. How's your house design coming along?" Jade and Rex had purchased a plot of land between their families' estates, and they hoped to build their house in the coming months.

"Same, same. We've got the plans pretty well set. We're meeting with the builder again next week."

"Let me know how it goes." Riley rubbed the ball of her foot. "I swear my feet feel like they've been bound. I'm gonna take a hot bath. Call ya tomorrow?"

"Sounds good. Miss you," Jade said.

Riley ended the call and headed for the bathroom, stopping in the living room to look over a photo on Savannah's bookshelf. Josh stood between his father and Hugh, the rest of his siblings fanned out to their sides. Each of the Braden men were striking, but as she looked at them all lined up with their radiant smiles and muscular physiques, it was Josh who drew her attention. *It's always been you.*

She set the frame back on the bookshelf. "Now I'm really losing it," she said aloud. "He's your boss. Delete that thought. Delete, delete, delete…"

Chapter Four

JOSH WOKE AS he did most mornings, with the crack of dawn lighting his expansive bedroom. He climbed from his king-sized bed, snagged a remote off of the bedside table, and walked in his boxers to the windows. He pushed a button on a remote and the blinds drew open, exposing a radiant view of Central Park. Josh had lived in New York for the past eight years, and at thirty-three years old, he was well aware of his good fortune. He'd built an empire around his name, and he didn't take his life for granted—how could he, when there was always someone who wanted something from him.

He stretched his arms and legs, as he did every morning, then sank to the floor and began his somewhat impaired exercise regimen of eighty sit-ups and push-ups, working around his all-too-familiar, morning wood. Josh had always had a healthy appetite for sex, even if he'd kept mum about the details to his overly curious brothers. But ever since he'd drawn a mental line in the sand between dating women he wanted to date and dating women he was supposed to date—and coming up short on the *wanting to* side—his body hadn't failed to remind him that those needs were still alive and well. Once that settled down, he showered to further warm up his muscles and headed out for his three-mile morning run.

He could navigate the streets of New York with his eyes closed. Every curve of the road, every lip in the sidewalk, every tree in Central Park had been ingrained in his memory from his daily runs. Whether it was raining, snowing, or hot and humid, he was out pounding the pavement. He needed something to relieve the stress of his chosen career. He hadn't expected to move so quickly up the ladder of fame. It seemed to happen almost overnight. One day he was showing his designs to his boss at an internship, and the next thing he knew, he was a full-time designer and his styles were gracing the red carpet on well-known, respected celebrities.

Josh jogged past a brown-haired woman power walking through the park. As he passed, he thought it might be Riley. At second glance, he realized it wasn't, but Riley remained on his mind. He'd wanted to help her feel at home in New York, and instead, he'd handed her over to Claudia, the wickedest woman in the business, and then later, he'd headed out for a meeting, which ended up being a big waste of time.

He'd been home in Weston when he and Riley had reconnected, and it had been nice seeing her there, a smile always on her lips, her eyes dancing with enthusiasm about everything from his brother Rex's relationship with her best friend, Jade, to the possibility of coming to New York. They'd hit it off right away, and now that she was here, he'd like to get to know her even better.

He'd noticed a difference in her eyes before he left the office the prior evening. She'd looked tired, which was to be expected, but he'd seen something else, too. Disenchantment, maybe? Could Claudia have killed her spirit already? The thought angered him, and he picked up his pace. He didn't think Claudia would be unnecessarily cruel, but she did have a strong reputation for being competitive, and for that reason, Josh had purposely refrained from showing her any of Riley's designs. He'd have to keep his eyes open.

An hour later, he walked through the front doors of JBD. Mia met him on his way in, dressed in her typical skinny jeans and blouse. She handed him a to-go cup.

"Espresso. I'm calling in ten minutes. You've got two messages from Madeline Stein, so please call her back already."

Madeline Stein. She was the last person he wanted to talk to, his date from the evening before: a willowy model with even fewer brain cells than the hundred pounds she probably weighed. That was definitely the last time he'd agree to a date in order to help the modeling agencies gain the right exposure for their models by being seen draped on his arm.

"Tell her I died," he said.

"No way. I'm not doing your dirty work," Mia said as they entered his office. "I did that the last two times, and as I recall, a few times before that, too."

Josh sat behind his desk. "Isn't that your job as my assistant? To fulfill my every whim?"

Mia placed her hand on her hip. "Not when your every whim means telling women that you're not interested in them. I don't even know why you accept the dates if you don't want to go out with them."

He thought of his older brothers Treat and Rex and how happy they'd been since they'd met the women they wanted to build their lives with, and he wondered if he'd be lucky enough to find that same type of connection. With each date he accepted, he looked for the qualities in a woman that he respected: intelligence, empathy, a sense of humor. He had yet to find a single one that he felt compatible with. *Compatible in the way I was with Riley back in Weston.* He pushed Riley from his mind and thought of an appropriate answer for Mia. *Because it's better than being lonely. Then again, maybe it's not.* "Because it's part of my job. I'm a designer. Everyone wants to be seen on my arm. Who am I to turn them down?"

Mia rolled her eyes. "Even I don't believe you're that generous."

He lifted his brows and frowned.

"Really? The pouty face? No way. I'm not making the call." She looked at her watch. "You have seven minutes before the conference call. Why don't you just pick up the phone and give her the big letdown?"

"Seven?" He wanted to talk to Claudia about Riley's desk situation. The file clerk's cubicle was unacceptable. "Give me ten." He pushed from his chair and flew out the door, Mia's voice trailing after him.

"Seven!"

HE FOUND CLAUDIA bent over Riley's desk.

"Claudia, I'm glad I found you."

"I came in early to go over a few things for the new line. I lost a few hours yesterday helping Riley." She wore a perfectly fitted Chanel suit, and her hair was pulled back in a smooth bun. Claudia looked every inch the designer, but Josh saw through that manicured exterior, and he'd picked up on the annoyed tone in her voice when she'd said Riley's name—a tone that anyone else might have missed.

Claudia had never really done anything egregious to any employees, and why she seemed to take issue with Riley was beyond his understanding, but he wouldn't allow it to continue.

"That's what I wanted to talk to you about. Why is Riley in the cubicle?" He felt his chest tighten when he said her name. He slipped his hands into his pockets, hoping to come across more casual and less personally interested.

"The desks in the pit were taken." She touched his arm and spoke in an alluring—and he was sure practiced—bedroom voice. "I'll move her out this week. Don't worry."

He had minutes before his conference call and no time for her games. "See that you do. Today," he said, and walked away. He'd have to keep a better eye on her manipulations. He turned and glanced at her one last time. She stood with her arms crossed, staring at Riley's desk.

"Was there something you were looking for?" Josh asked.

She spun around. "Not at all. Just thinking." She stalked away.

It must suck to be that competitive and insecure. If she'd been anyone else, he'd have felt sorry for her, but if she wanted to become a designer, she needed to spend more time honing her design skills and less time worrying about who else might pass her along the way.

Mia grabbed his arm and pulled him into a conference room. "I have Peter on line three. They're talking the Bliss line. Ready?"

Bliss. His favorite new clothing line. He nodded, plastered a smile on his face, and went to work selling his line to Peter Stafford, the head of one of the first modeling agencies to have taken a chance on dressing his models in Josh's clothes years earlier. Peter had helped Josh's name reach the status he now enjoyed, and because of that, he'd hired his niece Claudia. He didn't know then what type of person Claudia was, and now he was too trapped by loyalty to let her go.

Chapter Five

RILEY FOLLOWED CLAUDIA to her new desk in the design studio, set among the other employees' desks and in full view of a wall of windows. Riley breathed a sigh of relief. She didn't know what miracle had occurred overnight, but she was thankful—and now even more inspired to do a good job and make her mark in the industry. She hadn't liked the feeling of oppression she'd slept with last night, and she'd awoken determined to change things before they had a chance to get any worse. She'd decided to try to become friends with Claudia. No matter how much Claudia might fight her efforts, Riley had to try.

"Clay, this is Riley Banks, our new design assistant." Claudia introduced Riley with what looked like a genuine smile.

Riley wondered if emotions were like hair color—after they'd been faked for too long, could a person forget what real emotions were?

"I heard you were starting this week. A pleasure," he said with a nod. Clay was a tall, gangly man, about Riley's age, with a flat top and pasty white skin.

"It's nice to meet you," Riley said, just as Claudia rudely dragged her away, leading her to a group of people hovering around a clothing rack. They were discussing the merits of A-line skirts versus flared skirts, and Riley wanted to jump in and give her two cents. *Depending on the material you used, a flared skirt can easily be made more formal, giving a woman more options for going from daywear to eveningwear, whereas an A-line is usually more casual. But an A-line can make the right figure pop.*

Claudia cleared her throat.

A woman and a man spun around, their faces pinched. "What?" they said in unison.

Riley noticed the blond woman remained facing the rack, a skirt in each hand. Her head moved back and forth from one to the other, as if she were watching a tennis match.

"This is Riley Banks. Riley, this is Simone, and K.T."

Riley swallowed the embarrassment of Claudia having interrupted their discussion to introduce her. Her smile felt shaky.

"Great to have you on board," Simone said, wrapping Riley in a hug.

"Nice to meet you, too, and thank you," Riley said.

Simone looked like…a *Simone*. She wore a colorful scarf around her slim shoulders, and her black hair was cropped in a severe blunt cut just below her ears. Her round, wire-rimmed glasses were perched high on the bridge of her upturned nose, and when she flashed a Julia Roberts smile, it softened her angular face.

Riley beamed. Between the overcrowded street, scary sardine-style subway that she couldn't even think about riding on, and Claudia's cold personality, Riley had begun to wonder if she'd ever fit in. Simone's friendly embrace and warm smile offered a thread of hope for Riley to hold on to.

"This is Chantal," Simone said, nodding toward the blonde who had her back turned to the group. She turned around, and when their eyes met, Chantal flashed a radiant smile. She was nearly six feet tall, and up close, her green eyes seemed even greener than they had when they'd first met.

"We met yesterday morning. Hi, Riley. I can't wait to get to know you better." Chantal air-kissed both of Riley's cheeks.

"How did you know my name yesterday?" Riley asked.

"Oh." She swatted the air with her hand. "Mr. B. told me, since I fill in at the front desk. It's always nice to be greeted personally, don't you think?" She didn't wait for Riley to answer. "I hear you're new to New York."

"Yes, I moved from Colorado." Riley barely got the words out before noticing that K.T., a twenty-something African American man, was sizing her up. He stood with his arms crossed, one hip jutted out and his foot resting on its heel. She bristled.

"Mm-mm-mmm. What do we have here? A bit of Juicy Couture?" He touched the sleeve of her dress. "And a girl who's not afraid to eat. I like that."

Riley stiffened. *Did you just call me fat?*

Claudia snickered, and Riley wished she could shrivel up and disappear.

He must have read her mind. "Girl, I want to go to lunch with you. Eating with these waifs is like, *Just wave the food in front of them and they survive on the fumes.*"

Simone swatted his arm. "Ignore him. He hasn't had his meds yet this morning. It's really great to meet you. If you need any help, just let us know."

Even with the food comment, Riley was relieved. She could see herself working with them. They teased, they hugged, and they were nice. It seemed Claudia was an anomaly—one Riley had to deal with. *I can do this.*

Claudia sighed. "Okay, now that that's over with, today you'll be going over all the line sheets for the Bliss line. I want you to ensure that all details and changes for the past two days have been made and sent to the corresponding staff. Why are you looking at me like that?"

"Like what?" Riley checked her emotions. She wasn't feeling anything negative at the moment. She had no idea what Claudia was referring to.

"Like you're too good for line sheets. These are critical. If one style number, price, color, or size is wrong, it can wreak havoc with the line. Updates need to be sent daily, but since you just began yesterday, we're a day behind." Claudia walked quickly toward Riley's new desk. "We'll be attending a trade show in two weeks, and we have a lot to go over, so let's get to work. Be sure the sketches are up-to-date, and remember, accuracy is everything. Match all changes to the line sheets. Double-check your work. Oh, and there was a photo shoot yesterday morning. When the trunk arrives, go through it and make sure we got all of our samples back. If anything's missing, call over to Phil and track the samples. Make sure those greedy models didn't walk off with our stuff."

"Phil?" Riley asked.

Claudia pointed to Riley's computer. "Phil Lancorn. Look him up in your company address book."

Finally, some real work. It might not be designing, but at least she'd get her hands on fabric. It was a step in the right direction.

"Okay, got it," she said.

"Good."

Riley watched Claudia walk away with her nose in the air. She mentally ticked off what was expected of her: Line sheets, trade show prep, sample inventory, and then she got to work.

BY TWO O'CLOCK, when the trunk of clothing showed up, Riley had finished all of the line sheets, confirmed receipt with the corresponding team members, and was famished. *No wonder everyone's so skinny. There's no time for lunch.*

Mia rifled through the trunk. "I need the fuchsia pencil skirt from his spring line."

"I haven't inventoried the samples yet," Riley said, flipping through her checklist of clothing that had gone out to the shoot.

Simone breezed into the room. "We've got Carlisle coming over at four. Where's the scarf that goes with the Bliss jumpsuit?" She flung clothes from the trunk onto the couch in the corner of the room.

"I swear, every time there's a shoot, something goes missing," Mia said.

Riley grabbed the garments as they were tossed about and tried to match them up with the inventory as quickly as she could. Claudia walked into the room just as Riley snagged a belt from Simone. "Let me just mark it off. Then you can whisk it away. I promise."

Claudia snagged the belt from Riley's hands. "Josh comes first. He needs this stuff now, not later." She snapped her fingers.

"How can I inventory if I don't have the items? It will only take a minute to go through these as they take them away." Riley watched Simone stand with a stack of clothes in her arms and head for the door.

"Wait! Please. Just tell me what you have and I'll write it

down. Rattle it off as fast as you can," she pleaded, then immediately cringed. Simone and Mia froze. *Oh no. Did I step out of line?*

"I like her," Simone said to Claudia.

Thank heavens. She snuck a sideways glance at Claudia and held her breath.

Claudia narrowed her eyes and crossed her arms firmly over her chest.

Shoot, shoot, shoot.

"Okay, here goes." Simone listed all of the clothes she had in her arms, and once satisfied that she hadn't missed an item, Riley followed Mia to Josh's office, taking copious notes on the pieces she'd taken as well.

"Thanks, Mia. I appreciate your help. We'll have to figure out a better system for this." Riley had her nose in her notebook and bumped into Josh's chest as she turned to leave. His hands caught her forearms. "Oh, sorry. I'm so sorry," she said.

"Not a problem. Slow down. What's the rush?" Josh didn't let go of her arms.

"I've got to inventory the samples from yesterday's shoot before everyone takes them away." She blinked several times, trying to break the energy that ran from his hands through her arms and made her heart beat triple time. When that didn't work, she shifted her body as if to leave the room, breaking contact with him altogether.

"Did you have lunch?" he asked.

"No time," she said, trying to think past her desire to say, *No. Let's go grab something.*

"I haven't given you a proper welcome to New York. Why don't we have dinner tonight?"

When Josh and Riley were back in Colorado, Josh had a way of looking at her that wasn't lustful or platonic. Something hard to interpret hung in the darkening of his eyes and the lifting of the right side of his mouth, and every time he had looked at her with that butterfly-inducing gaze, she'd wanted to kiss him and run away at the same time. Now she stood frozen beside him, trying to interpret that exact look as he cast it in her direction. Only this time there were spectators—and she was his employee—and what made her stomach ache and shivers run through her body was that she couldn't decide if what she saw was an implication, a stifled desire, or if she was a crazy employee slash friend wanting more than he had to offer.

Dinner? Like a date? No, he doesn't mean a date. He means a work thing. He's being polite.

"Aren't you forgetting something?" Mia asked.

Claudia entered the room behind Josh. "Riley, the trunk is emptying," she said in a singsong voice.

Josh arched a brow at Mia.

"Your dinner with Peter Stafford?" Mia said.

"Right. Come with me," he said to Riley.

"To your dinner with Mr. Stafford? I couldn't—"

"You can, and I'd be honored if you'd join me. It would be a great chance for you to see how the industry works." He searched her eyes.

"She's got to prepare for the trade show," Claudia said sternly.

"Yeah, and—" *Dinner with Josh and Peter Stafford?*

"That's in two weeks. There's plenty of time. Six? I'll pick you up at Savannah's?" Josh didn't wait for an answer. "Now, slow down. Go do your inventory. And, Claudia, she'll need to leave by five to get ready."

Riley walked tentatively past Claudia, averting her eyes from the daggers that Claudia had been casting ever since she'd entered the room—heck, ever since Riley had arrived at JBD.

Chapter Six

RILEY WAS THANKFUL to be buried in work, allowing only moments of worry about whether dinner with Josh was meant to be a date or a work assignment. The way he'd touched her arms didn't feel very businesslike. Then again, having dinner with Josh and Peter Stafford, head of the biggest modeling agency in New York, was definitely all business. *I'm overthinking the situation.* Of course, he had asked her to a business dinner, a welcome-to-New-York dinner, as opposed to a date. *Or had he?*

As soon as she left the office, sheer panic stepped in, filling the space that work had occupied before. Her nerves tangled and fought, making her feel sick to her stomach. She took a hot shower, going over possibilities in her mind. If it was a date, how should she dress? How should she act? She'd been so comfortable with Josh back in Weston. Why was she so nervous now? What if she said something awkward and embarrassed herself in front of Peter Stafford?

She tipped her face up to the spray of the shower to wash away the bombardment of what ifs. What advice would she give Jade? She thought about that as she dried off and stepped from the shower. *Just be yourself.* Jade was beautiful, smart, and funny. Being herself worked. Riley looked in the mirror, feeling like a drowned rat. She needed to bring in the cavalry. She needed support. She reached for her cell phone.

Jade answered on the first ring.

"Tell me I'm beautiful, smart, and funny," Riley begged.

Jade laughed. "Why?"

Riley sighed as she sat on the toilet lid. "Because I'm having dinner with Josh and Peter Stafford tonight. Do you know who he is?" She didn't give Jade time to answer. "He runs the biggest modeling agency in New York. Can you believe it? And I have no idea if it's a business thing, a date, or what, and I don't look like the spit-skinny models, and I'm from small-town Weston, not New York City, so who knows how many ways I'll mess this up."

"Oh, is that all?" Jade teased.

"Jade! I need support. Please? Someone told me today that I'm not afraid to eat. That's code for *fat*, and now I'm not sure if I should just pretend to eat when I'm with Josh and Peter frickin' Stafford. I'm so nervous I could puke. I probably won't eat anyway."

"Oh my gosh. You're kidding, right?"

"Jade." Riley closed her eyes and took a deep breath.

"Come on, Ri. You know how pretty you are. You turn heads everywhere you go. You have curves and you know how to work them. Guys love that."

"I don't think New York guys do."

"Really? Josh is a New York guy now. And you know the way he looked at you before he offered you the job."

"How could I forget?" Riley asked.

"And remember that night at the concert? I swear, Ri. The man didn't give you thirty seconds with the rest of us. He whisked you away."

"We were talking about fashion. He was probably just interested because I wasn't a complete novice. He never made a single move on me, Jade." *I swear the butterflies in my stomach are taking steroids.*

"For a smart girl, sometimes you're a real dunce. Look, it's Josh Braden. Think of him as the boy from high school. Be yourself. You're charming and witty. You're gorgeous and smart. Ri, you're so likable that I can't imagine anyone *not* liking you."

The sincerity in Jade's voice settled Riley's nerves...a little. "You really think so? I don't even know which fork to use in a restaurant."

"Google it," Jade joked.

"You laugh, but I will before he picks me up."

"Josh is picking you up?" Jade asked.

"Yeah."

"It's a date," Jade said emphatically.

"Why? Just because he's coming to get me? I don't know where anything is around here and I'm petrified of the subway, but I promised myself I'd start taking it tomorrow. I think Josh is just being nice." *Oh gosh, a date?*

"I don't know. You're asking me to define something that's hard to figure out. I don't know how things work in New York, but if it's a friendly dinner, you know, you meet them at the restaurant. How did he ask you?"

This was getting more stressful by the second. "Well, he said that he hadn't given me a proper welcome and asked if I wanted to have dinner with him. Then Mia said he had this dinner engagement with Peter Stafford, and he asked me to come along."

"It kinda sounds like a date, but also like he was being nice because he brought you into New York, you know, welcoming a friend."

"See," Riley said. "That's what I thought, too."

"Well, it doesn't really matter what it is. You're his employee, so be professional and be yourself. You'll know it's a date if he brings you flowers, or kisses you when he sees you."

"Do guys even bring flowers to girls anymore?" Riley asked.

"Rex does, but he usually picks them from the garden." Jade laughed.

Riley glanced at the clock and her pulse quickened. "I have to get ready." She was mentally ticking off her potential outfits for the evening. "He'll be here in twenty minutes. Wish me luck."

"You don't need it. You're going to have a great time and they'll both love you. Call me after?"

"You got it. And, Jade?" Riley hoped she was as good of a friend to Jade as Jade had always been for her.

"Yeah?"

"Thanks for everything."

Riley dried her hair and put on her makeup, then stood in front of the closet, wishing she'd had time to shop for something new. She'd already worn two of her designer outfits, and she had only two more. Tucked in the back of her closet was the one dress that she'd made just before coming to New York. It was a bit racy for a work-related dinner engagement, but it did accentuate her curves in all the right places. She pulled it from the closet and slipped it on.

The black sheath hugged her curves, and the scalloped hemline rested just above her knees, not too short for a professional dinner, though a bit snug. The scooped neckline slimmed her bust, and she'd cleverly designed the sleeves with cutouts at the shoulders and tightly fitting material around her biceps. Riley might not be model thin, but she had well-defined shoulders, and they drew attention away from her slightly thick waist.

She spritzed on Gucci Première perfume, which she'd gotten at a great discount when she worked at Macy's, and slipped her still sore feet into a pair of black-and-white Marc Jacobs pumps. *Thank you, Macy's.* She stood in front of the mirror and surveyed herself from head to toe. Her hair never let her down. It was her easiest and most pleasant attribute, not too thick and with a natural wave she could accentuate with a twist of a brush. There was no denying the width of her hips or the fullness of her breasts, and even if her waist carried a few extra pounds, she was pleased with how she looked in the dress she'd designed. She shook her head, giving her bangs a playful look as they swept in front of her eyes. Date or not, she was ready, and she looked darn good.

The knock at the door shattered her confidence. Riley froze, her eyes wide. Suddenly she had to know if Josh had asked her on a date or not. She walked into the living room and stared at the door. *Move. Answer it. I can't. You have to.*

With the next knock, Riley took a deep breath and reached for the doorknob.

Chapter Seven

JOSH CHECKED HIS watch. *Five fifty-five.* He was sure he'd said six o'clock. He hadn't actually picked up a woman at her apartment in months. Most of his dates were arranged by acquaintances or friends—favors for women who were trying to find a place for themselves in the fashion industry. He'd typically sent a car to pick them up or he'd met them at the intended location. That strategy had kept the option of being intimate up to him, not up to circumstance. The idea of dating women he rarely thought about the next day didn't used to bother him, but over the past year, as he'd watched Treat fall in love with Max Armstrong, and more recently, Rex fall in love with Jade Johnson, he found himself longing for the contentedness they'd found. The way his brothers looked at Max and Jade made Josh long for the same connection, and the way Max and Jade returned that adoration, with looks of love that were nearly tangible and loving touches as they passed by, only made him want it more. It was time. He'd spent years dating whomever he was expected to date. Now it was his time to choose for himself.

The door swung open and Josh's jaw dropped. He'd seen more models than he could count, and he'd dated some of the most beautiful women in the country, and yet, standing before him, Riley Banks surpassed them all in a stunning black dress. She looked wholesome and sexy. She looked *real.*

"Hi," she said with a wide smile, fluttering her gorgeous, thick lashes.

"Wow, Riley. You look gorgeous." Josh leaned forward and kissed her cheek, inhaling deeply. "Not many women wear Gucci Première. It's one of my favorites. With hints of bergamot and blackberry mixed with the musky scent of sandalwood, it's the perfect scent for you."

"You noticed?" she said softly.

He saw the wonder in Riley's eyes and felt as if his discerning senses were showing again. He'd always been so entrenched in the fashion industry that he tended to memorize scents, textures, and of course, designers, and he'd instinctively noted people's favorites. It was one of his greatest pleasures, knowing the things that made people happy, though he was well aware that his ability to determine designers and such might be off-putting to others, or seem snotty. *I'll have to watch that.*

"Sorry," he said.

"Don't be. I like that you noticed."

Josh had yet to use the tidbits of information he gathered for anything other than courting buyers, but something told him that he might want to put some of Riley's favorite things to use.

"Who's the designer?" he asked, eyeing her dress.

Her cheeks flushed. "It's...one of mine."

"You designed this? Riley, it's incredibly hot. I love the attention to detail around the hemline and the peekaboo shoulders. This should be on a runway." *She really does need to design.*

She touched the waist nervously. "Really? You like it? I was worried about wearing it."

"I don't like it. I love it, and you should be proud to wear it. You really do have immense talent."

"Thank you," she said, blushing again.

"These are for you." He held out the bouquet of red-tipped yellow roses, and when she reached for them, his fingers brushed hers, sending an unfamiliar yearning through him. It had been so long since he'd felt true desire that he almost didn't recognize it. When he'd stopped to pick out flowers for Riley, there had been no question about which flowers to choose, and as he left the florist, he realized that the last time he had stopped to personally pick out flowers for a woman had been when he was in college.

"They're gorgeous," she said. "Thank you. Please come in. I'm sure Savannah has a vase somewhere."

He followed her into his sister's apartment, unable to keep from noticing her curvaceous hips as she walked away. He tried not to stare, but found himself reeled in, and followed her into the kitchen.

Riley pushed a pile of sketches to the side, then began opening cabinet after cabinet. "I don't see one, but I'm sure she has one."

Josh picked up one of the sketches. "Do you mind if I look?"

"They're not very good. I was just playing around the first few days I arrived in town. I haven't had much time to sketch since then."

"Riley, these are really good. You have a unique style. Your lines are sleek but feminine, and these high necklines are the opposite of what I've seen on these types of pieces." He watched her fumble in the cabinets, avoiding his gaze, and he realized he was embarrassing her. He set the impressive drawings down and picked up a box of gingerbread cookies.

"You caught me," Riley said. "My sinful secret. Comfort food."

Another favorite. He set down the box and grabbed a wide-necked bottle from next to the refrigerator. "This might work."

Riley smiled, then narrowed her eyes. "That looks like an old bottle of wine or something."

"It works, right? In fact, I think it's pretty with the green tint and its short stature. Let's see." He took the flowers from her, trimmed the ends, then arranged them in the bottle, leaving some stems longer than others and creating a textured layering of the flowers.

"It's almost scary how good you are at designs. I never would have thought to use that bottle for these. It looks like it belongs in a magazine," she said.

"Maybe I'll be a florist in my next life," he joked.

Riley's smile began to fade, and Josh noticed the way her fingers fidgeted. She was so cute when she was nervous that he reached out and touched her cheek without thinking. When her eyes searched his, he realized his mistake and withdrew his hand.

"I'm sorry. I don't know why I did that. You looked nervous, and I guess I was just trying to let you know you didn't need to be."

She dropped her eyes. "It's okay."

"Riley, I'm nervous, too, but there's really no need for us to be. We've known each other for years. Let's just go out and pretend we're back in Weston, hanging out at the concert." He'd felt so comfortable with her back then. He almost wished they were back in Weston now. Seeing that tight dress hugging every inch of her body only made him more confused. He battled his growing desire to pick up where they'd left off in Weston, to have that close friendship that might have quickly become so much more if they'd remained back in their hometown. He was her boss. He had to walk a fine line.

She fidgeted with a seam on her hip. "That sounds…great. I was really nervous. I didn't know if this was a date or a business dinner. I know that's silly. I mean, why would it be a date?"

Josh felt like he'd been punched in the gut. He'd thought of the evening as something of a date—a date that had been saddled with Peter's dinner engagement. He considered telling her as much, but she was already moving more comfortably, less constricted by nerves.

"Shall we go?" He hated the disappointment he heard in his own voice and made a mental note to check his emotions before speaking again. Had he been out of the real dating game for too long? Had he not asked her on a real date? Mildly annoyed with himself, he followed her out of the building and into the waiting car.

Outside, Josh opened the car door for Riley. "You have a driver?"

The shock in her wide eyes was so different from the privileged look on his typical dates' faces. They'd expect nothing less, while Riley probably found it excessive.

"I wasn't sure how comfortable you'd be in a cab," Josh explained.

"I don't mind cabs so much. It's the subway that I still need to conquer," Riley answered.

Josh chalked up another thing he liked about her.

Chapter Eight

PETER STAFFORD WAS a darkly handsome man, graying around the temples, with piercing blue eyes and copper skin. He stood when Riley and Josh arrived at the table. He was not quite as tall as Josh, but he looked very debonair in his dark suit and crisp white shirt.

"This is Riley Banks, our newest design assistant and a very talented future designer," Josh said with a proud smile.

How many times will he make me blush? "It's a pleasure to meet you, Mr. Stafford." In the car on the way over, Riley had played Josh's words over and over in her mind. *Let's just go out and pretend we're back in Weston, hanging out at the concert.* She hadn't realized how much she'd begun to hope that the evening was a date until she'd heard him say those words. Why had he brought her flowers? Maybe it was a New York thing. But what about the kiss?

Mr. Stafford kissed the back of her hand in greeting. "Please, call me Peter."

Well, that's a kiss too, and he's definitely not a date. It's a New York thing, she thought with a pang of disappointment.

They settled into their seats and ordered dinner. Riley was relieved when the waiter returned with a bottle of wine. She needed something to settle her nerves.

"Josh, how's my favorite niece?" Peter asked.

Josh glanced at Riley, then looked back at Peter. "She's well, Peter. Claudia's doing just fine."

Claudia? Peter's niece? Oh, no. Riley tried to blink away the surprise from her eyes.

"Good. Glad to hear it," Peter said.

Riley watched Josh reposition himself in his chair and spend an extraordinary amount of time refolding his napkin. *No wonder she still works there.*

"She's been with JBD for what, five, six years now?" Peter asked.

"Yes, that's right," Josh answered.

"Any movement toward full-fledged designer?" Peter asked.

Josh cleared his throat. "We're working in that direction." He sipped his wine, his eyes darting to Riley and back.

"Good," Peter said, finishing his wine. "Everyone needs a break. I remember when I first dressed my girls in your line, Josh. That was a big risk, and I'm glad I took it," he said.

Josh nodded. "It was a risk, and I appreciate your ability to see my potential."

Peter poured himself another glass of wine. "Yes, well, you're welcome."

By the time the waiter brought their salads, they'd finished the bottle of wine.

Peter ordered a second bottle of wine, and when it arrived, he filled their glasses and made a toast.

"To our incredible industry," he said.

Riley and Josh lifted their glasses to his, and as Riley sipped her wine, she noticed Peter staring at her. He arched a brow, and Riley looked away.

What was that about? Focus on your salad. Riley fumbled with her napkin, and realized that she'd forgotten to Google which fork was the salad fork. For a moment, she froze—panic-stricken. Between Peter's professional demeanor slipping toward flirtation and the news about Claudia, she could barely think, much less process silverware etiquette. She eyed Josh's silverware, figured out which of his forks he'd picked up, and she used the same one. *Catastrophe averted.*

"Tell me, Riley, how did you land in New York with JBD?" Peter asked.

"It was happenstance." She looked at Josh, not sure how to answer. *His brother referred me? I'm his brother's girlfriend's best friend?* They'd known each other growing up, but if she revealed that, wouldn't Peter ask her why she hadn't come to work for Josh sooner?

Josh came to her rescue. "Riley won two awards for her designs while she was in school, and when I was home visiting my family, I asked to see her portfolio." He looked at Riley and smiled. "Her work was too good to pass up."

How did he know how to say that so eloquently? She breathed a little easier. She'd have to remember to prepare for every possible scenario in the future. *Who am I kidding? This will be the last dinner with Josh's business associates.*

"Wonderful," Peter said. "And tell me about yourself. Do you have hobbies?"

Why are you so focused on me? She looked at his empty wineglass, silencing a groan. *Why do some men get tunnel vision when they drink?* Riley wasn't prepared to answer personal questions. Peter filled her glass again, and she took another sip while she thought of an answer. As it trickled down her throat, she remembered Jade's advice. *Be yourself.*

"I don't have many hobbies. I love people, horseback riding, and, well, designing. Back in Weston, I worked at Macy's, which wasn't glamorous or exciting, but it was fast paced and I enjoyed dealing with the customers. In my free time, I sketched designs, sometimes for hours on end."

"Do you miss Weston?" Peter asked.

The way he watched her, hanging on her every breath, gave her pause. She might have had a few drinks, but now there was no question. She knew a flirtatious look when she saw it.

She shot a look at Josh, who was also watching her, and the pressure sent her pulse soaring. "I miss my friends, but I'm where I want to be. I've wanted to design forever, and now, being among Josh and his team, watching it all come to life, it's like breathing new oxygen after being on a lung machine. It's invigorating."

"I assume Riley will be coming with you to the Bliss line meetings?" Peter asked Josh.

"We can arrange that," Josh said.

Peter's eyes darted between Josh and Riley. "Forgive me for asking, but I'm a pretty forthright guy." He looked directly at Riley and asked, "Are you two…?"

Oh no. I'm dead. Are my feelings that transparent?

"No," Riley said as fast as she was able. She shot another look at Josh and was surprised to see something that resembled hurt in his eyes. What had she done wrong?

Josh folded his napkin in his lap and took a drink of wine. She tried to catch his eye, but he was looking past Peter with a determined stare. She followed his gaze. He was staring at the back wall of the restaurant. *He's avoiding me. What have I done? I rattled on about Weston and Macy's. I've embarrassed him.*

"Would you excuse me, please?" Riley stood, forcing a smile

when both men stood as well. "I'm just going to run to the ladies' room." *And drown myself in the sink.*

JOSH'S BLOOD BOILED. Peter was not a man who incited conflict, and Josh was not at all prepared for the feelings that surged forth when Peter had asked if he and Riley were an item. He was still weeding through the whole date-versus-business-dinner conversation he'd had with Riley.

Josh wasn't known for giving up easily. He didn't get to where he was in the fashion industry by rolling over and playing nice. He worked hard and he took chances—chances that had led to his success and that he'd become known for.

Once Riley was out of earshot, Josh sat up straight and addressed Peter. He felt indebted to Peter for helping him make a name for himself all those years ago, but employing Claudia was payment enough, and Peter had obviously had too much to drink, so Josh took a professional approach. "Peter, Riley and I are not an item, but I'd appreciate it if you didn't approach her in that manner."

Peter sat back and crossed his legs. He lifted the left side of his mouth in a coy smile. "So you do have eyes for her? I knew I picked up on something. I apologize if I embarrassed you."

Josh held his stare. "I'm not sure what I have for her, but I would appreciate it if you'd refrain from stepping in and making it more difficult for me to figure out."

Peter leaned forward. "Message received. Childhood sweet-hearts reunited?"

I wish. That would be a lot easier to figure out. "No. Crush perhaps, not sweethearts," Josh admitted. He watched the direction Riley had gone in. The way his muscles ·tensed just having this discussion with Peter took him by surprise.

"If I might give you a bit of advice, Josh, getting involved with an employee can create a sticky situation. One you might not want to get tangled up in. That's how scandals are made."

Josh laughed. "I hardly think she's the scandalous type." He'd already gone down that line of thinking, and he wasn't sure of anything past knowing that when he saw her, when he touched her, even just their fingers brushing against one another sent something through him that he hadn't felt in a very long time. When she was nervous, when she blushed, and tonight, when she practically ran from the table, he found her adorable and wanted to wrap his arms around her and kiss the smooth skin of her cheek. He'd enjoyed their time together in Weston, and that was enough for him to know that he wanted the chance to see if there was more to it. More to them. Even if she was his employee. He'd figure that part out later. Right now, he didn't need Peter Stafford stepping in and wooing her, and he realized, he needed to find a way to let Riley know what he was feeling without scaring her off.

"They never appear to be the scandalous type until it's too late." Peter lifted his glass and looked down the bridge of his nose at Josh. "I have a new idea brewing that I want to talk to you about after the New Year. Let's see how tonight goes."

Chapter Nine

WHEN RILEY RETURNED to the table, Peter and Josh were discussing fashion. Relieved, Riley placed her napkin in her lap and listened, hoping to redeem herself with an intelligent comment of some sort. No longer hungry, she pushed the food around on her plate.

"I want class. Old-time class, not the typical New York cheesy trends. This means we stick to the more refined pieces of your Bliss line," Peter said.

Uh-oh.

"I don't believe any of the Bliss pieces are *cheesy*," Josh retorted.

"No, no, they're certainly not. I just meant to stick to the finer fabrics. Pencil skirts rather than flared, wool and silk, maybe a little leather. Something the older generation might take pride in wearing." Peter lowered his chin and looked at Riley from a discerning angle. "Don't you agree, Riley?"

Please don't put me in the middle. Wishing she could pick up a knife and slice through the tension, clearing a friendly path, she took a deep breath and said, "Actually, I find all of Josh's pieces refined, but I do understand the desire to attract a more mature audience." *Supportive yet discerning.* She shot a look at

Josh, who nodded, with an appreciative smile.

To a neighboring table, they probably looked like they were having a meaningful business meeting, but to Riley, who felt like a fly on the wall watching a silent game of one-upmanship, the exchange was unsettling.

"Riley, I'd be curious to see your designs. You don't mind, do you, Josh?" Peter smiled, and behind the facade, Riley saw fierce competition in his eyes.

Josh lifted his drink like he was going to toast. "Go right ahead. She's by far the most talented designer I've met in the past few months. She has a long career ahead of her."

Ohmygoshohmygosh! I do? Riley clutched her napkin in her lap to keep from jumping up and hugging him, and then she saw the way he sipped his drink, watching Peter above his glass. Was he using her as a playing card? Was he challenging Peter? *Oh no, what have I gotten myself into?*

JOSH PAID FOR dinner, and when they stood to leave, he was quick to pull out Riley's chair and put a possessive hand on her back.

"Peter, as always, it's been a pleasure. Have your secretary call Mia and schedule a meeting," Josh said with the most gracious smile he could muster while biting back his annoyance at the way Peter had tried to rile him and the way he'd reacted.

"I'm heading to Switzerland with my brother's family for the holidays. I'll schedule a time for after the New Year." Peter kissed Riley's cheek. "The pleasure was all mine." He shook Josh's hand. "I look forward to seeing this all come together."

Josh heard the double entendre loud and clear. "So do I," he said.

"Thank you for allowing me to join you for dinner. It was wonderful to meet you, and I'm honored to be included in the upcoming meetings," Riley said.

IN THE CAR, Josh wrestled with the conversation he'd had with Peter. The intent of their date—that wasn't a date at all in Riley's eyes—was to welcome her to New York, show her a good time, and get to know her better, and he wasn't going to let anything waylay his plans.

"That went well, don't you think?" he said.

"Yes, he's very nice." Riley played with the edge of her purse. "So, Claudia is his niece?"

He'd almost forgotten that relationship had been revealed. "Yes. Peter helped me get started in the business years ago, and when Claudia graduated from college and needed a job…" He shrugged. "I'm a loyal guy. What can I say?"

"I guess that explains a few things. I sort of wondered how you guys got connected. She seems…different from the other employees," Riley explained. Before he could respond, she said, "Josh, I'm really sorry if I embarrassed you with Peter. I didn't mean to talk about Weston like I was some cowgirl hick. I'm mortified."

"Is that what you think went on in there?" Josh couldn't bear the way she stared at her hands and sat stiffly beside him. It was a beautiful evening, and he was determined not to let Peter's comments ruin it. He reached over and lifted her chin until her eyes met his.

"Riley, you didn't do anything wrong. Your personality

sparkled. I love how much enthusiasm you have for life, for people, and of course, for designing." Boy, he wanted to lean forward and kiss her luscious lips, tangle his fingers in her hair, and press her full body against him.

Her lips parted, but no words came. He watched the tip of her tongue move slowly over her lower lip and he felt himself staring. He shook his head to stop his brain from wondering how her lips would taste on his.

"Peter's questions about us, and his intense interest in you, were his way of telling me that he was…interested." There. He'd said it. At least part of the truth.

"In me?" Riley laughed. "Did you have too much wine? I'm nobody. He was just being nice. I'll bet he treats all the women that way—and better."

She looked away, and he drew her chin back once again, lowering his voice to what he hoped was an honest, meaningful tone. If she saw Peter as someone who treated women a certain way, surely she saw Josh as the same type of person. They weren't so far removed in the industry, after all.

"Riley, I've known Peter since I began designing, and I can assure you that he does not treat all women that way. In fact, I have never seen him so forward with a woman that accompanied another man." He waited for understanding to dawn on her. She glanced down, and when she looked up at him again, the green in her eyes caught the light, and a hint of that spark that he'd seen while she'd spoken of Weston returned, hidden behind a shroud of confusion.

"But…this was business, and surely he knew that," she said. She shook her head. "It was business."

"That's what you tell me." Josh smiled, but inside he cringed, knowing he was pushing the limits. She might not want anything more from him than a job.

"But I thought…you said just to pretend we were back home." She clung to her purse.

"It's not what I'd hoped for," he admitted. "I saw how nervous you were, and I wanted you to be comfortable."

"Not what you hoped for? You mean the flowers, the kiss—"

"I don't ask women on dates very often, Riley. I'm out of practice, and stupid me, I thought yellow roses with red tips signified a growing attraction between friends."

"They do?"

She sounded breathless. Josh felt a stirring in his groin, a constriction in his chest.

"They do." He searched her eyes for an indication that she felt the magnetism that was drawing them together like metal to magnet. "Red alone is romantic love; yellow adds friendship, hopes, and promises."

"Hopes," Riley whispered.

"Red alone," he said. "Maybe one day. Riley…"

She licked her lips again, and this time he let his body lead them. He took her face in his palms and kissed her softly, soaking in the sweet taste of wine on her tongue and the warmth of her mouth, and finally, the release of tension as she kissed him back—tentatively at first, then harder, meeting his passion with her own, probing his mouth with her tongue. Josh could have kissed her for hours. He forced himself to pull away for fear of taking things any further in the backseat of his company car. He had to gain control of his emotions.

They stared into each other's eyes, the air between them sexually charged. Her chest heaved with every breath. He longed to kiss her again, to touch the milky crest of her breast, which had been taunting him all night. Instead, he took her hand in his and fought his desires. He might not have dated for a long time, but he knew the risks of going too fast—and even if he hated to admit it, Peter had a point about scandals. He wasn't worried about himself in that regard, but heaven only knew what kind of torture Claudia would put Riley through if she knew how Josh's feelings were taking flight.

"Let's go see New York," he managed. He couldn't erase the smile from his face if someone paid him to do it. His heart danced with renewed energy, and as he looked out the window, even the lights of the city seemed brighter.

"Jay," he said to the driver. "Longacre Theatre please."

"Yes, sir," Jay said.

A nervous smile lingered on Riley's face, worrying him. Had he misread her? Overstepped the boundary of their friendship?

"Do you regret our kiss?" he asked.

"Regret?" she asked. "No, definitely not." She smiled and squeezed his hand.

He found her nervousness endearing and breathed a sigh of relief to know she didn't regret the kiss he adored. For the first time in months, Josh felt like he had something to look forward to besides work. A country song came on the radio, and he reached for the rear controls to change the station.

"No, please. He's my favorite," Riley said.

"Who is it?"

"Hunter Hayes. 'Wanted' is my favorite song ever."

"Wanted." Hunter Hayes. Josh made a mental note of her favorite artist.

"The city is so beautiful," Riley said as she craned her neck, looking up at the illuminated signs as they passed. "This is so different from home. You know, I used to look at pictures of New York and think that I couldn't wait to get there and experience it, and now that I'm here, I know that I never could have imagined what it would have done to me." She turned back to Josh with a wide smile. "It's like just being here pumps me with energy. I want to experience it all—the lights, the nights..." Her smile faded.

"What is it?" Josh asked.

Riley groaned. "Oh, nothing about tonight. I'm just a little afraid to take the subway, and I'm realizing that I really need to."

He squeezed her hand, an idea taking hold. "We'll see if we can take care of that."

"How?" she asked.

"We'll see."

Riley turned back toward the window. "Look, there's Tiffany's." She whipped her head around. "Oh my gosh. I sound like such a tourist. I'm so sorry."

She was too cute. "Don't be. I love it."

As they neared the theater, his nerves became addled again. Paparazzi were known for stalking theaters and restaurants. Luckily, Jay was adept at evasion. He'd worked for Josh for five years, and in that time, had never let him down. He drove two blocks past the stone-faced theater and turned down a dark street.

Josh told Jay they'd walk home and opened Riley's door for her.

"Didn't we just pass the theater?" Riley asked as she stepped from the car.

"We're just avoiding the media hounds. I don't think you want to deal with Claudia seeing us on the front page of the newspaper tomorrow, do you?"

Her eyes grew wide. "Goodness, no."

He couldn't fight the urge any longer. He leaned in and kissed her quickly on the lips, wanting to do so much more. As he pulled away, she leaned in and deepened the kiss, telling him everything he needed to know.

"Come on," he said, taking her hand in his. They hurried around the corner.

"Mr. Braden, what a pleasure to see you." The older gentleman who greeted them inside the back entrance had thinning gray hair and wore a white dress shirt and gray slacks. "Ms. Banks, we hope you enjoy the show."

Riley squeezed Josh's hand. "Thank you," she said.

When Josh made the arrangements for the tickets, he'd also prepared Frank Rimmel for their entrance. He could see by the light in Riley's eyes that she felt as special as he had hoped she would. "Frank has run the doors here for twenty years. Thank you, Frank," Josh said, and followed the concrete hallway through a maze that grew more magnificent with each step. They wound their way down a heavily traveled red carpet to center-stage seats.

Riley let go of Josh's hand as she took her seat, and Josh felt the emptiness like a missing friend. *How could that happen so fast?*

"This is so exciting. How did you get tickets so quickly?" Riley asked with wide eyes. She scanned the stage, the audience, and finally Josh. "Thank you for taking me here."

"The show is called *First Date*. I thought it was appropriate, so I made a few phone calls," Josh answered. He slid his hand into hers.

She looked at him with warmth in her eyes, and as she leaned toward him, he thought she might initiate a kiss. She whispered, "*First Date?* Really? You're so thoughtful. This is incredible. It's so majestic but so intimate at the same time. I don't think we're in Kansas anymore, Toto," she joked.

In the flash of her words, Josh was thrown back to the concert once again: comfortable and happy and full of wonder about the woman who had reentered his life without warning.

The musical comedy began, and Josh watched Riley more than he watched the show. Her laugh was loud and hearty and anything but feminine. She threw her head back with her mouth open and roared; tears of joy streamed from her eyes. Her enjoyment was infectious, and Josh found himself not curtailing his own laugh for the first time in years. He was so used to making sure he was projecting an appropriate image for a man of his status that he hadn't realized how much of his life had been impacted by his career. Or perhaps *limited* was a better word.

By the time the show ended, Riley's tears of laughter had washed away most of her makeup, revealing the natural beauty that lay beneath. Her high cheekbones shone pink, and her thick lashes set off the glow of yellows and greens in her hazel eyes. Josh felt a tug in his heart, the speed of which threw him for a loop.

As they headed for the front exit, Riley slowed her pace. "Shouldn't we go out the back?"

He'd been so caught up in her that he'd almost forgotten. "The back will be swarming with people trying to get autographs. We're better off going out the front with a bit of cover." The last thing he wanted was to let go of her hand, but if he had any hope of shielding her from the media, they had to exit separately. Chances were strong that there wouldn't be any media out front. Photographers usually stalked the back entrance after the shows to take pictures of the actors.

The thought of anyone but Claudia seeing them holding hands didn't bother Josh, but Claudia could make Riley's life miserable. "Riley, we should walk out like we're not together. I'm really sorry, but just in case. It's probably for the best. You can leave first, and I'll follow. Go to your left and I'll meet you around the corner."

"Oh, good idea. You're so sneaky." Riley laughed. She let go of his hand and whispered, "I feel like I'm sneaking around in high school or something."

"Me too, but you're the last person I want to sneak with," he said honestly.

She frowned, and he realized she thought he meant something other than what he'd intended.

"I mean I'd rather walk out holding your hand, but I don't want to give Claudia a reason to treat you any differently."

"Why do you let her be that way?" Riley asked.

"I don't let her. Claudia is who she is. There's no changing her personality, but she's the best design assistant anyone could have, and...she's Peter's niece."

Riley flushed and looked down.

"What?" Josh asked.

"I thought you two were, you know..."

Josh shook his head. "What on earth would make you think that?" If Claudia had planted that seed in Riley's mind, he'd speak to her first thing in the morning. *That* was going too far.

Riley shrugged. "Something about the way she was around you the day we met."

"She's a master at manipulation and creating false impressions. I'm aware of her tricks, but I didn't think you'd really buy into them." *Or I'd have cleared it up right then.* Josh would straighten that situation out tomorrow as well. No more of her invasions of his personal space. It was high time he stepped up and gave Claudia a few rules.

Riley shrugged. "It was hard not to."

"Wait, you don't think that I…No, no, no. I have never and have no interest. Riley, really?" How could she think he'd ever fall prey to Claudia's games? *Do I come across as that much of a player?* Josh hadn't realized that the image he projected of himself could be so clearly misconstrued by those who knew him. Then again, he'd only begun to get to really know Riley. Growing up together in a small town where family feuds ruled out friendships and crushes grew from afar didn't exactly offer a chance to develop a well-rounded view of a person.

"Sorry. I know better now, but then…"

Josh let it drop. At the exit, he watched her walk alone down the busy street. Every second made him feel more like a heel. *Screw this.* He hurried down the sidewalk and clasped Riley's hand before she turned the corner.

She started. "Wait. They might—"

He kissed her—hard—and when her body relaxed in to him, he kissed her longer, deeper. When they drew apart, she was breathless again. He was beginning to enjoy the haze of desire in her eyes each time their lips met.

"I'm not hiding, Riley. I'll deal with Claudia and make sure you have nothing to worry about, but I'm not going to let one woman rob us of these moments." Josh breathed fast and hard, bowled over by his own desire to go public about their relationship. Even if it appeared to be in the beginning stages, it had been silently incubating for years, testing his willpower when he was younger and waiting at bay ever since. He wanted to tell everyone—his family, his employees, his colleagues.

Riley blinked at him in silence.

His gut wrenched. "Did I misunderstand? Are you not interested in seeing each other?" *He held his breath.*

"No." Her eyes grew wide. "I mean, I didn't realize how much I wanted this. I do. I want this."

He let out a relieved breath.

"But, Josh, I'll be a laughingstock. A cliché. *Girl sleeps her way to the top.* I'll be tomorrow's water cooler chat, and I don't want that."

She was right. The problem was, Josh wasn't willing to let her go before they even got started. He respected her, and he didn't want her to be uncomfortable, but he also wanted to be with her.

"Does that mean you want to sneak around?" Josh asked. Before she answered, he guided her around the corner of the building, beneath a blown-out light and out of eyesight of any passersby. He wrapped his arms around her waist and lowered his lips to hers again, pressing his hips against hers—and, wow, she felt incredible. He ran his hands along the curves of her hips, memorizing the feel of them for those moments when he wouldn't be able to reach out and touch her. He kissed her neck, her shoulder.

"Yes," she said in a rushed whisper. "Yes, I want to sneak around. I know that sounds stupid, but I just got here, and I'm already fighting an uphill battle."

He ran his finger along her collarbone.

"Okay," he said, looking into her eyes. "Sneaking around it is, but just for the record, I hate it already. It's been so long since I've felt enthusiastic about anything other than work, and Riley"—he lifted her chin so their eyes met—"you stir all sorts of excitement within me."

When Josh had offered Riley the job back in Weston, he'd

planned on showing her around New York, getting to know her a little better, and figuring out if what he felt in Weston had been real. He no longer needed clarification. His body ached for Riley. He wanted her. He needed her. From the sultry look in her eyes, he thought she felt the same, but he also didn't want to rush her.

RILEY HEARD HIS words, but her heart had leapt into her throat and stolen her voice when he'd said, *You stir all sorts of excitement within me.*

"Riley?" Josh touched her arm. "Do you want to take a walk?"

My pulse is racing. I could jog if you wanted to.

He closed in on her again, pressing her back against the wall, and he settled his cheek beside hers. Riley breathed in his rich, distinctive scent, which seeped right into her body, and drew her hands to his waist.

"You smell *so* good." *Shoot. Did I say that out loud?* She closed her eyes.

"It's Clive Christian," he whispered in a deep, seductive voice. "They say that for four thousand years it's been used to draw soulmates together."

She swallowed a whimper of desire.

He slid his mouth toward her ear, exposing his neck too close to Riley's lips. She could practically taste his skin. She bit her lip to stop herself from doing just that.

Josh kissed the edge of her ear. "Are you sure you want to sneak?" His breath was hot against her skin. "Because there's nothing I'd rather do than hold your hand when we walk down

How could she tell the man she'd dreamed of for years that she didn't want to hold his hand, when she really wanted to do so much more?

He drew back. His eyes said, *I want you.* His hands on her waist choreographed, *I need you,* and Riley wondered if he could read her desires just as easily. But her mind struggled with a thought she tried to push away.

He's my boss.

She swallowed hard, reaching for her voice, which was buried beneath a thick stream of lust. "I'm...sorry. Yes," she managed.

He kissed her on the cheek. "I respect your decision."

Josh took a step back, and Riley swore she felt her heart trying to claw its way through her chest to join him.

"Shall we?" He motioned toward the sidewalk. *I want you* lingered in his eyes.

Riley tried to ignore the battling voices in her head. *Sneak around? Are you stupid? You don't tell someone like Josh you want to sneak around. You don't even want to! I have to. Claudia will make my life a nightmare. You're insane. Point taken. I'm talking to myself. Stopitstopitstopit.*

They walked along Times Square. Josh pointed out shops and talked about the different districts in the city, and as he spoke, Riley's mind wandered. The combination of high-rise buildings, neon lights, and the rush of cars should have held her transfixed. New York was everything Weston was not, but she was so taken with everything about Josh that the streets, which surely breathed life into the air, were muted by the bubble of romance that had formed around them. The memory of her hand in his was so strong that when she made a fist, it was his

61

palm she felt on her fingertips. She licked her lips and tasted Josh's sweetness. The smell of his cologne was pungent, and with every shift of the evening air, it reminded her of how close their bodies had been only moments earlier. When she concentrated really hard, she could recall the faint scratch of his five-o'clock shadow as it grazed her cheek.

A cab blew its horn, startling Riley.

"You okay?" Josh asked.

"Yeah." She shook her head to try to escape the dreamy state she'd fallen into. Times Square came back into focus. "This is beautiful. Does it go on all night? The people, the lights, the cars?"

"Pretty much." He reached for her hand as they crossed the street and then quickly pulled it back. "Sorry."

"No, I'm sorry. I know this must seem really stupid to you, but I don't want Claudia to have anything to hold over my head, and I know New York is a really big city and the chances of her or someone she knows seeing us is probably slim, but—"

"Not as slim as you might think. When the media is in need of gossip, I'm definitely a target," he said with a shake of his head.

"Just so you know, that's not very comforting." *This is going to be harder than I thought.* "I really want to have a chance in the industry, and I can't do that if I start out with a reputation of dating not just the boss, but...well...*you.* Famed, iconic fashion designer Josh Braden." *I sound like a fan girl.*

He slowed his pace. "I don't think it's stupid at all. I might not like sneaking around, but that's just me being selfish because I haven't wanted to hold a woman's hand or take her face in my hands and kiss her until she forgets her name—" He stopped walking and stepped toward her.

Kiss him. Just do it. Riley was lost in the thought of what he wanted to do. She couldn't move, could barely think past what that kiss would feel like.

"In forever," Josh said. "And you spur all of that in me." His eyes searched hers. "When we were together back home, I felt something, but I wasn't sure if it was real or not."

He looked away, and Riley's breath caught. His profile was even more striking set against the backdrop of Times Square.

"I felt it, too," she whispered. She wasn't sure if he'd heard her, and she wasn't brave enough to say it again.

"I understand why you want to be careful, and as I said, I respect your decision," he explained. "That doesn't mean it'll be easy, and if I stand here looking at your beautiful face, I'm liable to do something that in no way resembles sneaking." Josh put his hand on the small of her back for a step or two. "Come on. I want to show you something." He shoved his hand in his pants pocket.

It was all Riley could do to keep breathing. She followed alongside him in silence, the sounds of the busy street fading behind them. When they crossed Fifth Avenue, they were swallowed by an enchanting hush. Unlike Times Square, there were no neon lights or open storefronts. It was as if they had walked into a secret world, and in that peaceful hush, Riley's pulse calmed and her mind cleared, and she was finally able to think clearly.

"Where are we going?" she asked.

"It's a surprise, but we're almost there. This is one of my favorite stretches of sidewalk. Can you feel it?" He held his hands out to his sides as they walked.

"The peaceful, magical aura?" Riley asked.

"Yes. I never really knew what to call it, but that's definitely spot-on." He put his hands back in his pockets, and Riley wondered if it was to temper his desire to hold her hand—or more.

They came upon busier streets and bright lights, and the serene hush vanished like a thought in the wind.

"Is that—" Riley felt her eyes grow wide.

"Grand Central Station." A smile stretched across his lips. "I've lived here for so long that I almost forgot how spectacular this place really is."

"It's brilliant," she said. "Are we going in there?"

"We are." He reached for her hand again, and she put it out without thinking. Their fingers touched, their eyes met, and for a split second everything felt perfect, and then the voice came back—*he's your boss*—and Riley drew her hand back to her side and looked away. *Maybe I made a mistake. He is my boss.* She looked back at Josh's hand. *But he's also Josh.*

"It's okay," he said. "Come on."

She followed him inside the exquisite building. Her heels clicked and clacked as they crossed the station. The impossibly high, arched, green ceiling grew from golden walls with thick columns. Riley took in the magnificent structure with glorious windows that allowed the moonlight to filter in, giving the evening an even more charming feel.

She and Josh walked past an enormous newsstand and under a portal. They appeared to be walking to another exit, and just before they reached it, Josh pointed to an escalator.

"Down there? Where exactly are you taking me?" she asked.

"I'll show you." He motioned toward the escalator, and Riley stepped on.

She clutched the railing as they descended beneath the ground. "This is a little nerve-racking."

"That's why you're doing it with me," he said.

They landed on a concrete platform with subway lines running in both directions.

"Josh," she said. She had a sinking feeling in the pit of her stomach. "I'm not sure I'm ready for this."

"Ri, look at me."

She did, but her eyes darted back to the platform and the dark tunnel just beyond.

"I'm right here," Josh said. "I'm not going to let anything happen to you. You are a smart, capable woman, and I don't want you to feel like there's anything you can't do. I promise that when we're done, you'll feel totally different about the subway."

She wished she could just tuck herself beneath his arm and cuddle up against his muscular body, hiding from any possibility of getting on a train.

"Trust me?" he asked.

She nodded.

"That's all I ask," Josh said.

Riley's legs shook and she held her breath as they stepped over the edge of the platform and onto the train. Josh held her arm in one hand and put the other firmly across her back long enough for her to find safety hanging on to a metal pole. She didn't mind that there was no place to sit. It gave her a reason to stand closer to Josh, and with her nerves tied in knots, she needed the security of being close to him. An older woman read the newspaper; her silver eyeglass frames slipped down her nose every few seconds, and she'd wrinkle her nose, then push them up with her finger, and repeat the act again a minute later. At the far end of the train, a group of high-school-aged kids gathered, laughing and smiling. Riley marveled at their ease.

Why am I so nervous? The seats were packed tight with people whose eyes were locked on the floor before them.

Each time the train stopped, more people got off the train, and by the third stop, Riley wasn't as nervous. She watched women and men in groups and alone, and the longer she watched, the more she realized that the subway *was* a way of life in New York. It was like taking the bus through Weston or Allure. She looked up at Josh, who was watching her intently, and she couldn't believe he'd take his time to help her through her fear. Then again, this was Josh Braden, who, as a fifth grader, had given his lunch to a boy who had dropped his tray in the school cafeteria. She'd almost forgotten about that incident, and as she looked at his handsome face, she realized that the boy he'd been was likely very similar to the man he'd become.

After the next stop, they settled into the hard seats, and soon there were only three other people on the train with them.

"It smells a little like cigarettes and stale food, but you can't smoke in here, can you?" Riley asked.

"It's from the people. Pack enough smokers into any confined space and you're bound to have some residual odor. I close my eyes and imagine the rumbling beneath me is a roller coaster, or a toboggan, and then I can actually smell it," Josh said.

"You can smell the crisp air of a snowy mountaintop? In here?" Riley asked with a smile.

"I'm a designer. I can design anything in my head. Then all I have to do is convince my brain to believe it. Try it," he said.

Riley closed her eyes and let out a sigh.

"Think about being back home. Remember that hill behind the high school?"

Riley nodded.

"Remember as a kid how everyone would sled all day when they closed the schools? Pretend you're there."

Riley knew exactly where he was talking about. The problem was, every time she and Jade had gone there, they'd spent half the time pretending not to stare at Rex and Josh. As she tried to force the smell of the Colorado winter air, thoughts of Josh brought the smell of Clive Christian cologne. Riley felt her cheeks flush.

"Is it working?"

"Better than I'd imagined," she said. When she opened her eyes, the last person was stepping off the train. "This is the Brooklyn Bridge stop. Isn't that the last stop?" She rose to her feet. "Don't we have to get off?" *Why are you still sitting down?*

"Everyone thinks this is the last stop." Josh rose to his feet and put one strong arm around her waist, pulling her against him. "We're all alone. No eyes, no ears."

He lowered his mouth, and Riley nervously rose on her tiptoes to meet him. *Last stop? Where are we heading?* The minute their lips touched, her anxiety fell away. She'd trust him to take her anywhere. When he deepened the kiss, she couldn't imagine how her legs were still holding her up. The train lurched to the side, and they drew apart. Josh held the metal pole with his free hand, stabilizing them, clutching her close with the other.

"See, there's no reason to be afraid of the subway," he said. "Just be smart. Were you nervous?"

Only about being so close to you. "Not really."

"Good. Everyone's got someplace to be, and you'll be taking the train to and from work. That's safe, Ri. I don't want you worrying about going places. The subway is a must in New

York."

"I know. I feel much better about it. I might not ride it alone at night for a while, but I think I can do the morning commute without worrying too much. It'll just take a little getting used to." She couldn't believe he had remembered her comment about needing to master the subway. His thoughtfulness tugged at her heart. "Thank you," she said.

"Here. Sit with me. The train's going to make a sharp turn, and when it does, you're going to see the most beautiful, forgotten subway station in New York."

"Forgotten?"

The train slowed, screeching against the rails as it made its way around the loop. Riley and Josh shaded their eyes and peered through the windows.

"Oh my gosh. What is that? It's so ornate. Josh, it's glorious." And just as fast as it had appeared, it faded back to concrete. Riley came away from the window with her mouth agape.

"It's built below City Hall. They renovated the station a few years ago, but they never opened it to the public. It's beautiful, isn't it? It's dark, so I know it was difficult to see," Josh said.

"It was incredible. Does everyone in New York know it's here?"

Josh shook his head.

"How did you know? Wait. Don't tell me if you found it with some other woman." She cringed at the thought. She'd seen the magazine pictures of Josh with beautiful models on his arm and she tried not to think about it. *Stop it. Everyone has a past.*

"You're so cute." He put his arm around her. "My real estate agent." He kissed her cheek. "He told me about it." He kissed her neck, and Riley closed her eyes, relishing in the motion of the train and the feel of Josh's lips. "At least in here we don't have to hide." He took her in another kiss, and his hand gripped her rib cage.

Heat rushed through her, and as the train slowed at the next station, Riley had only one thought. *I'm already sick of sneaking around.*

Chapter Ten

THIS IS A dream. It has to be. Riley stood at the entrance of Savannah's apartment—her choice. Josh had invited her to his apartment, but she worried that being seen coming or going from Josh's apartment might raise eyebrows. She hated worrying about that, and when they were kissing on the train, she'd been ready to forget about sneaking around, but when the cool night air hit her cheeks, she realized that reality would be waiting for her at eight o'clock the next morning.

From the first time Josh's lips touched hers, Riley had a hard time thinking about anything else. The musical had been a romantic and very enjoyable distraction, and helping her overcome her fear of the subway was the most thoughtful thing he could have done, but now, holding Josh's hand, knowing they were on the cusp of crossing the line between employee and lover, all she could think about was being close to him.

Her fingers trembled as she fumbled with the key. Josh reached around her, pressing his body against her back, and put his hand over hers, settling the key into place. His breath was hot on her neck, and she closed her eyes as he turned the key, soaking in the feel of him against her.

The door swung open, and Riley's nerves caught fire. *Oh my gosh! I'm going to have sex in his sister's apartment. This is wrong on so many levels.* Josh wrapped his arms around her from behind, kissing her neck, then nibbling her earlobe and whispering in her ear.

"Let's go inside so I can kiss you some more."

Who cares about wrong? Riley spun around and grabbed the collar of his shirt, pulling him into the apartment. He kicked the door shut behind them. She'd stifled her desire for him for too long. She wanted him, and she wasn't going to let something like who owned an apartment stop her from doing what her body and heart had been yearning for forever. The need was too great. She worked the buttons on his shirt as they made out like horny teenagers on their way toward the bedroom. It'd been too long since she'd felt such a craving for wantonness. Josh pulled back long enough to rip his shirt off and toss it aside. He reached for her dress, and Riley reached for the light switch.

"I want to see you," he said.

Not after all the skinny models you've dated. "I'm a little embarrassed," she admitted.

He cupped her cheek with his hand—a mannerism that she'd already come to long for—and whispered, "You're the most beautiful woman I've ever met."

I don't care if it's a lie or the truth. You just got major brownie points. She reached for a candle on the bookshelf. "Okay?"

"Perfect." Josh took a pack of matches from the shelf and lit the candle, then set it down on the bedside table. He pulled his wallet from his pocket and set it beside the candle.

There were only three steps between them, but three steps felt like a giant abyss. Riley moved toward him, and he met her halfway, reaching his hand beneath her hair and gripping the base of her head. His hand was large and warm, and as he pulled her into a kiss, she wanted to touch him, to feel her skin against his, but she hesitated. *Will he think I'm too forward?* His tongue explored the curve of her mouth and the fullness of her lower lip; then he took her lip between his teeth, sending a sizzling need through her revved-up body, and just when she couldn't hold back any longer, he raised her dress over her head. He kissed her again, and she reached for the button on his pants, drawing them down without ever missing a beat of his warm mouth against hers. Josh stepped back, raking her body with a slow, hungry leer.

"Riley, you're exquisite."

She looked down at her black lace bra and the line of her thong. What she saw was so different from what he did, but somehow, the way his eyes lingered over the curves of her hips and the fullness of her breasts gave her confidence. She stepped out of her heels slowly, savoring the heat that filled the space between them. She wanted to remember this moment forever. His sculpted chest and arms were so different from what she'd envisioned beneath his fine suits. Even her fantasies hadn't come close to the hardness and definition of his perfect body. *He's so handsome.*

There was no music, no other noise in the room besides their heated breaths. Riley swore she could hear her heart thundering against her chest. Moonlight filtered in through the curtains, casting shadows that danced with the light of the flickering candle across the thick comforter. When Josh reached for her, Riley closed her eyes, wanting to luxuriate in the feel of his hands as they explored her, and she didn't want to think past the next few breaths. She pushed away the worry of tomorrow, and when she felt Josh's breath on her cheek, she opened her eyes.

He kissed her again, and she wrapped her hands around his muscular back. His skin was hot, his muscles rock hard beneath her palms. She slid her hand to the curve of his back, just above the waist of his boxers, wishing she could stop her fingers from trembling. Riley had been with only three men, but she was able to distinguish the difference. The nervousness she felt was caused by more than just being with any man. She was trembling because the man she was with was the only man she'd ever really wanted. *Josh.*

She'd dreamed of what his mouth would feel like on her for so long that she nearly melted beneath his touch.

Josh guided her down to her back on the bed, perching above her and looking deep into her eyes. He brushed her bangs from her forehead and smiled. "You okay?"

Riley's voice was lost in his touch. "Mm-hmm" was all she could manage.

"I don't want you to do anything you don't want to, Riley. I wanted to take things slowly, but…"

She reached up and touched the prickly shadow that'd formed on his cheek. He was no longer Josh Braden, designer, employer. He'd become just Josh, the sweet, sexy man she'd had a crush on for years. No way was she going to stifle one more urge.

"I don't want to go slow," she said.

RILEY'S CURVES WERE luscious and full, different from all the other women Josh had been with. She moved with him, not at him like most women did. His other dates were always directing, showing, taking. But not Riley. He wanted to rip that thong from her body and plunge into her, deep and hard, but he held back. He wanted to savor their passion, to live in it while it was new and unscathed. Who knew what tomorrow would hold? Josh had lived his whole life for tomorrow. Tonight he was living for *now*.

He lowered his mouth to hers again, feeling the satisfied fatigue of her kiss and arousing all sorts of licentious desires within him. Josh wanted *more*. He wanted to be as intimate as he could with Riley, to taste every inch of her. He hadn't done that with a woman in years. It was such an intimate act, something he'd never do with a woman who was using him to move ahead, or with someone he didn't see a future with. He was different from many men in that way, and when he was younger, he'd worried about that moral guideline, wondering if he were somehow strange to hold such a thing in high regard. Now, with Riley lying beneath him, her eyes filled with trust, her body open to him, and her heart filling his, he knew he'd been right to savor the sacred act.

"Ri, open your eyes. Be with me," he whispered, bringing her eyes to his, needing that closeness. She smiled, and the emotions swimming in her eyes nearly did him in. He reached for her hands, lacing them together, and he knew that come tomorrow, he'd have a hell of a time keeping his feelings for Riley a secret.

Chapter Eleven

RILEY AWOKE TO the sound of her cell phone vibrating on the bedside table. She reached for it without opening her eyes, and then she remembered the night before—and the missing piece. *Did we say goodbye?* She shot up in bed, pulling the covers against her chest. Her eyes scanned the bedroom. Josh's clothes were gone, his wallet, too. *Thank goodness. Oh no. Did he sneak out? Like a one-night stand?*

Her phone vibrated against her cheek, and she clicked the Talk button. "Hello?"

"You were supposed to call me last night."

"Jade," Riley whispered frantically into the phone as she climbed from the bed. She didn't know if Josh was outside the bedroom door, still in the apartment.

"What's wrong?" Jade asked.

"Nothing. Everything. Hold on." She set the phone on the nightstand and pulled on a T-shirt and underwear, then picked it back up. "It was a definite date."

"Why are we whispering?" Jade whispered.

"Because I can't remember saying goodbye to Josh after...you know."

"You and Josh?" Jade screamed into the phone. "Really?

This is wonderful!"

"No, it's not. I mean, it's wonderful, yes, but it's also crazy scary." She tiptoed into the living room and, seeing that she was alone, breathed a sigh of relief.

"Why is it scary?"

"Because. Now I'm sleeping with my boss, and you know Cruella will eat that up and spit me out for all to walk on." Riley noticed a note on the counter in the kitchen. "Hold on," she said as she retrieved and read the note.

Good morning, beautiful. Back soon. J.

"Oh my gosh."

"Riley, clue me in here," Jade urged.

"It's a note from Josh. He's coming back. What time is it?" The sun was just beginning to rise over the crest of the trees.

"Six your time," Jade said.

"Isn't it like four in the morning there? Jeez you get up early to take care of those animals. Why would he leave and then come back before six in the morning?" Riley went into the bathroom and turned on the shower. There was a freshly used towel hanging neatly on the towel rack. "He showered," she said.

"And you what? Slept through him getting ready and leaving after you had sex?" Jade's voice carried an entertained tone.

"Ugh. I must have. I don't even know what time we fell asleep."

"That's some good sex," Jade said. "Really, think about it. When's the last time you had sex and didn't want to push the guy out the door afterward? You're not exactly the sleepover type."

"Shut up. It's not like I'm a slut," Riley spat.

"No, but you are really picky, which tells me one thing loud and clear. Josh Braden is good in bed."

Riley turned off the water of the shower and sat on the toilet lid, thinking about the evening before. Josh had touched her with such care and attention, like he was savoring every moment as much as she'd been. "He was, but it was more than that. When you and Rex finally got together for good, did you feel like everything he did felt right?"

"What do you mean? He's a man, and no man does everything right." Jade laughed.

"No, I mean like every touch felt right. With most guys, when they touch you, they're rushing ahead and ready for the next step. You know, kiss, boob, coochie, boom. It wasn't like that with him." *Open your eyes. Be with me.* A chill ran up her spine with the memory.

"Sometimes that's nice, the rush of hot sex, but yeah, I know what you mean. So, what now? How will you handle Cruella?"

Riley blew out a breath. "That's the worst part. I told him I'd rather sneak around than let her know."

"No, you did not."

"Yes, I did. Oh, Jade. I'm such an idiot. He was ready to talk to her and tell her that we were seeing each other, and I kinda freaked out about being seen as the woman who slept her way to the top."

"Well," Jade said, "if you're gonna sleep your way to the top, you skipped all the in-between steps."

"Shut up. You know what I mean. I want to be taken seriously. Yes, I'm sleeping with Josh, but I'm not doing it to advance my career." Riley wondered if she'd made a mistake following her heart instead of her head. "I should end it, shouldn't I? Before we get any closer?" Even the thought of ending things with Josh brought a lump to her throat.

"Look, if Rex and I can overcome a family feud that had gone on for longer than we'd been alive, then you and Josh can survive rumors. Tell me this. What do you really feel for him?"

Riley shook her head. "I don't know. I like him. A lot. Maybe more than a lot, but maybe that's just because it's new and exciting. You know how that works. Sometimes, after a month or so, that initial glow wears off. What if it does and then I've ruined my career for good?"

"You know you're only kidding yourself, right?" Jade asked. "You've liked him since grade school. This isn't new. It's just now *revealed*. How can you deceive your own mind like that?"

Riley sighed. "I'm not. Okay, maybe I am. It's like all those years of watching him from afar—"

"Fantasizing about him late at night," Jade said.

"Maybe."

"I did about Rex, so I know you did about Josh."

"Fine, okay. I fantasized about him since the day my hormones kicked in, and the fantasies only grew stronger every time I saw him. It was easier when I was away at school. Then I could sort of put those thoughts away for a bit," Riley admitted.

"I know the feeling, but, Ri, this is real. This is happening, and you know you don't want to end it," Jade said.

A knock at the door pulled her from her thoughts.

"Someone's at the door. That has to be him. I gotta go. Talk later?" Riley asked.

"Yes, and, Ri?"

"Yeah?"

"There's nothing wrong with following your heart. Let yourself be happy."

Riley set the phone down and answered the door.

"Hi." Josh kissed her on the cheek and handed her a warm Starbucks cup. He breezed past her like he'd been handing her coffee every morning. He wore a pair of jogging shorts and a sweaty T-shirt and carried a garment bag and a gym bag over his shoulder.

"Hi." Riley closed the door and leaned against it, holding the warm cup between her hands. *Let me be happy.* The warmth of the cup didn't compare to the warmth in her heart as she watched Josh in all his incredible handsomeness swing the bags onto the couch and come toward her with open arms. When he wrapped her in his strong arms, his skin was icy cold and slick with sweat, and still, when he kissed her, she nearly melted, and when he whispered, "I missed you," into her ear, she was a goner. There was no way she'd end things with Josh to save herself from gossip. She froze against him. What was she supposed to do now? Go to work and act like nothing happened between them, like she'd basically asked him to do? How could she do that when what she really wanted to do was fall into his arms again and kiss him like there was no tomorrow.

"You okay?" he asked. "Is the coffee all right?"

"Yeah, perfect," she said.

"What is it? What's wrong?" His brow furrowed, and the concern in his eyes was genuine.

How could she tell him what was racing through her mind?

"Riley? Am I missing something? Should I have not come back?" he asked.

"No, no. It's not that. It's just…" *I like this too much. I want to wake up to you. I want you to bring me coffee. I just don't want to be known as the woman who made her career by sleeping with you.*

"Babe? What is it?"

Babe? I love that.

Riley turned away so he couldn't read her expression. She knew her eyes revealed her emotions. Jade had told her that hundreds of times.

She felt his arms around her. He rested his cheek against hers.

"Whatever it is, we can figure it out," he assured her.

Riley sighed. "Do you really want to do this?" *Why do I sound so scared? I hate that.*

"This? You mean"—he pressed his body against hers and kissed her cheek—"or *this* as in you and me in general?"

"This as in you and me in general." *Please tell me you do. No, please tell me you don't. Ugh!*

He pulled back and narrowed his eyes. "Forget what I want, Riley. What do you want? What will make you happiest? I don't ever want to thrust myself upon you. If you don't want to explore what's between us, I'll understand, and your job will be safe."

"No." She reached for his arm and felt his muscles tense beneath her fingers. "Josh, there's no doubt in my mind that I want you, and I don't want to hide and scheme. But I don't know if I can survive a gossip storm before I even have a chance to prove myself."

He pulled her close once again, holding the back of her head so her cheek rested against his chest, safe and warm.

"Oh, babe. This is not an easy thing to figure out." He pulled back and smiled, then cupped her cheek and kissed her. "But I want to figure it out. Let's talk about it." He took her hand and led her to the couch.

"Where'd you go this morning?" she asked.

"Running; then I swung by my place and grabbed clothes

and toiletries."

"You ran with your bags?" she asked.

"No. Jay brought them over. I didn't want you to think I was taking off after last night, but I'm kind of neurotic about my daily run. Was it okay that I came back?"

"Yes, definitely. But why did you—instead of getting ready at your place, I mean?"

"Riley, I wanted to exercise, not be away from you. I want to spend time with you, and if you're most comfortable that we do that in secret, then I'll steal every secret second that I can get. Besides, what kind of heel doesn't bring coffee the morning after a night like that?" He ran a hand through his hair. "I probably should have asked you first. I'm sorry. I didn't even think that I might get in the way or throw off your mojo. Women have rituals in the mornings." He laughed. "I'm a big boy. I can get ready at my place, no sweat." He stood.

Riley pulled him back down. "Josh, that's not what I meant at all. I've never met anyone like you. Most guys would be out the door and thrilled with it. You surprised me, that's all. Stay. Please stay."

He caressed her cheek. "I'm not most guys."

"Yeah, I know that. Most guys wouldn't offer to talk through a concern, either."

He raised his eyebrows. "It is a tough one. There aren't many choices. We can go to work and act like nothing is going on and see where our relationship goes, or we can go to work and face the music and endure the rumor mill. There is no middle ground. I'm up for whatever you think is best."

"You really are too good to be true. Aren't you worried at all about dating an employee? A brand-new assistant? You're not just my boss, Josh; you're a fashion icon. You run JBD. No, you *are* JBD. Doesn't it worry you to date someone from work, or..."

"Or what?"

Riley looked him in the eye and asked what had been nagging at her all morning. "Or have you dated people at work before? Are they used to it? You know, models come and go from JBD all the time."

Before she could blink, Josh was on top of her, holding her hands above her head and kissing her neck. Riley shrieked in surprise and delight.

"Really? Is that what you think I do? Find lonely assistants and models to sleep with?" He lifted her T-shirt and kissed her belly. "Because let me tell you something, missy, not only have I not dated anyone from work, but I've never dated anyone like you before." He tickled her ribs until she was screeching with laughter.

"Okay. Okay," she said through broken laughs.

He lowered his mouth to hers and kissed her again. *I could get used to this.*

"I think we're in trouble," he said.

"Yeah, I was thinking the same thing."

Chapter Twelve

JOSH SAT IN his office looking over a portfolio and trying to stop thinking about Riley. When he'd seen her standing by her desk, it had taken all of his willpower not to wrap his arms around her, and his body had reacted in ways reminiscent of his teenage years—even back then the mere sight of Riley incited a rise within his pants. He'd had to retreat to the safety of his office to regain control.

Mia peered into his office. "Treat's on line two for you."

"Thanks." He picked up the phone. "Treat, how are you?" He hadn't seen Treat since he and Max announced their wedding date a few weeks earlier.

"Great, and you?" Treat's voice was comforting, familiar.

"Better than ever. What's up?"

"Max and I are coming into town tomorrow. I'm sorry for the short notice, but I've got a business thing, and I thought if you're free, you could meet with Max about her wedding gown."

"Sure, whatever you need. When?"

Mia peeked into his office and he waved her in.

"I'll be done with my meeting around four, and we can meet anytime after that," Treat answered.

Josh covered the receiver. "What's on my plate tomorrow evening?" he asked Mia.

"Nothing. I already cleared it for Treat." She beamed.

Josh thought about Riley and wondered if Treat would mind if he brought her along. He turned his attention back to their call.

"You already cleared my schedule with Mia?"

"Hey, you're a busy man, and so am I." Treat laughed.

"It's cool. Actually, it's a big help. Do you mind if I bring Riley along? I'd love to hear her thoughts about Max's dress." Josh watched Mia raise her eyebrows. He covered the receiver again. "Did you need something else, Mia?"

"Just to let you know that Claudia is beyond evil today. I thought you might like to know."

His nerves twitched just thinking about Claudia treating Riley badly. It was one thing to allow her to remain as an employee out of loyalty and another to allow her to abuse his sense of loyalty and do harm to others. *Is my relationship with Peter worth this?* If only it were that easy to decipher. In the fashion industry, someone like Peter could make or break a designer's career, and vice versa.

"Oh, and don't forget," Mia added, "you have a seven-o'clock conference call tonight. Do you need me to be here?"

He made a mental note to have a stern talk with Claudia and to delay his date with Riley. "No, I can handle it. Thanks, Mia." He watched her leave the office.

"How's it going with Riley working for you?" Treat asked.

He knew his brother well enough to hear the silent question carefully wrapped within the verbal one, and he chose to ignore it. "She's doing a great job."

"And?"

"What makes you think there's an *and*?" He'd never been able to pull the wool over Treat's eyes. He didn't know why he expected to now.

"Josh, you brought her to Dad's for lunch a while back. You've never brought a single woman to Dad's for anything. Am I to believe that you were just being nice by bringing her to lunch because she's from our hometown?"

Josh leaned back in his chair. He'd spent years watching Treat in action. His brother owned resorts all over the world; he charmed some of the smartest businessmen into deals no one else would ever be able to secure. Josh had learned a lot about negotiations and manipulation from him, and now he couldn't come up with a single sentence to waylay his brother's inquiry.

"That would be nice, yeah," Josh said with a smile.

"Yeah, okay, so we'll pretend. You're still young. You have time to figure these things out."

Josh rolled his eyes. "Okay, fine. Let's cut to the chase. Riley and I just started dating. Yesterday."

"Yesterday? Wow, you did well. She's been in New York for a week and you held back a whole six days."

"Ha-ha," Josh said. "It wasn't my plan to date her when I brought her here. It just kind of happened. And I like her. A lot."

"Wait a second. Josh, you just admitted to dating someone. You haven't admitted to a single date in six years. Which takes this dating situation to a whole new level. You know that, don't you?"

He really was losing his grip when it came to all things Riley. Josh never talked about his personal life with Treat or anyone else. He'd been photographed with models and celebrities, and he'd never once opened his mouth to the media or to his family about the depth, or lack thereof, in his relationships with any of them. What was he doing? And why did it feel so good to talk about her?

"Treat, can we keep this just between us?"

"You know Max will be there to discuss the dress, right?" Treat pointed out.

"Between the three of us, then? Seriously. Riley wants to keep it on the down low for professional reasons."

"She does or you do?" Treat pried.

"She does. I was ready to tell everyone, but she doesn't want to be seen as sleeping her way to a career, and I don't blame her."

"Wait. You were ready to go public after one date?" Treat asked.

Josh hadn't thought of it that way. Had it really been just one date? He felt so close to her already. From the moment Rex had asked him to look at Riley's portfolio, the feelings Josh had had for her all those years growing up came rushing back. He'd been drawn to her again, like he'd been waiting for her his whole life and never realized it. Everything about being with her was different—better—than with any other woman. *That's why I was so ready to shout it from the rooftops after the play. Because it's Riley.* "Yeah, I guess I was," he admitted. "I don't know what it is about her, Treat, but she makes me happy. Happier than I've been in years."

Treat laughed. "I never thought I'd hear those words from your lips, bro. I'm happy for you. Who would have thought you'd end up with a girl from our little hometown? Wait till Dad hears this. He'll be in hog heaven, making all sorts of plans for you to move back home again."

"Not happening," Josh said, and just in case, he added,

"Promise me, Treat, not a word to Dad or anyone else. This is Riley's choice to keep things hush-hush. I respect her wishes, and I'd like you to as well."

"Josh." Treat used his most serious tone, and Josh pictured his dark eyes narrowed, his brows pulled together, and his arms crossed over his broad chest. "Riley might be okay with this, but are you? Rex and Jade tried to keep their relationship a secret, and it was really stressful for both of them. Are you sure this is the best route for a relationship you might want to build a future on?"

As the oldest, Treat had always stepped in with sound advice. Josh had been thinking about the same thing, and he didn't know the answer.

"If we tell everyone, she could go through hell on the career front. She'll get hurt more than I will. People expect me to date anyone I want. In fact, they'd probably applaud me for dating a newbie employee. People are so messed up. But Riley? They'll tear her down and rip her to shreds." His chest tightened. "She'll be tagged as the girl who slept her way to the top, and she'll run the risk of not being taken seriously. There is no easy answer, but I do think I'd rather be uncomfortable than have her being hurt from every angle." He ran his hand through his hair, hoping Treat might see an avenue that he hadn't. "Treat, what would you do?"

"Whew, that's a tough one. I guess you're doing the right thing. Small-town girl in a new city, cutthroat business. There's no easy way around this. Even if you date for a year, and she gets a promotion in that time period, she's still going to be tagged as that girl." Treat laughed. "Bro, you really know how to come out of the closet, don't you? First you say nothing, and when you finally do come clean, you do it with the most difficult situation you could possibly get involved in."

"Tell me about it."

"Riley's a nice girl. Jade speaks very highly of her, and Jade and Max have gotten really close since she and Rex got together. So, my best piece of advice is to be sure of whatever it is you want before taking it public. You're a Braden. You can weather any storm. But women, they're different. Even the tough ones are sensitive. They care about what people think far more than we do, and Riley's bound to get caught in some crossfire that she's unable to handle."

"Yeah, I know. Thanks, Treat. Hey, does seven work for you tomorrow?"

"Yeah, seven's fine. Should we meet you at your place?"

My place? Josh realized that he was already thinking of wherever Riley was as where he would be. He really was moving fast. But it was what it was, and he had no intention of changing it. As long as Riley wanted to keep their relationship a secret, she wouldn't be staying at his place, and they'd have to show up at the restaurant separately so they didn't give the impression of being on a date. That meant no touching, no holding hands, no…*Ugh.* This was going to be torture.

"Do you care where we eat?" Josh asked.

"Never, why?" Treat answered.

"Riley is staying at Savannah's until she finds an apartment. Why don't we have dinner there? I can whip something up, or have something delivered, and then the stress of being seen together is out of the picture."

"Works for me. Where's Savannah?"

"She's in LA for two weeks. She let Riley stay there until she found an apartment."

"Sounds good. Does Savannah know you're doin' her

roommate?" he teased.

"Wow, Treat. That's a little raunchy, don't you think? And no, she doesn't know. No one knows."

"I'll bet Jade does."

"Maybe," Josh said, wondering if she did.

"It'll be nice to see you."

"You too, Treat, and thanks for keeping this between us."

"Do me a favor, Josh. Have a backup plan. Things like this don't stay hidden for long. I think Rex and Jade lasted for less than two weeks before Rex lost it and had to tell everyone. Figure out your what-if plan, and make sure she doesn't get hurt."

"That's exactly what I was thinking. You taught me well."

Chapter Thirteen

"TRADE SHOWS ARE one of the most important aspects of our jobs," Claudia began. "We are a reflection of JBD, therefore"—she ran her eyes slowly down Riley's cream blouse and black pencil skirt, both of which were not high-fashion pieces, but they were stylish and professional—"you need to represent JBD. Get something from the closet. If you can find something that fits."

Riley clenched her jaw. *Let it go. Just let it go.* "I'll do that."

"You need to be there an hour early to set up the booth. Be sure the layout is perfect."

"Aren't you going to be there?" Riley asked. This was to be her first trade show. She had no idea how Josh liked things arranged.

"Yes, but I'll have things to do. I'll join you right before we open. And the show is trying something different this year. They're doing an evening premier, not morning, so plan on sticking around until ten at least. This is their first pre-Christmas show, and if it goes poorly, it'll be the last."

"Are there guidelines for the booth arrangement?" Riley's pulse sped up with the sneaking suspicion she was being set up to fail.

"Simone can fill you in on those details." Claudia waved a dismissive hand in the air, and when Riley waited for further direction, she snapped, "What?"

Riley blinked several times. *Are you for real?* "You made such a big deal about the trade show, I figured there was much more to it. I feel like I have no information. What do I put up? What about accessories? What can I expect at the show? Is it okay to show buyers alternative clothing arrangements? Accessories?" She had a million questions, and by the pinched look on Claudia's face, she knew she would walk away with all of them unanswered.

"Simone. Go see her." Claudia spun on her heel and walked away.

Riley gritted her teeth and headed for Simone. *Simone. Go see her. What am I? A dog? A child?* Riley was by no means a wallflower, and if anyone back home had treated her that way, she'd have set them straight, but she couldn't afford to piss off Claudia. She needed to learn the ranks. *Learn the ranks.* Riley stopped in her tracks. Maybe she'd been playing Claudia all wrong, acting strong, taking direction without question. She'd seen women like Claudia before. Claudia needed to be the queen bee, and luckily for Riley, she didn't mind being the unwanted stepsister. At least for now.

Instead of seeing Simone, she headed back to Claudia and approached her with a furrowed brow.

"What?"

"I know you said to see Simone, but I really want to learn from the best." She lowered her voice to a whisper. "And Josh says there's no one better than you. I really wish you'd show me around a little. It's obvious that you know exactly what needs to get done, and according to Josh, no one does it better than you." She opened her eyes wide and covered her mouth. "Oh goodness, please don't tell anyone I told you that. Josh probably didn't mean for it to be public knowledge." She bit her lower lip, then turned, fidgeted with her hands. "Never mind. I'm sure I'm overstepping my bounds." Riley took a step away.

"Stop," Claudia said.

Riley bit the insides of her cheeks to ensure a smile wouldn't suddenly appear and give her ruse away.

"Josh told you that, did he?" Claudia held Riley's gaze.

Riley hurried to her side, feigning a worried glance around the room, then whispered, "Yes, and so I just thought...well...that it would be best to learn directly from you. You obviously know what you're doing."

"Of course I do." Claudia lifted her chin. She tapped her pen on the desk, then shot to her feet. "Okay, but I don't have much time, so pay close attention."

Riley followed Claudia into another room, this one stocked with banners, brochures, and various racks and displays. Claudia pulled a binder from a shelf and leafed through it.

"These are photos of our previous displays. Results from each show are noted behind the images. Obviously, the designs must change from show to show, and the setup needs to be fresh as well, but I use this and pull ideas from each to create something new. Whatever you do, do not ever duplicate a display. Buyers are smart, and they have great memories for details. You have to be on top of your game. Memorize every item we bring to the show as well as our stock on hand."

"How can I possibly do that in two weeks?" Riley asked.

"You'll have to study the line sheets day and night until then. All of them. I always make sure to read through the tech packs, too, so I know what stitch is used on each garment."

Of course you do. "Oh, you are so smart. Okay, I'll do my best."

"Your best?" Claudia turned stern eyes on her. "You cannot *do* your best. You have to be perfect. There's no room for flustered newbies at the trade shows."

Then why am I going? "Of course. I won't let you down. I'll stay late and study them."

"Why don't you take them home tonight? I always find it easier to concentrate at home," Claudia offered.

"Really? I'm allowed to take them out of the office? I figured this stuff was proprietary."

"Oh, don't worry. If I say it's okay, it's okay." Claudia smiled and touched Riley's shoulder.

Riley tried not to bristle against her touch. "Thanks, Claudia. I really appreciate your help. I won't let you down." Why hadn't she thought of being a kiss up before today? Worked like a charm. Unless…Was this a setup of some sort? Was she going to get in trouble for taking them out of the office? She had a sinking feeling in the pit of her stomach and tried to will it away.

Riley studied the books for the next two hours, taking copious notes of the details she'd need to remember. As she headed back to her desk to review the line sheets, she saw Josh coming toward her, Mia by his side.

"Hey, Riley. How's it going?" Mia asked with a wide smile.

"Great. I'm really excited about the trade show." She tried not to make eye contact with Josh, but she felt his alluring eyes on her, drawing her in, and she couldn't remain evasive. She lifted her eyes. *Oh great, now I want to kiss him.* "Good morning, Josh."

He smiled, and she felt a rush of excitement all the way to

her toes.

"Riley," he said easily. "Have you found Claudia unusually wicked today?"

"Wicked? No. In fact, she's been nothing but pleasant today. It's been a nice surprise." *And a shocking one. I don't trust her.*

Mia's eyes darted between the two of them, and Riley realized she was staring at Josh with a girl-crush smile on her lips. "I've got to get to work," she said and rushed past them. Mia's voice hung in the air behind her.

"A little skittish today?" Mia asked.

Riley slowed her pace to catch Josh's response.

"Aren't all new employees?" he answered.

Thank you. She breathed a sigh of relief. Back at her desk, she sat down with the line sheets spread out before her for the Bliss line as well as the previous two seasons. She opened her desk drawer and reached for a pencil without looking. Something pricked her finger. She brought her bloody finger to her mouth and looked around before glancing in her desk. She wished she knew what Claudia was up to now. She did flip on the *nice* switch awfully quick. Riley wanted to believe that Claudia was just being nice after her suck-up act, but could she change her tune that fast—or at all? *If she's playing a prank after being so nice, I'll*—She looked into the drawer, then quickly rolled her chair to block the view from her officemates. She reached into the drawer and withdrew an orange rose. *Josh.* Her heart skipped a beat. She opened her purse and stuck the flower inside. As she was closing her purse, she found a note. She hid it in her fist and headed to the ladies' room. She wasn't going to be caught blushing at her desk.

After locking herself in a stall, she opened the note.

Beautiful Riley, please forgive me, but I have a conference call tonight. Can we move our date to 8? Can't wait to see you. I'll pick you up at Savannah's. Wear something scruffy. Yes, scruffy, not nice, not designer, not pretty.

—J

Scruffy? What does that mean? Do I even own anything scruffy?

FIVE O'CLOCK FOUND Riley hovering over line sheets. In her mind, she saw a blur of sizes, colors, and stock numbers running like a pattern on repeat.

"How's it going?" Claudia asked.

Riley started at her pleasant tone. "Great. It's a bit hard on the eyes, but it's going well. I've got some great ideas, and with another two weeks of studying, I think I'll have this information ingrained in my mind forever."

"Good. Remember, it has to be perfect."

"Perfect. Got it." Riley saw Josh heading their way, and she trained her eyes on the paper once again.

"Claudia, how's our newest employee coming along?" Josh asked.

"Oh, she's coming along," Claudia answered.

Claudia's seductive tone caught Riley's attention. Claudia touched Josh's arm and fluttered her lashes.

Oh no, you did not just do that. Riley tightened her fist around her pencil.

"I'm giving her a few extra pointers," Claudia said.

Riley clenched her jaw against the green-eyed monster that had snuck into her mind, but she could feel the heat creeping up her neck, the tightening of every muscle in her body. She dropped her eyes back to the line sheets and stewed.

"Thank you, Claudia. I knew you'd step up to the plate," Josh said.

"Always," she replied in that bedroom voice again.

I bet you do.

"Josh, I wanted to talk to you about a few things. I'm tied up for a bit, but will you still be here in an hour?" Claudia asked.

At that, Riley pushed from her chair, sending it skittering a few inches backward. In the most casual voice she could muster, she said, "Excuse me. Nature calls." She brushed past Josh, sure she was leaving a trail of smoke in her wake, but she was too annoyed with Claudia to care.

Chapter Fourteen

JOSH SPENT THE afternoon dealing with buyers, meeting with his accountant, and taking phone calls. He watched the minutes tick by, the phone pressed to his ear.

"There's just one more thing I want to say," Peter Stafford said.

Josh had been on the phone with Peter for the past twenty minutes, and he was anxious to wrap up their conversation.

"Josh, I'm sorry for appearing forward with Riley Banks. I wasn't myself that evening," Peter said. "And I'm afraid I embarrassed myself."

It had been Peter's interference that had sprung Josh into action. He was glad for the push, but he wasn't about to let Peter know that. *Never let a business associate have the upper hand*—another of Treat's lessons.

"I thought something was a bit…off," Josh said.

"You have my sincerest apologies, and if I made Riley uncomfortable, I am truly and deeply sorry. I will apologize to her when I see her at the meeting after the New Year."

Josh waited for Peter to elaborate on why he'd gone down that road with Riley, and when he didn't, Josh let it drop. He accepted Peter's apology, and by the time he came up for air, it was six forty-five.

He went to the design studio and was surprised to find that Riley and most of the staff had already left for the evening. With fifteen unspoken-for minutes before his conference call, he headed back to his office and called Riley's cell.

"How's my secret girlfriend?" *Girlfriend.* He liked that.

"Tired and cranky," she said.

"Too tired to see me?"

"No way. You can take my crankiness away," she said.

He loved her honesty. "Does your crankiness have something to do with Claudia's pawing me this afternoon?"

"I must sound like a whiny, jealous girlfriend, don't I? I'm really not. I swear. But there's something about her that I just don't trust," she said.

"That makes two of us," Josh said. "Do you trust me?"

Riley waited a beat too long to answer.

"Ri?" Josh had been so young when his mother died, and he'd watched his father remain true to her year after year, both of which had driven him to be more careful with his emotions. He'd craved the same powerful love as he'd watched his father harbor, believing that if he did all the right things, then one day he'd have that same amount of love for a woman. Even as a teenager, he'd been able to control those urges, to analyze his feelings, and if he hadn't felt something bigger than lust for a girl, he hadn't taken her to bed. Josh knew he was different in that way, but he always imagined that when the right girl came around, she'd respect that about him and appreciate it. It was time for Riley to get to know him better and understand the man he'd always been.

"I do trust you, Josh. But I don't know much about your life in New York, so I have no idea what things were like before me."

Josh took a deep breath and sat on the leather couch facing a wall of windows behind his desk. He stretched his long legs out and leaned back, glancing at his watch. They had only minutes; it was not nearly enough time to say the things he wanted to say. Instead, he simply replied, "Don't believe everything you think, Ri, okay?" He wished she were beside him, snuggled in beneath his arm so he could kiss the top of her head and explain his past.

"How do you know what I think?" she asked.

"I know what people think. Trust me, Ri. Tonight we'll talk." A knock on his door caught his attention. "I gotta run. I've got a call at seven, but I'll be there at eight, okay?" The door opened slowly and Claudia came in.

"Have a sec?" Claudia asked.

Josh held up one finger. "Eight?" he said into the phone, feeling a bit like a bug caught in a spider's web. He really wanted to tell Claudia about him and Riley, just to remove the secrecy and tension. The knots in his shoulders were nothing compared to the wrath Claudia could unleash once she found out about them. *Maybe I should have terminated her ages ago.* His loyalty to Peter was like a noose around his neck that he'd never minded until Riley came back into his life.

"Sure." Riley's voice was almost a whisper. Then the line went dead.

Josh stood and ran his hand through his hair. Running on little sleep had left him fatigued, and he needed a hot shower—and time with Riley.

"I've got a call in two minutes. Is it quick?" he asked.

Claudia flashed an unusually warm smile, sending a chill of worry up his back.

"I'll come back. I have some work to do anyway." She closed the door on her way out, and Josh breathed a sigh of relief—for the moment.

Twenty minutes later, he was reaching for his coat and keys when there was a soft knock at the door and Claudia pushed it open.

"I saw the line light go off. Have a minute?" She didn't wait for an answer.

Josh leaned against his desk and glanced at his watch. "Just one," he said.

She sat on the couch, her leather skirt hiked up to the top of her thighs. She swung her long legs out and crossed them at the ankle. "Riley's making strides," she said.

Josh let out another relieved sigh. "That's great."

"She's got a long way to go, but I think she's really working hard to find her way."

"She's very talented. I wouldn't expect anything less."

Claudia leaned forward, her elbows on her knees. Her blouse bloomed open, revealing more cleavage and the edge of a lacy cream bra. Josh averted his eyes.

"You're making me nervous," Claudia said. "Can you just sit for a minute? I don't bite."

He half expected her to say, *Unless you want me to.* He didn't budge. "What's up, Claudia?"

She pursed her lips. "I just thought we should catch up a bit. We haven't really spoken about anything...special...you wanted me to do lately. You know, designs, or any special preps for the Bliss line. I just wanted to be sure I was prepared for *whatever* you might need."

Josh swallowed the bile that rose in his throat. Claudia was an attractive woman, and there was no denying her seductive ways, which might strike a powerful hold on a different sort of man. But Claudia's blatant abuse of Josh's loyalty to her uncle repulsed him, and as he watched her playing out her seductive ruse, he wondered if his loyalty to Peter was worth it.

She dug around in her enormous Louis Vuitton bag. "I met someone the other day, an editor for *Vogue*. Someone new."

"Someone new? I haven't heard of anyone new coming to *Vogue*." Now he was interested. Surely his publicist would have the details before Claudia.

"He's not there yet. But he will be." She looked up quickly, and the contents of her purse dumped over her legs and onto the floor. "Oh, shoot. I'm so sorry."

Josh bent forward to help her pick up her belongings. With a handful of lipstick containers, eyeliner, and her wallet, he lifted his eyes to return them and came up eye to eye with Claudia, her lips an inch from his.

"Thank you," she whispered. She ran her tongue slowly over her lower lip. "I really appreciate how highly you think of me, Josh, and if ever I can do anything for you..." She let the end of her sentence hang in the air between them.

Josh pushed to his feet at the same time she did and they knocked heads. Claudia's lips brushed his cheek, and she grabbed her forehead.

"I'm sorry," Josh said. "Are you okay?" This was the last thing he wanted to deal with. *Freaking Claudia.* Did she have to pull this right now?

"Yeah," she whispered. "Oh, gosh, I got lipstick on you." She rubbed his cheek with a firm stroke of her thumb.

Josh stepped back. "I can get it," he snapped. He grabbed a tissue from the desk and swiped at his cheek. "Claudia, I know you're willing to...go the extra mile to become a designer."

"Yes, I am," she said with lust-filled eyes.

"No one sleeps their way to the top at JBD. Skills will get you where you want to be. Spend some time coming up with fresh ideas; no more new takes on old themes. Give me something I can grab hold of and run with."

She sidled up to him, pressing her hips against his. "Oh, I've got something you can grab hold of."

Josh made a disgusted *tsk* sound and pushed her away. "Claudia, you're an attractive woman, but this"—he ran his hand back and forth in the space between them—"is never going to happen. Let your work stand for itself."

Her eyes caught fire. She threw her shoulders back. "You have no idea what you're missing, Josh Braden. We could make a great team, and I don't mean just in the design studio."

Josh ran his hand through his hair. He was tired of playing games with her. Hadn't he made himself perfectly clear? Claudia had worked in the business long enough to have established relationships with media, buyers, and designers. She could work anywhere, and he was about ready to have a little talk with Peter and cut her loose. This *take-me-now* game had gone way past a girl trying to just sleep her way to the top, but a scandal devised at the hands of Claudia Raven would be painful and humiliating—though not unrecoverable.

"Claudia—"

She held her hand up and stopped him from speaking. "It's okay, Josh. I get it. I'm a great assistant, but I need to be a better designer. That doesn't change the fact that I'm attracted to you and have been since the day I set eyes on you."

"Claudia, you're attracted to what I stand for, not who I am." He had to stop this train wreck before it got any more out of hand. "I'm involved with someone." There, he'd said it

UNRAVELING THE TRUTH ABOUT LOVE

without mentioning Riley. *Chew on that for a while.*

The anger in her eyes faded, replaced with a shadow of hurt. The harsh line of her mouth softened. "Please, don't play me for a fool. You're not attracted to me. I get that. There's no need to make up a fictitious girlfriend. Attraction isn't everything," she said, moving closer to him.

"Stop, Claudia. Whatever made-up game you have in your head is not going to happen." He took a deep breath. "If you value your job, then please stop these antics."

Claudia gritted her teeth. "Well, then, fine." She picked up her purse and headed for the door.

"And, Claudia?"

She turned to face him with watery eyes. He almost felt bad for her. "Let's not make anyone's life miserable because of this, okay? We're all professionals. I don't need you stomping around or making things uncomfortable. I expect a professional workplace with no ulterior motives."

"Yes, sir," she said, and stormed out the door.

Chapter Fifteen

NOT PRETTY, NOT designer. Scruffy. Riley stood before her dresser, wondering just what scruffy looked like. She was used to trying to look good, not bad. *Scruffy?* Josh would be there in ten minutes, and she was stuck. She hadn't been able to concentrate on the line sheets after hearing Claudia's voice in the background when they were on the phone, and no matter how she'd tried to quell her jealousy, the prickling at the back of her neck would not go away. Even though she knew Josh would never go for someone like Claudia, her mind began to wander. Would he tell her if he slept with her just once? What if he had and he'd left Claudia wanting more? Could that be the driving force behind Claudia's cattiness?

There was a knock at the door. *Shoot.* Still in her work clothes, minus the heels, she hurried to the door and pulled it open. A very sweaty Josh stood before her, wearing sweatpants and a wrinkled T-shirt. A Mets baseball cap was pulled down low over his eyes, and there was a glowing smile on his lips.

"Ah, scruffy." Riley smiled. *Still drop-dead gorgeous.*

He closed the door behind him and took her in his arms, kissing her like they hadn't seen each other for weeks, leaving her heart soaring.

"I've waited all day to do that," he said. "You smell incredible."

Riley crinkled her nose. "Yeah? Um." She looked at his sweaty T-shirt.

"Sorry, I ran over. I was late getting out of the office, so I headed home, showered, changed, then ran over." He looked at his sweaty chest. "I guess I could have waited to shower. Nasty habit...shower after work, shower before working out." Josh smiled. "I guess there are worse things to be than an over-showerer. In any case, I respect your desire to keep things secret, even if I hate it, and if that means I get a few extra runs in, then so be it."

Riley pulled him close and kissed him again. "Now I feel bad. I have no idea where you live. Was it far?"

"Not bad, a dozen blocks or so. I'd say no sweat, but..." He waved at his sweaty shirt. "I'm sorry about that, but there's a price for anonymity."

"I happen to find sweat very sexy." Riley ran her finger down his chest.

"You're not sidetracking me tonight. At least not yet." He looked at her outfit. "Did you get my note?"

"Yes, and it was really sweet, but kinda risky, don't you think?"

"You're a clever girl. I knew you'd keep things under wraps." He took her hand. "Come on. Let's find you some scruffy clothes."

They went to the bedroom and rifled through her drawers.

"Jeans, jeans, and more jeans. Yup, you're from Weston all right," he teased.

"I have sweatpants," she offered. "Where are we going, anyway?"

"Sweatpants. Perfect. Throw them on with a sweatshirt. Do you have a hat?"

"Sorry, left my cowgirl hat back in Colorado."

"I've got a baseball cap in my gym bag. Come on, babe. I'll give you privacy and wait for you in the living room." He left her alone, and Riley found herself getting excited about whatever scruffy thing they might be doing. For the life of her, she couldn't imagine anything scruffy in New York City, especially something that Josh might do. She slipped into the shower quickly, then threw on her sweats.

In the living room, she found Josh wearing a Mets sweatshirt, stretched out on the couch, his feet propped up on the coffee table.

"You, my dear, look spectacular," he said, coming to his feet and kissing her cheek.

"By the way, thank you for helping me conquer my fear of the subway. That was one of the sweetest things anyone has ever done for me, and it makes getting to work much easier. Thank you," she said.

"I couldn't have my secret girlfriend being scared of getting around town, now, could I?" He kissed her again. "Mind if I rinse off?" He grabbed his gym bag and headed for the bathroom. Ten minutes later, he met her in the living room with a Mets hat in his hand. He placed it on her head and tugged it down low. "Now it's perfect."

"Nothing like having hat hair," Riley said. She never minded wearing hats. It was the aftereffect that wasn't very appealing. But she was game for anything with Josh.

"Hey, don't knock hat hair. Some men find it wildly attractive. Have you eaten?" he asked.

"No, you?"

He shook his head. "Come on. I'm dying to go be normal for a while. I've had a wicked night." He grabbed her keys and pulled her out the door.

"Already? Gee, and I was hoping to get wicked later." *Did I say that out loud?* Riley was surprised to find how relaxed she was with Josh. Even the jealousy she'd felt about Claudia had fallen by the wayside.

"I like the sound of that." He planted a kiss on her cheek.

Her hand fit perfectly into his as they hurried down the stairs and onto the busy street. The cool night air chilled her cheeks as they walked block after illuminated block. Riley was mesmerized by the way everyone moved with quick, purposeful strides. The lights of the city sparkled from every window. Riley could see why people fell in love with New York, but her mind didn't linger for long on the city. It was too consumed with, and distracted by, Josh. To Riley, New York was no match for Josh Braden.

"So, is this our disguise?" she asked, pointing to their sweatpants.

"Yup."

"Cool. We're incognito. I love it."

Josh slowed his pace as they passed Lenny's. "Dinner. I almost forgot." He backtracked, and they entered the deli. Josh swung his arm around Riley's shoulder as they waited their turn.

"This is what New York is all about. Lenny's on a cold night." He kissed her cheek.

Who cares about Lenny's? This *is what New York's about.* She snuggled into his side.

Josh ordered turkey subs and Diet Cokes, and with the full bag in hand, they headed back into the night.

"What if I hate turkey?" she asked.

"I'm sorry. Do you?" Josh asked.

"No, and I loved that you ordered for me. I've just always wondered what a guy would do if they ordered something that a woman didn't like."

"Most of the women I'm set up with don't eat, so it's not usually a problem."

Riley flinched and stopped walking. "Josh, I'm not those girls, and if you're hoping to make me one, this isn't going to work. I eat. I like to eat, and I'll never be model thin."

Josh spun around and began dragging her back the way they'd come.

"Where are we going?" she asked.

"I'm taking you back to the apartment. I mean, if you're not going to stop eating for me, what's the use of pretending?" He drew his eyebrows together and pursed his lips, pulling her alongside him.

Riley laughed as he swung her into his arms.

"See how silly of an idea that is?" Josh asked.

It felt so good to have his body against hers again. She'd thought about him all afternoon, and the emotions she'd been holding in now wrapped themselves around her heart like pythons, tightening with every breath.

"Babe, I meant what I said last night. You are the most beautiful woman I have set eyes on in a very long time." He kissed her deeply, then set her back on her feet. He reached down and lifted her chin, another Joshism that stole her heart every time he did it.

"Riley, you are my breath of fresh air. I'm a designer by trade, just like you will be one day, but inside, I'm just Josh Braden, Weston born and bred. I live in New York, but that doesn't mean that I have the values and morals of a fast-paced racy city."

Every word he spoke made her heart open up to him a little bit more. He was so different from most men Riley had dated. They sailed the surface, while Josh dove deep. She touched his cheek, then rested her head on his chest.

"Thank you," she whispered. "Because I can only be me. I'm not perfect by any means, but it's who I am, and I like who I am."

"So do I."

Chapter Sixteen

IT WAS ONE thing for a man Josh's size to run through Central Park alone at night, but walking through Central Park at night with Riley was a whole different story. He eyed every man who walked by, sizing them up before they got too close. Josh had never had a lick of trouble in the park, but like any New Yorker, he'd heard plenty of stories.

Josh didn't have a plan for the evening beyond dressing in a way that would hopefully render them unrecognizable. He didn't have a plan for any part of what was happening between him and Riley, but he had faith that they'd have a wonderful night.

"This is so pretty," Riley said as they strolled along the path that ran through the park.

"This is my favorite bridge. I love how it's tucked into the park, like a hidden jewel." They walked up the gentle arch of the bridge and stopped to admire the water below. Moonlight illuminated the nearly bare trees and danced off the water below Gapstow Bridge.

Riley leaned over the edge and said, "It's so peaceful compared to the streets. If I close my eyes, I can pretend to be out in the country somewhere."

"You'd have to work hard to ignore the city noises." Josh came up behind her, pressed his body against her back, placing one arm on either side of her. He kissed her neck. "CK One?"

"It's scary how well you know perfumes." She turned to face him. "This is so romantic."

"Lenny's really pulls it all together," he teased.

She pressed her hands flat against his chest. "Believe it or not, it does. I just love being with you. I don't care what we eat or where we go. I like your company."

He lowered his mouth to hers again, kissing the cold from her lips. Feeling gluttonous for kissing her so often, he pulled away.

"I'm sorry. I could do that all day," he admitted. "Let's sit down."

They walked over the bridge to the edge of the water and sat on the cold grass. Riley leaned against his side, and Josh wrestled with how—or if—he should tell her about Claudia and what had happened earlier in the evening.

"Do you do this a lot? Come here, I mean?" Riley asked.

"Not anymore. When I first moved to the city, I came about once a week to walk through the park and just enjoy it, but then life got too busy." He shrugged. "Now I run through it, but I almost never come to just enjoy it." He squeezed her against him. "That's why I wanted to bring you here, so we could enjoy it together."

"I love it. Thank you."

Josh opened their sandwiches and they began to eat. He was ravenous after running and working all day on nothing more than a few energy bars. He ate half of his sub in a few bites, then leaned back and watched Riley. He hadn't noticed it the night before, but when she chewed, a dimple appeared just above the right side of her mouth.

She looked away and covered her mouth.

"You're cute when you eat," Josh said. The surety of his feelings for her were solidifying with every moment they spent together—and every second they spent apart. He couldn't hold back any longer.

"Listen, Riley, I really like spending time with you, and I know we haven't shared our deepest secrets yet, or had any history together to speak of, but I want you to know how I feel."

She placed her hand on his knee. He covered it with his own and wished she'd never be farther away than she was right then.

"Me too," she said.

"I want you to know who I am, not who everyone else thinks I am. I'm a really private person." He saw her eyes grow wide and read the disbelief in her eyes that he'd been expecting. "I know I have a public life, but I'm a private person by nature. You've seen the pictures of me with a different girl on my arm at every event, smiling for the camera, often even looking at them like they were special, like they were everything, but that was all a farce. That's the persona that's expected of me. I can count on one hand the women I've had any sort of real relationship with."

She dropped her eyes then and bit her lower lip. "Was Claudia one of those women?"

"I told you she wasn't, and she'll never be." He touched her cheek and held her gaze. "Not once, not ever."

She nodded. "Okay. I believe you."

"I've dated three women for five or six months, and while they were relationships of sorts, they were never anything real.

They were time fillers, and I think that's what I was for them, too. They were all between my last year of college and the two years after. I live a really busy life, and making time for a woman wasn't ever a priority. Once I opened JBD, I was handed dates, and when you have everything at your fingertips, none of it means very much. The people you're connected with are there for your status, or what you can do for them. I knew I wouldn't find a meaningful relationship in the mix, and I wasn't looking."

"I guess I know what you mean," she said. "I'd never date you for your status. I hope you know that."

He laced his fingers with hers. "Yeah, I do. Ri, I'm not telling you this because I worry about your reasons for being with me. I'm telling you because I want you to know that I'm not a player. I'm not what I appear to be in the magazines, and I don't want to be that person. You know about my mom dying when I was young."

"Yeah, that must have been awful."

"I don't really remember much about her other than what I've been told throughout the years. I was too young, I guess, but between Treat and my dad, I feel like I know everything about her, like she was there for all those years, even though she wasn't."

"That's nice, right? I mean, it would seem worse if you didn't know what she was like. This way you have a picture of her, an idea of her personality," Riley said.

"Yeah. Treat spent years talking about her like she was right there. He'd tell me stories she'd told him, and he'd try to talk like she did. I'm really lucky that he did that, because while my dad filled me in some, too, I was always afraid to ask him too many specifics about her. He's always missed her so much."

One of the earliest memories Josh had was at his tenth birthday party, when he turned to his father and said he wished his mother could have been there. His father's eyes filled with tears and his voice with emotion when he said, "She's right here with us, son."

"My dad has never strayed from the memory of my mother, at least as far as any of us knows, and that's so honorable. To me, that's what love is. It's a commitment for a person that goes beyond their being physically present, and maybe it's even beyond being defined."

"So you believe in true love?" Riley asked. "Real, heart-pounding, breath-stealing, forever and beyond love?" Her eyes lit up.

"I guess I do," he said.

"And what about lust?" She wrapped her arms around her knees, pulled them in to her chest, and crossed her ankles, looking at him expectantly.

"Lust is definitely real." *And very much alive in me for you.*

"But what role does it play in love?" She scooted closer to him.

"I think there's lust in love. I mean, how boring would it be without a bit of tawdry lust?"

"And desire? Different from lust?" she asked.

"You are full of questions. I think so. Desire is a want, a craving, an urge, and it can be felt for anything. I can desire ice cream or I can desire you." He touched her cheek. "While lust goes way beyond, and to me, lust encompasses only a sexual urge. I don't lust for a run in the park, but I lust for your naked body beneath me." *Even now, in the park.*

"And"—she lowered her voice to almost a whisper—"do you think what your parents had included those attributes, or were they just in love? I think there's a difference. Like with my parents, I know they're in love. I can see it in the way they look at each other across the room, but I'm not so sure about desire or lust. I think what they have is comfortable, and maybe that happens after so many years. I don't know. But I'd like to think that desire and lust can be part of love forever."

Josh thought of the look in his father's eyes when he was down by the barn, taking care of his mother's horse, Hope, and he had no doubt that what his parents had included all forms of love. "I think it can be, but I'm not naive. Life gets in the way of lust and desire sometimes, and I can see how after coming home to someone night after night it might be hard to leave the stress of the office behind, but that doesn't mean that desire or lust is gone." He looked at the water and realized that he had never thought about these things until just now. "I think it takes effort to recognize that outside stress can take over if you let it. Couples need to make time to be intimate and maybe do things that are outside of the norm to spice things up every few years, but yeah, I think desire and lust can remain if you help them."

Riley nodded and leaned her chin on her arms. "You might be right."

"What's worrying you?" he asked.

She shrugged.

"Really, Ri, I sincerely want to know. Remember, I'm that guy who likes to talk. I love sex as much as the next guy, but not in place of really knowing someone."

"It's just...I see how happy and committed Rex and Jade are, and believe me, neither of us saw that relationship coming." She smiled. "I just hope I can have that someday."

"Rex is a very passionate guy, always has been. He protects

115

the things he loves fiercely. He stands up for what he believes in and fights what he doesn't." Josh had spent his life feeling less manly than Rex, the brother he saw as the epitome of masculine and heroic, and he wanted to be honest with Riley, even if it was embarrassing. If she wanted a *Rex*, that wasn't him.

"Ri, I'm not Rex, and I never will be. I don't have that same outwardly apparent level of anger, or passion, or whatever it is that he has that makes him so…macho. I have the same level of love and passion, and I stand up in my own way, but I'm not someone who will get into a fistfight. I'm the guy who works things out with methodical, rational thought. I'm big and I'm strong, but I just don't handle myself in that way. I never have, and I probably never will."

"That's one of the things I admire most about you," she said, cocking her head to the side. "I don't want someone like Rex. I hope that someday I'll be loved to the ends of the earth the way Jade is, in whatever form it comes. And I'm not asking you to love me, Josh. I'm just talking. You asked; I answered. I'm not under any weird illusions or trying to pressure our relationship into being anything more than it is." She shrugged.

"I don't know how any man could not love you to the ends of the earth." The words were on the tip of his tongue. *I love you.* It was too soon. He'd scare her away if he said them aloud. It even scared him a little to think about saying them so soon. Instead, he took her hand in his and took a deep breath in preparation for sharing part of what had been nagging at him all afternoon. He'd get to Claudia soon enough, but first he needed Riley to understand the type of man he really was.

"Ri, I'm not really like any of my brothers. I've been thinking a lot about Treat, and I'm probably more like Treat than Rex, but I know myself, and I could never give up my career the way he did for Max, no matter how much I loved the person. I enjoy what I do too much, and I know that sounds self-centered. When you fall in love, you're supposed to be willing to give up everything for the other person. I'm just being honest with you."

Riley sat up straighter. "Why would you even think to say that? I'd never want you to give up your career, any more than I'd expect you to want me to give up mine."

He'd expected her response, which opened the door for him to continue. He knew what he was saying was true, and Riley deserved to know it, too.

"Look at Rex and Jade. They weren't able to keep their relationship a secret for very long, and I just want to be sure you know what you're getting into if you get involved with me," he explained.

"*If* I get involved with you?"

"You know what I mean. Involved for the long term." The conversation was becoming too heavy, and there was much more to say and much more he wanted to know about Riley. He took a deep breath and said, "I just want you to know where I stand. I'm not trying to scare you off, Riley. That's the last thing I want. You deserve to know."

Riley looked away, and tension filled the silence.

"Do you want to walk a bit?" Josh offered.

They threw away the remains of their subs and he reached for her hand. Holding in his thoughts was making Josh's stomach ache. He needed to get the rest of what he had to say out in the open. Now. "I need to tell you something," he said.

"Sounds serious."

"I'm an honest guy. I just don't know how to be any other way, not with the people I care about. And I want to be honest with you." He stopped walking and placed his hands gently on her arms. "There was an incident with Claudia tonight." He felt her stiffen beneath his touch. "She came into my office and made it very clear that she wanted to be with me. Sexually."

He watched Riley swallow that chunky, awful pill.

"I made it clear to her that it would never happen, and I told her I was involved with someone. I didn't tell her who, and I'd never do so without your consent, but I don't want her pawing after me on any level. And I made it quite clear to her that she's not to take my denial out on the office staff. There's no way she didn't understand what I said."

Riley looked down, but not before Josh spotted the worried shadows within her eyes. "Josh, you don't have—"

"Yes, I do. I don't know where you and I are headed, but I want to go wherever it is for however long it lasts, and we can't do that if Claudia is always undermining our relationship. I never want you to worry, especially about her." Josh felt like a weight had been lifted from his shoulders. That was only the first step in a long line of things that would need to happen to clear the way for them to have a relationship, but it was a start.

"Thank you for that," Riley said.

They walked in silence, and as Josh opened his mouth to break it, Riley beat him to it.

"I can't blame her, really. I mean you are charming, even if a little too handsome."

"Too handsome?" He grinned. He'd never met a woman who could take a threatening situation and turn it into a joke. "What does that even mean?"

"Oh please." Riley laughed. "It's like walking around with a Photoshopped model. I love it, but whew, I can't take my eyes off of you, so how can I expect anyone else to?"

Josh shook his head. He knew that women found him attractive. He'd graced magazine covers and been told how handsome he was all of his life, but that didn't mean Josh gave it any credence. Hearing it from Riley—that drove it home and meant more to him than any magazine cover ever would.

"I want you to know, to really understand and believe, that as long as we're together, I'm fully committed. You'll never have to worry about me straying with anyone else. Especially Claudia. There is something I need to ask you," he said.

"Go ahead, but the answers are no, I won't wear edible underwear, yes, I will make out in a movie theater, and…well…we'll leave the rest up to your imagination."

I'm the luckiest guy on the planet. "Really? No edible underwear?"

"Well, maybe you can convince me," she teased.

"While I think about you in edible underwear, we probably need to come up with a backup plan in case—or for when—people find out about us. I've always thought of myself as a patient guy, but I'm not so sure I can publicly deny my feelings for you for very long, and I know it may mean trouble for you. Even if I do talk to Claudia, she's just the tip of the iceberg. You probably will encounter gossip about sleeping with the boss, which hurts me to admit, but…So I think we should try to come up with a strategy for how we'll handle things if and when people find out. A way that will protect you as best we can."

Riley walked in front of him, then turned around and stopped, forcing him to stop walking, too. She stood on her tippy-toes and kissed him. "Can I just say that I love how you think about me? There aren't many men who would worry about a woman's feelings as much as you do, and there aren't many men who would want to take steps to protect them in a situation like this. Thank you."

He pulled her to him and dipped her over his arm, lowering his mouth to hers and kissing her like she was a movie star on a stage.

"I can't *stop* myself from thinking about you," he said as he brought her upright once again. "I am worried about you having to deal with gossip or whatever our relationship might stir up. The last thing I want is for you to feel uncomfortable about us in public or at work."

She put her head on his shoulder as they strolled by the water. "I don't have an answer. Any way I look at it, it's torturous. I guess I could quit working for you and try to get another job, but I know from experience that it won't be in fashion design."

He heard the regret in her voice. "That's not even an option. Your design skills are superb. Maybe it was a mistake to have you learn the nitty-gritty of the business first. I should have brought you in as a designer."

She squeezed his arm. "You think I'm *that* good?"

"I know you're that good."

"Then why couldn't I get a job after college?"

"Probably because this business has more to do with who you know. There are hundreds of applicants for every position. Right out of school, probably none of the people reviewing your résumé even looked at your portfolio. I'm glad I did. You should have come to me years ago," he said.

"You're kidding, right? We avoided each other because of the family feud between your family and the Johnsons. Besides, I'd never dream of using our friendship like that," she said.

He arched a brow at her.

"Rex brought it up, not me," she explained.

Josh laughed. "I know that. I just love to see you get riled up. But I do wish you'd have come to me earlier. Think of all the time we've missed together."

Riley stroked his arm.

Josh couldn't stop wondering if they'd have an issue if Claudia didn't exist. Would Simone or K.T. or any of the others feel like she slept her way to the top? The questions formed an endless circle in his mind.

"Well, like I said before, we should just keep things quiet," Riley said. "Who knows? You might not even like me tomorrow."

"You mention edible underwear and twenty minutes later you think I might not like you the next day? I am male. I'm still thinking about the edible underwear."

"If you wear it, I'll wear it," she said.

"Now we're talking." He laughed, but he was still worried about what Treat had said. They did need a backup plan. At some point, something would come to light, whether by accident or on purpose, and they needed to be able to deal with it proactively, not reactively.

"What are you doing tomorrow night?" he asked.

"Studying line sheets for the trade show."

"How about taking a break for dinner with me, Treat, and Max at your place? A double date." The thought of being together as a couple in front of his family was a big step for Josh, and he felt his chest swell with joy.

"Really? What are they doing here? I'd love to see them."

"Treat's here on business, and I'm designing Max's wedding dress. It'll be fun. We'll bring in food from anywhere you want." They left the park and headed back toward her apartment.

"I *can* cook, you know. My mama did teach me that," Riley said.

"Mm. You can cook and you're beautiful? I'm a lucky guy." There were fewer people on the street, making their walk back much quicker than their walk to the park. Josh slowed his pace, wanting to savor the normalcy of the evening. Being with Riley in the park reminded him of his high school years, when he'd watch her in the schoolyard with Jade, or walking around town with her girlfriends. His body remembered those stolen glances, too, and the rush of adrenaline that soared through him returned. He smiled at the memory, and when he looked at Riley, a peaceful smile on her lips as they strolled hand in hand, he wanted her to know that his feelings for her had started well before a few weeks ago.

"Riley, I've never admitted this to anyone, but I had a pretty bad crush on you in school."

"No way. I had a wicked crush on you, too, but you were a Braden boy and way out of my league."

"That is the stupidest thing I've ever heard, and I've heard it my whole life. We're just a family. We're nothing special." He'd always been proud of the Braden name, but he hadn't been blind to their reputation. He and his siblings had been seen as the *untouchable Bradens*: too good-looking for just anyone to go out with and too wealthy to be treated like everyone else. It was the one aspect of being a Braden that had always bothered him. Luckily, as the years passed, people matured and some of that air had fallen way.

"You were the hottest guys in town, and Savannah? She was like a model even in grade school, with that gorgeous auburn hair and her extroverted personality. I swear, I was so jealous of her confidence."

"I remember you being pretty darn confident and definitely

gorgeous. You and Jade were always together, and we had to avoid Jade, so I could never approach you, but there were times that I'd see you and Jade hovering close together, laughing about something, or in town shopping, and I was so drawn to you. I remember just watching you, wishing I could gather the courage to talk to you. And, well, this is embarrassing, but I remember thinking about you way too much *after* I'd seen you."

"Yeah?" she asked as they climbed the steps to her apartment.

"Oh yeah. Way too much."

"Well, that feud took a toll on all of us. Jade was lusting after Rex and I was always thinking about you," Riley said. "Gosh, I can't tell you how many times I wanted to cross that invisible line just to hang out with you at the fall festival or after school when everyone was just hanging around."

"I think it just makes things sweeter for us, having all that time to dwell on our private thoughts about each other."

"Fantasies?" she teased.

"I'll never tell." At the top of the stairs, Josh took her hand and brought it to his lips. "Thank you for a wonderful evening, Ms. Banks."

"Is this my kiss good night?" She draped her arms around his neck.

"I don't want to push myself on you." The lie turned his stomach. He wanted nothing more than to open the door and carry her into the bedroom and have his way with her, but he wanted—no, he needed—to give her time and space to think. They were moving fast, at least his heart was, and he wanted her to have time to process her feelings.

"Push. Please push." She kissed him hungrily.

Who cares about thinking space?

Chapter Seventeen

THE NEXT MORNING, Riley jumped up at the vibration of her cell phone. She wasn't surprised to see that Josh was gone, but she was surprised at how natural it seemed for him to have spent the night again and for her to know he'd be back shortly after his run.

"I'm sorry. I should have called you last night," she said to Jade.

"Darn right you should have," Jade said with a smile in her tone. "I hope you have a good reason not to have called."

"Too good." Riley got out of bed and threw on a T-shirt. She went to the kitchen, and when there was no note on the counter and Josh's gym bag was gone from the couch, she felt a stroke of panic shoot through her. "We're still not telling anyone about us," she said, distracted as she headed for the bathroom.

"What are you doing? You're breathing really hard," Jade asked.

"Walking into the bathroom." She flicked the bathroom light on and nearly dropped the phone when she saw, *Back soon. Don't shower without me. Xo, J*, written in lipstick on the mirror, surrounded by a big red heart.

She breathed a sigh of relief.

"Hello?" Jade said.

"Sorry. I just woke up."

"I hear you're having company tonight. I wish I was gonna be there. It's like we're back in college again, in different states, catching up via phone all the time," Jade said.

Riley missed seeing her best friend, but she wouldn't trade a minute of her time with Josh for anything. Not even Jade. *Josh.* What was she going to do about him? He'd get sick of hiding out, and wouldn't she, too? Didn't she want a real relationship where they could be seen in public without wearing disguises?

"Hello?" Jade repeated.

"I'm sorry. I'm just distracted. I don't know how you did this sneaking around stuff. I am always so worried. Even when I'm not thinking about it, I'm thinking about it."

"I told you what to do. Just come clean and let Cruella deal with it," Jade said.

"That's easier said than done. She came on to Josh last night."

"No!"

"Yes. He set her straight, but she'll have a bigger reason to hate me when she finds out, and let's be honest, it's only been two days. *Two days.*"

"Who are you kidding? It's been fifteen years and you know it. You dug him in school; you know you did," Jade teased. "Don't you believe for a second that while I was crushing on Rex I didn't notice you lusting after his brother. I've said it before and I'll say it again. We both loved them from afar, and it was really hard."

Riley had liked Josh back then, but she'd pushed him out of her mind through college, and even in the years that followed—

until that night at the concert, when she'd felt the door to her heart crack open. Over the last two days, the power with which those bottled-up feelings she'd tried so desperately to ignore returned made her feel like a love-starved kid.

"Okay, fine, you're right, but you know me, Jade. I've never fallen for a guy so hard that I want to be with him every second of the day, and certainly not after two days. Do you think it's just the whole new city, hot guy thing?"

"Do you?"

Only Jade would push her to the wall. "Honestly? No. But doesn't that make me one of those stupid girls who throws caution to the wind and gets swept away on the fallacy of love?"

"Hey, I take great offense to that," Jade said.

"You know what I mean. You and Rex lusted after each other forever. I had a crush, and apparently Josh had a crush, but not like you two did. The way you two looked at each other for all those years? I swear you two burned a scorching path between you that everyone else could feel, even if you couldn't act on it. You guys were on fire. What if his desire for me fades? How do you know when love is enough?"

"So the sex isn't hot?"

"No, the sex is steamin' hot. And it keeps getting hotter. But I don't want to end up like my parents. I want heat forever. I wanna be chased around the living room when I'm fifty, swatting at my horny husband." Riley thought about the way Josh was an eager, pleasing lover and about how she came alive when she was with him in ways that she never had before. The fear of becoming like her parents must be clouding her thoughts. *We're just as hot as Rex and Jade.*

"You can't know, Ri. You're asking for assurances that no one can give you. I know what you're worried about. You don't want to be like your parents. You're afraid you guys will get too comfortable with each other. Even those couples that start out hotter than me and Rex sometimes end up with no spark at all, and then the ones who started out warm end up kinky and hot. You have to go with your gut. And we do control those things, you know."

Riley was brushing her teeth, listening to Jade. She rinsed her mouth. "What do you mean?"

"I mean that when things cool off, we turn up the heat. Jeez, Ri, you're the one who told me to go for it. Why are you worried? Maybe you don't like him as much as you thought you did."

"No, that's not it." She closed her eyes and let Jade in on her secret fears. "The problem is, I like him way more than I thought I did, and it's scary. I think of him all the time. When he calls, my pulse races. When he kisses me… Oh, Jade, it's so much more than toe-curling sex. We're so comfortable when we're together, even with the sneaking around. It's like we've been together forever. Is that a good thing or a bad thing? I'm so confused. And hiding it all at work just totally sucks."

"It's all good, except the *hiding it* thing. I wish you weren't stuck with that. That's really stressful."

"I could quit and then there would be no issue." Riley heard the regret in her own voice again, as she had the night before.

"You're insane. He'd never want you to do that. This will work out. These things always do. Besides, he set Cruella straight. Maybe she'll quit."

"I don't want her to quit. I just want her to be nice. Besides, it's not just her. Everyone will think I slept my way to the top. Cruella's just the most vicious of them all." Riley paced the hallway. The conversation was making her nervous. She didn't want to think about Claudia finding out about her and Josh. "Enough about me. How are you? What's going on?" she asked.

"I'm great. You're coming home for Christmas, right?" Jade asked.

"I promised you an outfit; of course I'll come home. Did you get the pic I faxed?"

"Yes, and I loved it. You're so talented," Jade said. "How do you find the time?"

"I don't eat," Riley joked.

"Oh no. You cannot become one of those girls."

"I never would," Riley assured her. "I gotta get ready to go to the office. Love you," she said.

"You too, Ri. Call me tomorrow. Let me know how things went with the family."

"You're a fool. They're your family, not mine." Riley laughed.

"They're not mine officially yet. We're not even engaged."

"Close enough. Gotta run."

Riley felt better after talking to Jade. She unlocked the front door for Josh and went into the bathroom to shower, then caught sight of the mirror and raised her eyebrows. As she debated taking a quick rinse before he arrived, the front door opened, and a minute later, Josh was leaning against the doorframe, glistening with sweat and looking at her with a hungry stare.

"I was just thinking about you," she said. He looked so sexy all revved up from his run. *And here I am in nothing but a T-shirt.* Under his heated stare, she felt bold. Her hands were drawn to his waist. She lifted his T-shirt and ran her hands up his sweaty chest, then kissed the center of his salty, rippled abs. Her body responded to the taste of him.

"I missed you," she said.

He lowered his mouth to hers, kissing her so tenderly her knees weakened.

"Riley, let me love you," he whispered against her lips.

Riley's breath caught in her throat as he slipped out of his clothes, his chest and leg muscles strained against his glistening skin. He held her gaze as he turned on the shower, then lifted her shirt off of her trembling body and led her beneath the warm spray of water. The bathroom filled with steam, but in response to Josh's tender touch, goose bumps rose on Riley's skin. He lathered a washcloth and gently washed her from shoulder to fingertips, lifting her arms above her head and doing the same to the sensitive skin beneath, sending another shiver right through her. With a soft touch, he gently ran the washcloth over her skin.

"I realized something when I was running this morning," he said in a breathy voice.

Riley closed her eyes as he moved to her other side and repeated the same sensuous caresses; then he moved behind her and placed his cheek against hers.

"I want you to feel how much I care for you," he whispered. He gathered her hair and placed it over her right shoulder. "Not just sexually." He continued as he washed her back. "You're an intelligent, kindhearted woman, Riley, and the more I get to know you, the more I want to cherish you."

Riley opened her eyes as he came around to her front and touched her cheek with his wet palm. She leaned in to the warmth of his hand. *Yes! Cherish me*, she wanted to say, but her heart had swollen, her throat tightened, and when she opened her mouth to speak, he kissed her. She felt his heat against her belly, hard and ready.

She reached for him and he touched her arm.

"We have all the time in the world. Let me love you. Sex can wait."

Every inch of Riley called out for Josh. Her heart was so full, and his words touched her deeper than any part of his body ever could. She closed her eyes, and she knew at that moment that she didn't want to hide what she felt. Not for her career, not to escape the wrath of Claudia. Not for anything.

Chapter Eighteen

JOSH WAS STANDING in Mia's office when the call from Peter came in.

Mia arched a brow. "Peter Stafford is asking for Riley Banks."

The call didn't come as a surprise. Peter had asked if he could see Riley's portfolio, but it still sent a wave of discomfort through Josh's gut. He contemplated bringing up his issues with Claudia to Peter, but then he realized that if he did so on the heels of Peter's conversation with Riley, he might look more like a jealous boyfriend than an employer dealing with a problematic employee.

"Put him through to her," he said with what he hoped was a nonchalant shrug.

"I swear, between you walking around with that contented look on your face all the time, Claudia running hot and cold, and now this? I feel like I'm suddenly working in the Twilight Zone," Mia said.

"What contented look?" Josh asked.

Mia rolled her eyes.

On his way back to his office, he swung by the design studio, where Claudia was busy hovering over a design table. He leaned over her shoulder and was surprised by the impressive design she was sketching.

"That's really interesting, the way you mixed the empire waist with the shoulder cutouts." He remembered the dress Riley wore out to dinner, and the similarities were striking. "How did you come up with this?"

Claudia leaned back and flashed a smile. "You told me to come up with fresh ideas, things that aren't redesigns of old trends. It took some soul-searching, but this is what came to mind." She touched his hand and he pulled it away.

"Claudia," he said in a stern voice. "I told you no more of those games, and I meant it."

"My apologies," she said, turning back to her drawings. "Old habits die hard."

"Hard or soft, as long as they die. Immediately."

He heard Riley on the phone and headed in her direction, feeling the heat of Claudia's eyes on his back.

"Yes, sir," Riley said into the phone.

The curiosity was killing him. Peter ran a modeling agency. He wasn't in the design business, which made Josh wonder if Peter had something more intimate in mind after all. He overheard Riley wrapping up the call. She spoke professionally to Peter. Josh thought of the deep, sensual tone she used with him in the privacy of each other's arms.

"Yes, I'll send them over, but again, I'm not looking to leave JBD. I'm quite happy here. Oh yes, I see. Thank you. That's very kind of you. Yes, sir. Goodbye." Riley pushed a stack of drawings into a pile and placed them on the corner of her desk before backing out her chair. When she turned and saw Josh, relief swept through her eyes. "I was just coming to see you," she said, reaching for him, then pulling her hand back and shooting a glance at the other employees.

He'd sensed a change in Riley that morning in the shower, but they'd hardly had time to get ready before leaving for work, and talking had been the furthest thing from his mind.

"That was Mr. Stafford," she said.

"Yes, I know." He wished they were somewhere private, where he could put his arm around her and feel her against him while she spoke, for no other reason than to calm that nervous look in her eyes.

"He wants me to send my portfolio over, but I don't understand why. He knows I'm happy working here. Should I be concerned or flattered?" She crossed and uncrossed her arms.

"Flattered, I think," Josh said, trying to keep his tone professional. "Would you like me to call him and see what he has on his mind?"

She shook her head. "No. Thank you, but no." She took a step closer to him just as Claudia stood and walked toward them.

Josh saw Riley's shoulders tense.

"How's the booth design coming along?" Claudia asked.

"Perfect. I'm about as ready as I can be," Riley answered.

Claudia nodded. "Super," she said in a friendly tone, and continued walking past them.

Riley let out a breath.

"You know you can ask me anything you need to about the trade show. I do know a little about this stuff," Josh offered.

"I know. I want to succeed on my own, and I will. I really am ready. I came up with a great design for the build out, too. We're one of a handful of designers who get to do a real build out, so I've designed it like a showroom. Claudia gave me all the materials I'd need the other day, and I am fairly good at putting outfits together."

He leaned in close and whispered, "And taking them off."
Then he walked away, hoping she'd think of him for the rest of
the afternoon.

"RILEY, COME HERE." Simone waved her over.

K.T. held up two slightly different white wool skirts.
"Which of these would you pair with an aqua-blue satin
blouse?"

Riley studied the two skirts, noting the higher waist on one
skirt and the barely noticeable embroidered edging on the other.
"I wouldn't pair either of them with it. True aqua is too harsh, I
think. How about something softer? A tame honeydew, or blue
violet, or light cyan maybe? What's the event?"

"Tame honeydew?" K.T. said. "Isn't she clever?" He set the
skirts down and headed down the hall for the closet.

"What's going on?" Riley asked.

"We're having a fashion war." Simone laughed. "A potential
buyer is coming in a few days, and K.T. refuses to let me put
the pieces together alone. He swears I'm missing a certain
something every time I put something together."

"Yikes, that sounds uncomfortable." *Competition never ends.*

Simone waved her hand, then pushed her round red frames
to the bridge of her nose. Riley had learned that Simone chose
her eyeglass frames to match her outfits, and today, with her
maroon-and-black plaid skirt and bright white top, the red
added a nice shock of color.

"He's just like a little kid. He wants his two cents heard.
Even if I don't use his ideas, he likes knowing he shared them.

No discomfort here." She looked down the hall at Claudia, leaning against a doorframe down the hall. "Except for her, of course. Have you noticed how hot and cold she's been lately?"

Riley wasn't going to get caught in that tangled web. "She's just overloaded," she said, and headed back to her desk thinking about Josh. After the uncomfortable dinner they'd shared with Peter, she didn't want Josh to worry over him. *We have enough real worries to think about.* She pulled out her phone and texted Josh.

Sorry about Peter.

Her phone vibrated a few seconds later. *No need to be. I'm a big boy.*

She mulled over a response and decided on being a little playful. *Yes, I've experienced that big boy and wish I could—*

"Texting during work hours?"

Claudia. Riley flipped her phone over and turned around, feeling the blush of heat on her cheeks. "Sorry. My best friend back home. I miss her."

"I'm sure you do. Listen, I'm working on some things for Josh. Could you run over to Phil's office? He said he had a few things from the shoot to send over."

Riley shot a look at the clock. There went her extra five minutes to draw. "But I inventoried them all and everything was returned," she said.

Claudia shrugged. "Something must have slipped through. It's only noon. You'll have plenty of time to finish your work." She flashed a smile that didn't reach her eyes. "Thank you," she said and walked off.

Riley sighed. She'd been working on some design ideas for Jade's Christmas outfit, and she was on a roll. She needed only a few more minutes to get her thoughts down on paper. She shoved the drawings in her drawer before grabbing her purse and heading out of the office.

She flagged down a cab, and no longer feeling playful or flirty, deleted the message to Josh.

Fifteen minutes later, she was standing before a baffled and balding Phil Lancorn.

"I have no idea what Claudia's talking about. We have no more items, and frankly, I'm getting tired of her accusatory ways."

"Maybe I misunderstood her. I'm so sorry. She must have said someone else's name. My apologies."

Phil breathed a frustrated sigh. "It's okay. We expect these things with newbies."

We expect these things? Riley was not the type of person to make mistakes that were *expected* of her. She knew Claudia's good mood had a hidden agenda. She was trying to make her look bad. She wouldn't give her the satisfaction. She headed back to the office with a plan.

Mia was more than happy to help Riley find the yellow scarf she'd seen Claudia carrying the day before. Mia rifled through the accessories in the closet.

"What do you need this for?" she asked.

Riley bit her lip. She didn't want to involve Mia any more than she had to. "I'm looking at a few outfits for the trade show, and I want to see if it'll go well enough with the brighter shades of the Bliss line."

"Love that," Mia said with a wide smile. She snagged the canary yellow scarf and handed it to Riley. "Just put it back when you're done."

"Sure. No problem."

Mia stroked her chin, studying Riley's pantsuit. "That's a

really great outfit on you."

Riley sensed sincerity in Mia's voice. Her eyes were bright and her smile genuine. Josh's faith in Mia reassured her, and Riley sensed that she could let her guard down with her. "Thanks, Mia. I don't have the money to wear all designer clothes yet, and back home dressing up meant wearing your best cowgirl boots and denim skirt." She laughed.

"Been there, done that," she said.

"Where are you from?"

"Southern Virginia. My father ran a dairy farm." She shrugged. "I think that's why I always wear jeans. It reminds me of home."

"You can get away with skinny jeans. You're about as big around as a string bean, besides, with your heels and your taste in blouses, you always look stunning."

"Thanks. It's all about comfort for me, and Josh doesn't seem to mind, so…" She shrugged.

Josh doesn't seem to mind much of anything, other than Claudia's attempts to seduce him. Riley smiled to herself.

"Mia, can you give me the name and number of the company courier?"

"Sure. I can have something couriered if you need me to," Mia offered.

"Really? Peter Stafford asked to see my portfolio. Josh knows. It's not for another job or anything like that. I was in the meeting with him and Josh the other night about the Bliss line, and he asked then, as well as when he called earlier today."

"Sure. Wow, that's big. Peter is known for turning down ideas, not asking for more."

"Really? Hm." She had no idea why Peter had requested her work, but she'd been up-front with Josh, and being open with the company and working through the JBD courier would send a clear and professional message to Peter. "Thank you. Oh, and I don't know why, but I have a feeling this is best done without Claudia knowing about it. She might think I'm doing something inappropriate."

"She'd be jealous as all get out. How are things going with Cruella?"

Riley froze. Had she heard her use that name? She ran through her calls to Jade and couldn't remember calling her from the office.

"Relax. We all call her that."

She let out a relieved breath. "Oh, whew. I thought you read my mind."

"Nope. Is she making your life miserable?"

Riley leaned against a shelf. "Only a little. Nothing I can't handle."

"She has a thing for Josh, so she puts all attractive new employees through the wringer."

"Really?" *Attractive?* The compliment made her day.

"Haven't you noticed the way she stalks him, showing up whenever you and Josh are near each other? I swear that woman's got him on a homing device."

Riley hated herself for what she was about to ask, but it didn't stop the words from tumbling from her lips. "Do you think they've ever...you know?"

Mia let out a loud, "Ha! Josh? No way. He doesn't even like dating the gorgeous women he's set up with. I can't figure him out. He's got women at his fingertips, and it's like he's waiting for Ms. Right. I have no idea what he thinks he'll find in a woman, but he doesn't like the typical snooty women he's introduced to. I just hope that when she shows up, she's as kind as he is, because the wrong woman could ruin that wonderful man."

I'm a kind woman. "You're so right. I hope so, too."

Mia looked at her then with narrowing eyes, and Riley thought she saw a secret lingering behind her gaze. *There's no way she could possibly know about us.* She thanked her for the help and went back to her desk.

Her phone vibrated as she sat down. She pulled it out and was surprised to see a text from Max.

Hi, it's Max. Jade gave me ur number. I hear ur with Josh!

Before texting back, she took a deep breath. She'd met Max at Josh's father's ranch when she was there for lunch right after Josh had offered her a job, and she had warmed to Max right away. Why did it feel like she was exposing their relationship publicly by confirming what Max already knew? And why did it feel so good? She texted back.

Yup! Pls don't tell anyone. Ur coming over 2night 4 dinner?

She tucked her phone under her leg and tapped her foot, waiting for the return text, renewed excitement rushing through her. After they'd been intimate that morning, she'd decided that she no longer wanted to hide their relationship, but she hadn't had the courage to tell Josh. She knew that once she did, there was no turning back. He was chomping at the bit to get things out in the open, and when she was at work, she wasn't quite as sure of her decision. *I wish I could decide once and for all.* She stared at the phone sticking out from under her leg. *Tell. Don't tell. Ugh! I can't decide!* Her phone vibrated again.

I never would. Promise. Yes. Can't wait 2 see U.

U 2, she responded, then tucked her phone into her purse and put them both in the drawer on top of her stack of drawings. She picked up the scarf and went in search of

Claudia.

Claudia turned from what she'd been working on as Riley approached.

"Found it." Riley held up the scarf. "Phil said he was so glad you remembered."

Claudia's jaw dropped.

"I'll just go put it in the closet." Riley walked away with a smirk on her face. *Two can play at this game.*

Chapter Nineteen

RILEY ANSWERED THE door wearing what Josh knew were her favorite skinny jeans, which she'd worn confidently in Colorado and hadn't worn since being in New York, a sheer, red drop-neck blouse, and a single gold necklace draped across her collarbone. She stood on her tippy-toes to kiss him, and Josh laid a hand on her hip.

"Wow, Ri. You look scorching hot," he said. "I haven't seen you in skinny jeans since we were in Colorado."

"The idea of being with Max and Treat made me feel a little closer to home, and the way you relish my body replenished my confidence in my curves," she admitted.

"I do love your curves." He ran his hand down her hip and squeezed her butt. "You look almost as hot as you did in your scruffy outfit," he teased. "Almost. There's nothing like sweatpants." Josh headed for the kitchen with an armful of take-out Italian food and wine.

"Thanks. I was gonna wear the sweats, but I didn't want to tempt your brother too much." She followed Josh into the kitchen.

"I doubt anyone could tempt Treat away from Max." He set the bags on the table and began removing the hot containers of food. "I've got mussels, fresh bread, pasta. Oh"—he held up two bottles of wine—"and wine, of course."

"Everything smells delicious," Riley said.

Josh opened the wine and poured two glasses, handing her one. He thought of their first date and how nervous she'd looked when they were in the kitchen together. Being with her now, he could hardly believe it had been only a few days. He felt like Riley had always been in his life.

"Don't you want to wait for Treat and Max?" she asked.

"Nope. This toast is to us. We've survived secrecy," he said, and kissed her lightly on her lips.

"Yeah, I wanted to talk to you about that." She ran her finger around the rim of her glass.

"Okay. Want to go sit in the living room?" Josh's stomach tightened. He still didn't have a backup plan in case his staff found out about their relationship, and the more he thought about how hurt Riley might get when they went public, the more he fretted about it.

They sat on the couch in the living room. Riley sat with her glass between her hands, her eyes trained on the wine. He watched her purse her lips, blink several times, and then draw in a deep breath.

"Did something happen at the office today that I should know about?" he asked. He was sure he'd have heard about it if someone had found out about them, but Riley wasn't the type to run to him for help.

"No, not really. I just…"

She looked up at him and there was no mistaking the warmth and desire in her eyes. The edges of her lips lifted; her eyebrows drew together. She set her drink down and took his hand in hers.

"I think I want to let people know about us," she said.

Josh opened his eyes wide. "Wow. I didn't expect that," he admitted. He'd begun to think that she was right to keep things a secret for a while longer.

"I know. Neither did I, but this morning in the shower, something hit me, and I just knew that you were the person I wanted to be with. Keeping it a secret feels like we're doing something wrong, and not in a good way." She smiled, but it didn't quite reach her eyes.

Josh thought he saw a flash of hesitation. His stomach twisted and his heart ached. He was conflicted. He'd wanted to tell the world about them, but after spending days trying to figure out the best way to approach it, he still came up empty. The more he thought about it, the more he worried about her career.

He was silent for a beat too long, and Riley pulled back from him. "You don't want to, do you?"

"I do. I'm just…I'm worried about you, Ri. Any way I cut this thing, you get labeled. I don't, but you do, and I hate knowing that it might turn your life upside down." The pain that crossed her face killed him, but he knew he was right. They would find a way to deal with the staff, but they had to figure it out before they revealed their relationship.

"Right. Well, if I'm willing to risk it, shouldn't you be?" She held his stare. "You're not ready. I get it. Okay." She laughed under her breath. "I definitely didn't expect this." She stood up.

Josh grabbed her hand. "Babe, sit back down, please."

"It's a bit humiliating, don't you think? To learn that your boyfriend…wait…maybe you realized that you don't want that?" Her eyes filled with tears.

"No, Riley, no." He stood and took her in his arms. "I'll do whatever you want. I only want to protect you. I'm happy to go into work tomorrow and tell everyone. I'll send out a press release if you want me to. I am only concerned because you were worried about your career, and I get that. You have a reason to worry. This industry is not very forgiving, or very accepting."

Riley flopped down on the couch. "This is so hard, Josh. When I'm with you, I really want to be with you—publicly, I mean—and when I'm at work, I see very clearly where the issues lie. But how many times can we beat this dead horse? We either have to jump in with both feet or…"

"Or?" *Don't even say it.*

"Or sneak around, using your sister's apartment as a love nest, I guess." She smiled.

He pulled her close again, relieved. "I'm sorry, Riley. This would have been much easier if I'd known that you felt the same way I did before you came to New York. Then I could have introduced you on day one as my girlfriend, and people would have been forced to accept it for what it was." *Or they'd have assumed that's how you got the job.*

"It's all so frustrating. And it's crazy. We've been dating for only a few days. Who throws away their career after only a few days? I swear I'm losing my mind. You know what? I don't really care anymore what people say about me. Throw me to the wolves. Let's just jump in with both feet." Hope danced in her wide eyes.

"It is crazy, and it's fast and probably not the smartest thing to pin our hopes on a week of crazy love, but I trust my heart, Riley, and my heart tells me that you're the woman I want to be with. If you're game, I'm game." His heart soared, but a tiny voice in the back of his head told him to be careful.

A knock at the door tore them from their decision.

"We'll figure this out, babe. I promise we will." He pulled her into another quick hug before opening the door.

Treat opened his arms with a gracious smile. His dark hair was thick and wavy, his chiseled face cleanly shaven, and his dark eyes were full of joy.

"Josh." Treat embraced him, patting him on the back. "Good to see you." Then he turned to Riley. "Riley, you look beautiful." He embraced her just as warmly; then he reached for Max's hand. "Come here, sweetness."

Max wore jeans and a cashmere sweater. Her dark hair fell past her shoulders, and her face was free of makeup, with the exception of eyeliner, allowing her natural beauty to shine through. She hugged Riley, then Josh. "So good to see you guys again." She stepped into the apartment and her eyes grew wide. "Savannah has great taste. I love that sofa and coffee table."

Even though Treat was wealthy, Max remained utilitarian in her views. She was careful with money, and she remained as down-to-earth and comfortably familiar as she had been the day Josh had met her.

"Want some wine?" Riley asked, heading for the kitchen. Max followed her, leaving Treat and Josh in the living room, where they made themselves comfortable on the couch.

"It's really good to see you, Treat. You and Max look great. Is everything going well? The house plans coming along?" Treat and Max had purchased property that adjoined their father's ranch.

"You know how these things go. There's a lot of hurry up and wait. Things are good, and Dad's doing well, strong as an ox," Treat said.

Their father had suffered through a minor heart issue a while ago, but he'd recovered quickly and was not someone who could be kept down for long.

"Good to hear. And the wedding plans?" Josh asked.

"They're coming along," Treat said. "That was one of the reasons I wanted to see you. You remember when *Vogue* magazine did that front-page feature on us?" He leaned his elbows on his knees.

"How could I forget? Dad teased us for two years solid." Josh deepened his voice. "'The Braden Men: Two of America's Most Eligible Bachelors.'" He laughed.

"Yeah, well, they want to do a story on the wedding," Treat said quietly.

"And you're not happy about it?" Josh asked. He was trying to focus on Treat, but his mind kept coming back to Riley.

Treat shot a glance at Max. "I don't really care one way or the other, but Max isn't very keen on the idea. She hates that stuff; you know that. So, I was thinking…media's gonna pick this up whether we agree to it or not, but maybe we can give them a different angle."

A different angle. Josh found himself staring into his brother's dark eyes and hearing him as he'd been as a teenager, when the two of them had been with Rex at the county fair. They'd hidden behind the livestock barn so Rex could watch Jade, and Josh had secretly been delighted because it gave him a clear view of Riley. He'd completely forgotten about that afternoon, and now it brought a smile to his lips.

"Hello?" Treat said, waving a hand in front of Josh's eyes.

"Sorry. Another angle, right. What were you thinking?" *Man, did I ever have a major crush on her back then.*

"How about we get them to focus on the designing brother instead?"

Josh sat back. "Are you kidding me? With everything that's

going on, you want me to invite the media into my living room?" Josh shook his head.

"Yeah, once I found out about you and Riley, I didn't think you'd go for it."

"Treat, it'd be like throwing her to the sharks. In your effort to protect Max, you'd toss Riley out there?" He shook his head.

"No. I was thinking more along the lines of you letting her help design Max's dress, and then she could use it as a way to gain media attention as a designer. Before you hired her, you said her portfolio knocked your socks off. She obviously has the skills. Focus the article on the wedding gown, and then you've got a reason to promote her if you want to, and she'll have credibility to use against any relationship backlash. Even if they claimed that you fed her the work, her work would stand on its own."

Josh patted Treat's leg. "You, my friend, might just be brilliant."

"Did you ever have any doubt?" Treat teased.

RILEY HADN'T BEEN nervous about having dinner with Treat and Max. They were both very down-to-earth and easy to talk to, but she had wondered how they might react to her and Josh as a couple, even with Max's enthusiastic text message. For that reason, Riley hadn't made any overt gestures toward Josh. Now that they'd polished off a bottle and a half of wine, she felt more comfortable, and when Josh moved his chair closer to Riley and draped his arm across the back with a wink, that wave of panic that she felt at the office when she and Josh were near each other didn't strangle her. She placed her hand on his thigh.

"We knew you'd end up together," Max said.

Riley thought back to the luncheon at his father's ranch in Weston and how easy they'd been together. She'd tried to ignore the butterflies she'd felt when she saw him, and she'd thought she'd done a good job of hiding her feelings from everyone else. From the look in Max's eyes, she realized that her acting skills were far worse than her design skills.

"How could you have known?" Riley asked.

A knowing smile flashed between Max and Treat. She touched his thigh. "For me, it was just the vibe between you two. You were so...compatible." Max shrugged.

"Vibe shmibe," Treat teased. "Josh used to watch her like Rex watched Jade. Once you guys reconnected, it was just a matter of time before all that lust took over."

She looked at Josh and touched his chest. "You used to watch me," she said. "I love that."

"I told you I did," Josh said. "Treat just makes it sound dirtier than it was."

"Okay, truth?" Treat asked. He didn't wait for an answer. "I knew the minute he brought you to Dad's for lunch. Josh isn't a wishy-washy man. When he makes up his mind, there's no changing it. He may take a wider path than some and navigate around a bit, but he always ends up where he said he would. When he moved to New York, he said he was going to be a top designer, and he did it. Two years later, he said he was going to try to compete with Vera Wang. The man made his mark. And when he hired Riley, he said, 'She's perfect for JBD.'" Treat splayed his hands. "Was there ever any question after that remark?"

Riley blushed. She'd heard Josh say that at his father's house. She'd thought he meant the company, not himself personally. Treat really did know his brother well.

Josh pulled her close. "She is perfect for JB, without a doubt." He kissed her cheek. "And she also happens to be perfect for JBD."

"Okay, now that y'all have embarrassed me, can we talk about Max's dress?" Riley heard her hometown drawl, the one she'd worked diligently to omit while in New York, and it felt so good to use it again without worry of being given an amused look.

"Yes, please," Max said. She leaned across the table. "First, Josh, thank you so much for offering to make my gown. It's really beyond kind of you."

Kind. There it was again, one of her favorite traits about Josh.

"I'm thinking of something very simple, without all that fluff and drama of most wedding gowns. You know me—simple and clean works best," Max said.

"Simple, clean lines. We can do that," he said, giving Riley's arm a squeeze.

"Max, I hope you don't mind, but I pulled a few drawings together, based on the conversations we'd had back home. I know I'm not designing your gown, but I thought of a few ideas that you might want to consider implementing." She held her breath, hoping Max didn't mind.

"You did?" Josh asked.

"Just a few," Riley said. "I was really nervous about showing them to you. Somehow it felt easier to show them to Max than my top fashion designer boyfriend. If she hates them, then you won't ever see them." She winked as she left the room to retrieve her sketches. When she returned, Josh had already started clearing the table.

"Why don't you and Max take them into the living room?" Treat said as he stood. "Josh and I can handle this."

"Men who tidy up? I like that," Riley said. She touched Josh's back and whispered, "I didn't mean to take over. I don't have to show these to her. I'm so sorry."

He kissed her forehead. "You can take over any part of my life that you want."

Riley's breath hitched. She squeezed his hand, then followed Max into the living room.

"I was thinking," Riley began, as she spread out her drawings, "you're all about comfort and a clean, pretty presentation. Everything you wear is focused around ease of wear and functionality, but well made. With your gown, I thought of the same qualities: a little tailored and decadent without being ostentatious. So, this was my first thought, something of a long, comfortable spaghetti-strap dress with a few modifications."

Max crinkled her nose. "To a wedding?"

Riley smiled. "Hear me out." She experienced the same increased heart rate that she had when she'd worked at Macy's and helped customers find just the right colors for their skin tone, choose accessories for their big night out, and find the perfect fit to complement their various body types. She pulled her favorite drawing out from the stack and spread it out in front of Max. "Yes, a wedding gown." She pointed to the spaghetti straps.

Max gasped, her eyes opened wide. "Oh my gosh."

"You hate it?" Riley had a sinking feeling in the pit of her stomach.

"No, I adore it. What's it made of? Are those hand-stitched designs or is the fabric printed? Treat, honey, come here, please," she called.

Treat and Josh came out of the kitchen, wiping their hands on dish towels.

"Look at that. How perfect is that?" Max's cheeks were flushed as she pointed to the drawing while she looked up at Treat and laced her fingers into his. "We're getting married in Wellfleet, where we fell in love. The resort overlooks the water. This is just perfect. Not too fancy, very beachy. It's perfect, isn't it, Treat?"

"Gorgeous," Treat answered.

"Oh, Josh! Why didn't you tell me that Riley hit the nail on the head?" Max pulled Riley into a tight hug.

Josh beamed. "She always hits the nail on the head."

"Josh, what do you think? You're the expert," Riley said. She held her breath as he picked up the drawing, narrowed his eyes, and shook his head. Her stomach lurched, fearing he didn't like it.

"You designed this after just talking to Max at my dad's that day?" he asked.

"Yes," Riley answered. "I was sort of thinking about it, and this is what came to me."

"Satin chiffon?" Josh asked in a discerning voice. His eyes darkened as he studied the image.

"Single layered," Riley said.

"I really like the curved shape of the neckline, the way it draws the eye to her face by narrowing as it comes down between the breasts. The single thin spaghetti straps, so feminine and natural." He ran his hand through his hair and nodded. "I never would have thought to do that on a wedding gown."

Josh seemed to really like her design, but the seriousness of his gaze and the intense scrutiny of the design left Riley feeling as if her body were made of eggshells. One wrong breath and she might fall to pieces.

"No train. Is this embroidery, appliqué, or printed, where it gathers under her chest and across the torso?" Josh asked.

"Light embroidery. Faded pastels: peaches, blues, yellows. It's a little different." She came to his side and pointed. Feeling the pressure of Josh's examination, she pushed the words out as fast as they would come. "See the way it's patterned across the bodice, but horizontally stitched? I'm thinking about one and a half inches or so, runs under the breasts and another half inch or so at the waist, then scalloped embroidery edging the lower part of the horizontal waistline." Riley let out a fast breath in an effort to ease her tangled nerves.

"I see that, and the arc across the hips, with just the stretch of white between that and the waist." Josh nodded.

Riley watched him, sure he was going to tell her that it was too different, or that it looked cheap.

Josh rubbed his chin, then looked at Riley, his brows still drawn together. "Why didn't you go for a traditional all-white wedding gown?"

Riley had known that she was taking a big risk when she'd chosen a cream gown with pastels. She'd weighed the potential feedback in her mind before going in that direction, and the worst that might have happened would be that Max or Josh would hate the idea. As she looked at Josh, she wasn't sure if he hated the idea or liked the idea, and all she could do was be honest with him. She took a deep breath, trying to quell her nerves before answering.

"Ri?" Josh said.

"It's what I felt." She glanced at Max, then Treat. "When Max was describing what she envisioned for their wedding, she didn't strike me as wanting a traditional wedding gown. Max has her own style, and her personality seemed more suited for a wedding dress that accentuated that style. Max, I'm sorry if I misinterpreted. We can do the same dress in white."

Max put her hand over her heart. "Me? Goodness, Riley, you hit it spot-on."

Relief brought a smile to Riley's lips and an excited pitch to her voice. "Really?"

"Ri, I was just asking," Josh said. "I wasn't judging. I wanted to know why so I could understand the process."

He didn't say it's cheap or awful! Josh turned back to the drawing, and Riley watched as his face morphed from the momentary softness, when he was explaining why he asked the question, back to the serious scrutiny as he once again pondered the design. She found his ability to switch from business mode to boyfriend mode and back again appealing. She bit her lower lip and waited for him to pepper her with more questions.

"You carried the same pattern in the bodice as you did down the front of the skirt, from the arch of the print down," Josh pointed out.

"Yes," Riley said nervously. "When you look at it as a whole, it gives the impression of a summer breeze, movement, I guess. That's what I was going for, but if you think it's too much, I can change it."

"No," Max said. "Please, I love this. Josh, I assumed I'd see fifty designs of fluffy white gowns. This is so...me. It's simple, light, airy, and I love the colors."

"Length?" Josh asked.

Treat stood. "It looks like it doesn't matter what length it is; you have a designer on your hands, and a really good one."

"I have more designs," Riley offered. She shuffled the papers. "I drew, like, twenty of them. They were so fun."

"When did you have time?" Josh asked.

Riley bit her lip. "I squeezed them in while I was on hold at work and on the subway." She shrugged, watching Josh's lips curve into a smile.

"Riley, you never fail to amaze me. I guess you've got yourself a designer, Max," Josh said.

Max squealed and jumped to her feet. "I'm so happy! I was kind of dreading this whole thing."

Riley's legs were frozen in place, her eyes locked on Josh, who was looking at her like she'd just attained world peace. *I did it. I'm actually going to design her gown. I can't believe it.* Max hugged her again, pulling her from her stupor.

"A girl should never dread her wedding day. Especially when she's marrying a man like Treat," Riley said. She wrapped her arms around Josh's neck and kissed him. "Thank you so much!"

"I'm so proud of you," Josh said.

"I know I kind of weaseled in, but I wasn't trying to, honestly. I just thought it would give her some ideas to bring into your designs," Riley said.

"You can weasel into my life, my work, my anything you want, Riley Banks," Josh said, pulling her close.

"I don't even know who you are anymore," Treat teased.

"What?" Josh held his arms out in question.

"All I can say is that whatever Riley is doing has made you a happier guy. Riley, why the heck did you wait so long?" Treat touched her shoulder.

"Braden boys are a little intimidating," she said with a laugh. "The truth is, I never thought anything would ever come from my crazy crush on Josh. First there was the whole family feud thing, and since I was in Camp Jade, I was clearly off-limits to Josh, and I never knew he liked me back then, either. Gosh, I liked him so much that it's embarrassing to admit." She felt her cheeks flush. "Then he moved away and became this amazing designer that all the world recognized, and I was just this small-town girl who adored him from afar." She reached for Josh's hand. "Now I wish I'd never wasted a second. I wish I would have taken a chance years ago and crossed that imaginary line defined by the feud and my friendship with Jade. I feel like we missed out on so many years together."

"That's exactly how I feel," Josh agreed.

Treat's eyes darted between Josh and Riley. "Have you found an apartment to rent yet?" Treat asked Riley.

She sat on an upholstered chair across from the couch. Josh sat on the arm of the chair, holding her hand. "I haven't even had time to look yet, but that's on my agenda for the weekend," Riley explained.

Josh opened his mouth to speak and Treat cut him off. "Josh, let's finish up those dishes and let the ladies drink wine so we can take advantage of them later." He grabbed Josh's arm and headed for the kitchen.

"I can do that," Riley said.

Max waved a hand at her. "This is their thing. Let them go."

A few minutes later, Treat and Josh returned to the living room, eyeing each other with coy smiles.

"Riley, Max and I have an apartment by Central Park. We're never there. Well, we're staying there now, but we don't travel here often. You're welcome to stay there if you'd like—that is, as long as Max doesn't mind," Treat offered.

"What a great idea," Max said.

"We're leaving town in the morning, so you can move in tomorrow afternoon if you want," Treat offered.

"I feel like such a mooch. First I'm borrowing your sister's place, now yours? I can't do that. Really, thank you, but I'll find someplace to rent. It can't be that difficult," Riley said.

Josh and Treat shook their heads.

"Babe, take the offer. It's a great place, and we'll be neighbors," Josh said.

"That makes it much more enticing, but I'd feel too guilty." Riley mulled it over. "What if you want to come to New York?"

"Then you'd stay with Josh," Max said. "It's a perfect solution."

"There'd have to be a lot of incentives for me to allow that," Josh teased.

"I don't know. You'd have to let me pay rent. That's important to me. I'm not a freeloader." Riley knew she couldn't afford much in the way of rent, but she'd find a way to pay whatever Treat thought was fair.

"How about this," Treat began, "since you'll be designing Max's gown, that's worth a couple grand at least, right?"

"I don't want to be paid to design her gown. That's fun for me and great practice," Riley insisted.

"With that attitude, you'll be a broke fashion designer. Fair is fair," Treat said sternly. "How about we take the price of the gown out of the total rent? I think a thousand dollars per month, month to month in case you don't like it, sounds fair."

"That seems awfully inexpensive," Riley said.

"She'll take it," Josh said. "Thank you, Treat."

"But—"

Josh cut her off. "Ri, this is the deal of the century, and the apartment has plenty of space for you to design. Just say thank you and let's get to the wine." He winked.

"Thank you," she said. *How did I fall into the arms of such a wonderful man with such a generous family?* Her mind spun with the idea of moving, Max's dress design, and the enticing way Josh was staring at her, like she was the only person in the room.

Chapter Twenty

SATURDAY MORNING, JOSH rose early for his run. He hadn't missed a run since moving to New York, and lately, the idea of leaving Riley, lying naked and alone in the bed they shared, made his morning run not quite as appealing as it once had been. He showered and slipped into his running clothes as quietly as he was able, then wrote a note for Riley and placed it on the kitchen counter.

He put on his running shoes and headed out the door, hesitating for just a second as he debated climbing back in bed beside Riley and missing his run—just this once. It was a slippery slope, and if he skipped one run, he'd have an even harder time getting out of bed the next day, and the next, and the next…

He jogged through Central Park, watching the sun climb above the trees, its warm rays filtering through the umbrella of bare branches. Dawn was his favorite time of day, before the masses began hurrying about, when the birds still lingered on the dewy grass and the ducks slept lazily beside the water.

When he reached the Dakota, he slowed to a walk and caught his breath. He withdrew the key from his jogging shorts pocket and entered his apartment. After spending time with

Riley in Savannah's quaint apartment, his seemed too big, too empty, and far too...cold. He remembered how proud he'd been when he'd purchased the eight-room apartment and how special he'd felt knowing he was walking into the same building where John Lennon had lived. Now, as he walked through the expansive living room to the balcony overlooking the park, he realized how silly that feeling had been and what it said about who he had been. When he'd come to New York, he'd pulled far away from his Colorado roots, trying to fit in with the other elite designers and, he now realized, worrying about his image and what other people thought of him.

After spending time with his family during his recent trip back home—two of his brothers now in love, his father still pining for his mother—he'd returned to New York wanting more. Riley seemed the answer to his prayers. Since she came into his life, he'd felt more fulfilled than any material item could ever make him feel. She fed his desire to love and be loved. *Love.* He knew it was crazy, falling in love so quickly, but he was sure the way his heart hammered in his chest when he thought of her—as it was right then—and the way she was always on his mind, every moment of every day, that he was falling deeper and deeper in love with her. When Treat pulled him into the kitchen and suggested that she rent his apartment, Treat had instinctively known that Josh had been on the verge of asking her to move in with him. He'd offered the apartment as a safety net. Riley could live there, or have the option of staying there, giving them the time to be certain about their relationship without the added pressure of a year-long lease or moving in together right away. *There's no rush*, Treat had told him.

Josh didn't need or want time. He was one hundred percent

sure of his feelings, but he didn't want to pressure Riley.

He crossed the hardwood floor, passing the hand-carved mantel above the fireplace and the pocket doors that led to the stately dining room. He couldn't remember the last time he'd used the dining room. In fact, he couldn't remember the last time he'd even walked into the guest bedroom on the other side of the apartment, either. He assumed his cleaning lady cleaned it, but he wouldn't know if she hadn't.

He headed down the hall toward the master bedroom. He stood in the center of his sitting room, arms crossed, surveying the rarely used room with the beautiful fireplace. *This could be Riley's design studio.* He wasn't sure how he'd handle finding time for Riley to design Max's dress while she was working under Claudia's supervision as an assistant. Designing at the office would raise all sorts of questions. He wasn't going to figure it out in the next five minutes, and he wanted to say goodbye to Treat and Max before returning to Riley's. He went through the bedroom to the bathroom, where he washed his face with cool water. He patted it dry and leaned over the sink, looking at himself in the mirror. He ran his hand through his hair and scoffed at his sweaty shirt. *Treat's seen me look worse.* Josh had no interest in spending any more time in the home he once took solace in unless Riley was by his side.

He left his apartment and headed to the next floor, where he found Treat and Max closing the door behind them.

"Josh, what are you doing here so early?" Treat asked.

"I came to say thank you." He hugged his brother, embracing him for a breath longer than usual. Treat had offered sage advice throughout his life, and he appreciated him for that and for the love he'd shown him over the years. When he disengaged from his brother's strong grip, he hugged Max. She felt like a fragile bird in comparison.

"Thanks for letting Riley design my dress, Josh," Max said. "I feel blessed on so many levels." She took Treat's hand with a smile.

"We'll see you at Dad's for Christmas?" Treat asked.

"Yeah, of course." He bit back his desire to bend Treat's ear for a minute more, and as Treat always had, he sensed his hesitation.

"What is it?" Treat asked. "You've got that look you always had as a kid when you wanted to ask Dad something but you were afraid to." He moved his head forward and stared at him. "And you're doing that pensive, biting-the-inside-of-your-lip thing you used to do. What's wrong?"

Josh looked down. Was he a fool? Was he missing some raging red flag? He was not used to dealing with such intense matters of the heart, and he needed guidance.

"How did you know?" Josh's words fell fast and determined. "When you knew you two were in love, did it scare the heck out of you and make you feel like you were on cloud nine all at once? Or is it just me?"

Treat broke into a wide grin as they headed into the elevator.

"Aww," Max said. "Little Joshy is in love."

Josh closed his eyes and shook his head. When he opened them, Treat had a serious look in his dark eyes.

"I'm gonna tell you what Dad told me about Max." Treat pulled Max close to his side. "'Ain't no use pretending that noose around your heart doesn't tighten every time you see that woman.'" He shrugged. "That's the best I've got for you, Josh. You know when you know, and love is like nothing you've ever felt before. It makes you question everything you've ever done and everything you've ever known." He kissed Max's forehead. "And it's the best thing that can happen to a guy."

"A noose around your heart. That's it exactly. Thanks, Treat. I just keep feeling like it's all happening so fast, but I don't want to slow it down. I just want to run with it. Forever," Josh admitted.

The elevator doors opened, and Treat held the front door open for Max and Josh to pass through into the frigid morning air.

"Then what are you standing around here for? Figure this out and move it along. Riley's a catch, and the fact that she's from Weston makes me think fate has stepped into another Braden's life." Treat opened the door of the waiting sedan. "I love ya, bro." He hugged him again and stepped into the car after Max. "Hey, you still have the key, right?" Treat had given Josh a key to his apartment when he first purchased it.

"Of course."

"Good luck. Love you," Treat said.

"Love you both, too." The words came so easily for them. Their father had always shown them love, verbally, physically, and emotionally, and by doing so, they'd each been comfortable showing love toward one another. Now Josh was ready to share that love with Riley. He watched them drive away before sprinting back to Riley's.

RILEY WAS PACKING her belongings when Josh burst through the door. His determined footsteps crossed the floor. She stepped into the hall, and Josh took her in his arms and kissed her, holding her so tightly she could barely breathe. It wasn't a sexually driven kiss, and the difference stole her breath. This kiss was laden with an energy that vibrated through him, seeping into her lungs, her heart, and—she swore—into her soul. This kiss held the promise of something so big, she could practically feel it swoop her off her feet. She could taste the tangy sweetness of it.

He drew back, his hands on her waist, his eyes searching hers, and a silly grin on his lips. "I love you, Riley Banks."

She couldn't breathe. Her jaw gaped and her heart slammed against her chest so fast she thought it might explode.

"There are just no two ways about it." Josh's words fell from his mouth fast and loud. "I love your quirky jokes. I love you when you're scruffy, and I love you when you're naked. I love the way you melt beneath my touch, and most of all, I love your kind and generous soul. Riley, you're one of the most genuine people I've ever met, and I...I...Damn it, Riley. I love you, all of you. You don't have to tell me that you love me. I just didn't want to hold it back anymore. You need to know, or...or I needed to tell you."

Riley could barely think past the rush of adrenaline soaring through her. Her stomach whirled and goose bumps rushed up her arms. "Josh" was all she could push from her lungs. She took a step forward, her palms against his chest, her cheek between them. His arms enveloped her. His heart beat against her cheek, sure and true.

She looked up at him, knowing she'd remember the sincerity and hope in his eyes forever. Her eyes watered, and her throat tightened. She swallowed, forcing her voice past the lump that had lodged itself there and hoping it would be as strong as the love in her heart. "I love you, too."

Chapter Twenty-One

MOVING INTO TREAT'S apartment didn't take very long with the help of Josh's driver, Jay, but from the moment she walked into the Dakota, Riley felt completely out of her element. The enormous foyer swallowed her, and between the eleven-foot ceilings, expansive living room, dining room, library, and three large bedrooms, she knew she'd been given a handout at one thousand dollars a month, and it embarrassed her.

Josh took her through the maze of rooms, each one bigger than the previous one, passing furniture so rich and finely made that she was afraid to touch it. *Do people really live this way?*

She unpacked her meager belongings in the master bedroom outfitted for a king and queen. A four-poster bed that she needed a footstool to climb into graced the center of the room between two eight-foot windows. Cherry furniture with elaborate carvings that could only be handmade lined the walls. A mirror larger than her bedroom wall back home hung above the oversized dresser. It looked like it belonged in an upscale showroom.

She escaped to the kitchen, hoping to feel more comfortable away from the expensive woods and textures. She was not that lucky. Riley lowered herself onto a barstool in the enormous kitchen. She'd always imagined that living in a lavish home would be exciting. She not only felt out of place, but she felt downright lonely, even with Josh just down the hall in the ridiculously large master suite. She pushed to her feet and flew into his arms when he came looking for her.

"You okay?" He rubbed her back.

"I've just never stayed anywhere like this before. It's huge. Why would he have such a huge place? I mean, even with Max, it seems really, really big. I thought he was so down-to-earth." She snuggled into him, wishing she were back at Savannah's.

"He is down-to-earth. Who he is isn't linked to the homes he owns. That's real estate, investments. Treat is the man you always thought he was. It's a bit big. I'll admit that. But don't judge him based on his apartment." He took a deep breath. "Riley, come with me." He took her hand and led her out of Treat's apartment, down the elevator, and into his own apartment.

"Where are we going? Don't tell me he owns two of these monsters," she said.

He withdrew the key from his jeans pocket and unlocked the door. "This is my home," he said.

Riley covered her mouth. *I'm such an idiot.* "Insert foot in mouth," she said. "I'm sorry. I'm just not used to these types of luxuries. And I'm not a handout. A thousand dollars a month wouldn't even pay for someone to wash his windows."

"Relax, babe. It's not like he needs the money," Josh said. He put his hand on the small of her back and guided her forward.

Riley hadn't spent much time picturing Josh's apartment, and as she walked through the lavish rooms, she realized that she saw pieces of him everywhere. Instead of velvet couches, like Treat's, his were leather and cloth, with chenille throws across the back and thick brown area rugs covering the hardwood. His apartment felt very masculine, very Josh. She glanced over the bookshelves, where she found not only books, but candles and other knickknacks. She picked up a heavy metal frog holding a magnifying glass and raised an eyebrow in question.

He shrugged. "He was cute."

She set it back down and picked up a picture of a very young Hugh standing beside a red car. "He looks happy."

"His first race. I took that right before he headed out to the track." She set it down and ran her finger along the books: a mixture of fine literature and recent fiction. "You're a reader?"

He shrugged again. "When I have time."

"Candles. For your hot dates?" she teased. Inside she winced, not wanting to hear the answer.

"I've never had a woman I dated in my apartment."

Riley spun around. "No way," she said.

"Way," he said. "I told you. I'm a private guy. My place is my place. It's the one place I can come and feel...I don't know...safe, away from the scrutiny of the public. Bringing a woman up here would bring that world in. I didn't want that."

She asked the question that begged to be asked. "What if you wanted to, you know..."

"They had apartments." Each word was laced with honesty.

"Eight years and not one single woman in your bed? Come on, Josh," Riley said.

"Eight years and not one woman in *my* bed," he assured her.

She couldn't imagine having that sort of self-control. It seemed unimaginable. Could he be saying what he thought she might want to hear? She searched his eyes and came away knowing that he was telling her the truth.

"So I'll be the first?" she asked, reaching for his hand.

"We'll see," he teased. "Hopefully the last."

She wrapped her arms around him and realized that he'd invited her over to his apartment after their first date. "Josh, you invited me here after you took me through the subway that first night, remember?"

"I remember that night very well, and I hope I never forget it," he said with a smile.

"But…if you've never had a woman here…"

He shrugged. "It's you, Riley. My heart always wanted it to be you."

"That's a lot of pressure for a girl," she said. She went to the mantel, which was decorated with family photos in mismatched, though expensive, wood frames. Pictures of each of his siblings, his father, and even one photograph of Max and Jade sitting side by side, smiled back at her.

"Your mom," she said, pointing to the one of Adriana Braden. His mother had been stunning, with auburn hair and green eyes, just like Savannah. In the photograph, her eyes sparkled and her mouth was open, her head angled back, as if she had been caught laughing.

"She's always around," he said.

She crossed the living room to the balcony, upon which were two iron chairs. "Your favorite place," she said, taking in Central Park below, the vast expanse of nature contrasted sharply against the concrete world around it. "No wonder you live here."

She spun around and found Josh smiling with that loving look in his eyes again. Her heart warmed as she went to his side. "I love it," she said. "This feels like you…only bigger."

He smirked.

She swatted his chest. "Stop thinking about sex."

He raised his eyebrows. "Wanna see the bedroom?"

She followed him down the hall and through a large sitting room with a magnificent fireplace. "Wow, this is incredible." She noticed a *Men's Journal* on the coffee table and more family photographs on the mantel. They walked through double pocket doors to the master bedroom, which was almost as large as the sitting room. The king-sized bed was placed off center, flanked by mahogany bedside tables, each topped with a lamp. The lamp on the left was more masculine than the one on the right, with a slightly darker shade and a chunkier base. The hardwood floor was partially covered with a deep white rug. In the corner of the room were two leather reading chairs with lights perched above and an oversized ottoman before them. Both of the chairs had soft-looking throws on them as well. In the center of the long dresser was a large framed family photo. Riley ran her finger over the children in the picture.

"Y'all were so young," she said.

"That was taken in Wellfleet, Massachusetts, with my mom. We used to rent a little cottage there when we were young. Treat actually bought it a few years ago. That picture was taken the last time she was there." He stared at the frame as he said it, as if memories were unraveling right before his eyes.

Riley went to the bed and sat, sinking into the thick comforter. "Who decorated?"

"You're really asking me that? I did, of course."

"Everything is made for a man and a woman, a very close couple, it seems."

Josh smiled. "I guess I always hoped to find you," he said, coming closer to her with a seductive look in his eye.

She patted the comforter. "This thing must be four inches thick."

"Six." He positioned himself above Riley, her feet between his, and leaned over her so she was forced to lie back on the bed.

"You are an overachiever," she teased.

"So? Do you see me differently now, too?" He ran his hand beneath her shirt and kissed her cheek, planting a trail of kisses down her neck.

"I know you a little better now," she said, lifting her head, baring more of her beautiful neck.

"You do, do you?"

"I always knew family was important to you, but being in your home and seeing your family so alive in everything you own, it makes me feel like you're the man I always thought you were." Riley closed her eyes.

"And who is that man?"

"The man from Weston who puts family above all else. The man with a heart bigger than all of New York City," she said in a breathy whisper.

Josh did a sexy striptease, then he teased and taunted Riley until she thought she'd lose her mind. And finally, he made sweet love to her.

After, as they lay together, he whispered, "I love you, Riley Banks."

"I love you, too, but I really loved your little striptease." She traced the line of his jaw with her finger, then kissed his chin. "How was the first woman in your bed?"

"Don't you mean the first and last?" He pulled her into his arms and kissed her. "Perfect."

Chapter Twenty-Two

RILEY HAD BEEN hunkered down, laboring over Josh's dining room table all afternoon and into the evening, adding the final touches to Max's wedding gown design. She'd changed into a cotton skirt that reached her ankles and a thin sweater, the sleeves pushed up to her elbows. Music filtered into the room through an intercom in the wall just beside the doorframe where Josh was leaning in his pressed jeans and polo shirt, a steaming mug of hot chocolate in each hand. She'd been working for hours, and Josh had tried to leave her alone and not hover like a needy boyfriend, but he found himself drawn to her, and every half hour or so he'd wandered into the room just to touch her shoulder or kiss her cheek. He loved knowing she was there. His apartment had felt different since she'd arrived. The starkness he'd felt that morning had dissipated. Now it felt more like home.

Riley set down her pencil and lifted her head, smiling when she noticed Josh. "Sorry I've been at it for so long," she said.

"I could get used to this." He handed her a warm mug.

"Mm. Thank you." She took a sip. "Now I see why you moved here. Until the sun went down, the warmth of its rays through the windows was so inspiring. I swear, if I were you, I'd forget the office and just stay right here." She ran her finger over the intricate carvings on the edge of the stately dining room table, upon which Josh had laid a worktop that he'd had specially made for the surface. "Of course, it does put a damper on the beauty of your dining room to have notes and drawings scattered about."

He pulled out a chair and sat beside her. "I never entertain, so the dining room has been unused for the most part. It can get too quiet here when I'm alone."

"I can see that. When I was talking with Max, I realized how much I missed working with the public. I know I have to learn the business, and I appreciate the opportunity, but I do miss interacting with customers."

"You'll do just that with the buyers at the trade show, and this"—he pointed to the wedding gown—"this will bring you to a whole other level. But do you think you'll be happy when you're a designer? There's a lot of pressure, even more so than when you're assisting, even though it seems the assistants do all the dirty work. And the people you're designing for, at our level, they're not Weston customers. Some of them are notoriously picky, conceited bastards. A designer's life is not as glamorous as it looks from the outside."

She reached out and touched his thigh. "I know. I'm not that naive. Josh, I know you love designing, but how do you really feel about the business of it? It's just you and me here, and I'd never say anything to anyone."

He looked at her then and knew he wanted to share this with her. There was no one in Josh's life that he'd shared his real feelings about the business with, and he'd often wished there were. He put his hand on top of hers, and when he opened his mouth, the words tumbled out without hesitation.

"My whole life I have wanted to design. I was the kid who would critique the other kids at school. Only in my head, of course, and I didn't do it purposely. It was like this little voice in my head would think, 'If only she'd worn black heels instead of brown flats,' or something equally as obnoxious. I'd watch Rex with all of his macho bravado, Dane with his penchant for risk taking, or Hugh and his need for speed, and for a while I wondered where I'd fit in."

Her eyes narrowed. "Oh, Josh," she whispered. "That's so sad."

"Not sad. It just made me work harder to figure out who I was. I'm loyal, dedicated—"

"Handsome, strong," Riley added.

"I guess, and I'm nothing if not honest. I'm a definite Braden in all those ways, but I think I'm just more like my mother in the way that I like things to have a certain aura about them. She was like that, from what Treat says. He used to tell me that some mornings when he was young he'd wake up and the living room furniture would be completely reorganized. He said she'd just smile, like she'd done what any normal person would have done, and she'd lift her palms to the ceiling and say something like, 'The energy in the room shifted' or 'The couch was blocking the sun from moving freely.'" He smiled at the memory. "Anyway, what I realized was that I'm every bit a Braden. I've got my father's masculine looks and strength, but my mother's design abilities." His father, Hal Braden, was Treat's height, and a rancher to his core, like Rex.

"And now that you're in the business? Do you ever regret it?"

"No, never. The business has changed, though, and you probably don't see it, but high fashion used to be exclusively for the wealthy. Fashion shows used to be the only way for buyers to get their hands on the new lines, but now, with the Internet and fashion at the world's fingertips, it's a whole different ball game. We have to stay three steps ahead at all times," he explained.

"I know. I've read a lot about it. It's no longer exclusively for the rich, but in some ways that's a good thing," Riley said.

"Absolutely. I agree, but it does mean working harder to set yourself apart. But it's like anything else these days. Look at music and books. The minute they went online, prices dropped and numbers increased. It's the way of the world."

"Do you ever miss the less stressful side of things? Do you miss Weston?" Riley asked.

"When I first moved here, I was so glad to be out of the small-town environment that I think I didn't miss it because of that. I finally lived someplace where the world didn't revolve around horses and livestock. I know that sounds snotty, but at first, I did feel that way. After a while, and recently, I've missed something that I hadn't even realized I'd left behind." He looked away, realizing that he was about to reveal one of the most intimate things about himself to Riley.

"What was it?" she asked.

Her voice drew him back, and the love in her eyes brought him the comfort he needed to continue. "Seeing real love. A love that wasn't driven by what someone could give a person, or their social stature. The one thing I had in my house that I've never seen replicated, except recently with Treat and Max and Rex and Jade, was the love my father had for my mother and the love he has always had for each of us. It's almost like a physical being rather than a feeling, as stupid as that sounds."

"But..."

"I know. My mother wasn't there, so how could I see it? Riley, my mom died, but my father's love for her is present in everything he does and says. He still talks to her, even now, so many years later. He swears she's still around the ranch." He searched her eyes for disbelief, but what he found was the complete opposite. Riley took his hands in hers and her eyes shone bright again.

"I believe that happens. I do. I think if you love someone enough, they never really leave. They're always there in spirit."

"You do?"

"Yes. I always have," Riley answered.

He shook his head. "I never questioned it until I was an adult, and then I worried that maybe my father was a bit *off*. But the love that drives him is so real, Riley. That's what I've missed most. Seeing that love alive in his eyes. Feeling that love that he has for me and my sister and brothers. That kind of love isn't all around you in the city—I doubt it's abundant anywhere. But it's always been there for me, and that's what I miss most. I want to feel that love in my home and in my life. New York is fast and furious. Not that I want to move back home, but I want the warmth and depth of the love that exists there in my life. Here, in New York." He moved his chair closer to her, settling her knees between his. "I missed that until you and I reconnected. I knew when we were at the concert that there was something about you that was different from anyone else. Riley, you filled that gap in my heart, and I hope that one day you feel the same way about me."

RILEY KNEW THE dangers of bad relationships. She'd seen

people fall out of love and she'd had too many friends feel second best to their boyfriend's careers or hobbies. The span of time that had passed since she and Josh had gotten together was shorter than the amount of time it took to get a gun permit. But she had to admit that she felt every bit as in love with Josh as he was with her.

"I'm not one of those girls who spent years planning her perfect wedding, or conjuring up details of the perfect man. In fact, now that I think about it, I've spent very little time of my almost thirty-two years on earth thinking about settling down at all. I guess I always figured that if it was going to happen, it would happen, and I'd know when it was right." Her heart swelled with love for him, and when she continued, her voice was thick with proof. "I didn't feel fireworks when we first kissed. I felt the earth move, Josh. And every minute we've spent together since has had that same soul-altering effect. It doesn't matter what we're doing—making love or working. I think of you when you're with me and I long for you when you're not. You fill my heart too, and I want to make you feel every bit as wanted as you make me feel, and every bit as complete. I lived a long time without you by my side, and now I can't understand how that ever felt right."

Josh pulled her onto his lap and kissed her. His kisses were heavenly. The way he moved his tongue around her mouth, exploring and caressing with each swipe of his tongue sent a shiver of heat through her. The impulse to make love to him came fast and hard. She kissed the line of his jaw, his neck, his collarbone. She couldn't stop herself from taking his neck in her mouth and sucking until he groaned. All the talk of love and forever had her heart reeling. She put her hand on his stomach, feeling the ripples of his abs beneath the thin cotton of his shirt, and the urge heightened like a wild animal being set free. She took his face in her hands and kissed him again. When he wrapped his strong hands around her ribs and lifted her to the table, she knew he was feeling just as feverish—crazed with urgency—as she was.

Chapter Twenty-Three

IT WAS THE week before Christmas and the week of the trade show. Days had passed in a flurry of preparations, and by the time Friday arrived, Riley felt like she'd sailed through the week on a cloud, so happy in her personal life that the business of the show preparation barely scratched her elated surface. The trade show was taking place Friday and Saturday, and on Sunday she and Josh would fly home together and spend their first Christmas as a couple in the homes of their parents.

She couldn't imagine her life being any more perfect. The only hindrance was keeping their relationship a secret, and they'd become a bit lax with covering their tracks outside of the office. Jay usually picked up Riley and then swung back to pick up Josh, but on rare occasions, like today, when they were running late, they rode to work together.

"Do you worry about showing up together?" Riley asked. They'd spent most of the previous weekend in bed, and when they weren't in bed, they were christening one of the other rooms in his apartment. Marking each one with their lovemaking. Claiming each piece of furniture with intertwined bodies, breaking the formality of each piece with every loving caress, every ravenous kiss.

"After the weekend we just shared, nothing worries me," Josh said.

She knew that wasn't true. They'd both vacillated a hundred times about telling the staff of JBD about their relationship. It had become the most painful decision Riley had ever had to make, and she was still on the fence.

"Josh, I'm not kidding," she said.

"Riley, we just spent days memorizing every curve of each other's body. Over the past week we've had picnics on the living room floor, moved your stuff into my place. *Our* place. Let's not bring the what ifs into our lives just yet. Can't I just revel in this happy place for a while longer?" Josh stroked her cheek. "I feel like we're finally having a seminormal life, babe. I've never kept pictures of women in my apartment. And now we've got that picture of us in our Mets hats from last weekend on the mantel and another in the bedroom. I love how our lives are coming together. I don't want to think about how arriving at work might rock the boat."

They'd taken the picture in Central Park the previous Sunday evening, wearing their sweats and Mets caps. Josh had held the camera at arm's length and they'd smiled like fools. She loved that picture, but she loved the one in the bedroom even more. An eight-by-ten framed photograph of the two of them, their heads angled toward each other on their pillows, fluffy white sheets surrounding their sexually sated faces as they gazed happily into his iPhone camera.

She looked out the window, thinking about how the work week had flown by, with days spent trying not to let their raging hormones give them away and working late into the evenings until they were sure the other employees had gone, then making out like kids on the couch in Josh's office. As much as she wanted to enjoy the last few days, she felt haunted by their secrecy, and at the same time, afraid to expose it.

Josh cupped her cheek and drew her eyes to his. "I love seeing your perfume bottle beside my cologne in the bathroom. And I love that even though we have two sinks, our toothbrushes hang side by side. I care about all of the rest—I really do—but all I want is to not think about it right now, okay?"

How could she ask for anything more?

WHEN THEY ARRIVED at the office together, no one seemed to notice, and for that Riley was thankful...sort of. She was about ready to just tell everyone they were together and throw caution to the wind, but Claudia had been more pleasant to deal with lately, and from what Josh had told her, Claudia's efforts were paying off. *She's giving you some fierce design competition*, he'd said. She was happy for Claudia. She understood being competitive, even if she didn't think Claudia handled things in the most appropriate manner. If she could progress on her own merits, then she deserved to, and that's what she'd told Josh. Everyone deserved a chance. The only chance Claudia wasn't going to get was a chance with Josh. He was one hundred percent Riley's.

"It's like a fairy tale come true, Jade." Riley paced the ladies' room floor Friday afternoon. "We couldn't be happier in our personal life, and I must be doing a good job at work, because he gave me a key to the office last week so I no longer have to ask someone to be there when I want to work after hours or on the weekends."

"So we'll be sisters-in-law one day? Awesome," Jade said.

"I don't know about all that, but…" Every time Riley thought of how close she and Josh had become and she began to think of a future together, she made herself stop. She didn't want to jinx their relationship.

"Girl, you've got it bad. No details, please. If Josh is going to be my brother-in-law one day then I probably shouldn't know all those things." She laughed. "What did you decide about work?"

Riley's nerves were wound so tight around the office that she was sure everyone could see the love she had for Josh dripping from her pores. When she and Josh were in the same room she avoided looking at him, and when Claudia was around, it took all her determination to keep her girlfriend instincts in check.

The night they'd had dinner with Max and Treat, they'd discussed no longer hiding their relationship, but somehow hiding felt safer. It had become a habit that she didn't quite know how—or if—she should break, and the conflicting feelings were tearing her up inside.

"We keep going back and forth. I mean, what are we supposed to do, make a general announcement? That seems weird, but not saying anything feels weird, too. What would you do?" Riley had been thinking about nothing else since she arrived at work at seven thirty that morning.

"I don't know. It's really none of anyone's business. Why don't you guys just live your lives without worrying about it, and when you're at work, be professional because it's the workplace, but don't hide anything on purpose. Not at this point. That could only hurt your relationship in the long run."

"Jade, I wish you were here."

"No, you don't. Then you wouldn't be having all that crazy

sex you're having. Besides, you'll be home soon and we'll see each other then. I got the fax you sent me of Max's dress this morning. You are amazing. I want you to design my wedding dress, if we ever get married. Oh, and I love, love, loved the last design you sent for me. I know you can't make it before the holiday, so can you make it for Easter?"

Riley covered her eyes. What had she been thinking, promising to make an outfit for Jade for Christmas? She hadn't been thinking at all. That was the problem. Her brain had been swimming in a river of love. "I'm sorry," she said.

"Don't worry about it. I have other dresses. I'll just pick one of those. I was trying to make you feel needed," she teased. "But it appears that Josh is doing a fine job of that on his own."

"Ha-ha," Riley said. "I'm really nervous. Josh wants to show the staff my design for Max's dress today at the monthly meeting. He thinks it will solidify my design capabilities in their minds, to sort of ease Claudia into accepting my skills. He says my design skills surpass hers, and I guess he's thinking of the future, if he moves me into a higher design position. Wow, that sounds weird. *My skills*, like I'm something special."

"You are something special, Riley. Josh is a smart man. Follow his lead."

"It's just been such a whirlwind. I keep waiting for the other shoe to drop. Can life really be this good?" Riley looked at her watch. She'd been in the ladies' room too long. Claudia would give her the stink eye. "I gotta go. The meeting's in a few minutes, and the trade show starts this afternoon, so I'm swamped."

"No worries. I'm here when you need me."

"Thanks, Jade. Wish me luck."

"You're made of luck. You don't need it."

Riley had never felt lucky a day in her life, until she and Josh reconnected. Now, as she prepared to face the entire staff—including Claudia—she wondered if luck would be enough.

Chapter Twenty-Four

RILEY SAT WITH her legs crossed in the packed conference room, her eyes darting from person to person. Simone and K.T. whispered among themselves. K.T. pointed to something on his tablet, and Simone let out a loud laugh. Clay scrolled through his cell phone messages, and Chantal tapped her pen on a black notebook that lay on the table. She had a pinched look on her face. Riley wondered how she must look to everyone else, with her right foot bouncing with nervous energy and her jaw clenched so tight her teeth hurt. She closed her eyes for just a second and reminded herself of what mattered: *I'm educated, knowledgeable, and eager. I can do this.* She opened her eyes and thought, *Correction. I'm a skilled designer. I will do this.*

Mia walked into the conference room in a long black skirt and white tuxedo shirt. Chunky black, white, and gold necklaces hung over her thin chest. Josh followed her into the room in the black Versace suit he'd dressed in earlier that morning. Riley knew he was wearing black boxer briefs beneath the finely made trousers. She felt heat rush up her neck and cheeks. *Ice. Think of ice.* But thinking of ice only made her think of ice cubes and all the dirty things she'd heard about people doing with them. *I'm turning into a sex maniac.* That thought brought a mischievous grin to her lips.

Josh touched the back of her chair as he walked behind her, and she gripped the portfolio she held in her lap tightly between her hands to keep from reaching back and touching his hand.

Once he moved to the head of the table and sat down, she let out the breath she'd been holding. It became more and more difficult to repress her feelings in front of her peers, and recently she'd found herself resenting the need to. *Is it a need or a desire?* She couldn't think about that right now. She had to focus.

Mia went over the agenda for the meeting and the details for the New Year's Eve party. Josh had told her about the annual JBD black-tie affair. Each year he made a speech, handed out bonus checks, and commended each employee for something they'd done well over the course of the year. Riley was sure the trade show would be a success, and she wondered if Josh would comment on her work at the New Year's Eve party. It was a big event for the employees. A time for them to feel honored and appreciated. She was looking forward to it and had already begun leafing through the JBD closet for possible gowns to wear. Mia had been setting aside the items she thought might fit Riley. Since the samples were made for models, size six or eight was considered large. With Josh's insatiable appetite for her, she felt just as sexy and appealing as she had when she'd left Weston—before stepping into the impossibly thin world of fashion design. *In fact,* she thought as she listened to Simone describe design elements she was struggling with, *I'm proud of myself for not falling prey to the overly image consciousness of Manhattan.* She cared about fashion—oh yes, more than she was willing to admit—but it did not define her. She was still the same Riley Banks that had left Weston so many weeks earlier. She still kicked back in her jeans and T-shirts. She still ate what she enjoyed and laughed louder than most men. Her confidence grew as she realized how far she'd come and how much more room there was to grow. By the time it was her turn to present, her frenetic pulse had calmed. She drew her shoulders back and held her head high.

Riley set her portfolio on the table. "My first trade show is this afternoon, and thanks to Claudia I'm fully prepared." She shot a glance at Claudia, whose nose inched toward the ceiling. Riley didn't like seeing Claudia gloat, but she had been the one to give Riley the information she needed in order to succeed with the show.

"The samples are ready and I've got everything Josh has ever designed memorized. Every stock number, every color, every stitch, and every piece of fabric. I think I've even memorized how many hours it took to make each piece. The show is allowing three designers premium space with substantial build out, and we've secured a spot, so we can't fail. In fact"—she looked at her watch—"the booth should be erected by now."

"Way to go, Riley. You'll knock 'em dead," Simone said.

"Thanks, Simone. As long as I knock their wallets loose, that's all I need." Riley avoided Josh's eyes, which were locked on her with what must look like professional pride to everyone else, but Riley could still feel his hands around her waist, as they'd been earlier that morning, his cheek against hers, the smell of his cologne seeping into her pores, and his voice in her ear. *I'm so proud of you. I can't wait for the day to be over so I can make love to a woman with trade show experience.* He'd made it sound so erotic. She cleared her throat in an effort to clear her mind and focused on sharing her design for Max's dress.

"I've been working on designs for a beach wedding dress for a friend," Riley began.

"Not just a friend, for the fiancée of one of America's Most Eligible Bachelors," Josh added.

Riley started at his admission. "Yes, that's right."

Claudia lowered her chin. "I haven't heard about this. Who might that be?"

Her question sucked the confidence right out of Riley's brain. She looked to Josh for direction.

"Who doesn't matter at this juncture," Josh responded. "Riley, please continue."

Riley shot another look at Claudia, now sitting back with a narrowed gaze locked on her. Her pulse sped up again. She feigned a cough, trying to regain her composure. *I can do this. I can do this.*

Her hands trembled as she lifted the design sheets. She reached for the back of a chair to support her weakened knees as she placed the drawings on the display boards. Every breath she took echoed in her ears. She scanned the images she'd spent hours laboring over, scrutinizing them for fault, and as she took in the fine neckline, the unique, intricate designs of the bodice, and the simplicity and flow of the skirt, a bit of her confidence returned.

She faced the people she'd spent weeks working with and hoped for a positive reaction. She took a deep breath and began describing her process.

"The bride is very utilitarian. Comfort and ease of wear are her primary concerns. The wedding will take place in the summer, and she's looking for a simple gown that doesn't scream of her fiancé's social stature, but rather whispers it with grace." There was a collective, *Mm*, around the table. Pleased at the response and worried by the frown on Claudia's face, she forced herself to continue.

"I opted for a spaghetti strap and a modified sweetheart neckline to draw the eyes up."

K.T. nodded. Riley's eyes drew back to Claudia, whose frown had turned to a devious smirk, the left side of her mouth curved up. She leaned back in her chair, crossed her legs, and leaned her right arm on the table.

Riley shot a glance at Josh, hoping to draw strength from him. He nodded just enough for her to see but not enough for anyone else to notice. Mia's eyes were wide. She nodded, then flashed a thumbs-up, encouraging Riley to continue.

She took another deep breath, drew her rounded shoulders back again, and went on to describe the materials she'd use for the dress, the lack of a long, bustling train, and the intricate and delicate embellishments. There were many questions about the printed designs, which she answered with confidence, and by the time she was done, Josh was beaming across the table at her, and the others were murmuring among themselves, with the exception of Claudia, who remained in the same position she'd been in when Riley had begun describing the dress. And with the same evil smirk on her lips.

Chapter Twenty-Five

YOU WERE AMAZING. I couldn't love u more. Xox.

Riley sat in the back of the cab on the way to the trade show staring at the text message. It had come in only seconds after the meeting was adjourned, while she'd been cornered by Claudia, who dropped the bomb that Riley would be on her own for most of the show. Claudia had *something to take care of,* and she wasn't sure what time she'd arrive.

She'd responded to Josh's text, and he still hadn't texted back. When the cab pulled up in front of the Javits Center, Riley shoved her phone into her purse, grabbed her bags, and headed into the frigid afternoon air. Mia had chosen the perfect dress for the occasion, and Riley loved knowing that it was Josh's design. It made her feel like he was right there with her. He had an evening meeting, and they planned to arrive back at the apartment around the same time. She didn't know what to expect. The preholiday show was a new event. Never before had the convention organizers done a show so close to a holiday, and according to Claudia, the success of this show would determine if they would continue this particular show in the future.

Inside the massive building, people were already shuffling about at top speed. She followed the signs to the exhibition hall and stopped cold. The JBD booth was front and center, built to look like an elegant fashion showroom, complete with enormous white, comfortable chairs and a circular coffee table, just as she'd envisioned it. It looked majestic compared to the rather plain tables and banners of the other exhibitors. She couldn't believe she'd designed this all herself. *I did it. I made it happen.* She threw her shoulders back, raised her chin, and proudly walked forward.

Riley began arranging the clothes, setting up displays, and placing materials for buyers on the counter. Her feet were already killing her. While Mia could wear sky-high heels every day of the week, Riley found that her feet were better suited to cowgirl boots, and she altered her footwear every other day from high heels to lower pumps. The heels Mia had picked out for her were stunning but torturous.

She reached into her purse to check the time and checked her text messages as well. Still nothing from Josh. She let out a sigh and turned off the ringer, then tucked her purse under the table drape.

"I don't think I've ever seen a booth look better."

Riley spun around. "Mia. What are you doing here?"

"You don't think I'd let Claudia leave you high and dry, do you? I saw her locked in a room with Josh, and I got Chantal to take over Josh's calls and came right down."

Locked in a room with Josh? She couldn't get lost in that garbage, not now, with such a big event moments away.

"Besides, Josh made it very clear to me to ensure that Claudia does nothing to impede your work." She shrugged. "I love these things anyway. We'll have fun."

"Mia, you're a lifesaver. Really, thank you."

"Simone's coming, too. She'll be here in ten minutes. She

was right behind me."

"Simone? Claudia's going to kill me if I have both of you here. She told me that it's usually just her and an assistant." Riley was relieved she'd have help, despite how Claudia might feel about it. She couldn't imagine how she'd run the booth on her own with an expected crowd of at least three thousand.

"Oh, baloney. That woman has hogwash coming out her eyes." Mia planted her hands on her hips. "She brings three or four people with her, and if they aren't there early and they don't stay late, then she reports them. What a jerk."

Riley tried to keep a straight face, but she wanted to do a happy dance, knowing that Mia disliked Claudia. Instead, she rode the safe side of the fine line.

"Whatever. We'll do a great job and Josh will be proud. That's what really matters. Claudia is just competitive. I don't think she's evil. She just has tunnel vision toward her goal of being a designer, and from what Jo—" She quickly caught her mistake. "From what I've seen, she's making great strides to produce more original designs."

Simone arrived at the booth in a flourish of hellos and carrying an enormous bouquet of flowers. "I brought goodies," she said with a melodic tune.

"That is gorgeous, Simone. I can't believe I forgot a bouquet. In the pictures I saw of the previous booths, most of them had bouquets. I'm so sorry." Riley groaned.

"Oh, please. Look at this build out. It's fabulous. Simone, tell me you didn't bring food," Mia said. "The last thing we need are greasy fingerprints on the garments."

"No, silly girl, although a hunk of chocolate right about now does sound good." She set the bouquet on the display table and winked at Riley. "Hey, there's an idea. We haven't spent any time with Riley since she started working with JBD. How about a girls' night after the show?"

"I'm game," Mia said.

"Sure," Riley said with a forced smile. *After the show?* She wanted to befriend these two women and was excited to go out and spend time with them, but she also longed to see Josh. She watched them work side by side and laugh at inside jokes. *What am I thinking?* Josh would be there no matter what time she got home. He loved her. *He'll always be there.* But finding time to bond with Mia and Simone—that invitation might come only once, and she wasn't going to blow her chance.

From the moment the doors to the show opened, the JBD booth was mobbed. Riley answered questions, suggested accessories and outfits, and she surprised herself at the depth of her knowledge about JBD. Thank goodness Simone and Mia were there, because just as Riley would catch her breath, five more questions were thrown at her.

"The show ends in half an hour," Simone said. "I'm ready to blow this joint. My feet hurt and I need a drink. Where shall we go, ladies?"

"I want to call Jo—" *Yikes.* "Jade, my friend from Colorado. I told her I'd call her when I was done. Do you mind if I call her quickly and tell her I'll call to chat tomorrow instead?"

Mia and Simone exchanged a shrug. "Sure," they said in unison.

"Great. I'll just be a sec." Riley grabbed her cell phone and headed for the lobby. She had only one text, and it was from Jade.

Good luck at the show! Xox.

She texted back. *Went great. Will call 2moro. Xox.*

She called Josh's cell, then remembered that he had a meeting and hung up before it rang. She sent a text instead. *Show was awesome. Mind if I go out with Mia and Simone? Home before midnight I think. Luv u. Xox.*

MUSIC BOOMED THROUGH the dimly lit club. Riley, Mia, and Simone sat in a booth by the bar, sipping their drinks and letting the stress of the day roll from their shoulders. Simone had ordered a round of seven and sevens. It was not Riley's favorite drink, but she could go with the flow for one night.

She looked around the bar, thinking about how different it was from a night out in Weston. Here everyone looked like they had money. The women had stylish coifs and expensive clothing. They wore sky-high heels, and every motion they made seemed practiced and graceful. The men's styles looked just as manicured, some with an artsy flare and others in suits that probably cost more than a month's worth of horse feed back home. Riley could be happy anywhere as long as she was with Josh, but she wondered what Jade would make of New York.

"That was a killer show. JB is gonna be psyched," Simone said. She lifted her drink to her lips and threw back her head, taking a hearty gulp. "And that, ladies, is what tonight is all about." When she smiled, her slim black frames slid down her nose a tad and she set them right back on their perch with her index finger.

JB? Riley realized that she might hear things about Josh that she would rather avoid. What if they told her they had a crush on him and then they found out she was dating him? *Oh no.* Or worse, they might dislike something about him and she'd have to pretend to not take offense. *Maybe this was a bad idea.*

"Riley, what's the scoop with you?" Mia asked.

"The scoop?" Riley asked.

Simone finished her drink and held up her glass toward the blond waitress. "I swear they should just bring two out at a time."

"You know, tell us about yourself. All we know so far is that you're a killer designer working as a design assistant, and you're from Josh's hometown," Mia said.

Riley furrowed her brow. "You know where I'm from?"

"Of course. We know where you worked, about your awards; we even know that you dislike Cruella as much as we do," Mia said.

Do you know I'm sleeping with Josh? "I don't dislike her. She's okay; she's just trying to move up." *And using all the wrong tactics.*

"Speaking of moving up, did you guys hear about her and JB?" Simone asked.

Mia's eyes opened wide. "No, please don't tell me he gave in to that snark."

Riley bristled.

"No, but I hear she tried…again. Wella—the night cleaning woman—told Chantal she saw Claudia storm out of his office late one night looking pissed and flustered," Simone explained.

"She deserves to be fired, if you ask me," Mia said.

"Sexual harassment, that's what it is. And JB can do so much better," Simone said.

Riley swallowed the urge to tell them about her relationship with Josh. She gulped down her drink. They clearly liked him enough to want him to be with a good person, but was she that

person in their eyes, or would she be seen just as Claudia was—
a career climber using sex to get to the top?

"I hear he is." Mia sipped her drink, her eyes on Riley.

Riley froze. *Does she know?* "Really?" she managed. The
waitress brought another round of drinks, and Riley took
another gulp to numb the pinch that was slowly creeping across
the back of her neck.

"That's what I hear, too," Simone said. "He's got a woman
stashed away somewhere. All I can say is that I hope she's not
witchy and backhanded. The guy's loaded, and you know, I
wouldn't kick that body out of bed for eating crackers."

Riley choked on her drink, coughing and fanning her face.
"Sorry, sorry," she said, catching her breath. "Went down the
wrong tube or something."

"Drink some more. It'll help." Simone pushed Riley's drink
toward her. "Anyway, I always thought Mia would hook up
with JB." She flashed a half smile and nudged Mia's arm, then
flagged the waitress for another round.

"Please." Mia rolled her eyes. "I'm an excellent assistant, and
he values that, but there's nothing more to it. He's like an older
brother to me more than anything else. Don't get me wrong. I'd
do him if he asked, but I'd never pursue him. I like bad boys.
You know that, Simone. Besides, he doesn't even take home
those gorgeous, airheaded, easy-lay models he dates. I think Mr.
B. is pretty picky, if you ask me. How about you, Riley? Have a
boyfriend?"

Yes, and you'd do him. Oh no, no, no. She finished her drink
and said, "Are you guys hungry? Want to get an appetizer?"

"Oh, we are so much more clever than your Colorado
friends, chickadee. Spill it," Simone said.

"Now, now. She's new to the city. Don't pressure her. She

has morals and values, and—"

"Really? I'm not some dumb hick, you know," Riley said. She accepted another drink from the waitress and took a sip.

"I didn't mean that," Mia said. She touched Riley's arm. "Really, hon. I was just joshin' with you."

Joshin'? Crap. "Okay, yes, I have a boyfriend, and he's great. I mean, we haven't been seeing each other that long, but he's…" She shook her head, thinking of the ways she could describe Josh: caring, loving, sensuous, gorgeous, smart, funny, an incredible lover. Instead she took the safe route. "He's pretty great."

"Does Mr. Great have a name?" Simone asked. She finished her drink and flagged the waitress down again.

Mia grabbed her arm. "Slow down there, woman. I can't drink as much as you."

"You don't have to. I'll drink yours," Simone said with a wink.

Riley was glad the conversation had turned away from Josh before she had to come up with a fake name for him. "Did you guys like the gown I designed, or did it pretty much suck?"

"You're kidding, right?" Mia gave her a stern look.

"No, I really want to know." *Anything to get away from the subject of Josh.*

"It was about the most original wedding gown I'd ever seen," Mia said.

"I'd even consider getting married if I had that gown," Simone quipped.

Riley let out a relieved sigh. "Oh, thank goodness. I thought y'all were just being kind in the meeting."

"*We all* were not just being kind," Simone teased. "Especially Cruella. Did you see the scowl on her face when she saw your design? I thought claws were going to come shooting out from the ends of her fingers. Seriously. What's up her butt with you? I see how she's hot and cold with you. Any idea why?"

Because I'm sleeping with Josh? Riley shrugged. "Don't ask me. I just do what I'm told." The buzz of the alcohol was beginning to settle in. She looked around the bar through the haze of alcohol, spying a dance floor she hadn't seen earlier. She began swaying to the music in her seat. She closed her eyes and imagined Josh there beside her. Oh, what she wouldn't do to make that come true.

"Okay, it's time." Simone said.

Riley's eyes shot open. "What?"

Simone and Mia climbed from the booth and pulled Riley along with them.

"Dancing. It gets rid of all the chaos in our minds. Come on, country girl." Simone tugged her along, and before Riley could protest, she was between Mia and Simone in the middle of the dance floor.

The more they danced, the fuller the dance floor became, until the three of them were practically squished together. Riley had a definite buzz. She could barely hear past the music. She hummed to the beat, enjoying herself without care of who saw her, and it felt so good.

Mia tugged her arm. "Come on," she said, and dragged her back to the booth. "Get your stuff."

"Why? What's happened?"

Mia showed her the screen of her cell phone. Riley squinted, pulled back, then drew in close again, trying to focus, but she was beyond focusing. "What does it say?"

Simone pulled her phone from her purse. "Me too. I wonder what went down."

Riley scrambled through her purse, fumbling with her phone to read the sole text message. When she did, she was even more confused. Mia peered over her shoulder, and Riley shoved her phone back in her purse.

"We've got to go to the office. Did you get a nine-one-one text from Josh?" Mia asked.

Riley shook her head, wondering how Mia's eyes could look so clear when she felt so light-headed.

"Are you okay to get home on your own?" Simone asked, slipping into her coat.

"Of course," Riley said. "Why are you going to the office?"

"Dunno. But when JB texts nine-one-one, we go. See you tomorrow at the show? I'm sure Claudia will have some excuse not to show up." Mia threw money on the table, then draped her purse over her shoulder and looped her arm into Simone's. "Hey, cowgirl, great to hang with you. We'll fill you in tomorrow if there's anything worth sharing."

Simone shoved two twenties into Riley's hand, then kissed her cheek. "You're so cute when you're shnockered. Be safe."

"Thanks. I had a great time." Riley watched them hurry out of the bar before taking out her phone and rereading the text from Josh.

We need 2 talk. Home later than expected. J.

Chapter Twenty-Six

RILEY SHIVERED AS she walked into Josh's apartment. It was almost one o'clock in the morning and she was still a little light-headed from the alcohol. She'd sobered up a bit on the cab ride over, stewing about what could have happened and worrying about whether someone had caught wind of their relationship. Maybe that wasn't the worst thing that could happen. Maybe it would be for the best, especially after tonight. It would be easier to fess up to dating Josh right away to Mia and Simone rather than letting the lies linger between them. *If someone found out, wouldn't he have called me first?*

She set her purse down on the table by the door, peeked into the empty living room and dining room, then headed for the kitchen, which was also empty. She walked quietly across the hall to the master bedroom, hoping Josh was there. The bed was empty. She pulled off her heels and flopped onto the bed.

What on earth is going on? She smoothed the comforter, thinking about their lovemaking and smiling at the thought. *Yes, maybe it would be for the best if our relationship was exposed.* She hated sneaking around and lying, and although they weren't being as careful outside of work, she still felt like a thief on parole. She'd seen pictures of Josh in the rag mags over the years and on the cover of the larger publications when his career first began to flourish, and she remembered how her heart had skipped a beat, breathing new life into the crush she'd worked so hard to tamp down. Each time she'd catch sight of one of those articles, she'd buy the magazine and look at it when she was alone at night. Then she'd force those feelings back into the confines of some well deep within her mind. Someplace where they wouldn't render her unable to think straight, as they had when they'd reconnected. Maybe now he wasn't quite as much of a reader draw as he once was. Maybe he was overreacting. After all, why would the media care if he was dating her? She was talking herself in circles again. She knew the answer to the relentless question. It wasn't the media he was worried about. If they took his picture, it would be happenstance, a space filler in some useless magazine in the About Town section. It was Claudia catching wind of that picture that worried him.

She slipped out of her clothes, hung them on a hanger to be taken to the cleaners, and ran a warm shower. She had to be at the show the next morning at seven thirty, and she'd get no sleep if she didn't relax. She pushed away the unsettling feeling in her stomach, writing it off as too much alcohol, and stepped into the shower hoping Josh would come home and join her.

At one forty-five she climbed into bed, chewing on the possibilities that something worse had happened. With no additional texts from Josh and knowing he'd texted nine-one-one to Mia and Simone, her stomach was doing somersaults. *We have 2 talk.*

Chapter Twenty-Seven

THE ROOM FELT like it was closing in on him. Josh's chest constricted, and he broke out in a sweat. *What the hell is going on?* It wasn't the room and it wasn't a heart attack, Josh realized, but the shattering of his heart. He sat behind his desk with his head buried in his hands, rehashing the last few hours and Claudia's accusations that Riley had stolen the design for Max's dress from her. *Riley? A design thief?* Any way he cut it, it would be her word against Riley's unless he could prove that Claudia was lying.

The last thing he wanted to do was upset Riley with Claudia's obscene accusation. He wanted to prove Claudia wrong here and now and go home to Riley without this crap hanging over their heads. He'd get to the bottom of this chaos if it took all night.

He knew a nine-one-one text would raise all sorts of questions, but tonight, with exhaustion and anger taking over his rational mind, he didn't care. He hoped that one of the staff could verify that Riley had been designing Max's dress while she was at work, or that she'd shared her designs with them. Anything to prove that Riley wasn't the one who had stolen the design. Why would she? She had Josh. Her design skills were flawless. She had it all. Why would she risk everything? *Why would she risk our love?*

CLAY AND K.T. had been no help at all. Both came into the office looking like they'd just rolled out of bed, with worry etched into their faces. Neither had witnessed Riley doing any work other than JBD work, though Clay claimed to have seen Claudia designing through lunch on several occasions. They'd left the office with a firm directive that what they'd discussed not leave the safety of his office.

Mia and Simone flew through the front doors and into his office. Having had another hour to think without Claudia in his face, he realized that he should have spoken to Riley before speaking to the staff, but it was too late for that now.

"We're here, boss. What's up?"

He lifted his frustrated gaze to meet Mia's voice. "Have a seat, ladies." He stood and paced.

"What is it?" Simone asked, shooting a worried look at Mia.

"There's been an accusation raised about Riley's wedding gown design," he began. "Do either of you know anything about this?"

The surprise in their eyes only frustrated him more. Surely someone would have seen Claudia rifling through Riley's things, or Riley poring over her sketches.

"What do you mean, an accusation?" Simone asked.

"She's been accused of stealing the design," Josh admitted through a clenched jaw.

"We just spent the evening with Riley, and she sure doesn't seem like someone who would steal a design," Simone said.

"This has to be Cruella, right?" Mia shot to her feet. When Josh didn't answer, she continued. "That woman will do anything to get ahead. How can you even trust a word she says?"

"Don't you think the same thoughts have already run through my head?" He sat on the edge of his desk and let out a long sigh. "She has proof, Mia. I was hoping that Riley had shared her designs with one of you, or that you'd at least seen her working on them. I've seen sketches in her apartment, but they were already drawn. I didn't see her working on them."

Mia shook her head. "I haven't, but that's not surprising. I can't imagine that she'd let everyone here know she was doing something other than straight JBD work."

"Good point," Josh said, chewing on the tiny nugget of hope.

"But then again," Simone added, "we have seen Claudia working on new designs. Remember, Mia? She showed us that pantsuit, the one with the thick belt and flared legs."

Man...

"I still don't believe it." Mia crossed her arms and paced. "What kind of proof does she have?"

Josh knew that he shouldn't divulge the details of the accusation or the proof that Claudia had presented, but his nerves were so tightly wound and anger strangled any patience that he might once have possessed. He was scrounging for something to prove Riley's innocence. One small shred of evidence, that's all he needed.

"Drawings. Scanned, dated, and recorded," he answered.

"Oh." Mia sat back down on the couch, her elbows on her knees. "What are you going to do?"

"What can I do? This is a serious accusation. I have to talk to Riley and hear her side of it." Josh tried to ignore the piercing pain shooting through his stomach.

"She'll quit. Heck, I'd quit even if I hadn't stolen the ideas. Just being accused of something so heinous would piss me off," Simone said. "You'd better be sure before you take that leap. From what I witnessed today, Riley could sell a double bed to the pope. She's got more people skills in her pinky than Claudia has in her entire body. She'll have no trouble getting another job, especially if she really did design that dress."

Tell me something I don't know.

Josh ran his hand through his hair, thinking, buying time before going home. No matter how many ways he turned the accusation, he didn't have a lick of evidence supporting Riley's efforts.

"Not a word of this to anyone outside these four walls. Got it?"

AFTER TALKING WITH the staff, Josh felt as if a giant hand had crashed through his chest and ripped out his heart. He stepped from the office into the cold night air, and instead of climbing into a cab or calling Jay to pick him up, he walked, crushing his anger with each determined step. *Could I have been wrong about Riley? Were there red flags I overlooked because of my feelings for her?* He walked by Savannah's apartment, where his intimate relationship with Riley had first begun. He stopped in front of Savannah's building, wishing he could go back to the nights when he and Riley had lain in each other's arms without this mess on their shoulders.

By the time he reached the Dakota, he felt like he'd been

through a war. His muscles ached, and his emotions were frayed so badly that he didn't trust himself to deal with this mess rationally until he'd had time to sleep and process the facts. Inside the dark apartment, he removed his shoes by the door, feeling the warmth of Riley's presence around him, and walked soft footed to the bedroom. The pit of his stomach sank at the sight of Riley tucked peacefully into his bed. Her beautiful hair fanned from her head like a halo. He swallowed past the lump in his throat. He couldn't accuse her of something so wrong. *This has to be a mistake.*

Chapter Twenty-Eight

RILEY AWOKE TO the alarm at six o'clock and reached across the empty bed. She bolted out of bed, hurrying into the hall wearing Josh's T-shirt and her underwear.

"Josh?" she called as she walked down the hall. She found him asleep on the couch in the living room. He stirred when she sat beside him, and when she kissed his forehead, he blinked awake.

"Hey," she whispered. "Missed you last night. Why'd you sleep out here?"

He scrubbed his face with his hand. "Hi. I didn't want to wake you." He pushed himself up to a sitting position.

"Please don't ever worry about that. I'd always rather be next to you. Why didn't you at least sleep in the guest room?" she asked.

"It felt too far away."

She kissed his cheek and felt him stiffen against her lips. "What's wrong?" She searched his downcast eyes. Something was wrong. Something was very wrong.

Josh cleared his throat. "Let me get some coffee." He pushed to his feet and started for the kitchen.

Riley was on his heels. "Why didn't you return my texts last night? Did something happen with Claudia? I know you texted Mia and Simone. I was with them last night when the texts came through."

Josh didn't respond. He put both hands on the counter and leaned over it.

"You're missing your morning run," she said. *This has got to be bad.*

"I know," he whispered.

She touched his back, hating the way he pulled away just slightly but enough to send a very strong message. "Josh? Have I done something?"

When he turned, his eyes were filled with love. Relieved, she took a step toward him. He looked away, and in that flash of an instant, she saw his eyes narrow, then close, stopping her in her tracks.

"Josh?" The hair on the back of her neck prickled.

"Riley, let's sit down."

She moved robotically to a chair. He sat across from her, but he felt a million miles away. Her mouth went dry, and she thought she might be sick as she waited for him to speak.

"Where did you get that design for Max's dress?" he asked.

She shook her head, thinking she'd misheard him. "*Where* did I get it? Do you mean where did I get my ideas from?"

He sighed, running his hand through his hair again. His eyes darted around the table, to the left of her, to her lap, anywhere but meeting her confused stare. When his eyes finally found hers, it was the rest of his face that sent the pit of her stomach on a downhill roller coaster. Worry lines streaked his forehead, and a deep vee had formed between his furrowed brows.

"Riley, Claudia said the design was hers."

Riley felt like she'd been kicked in the gut. She pushed to her feet, sending the chair flying backward. "What? That little witch. You know that's not true." Her entire body shook. She crossed her arms in an effort to stop them from trembling. Her lower lip shook, and she bit it, holding it in place. *Don't cry. Don't cry.*

"Babe," he said.

She wished that endearment didn't remind her of just how much she loved him. "Josh, you know this isn't true. You were there when I showed it to Max. You saw the drawing. You saw me laboring over the design right there at your dining room table." *Don't cry.*

"I saw the sketch when you showed it to Max, but I didn't see you draw it." He looked at her then with a mixture of disbelief and empathy—or maybe it was pity, she couldn't tell.

"Don't look at me like that. I didn't steal anything. I can prove it." She didn't mean to yell. She swiped at a tear that had broken loose. *Prove it? I have to prove something to you?* "I can't believe this. You'd believe Claudia over me? It's me, Josh. Remember?" There was no stopping the flow of angry tears. She sucked air into her constricted lungs. "Remember me, Josh? The girl you said you loved? Do you really think I'd do something like that?"

He dropped his eyes. "I didn't want to believe it, but she showed me scanned sketches of all the drawings, dated well before you showed the dress to Max. I accused her of lying, of stealing. I accused her of everything I could think of. Then I had to watch her click through image after image on her computer of scanned clothing designs she'd supposedly sketched. Designs I'd never seen before, with the exception of Max's wedding dress and one dress that I had actually witnessed her designing earlier in the month. *Witnessed, Riley.* Why didn't I witness you drawing the wedding dress in the first place? You have to believe me. I didn't want to believe her—even when her proof was indisputable. So I talked to the staff and—"

"You talked to the staff?" *This can't be happening.* "You've humiliated me without any proof."

"Riley, no one has seen you drawing anything besides JBD work."

He looked at her then, and this time the meaning was clear. Pity. Before the sobs tore from her chest, she stormed from the room.

"I don't believe this," she spat.

In the bedroom, she threw her clothes onto the bed. She was shaking so badly that she kept dropping them on the floor. She heard Josh enter the room, felt his arms touch her from behind. She stopped for a beat, then twisted away.

"You're not the man I thought you were," she said, more sad than angry. She scooped the clothes into her arms, grabbed the few pairs of shoes she could hold on to, and headed for the front door.

"Riley, wait. Let's talk about this."

She hooked her purse with her finger and turned to face him. He stood with his shoulders rounded forward, his hair askew, and bags under his beautifully sad dark eyes. She loved him so much that every fiber of her being ached at his accusation. She couldn't stay in that apartment. She couldn't stay with him. No matter how much she loved him, she knew she had to leave. She gathered all of the courage she could muster, gripping the clothes tightly against her body—a shield between her and the hurt—and when she spoke, she barely recognized the sound of her own broken voice.

"The man I love would never have believed this farce in the first place. I'll stay at Treat's, and I'll get my stuff at some point. I'll move out of Treat's when I go home. I'm sorry, but please find someone else to run the show. Mia and Simone are great. They'll do it." She reached for the doorknob just as Josh touched her shoulders.

He rested his forehead on the back of her head. "Please, don't do this."

She clenched her eyes shut, damming the tears. Her heart screamed, *Turn around! Hold him! Love him!* Her mind screamed, *Someone who loves you doesn't do this.*

"You already did," she said.

Chapter Twenty-Nine

DAMN! JOSH STOMPED through the apartment, up and down the hall, through the living room, and finally, into the master bedroom, where he leaned on the dresser and stared at himself in the mirror. His hair was a mess; his eyes were bloodshot and angry. He wanted to punch something. He wanted to scream. He wanted to rewind time and *witness* Riley draw that original drawing. He gritted his teeth, clenched his jaw, and paced the floor until his chest and stomach hurt so badly he had to get the poison out. He raised his arms toward the ceiling and cursed.

The veins in his neck pressed against his skin. His face felt white-hot. How the heck would he fix this mess? He stomped to the front door and swung it open. He'd apologize to Riley. He'd take her in his arms and work this mess out. *Then what?* What if he'd been wrong about her? What if she did steal the design? *I'm not wrong. She's a good person.* But what if...

He closed the door, taking relief in the fact that it was Saturday. He had time to think. To plan. *To mourn.*

UNRAVELING THE TRUTH ABOUT LOVE

RILEY FLUNG HER clothes on the foyer floor and crumpled onto the living room couch, sobbing. How could this happen? Yesterday she was on cloud nine, and now her career—and her relationship with Josh—were over. Kaput. Done. She sobbed until her chest and throat ached and she had no more tears to cry. She punched the couch pillows, then stood and paced. She wished she could climb out of her skin and hide. Riley threw herself onto the center of the living room floor and curled up in the fetal position. *How could anything hurt this much?*

She couldn't think past the ache of mistrust Josh had shown. He should have come to her first. Now everyone knew that she'd been accused of something she didn't do—of something Josh believed she did.

She dialed Jade's number. Jade answered on the first ring, and the sound of her voice drew more sobs from a well deep within Riley's body that she didn't know existed. How could something hurt so much?

"Ri? What is it, hon? What can I do?" Jade urged.

"I...I wanna come home." That was it. She had to go back to her safe existence. No one in Weston would ever accuse her of something so vile.

"Oh, honey, of course you can come home. Ri, honey, tell me what's going on. Did something happen? Did Josh do something?"

Riley pushed through the pain and humiliation and told her best friend exactly what had crushed her will to go on.

"Oh, hon. I just can't believe Josh would believe any of that," she said. Her voice was like a warm hug—an embrace that part of Riley wanted to rebel against and push away from so she could wallow in the ache of Josh's faltering faith in her and another part of her wanted to run back into just to feel that she was loved.

There was no hiding from the excruciating pain. She had to face Josh head-on or give up. How could she love someone who didn't trust her? But she *did* love him.

"Well, he does," she said to Jade. "What should I do? Should I talk to him some more? I mean, what can I say? There was no one watching me draw Max's dress. I mean, I had to hide it from Claudia or deal with her wrath. There were no eyewitnesses."

"Take a deep breath, Riley. Let this mess blow over, then talk to him. It's Saturday. Talk to him tomorrow, when you're less upset. That way you can fix things before Monday."

"I don't know if I want to fix things. I'm not sure I'm cut out for this backstabbing business after all." *Or a relationship with Josh.*

"I can't give you the answers, but I wouldn't make any final decisions today," Jade said.

"I told Josh to get someone else to run the show," she admitted.

"Then Cruella wins. Hands down."

She knew Jade was pushing her in the same way that she might have pushed Jade if she were in a similar situation, but it hurt so darned much.

"So come home. Give up," Jade urged.

Riley wiped her eyes as reality dawned on her. Jade was right. If she gave up, Claudia won. Even if she didn't carry on her relationship with Josh, she couldn't let Claudia define her career. "Sometimes I hate you," Riley said.

"I can accept that. Now get your butt in the shower, show up on Josh's doorstep, and tell him that you're doing the show. Then hold that beautiful head up high and don't let all this bull weigh you down. You'll figure this stuff out. And if you don't, you can come home to me. I'll open a bottle of Middle Sister margaritas, and we can drink all the hurt away."

She heard a forced smile laced with worry in Jade's voice. Riley sighed. "And what about Josh?"

"That's a hard one. I get why you feel he doesn't trust you, but also, he's a businessman, and there's that to consider. He has a company and a reputation to protect. Riley, without talking to him, you can't know where he's coming from. Maybe he's as confused as you are."

Riley wiped her remaining tears and took a deep breath. "Okay. I'll try, but I might end up on your doorstep tomorrow."

RILEY STOOD IN front of Josh's door with her hand perched to knock. There wasn't much she could do about her red-rimmed, puffy eyes or the deflated feeling in her chest, but at least she looked good. She wore the other JBD outfit Mia had picked out for her, and the form-fitting navy dress gave her a modicum of confidence. She'd been practicing what she was going to say for the past thirty minutes, but when Josh opened the door wearing his wrinkled clothes, his eyes also puffy and bloodshot, his hair still askew, it completely derailed her.

"Riley," he said in an exhausted whisper. He stepped back and opened the door wider. "Come in, please."

The little confidence she'd mustered shattered with his broken voice. Her eyes filled with tears, and she squeezed them shut. "Shoot."

His arms were around her then, holding her against his

chest. His lips on the top of her head, kissing her in a way that pulled more tears from some invisible well deep within her.

"I'm so sorry," he whispered. "I should have come to you first. I should have fired Claudia ages ago, but she's Peter's niece, and he did so much for me. I've always felt indebted to him. But I'm done worrying about him."

Riley cried into his wrinkled dress shirt. She wanted to stay right there in his embrace, with his kind words bathing her like his hands once had, but she wanted to push him away in equal measure. *How could you do this to me if you love me? Why does love hurt so much?*

Josh shut the door behind them, Riley still in his arms. "Can you forgive me?" he asked.

She pushed away then, just enough to see his dark eyes staring down at her with the most intense stare she'd ever seen, strangling her words once again.

"You don't have to forgive me. Just know we'll figure this out together. You're right, Riley. I can't imagine that you'd have done something like this. I just couldn't see that clearly last night."

"This whole thing sucks," she finally managed. She pulled away from him, set her chin straight, and pulled back her shoulders. She had to do this. "I'm really hurt that you'd even consider what she said as true, and I'm beyond humiliated that you've spread this to all of the staff."

"I understand," he said. He ran his finger along the line of her jaw. "Riley, please believe me when I say that I did that in an effort to clear your name. I was hoping someone would have seen you designing."

"Oh, right, like I'd let anyone know I was doing something other than JBD work." She turned away. "Listen, I don't know what to do about this—you, me, my career—in the long run, but I'm going to honor my commitment. I'll go run the show and I'll be at work Monday."

She watched him swallow, then cross his arms. "What are you telling me?"

"I don't know," she said honestly.

"You don't want to be with me?" Josh asked.

The hurt in his voice rivaled the ache in her own soul. "How together are we, Josh? We're a secret love affair." The words surprised her as much as they did him. He reached for her, and she stepped away, unsure of what she was doing, much less saying. "I love you, but I'm hurt. Beyond hurt." She grabbed the doorknob and swung the door open.

"Riley, wait," Josh said.

Riley closed her eyes, unable to form a rational response or even weed through her tangled feelings to know if she should listen to him or not.

"Claudia won't be at the show today. I know she was sched- uled to run it with you, but I've told her not to. Until this is figured out, I don't want you two in close quarters. She assured me that until this was figured out, she wasn't going to talk to anyone about it, so at least it isn't public knowledge."

With her eyes locked on the door, she asked, "Should I not do the show?"

"No, you can. I just didn't trust her."

That was enough to allow her eyes to meet his. Those five words meant that he did trust her, at least more than he trusted Claudia. She realized that didn't say much, but at least it was something. And right then, Riley needed something to pull her through the morning.

Chapter Thirty

JOSH NEEDED HIS morning run more than he ever had before. He ran like he was being chased through the park, in and out of the streets, until finally, he ended up in front of the JBD building. He'd rip the office apart if he had to. If Riley was designing Max's dress while at work, even when using stolen moments, there had to be some proof.

He stormed through the doors and into the design studio.

Claudia looked up from a drawing table with a smile. "Hi, Josh. I thought I'd be alone this morning."

His sweat-covered body was ablaze. "What are you doing here?" he snapped.

"Sketching." She tossed the answer as if she hadn't a care in the world.

"Sketching." *Sketching, my butt.*

"Yes, refining one of the designs in my portfolio. Wanna see?" She lifted her brows, and her green eyes sparkled, inciting a surge of anger within him.

"No." He clenched his fists and stomped past her to Riley's desk.

He pulled each drawer open, rifled through them, then slammed them closed.

"What are you doing?" Claudia asked.

Ignoring her, he continued his search, pulling out her file drawers and leafing through each and every folder. If there was proof, it was there somewhere. He felt Claudia's eyes on his back, and that just spurred his vehemence to clear Riley's name.

Ten minutes later, and having come up without any evidence of her drawings, he turned on Riley's computer.

"You need her password," Claudia said.

He glared at her.

"It's *WestonGirl4Life*. Number four, all one word, initial caps."

Josh narrowed his eyes. "How do you know?"

"It's my job to know the passwords on all design computers, remember? You added that to my duties two years ago, when you were trying to find something or other."

My mistake. Josh sat in Riley's chair. Her scent was everywhere, momentarily distracting him from his anger. While the computer booted, he thought about their conversation earlier that morning. He'd been so relieved to see her that he'd almost teared up, and when he'd held her, he'd wanted to tell her not to go to the show, but to stay with him. They could make love and figure out this mess later. He felt like she'd been ripped from his arms—and he knew she hadn't been ripped at all. She'd been pushed, and he was the one who had done the shoving.

"Did it work?" Claudia asked.

Her voice pulled him from his thoughts. He typed in Riley's password, and her JBD home screen came to life. He didn't answer Claudia. The less interaction with her the better until he knew the truth about her accusations. He went through Riley's files, feeling slightly voyeuristic; then he clicked over to her JBD email account. He went through anything with an attachment, hoping for something that would validate her innocence. Coming up empty once again, he went to her scanned documents. Maybe she'd have done the same as Claudia and scanned them into the computer. A few clicks later, nothing was revealed. Riley appeared to be the typical JBD employee doing her job.

She's not a typical employee. She's talented beyond belief. She's honest and more Weston than New York. He spun around in the chair, scrutinizing Claudia as she leaned over the drawing table. *She's not honest. More Alcatraz than anywhere else. Something's not right.*

RILEY TRIED TO ignore the differences she felt in Mia and Simone and concentrated on the mass of buyers instead. She was taking an order and had stopped writing to present an accessory ensemble to the buyer when the flash of a camera went off. She looked up, and two clicks later, she was seeing spots.

She smiled at the photographer, pleased that JBD would be included in the event's media coverage.

Mia squeezed between Riley and the camera.

"Riley, why don't you take our buyer someplace a little more private?" Mia asked.

Riley turned back to the buyer, watching Mia in a heated discussion with the photographer out of the corner of her eye. When the photographer left, Mia whispered something to Simone, before grabbing her phone and heading to the ladies' room.

Another wave of buyers came through, and as Saturday

afternoon turned to evening and the show finally came to an end, Riley was surprised to realize that she hadn't thought about Claudia all afternoon, while thoughts of Josh pressed in on her every thought. Maybe she could get through this. Maybe it would pass without a lot of fanfare. Feeling mildly better, she wished Jade were there to go out for a drink or even just to be there to give her strength to deal with all the stuff swirling around in her head.

She packed the brochures and correlated the orders while Mia and Simone prepared the clothes for shipment back to the office.

The last thing Riley wanted was to go home to Treat's empty apartment. She didn't want to be alone. She wanted to be in Josh's arms, listening to him telling her it had all been a mistake, but she knew that wasn't going to happen. She looked at Mia and Simone, hoping she could catch a break, at least with them. They hadn't said a word about Claudia's accusations, and she didn't like it hanging between them like the white elephant in the room. She steeled herself for rejection.

"Hey, do y'all want to have a drink tonight?" Riley cringed at her hometown drawl.

Mia and Simone exchanged a glance, sending a clear, painful reminder of the accusations that hung over her head like a dark cloud.

"I've got a date," Simone said and turned away.

Mia grabbed Simone's arm and cast a harsh look in her direction.

Simone made a *tsk* sound, rolling her eyes. "Fine," she huffed.

"Sure," Mia said.

A new worry entered Riley's mind. What if they believed

that she really had stolen Claudia's work, and they'd agreed to go for drinks just to give her a hard time about it? It was one thing to dislike a coworker, but calling her a thief took it to a whole new level.

"You don't have to," she said, feeling like she'd jumped into a night out with Mia and Simone too quickly. Maybe what she really needed was to go home and talk to Josh.

"Yes, we do," Mia said.

Chapter Thirty-One

THEY CHOSE A quiet bar that was off the beaten path. Mia and Simone sat on one side of a booth in the back corner. Riley sat across from them nervously chewing the inside of her cheek. *What was I thinking?*

"Wanna talk about it?" Mia asked.

No. I want to hide under a rock. She let out a sigh. "Not really," she admitted.

"Did you do it?" Simone asked.

"Simone!" Mia punched her arm.

"No, I didn't do it," Riley spat. She tried to hold back the rush of tears that welled in her eyes.

"I know you didn't," Mia said.

"That's not what you said earlier," Simone said.

"Why are you such a bull today?" Mia said to Simone. "I said that I didn't know what to believe, and I don't, but I'm more inclined to believe Riley than Claudia."

"Aren't we all," Simone agreed. "Riley, you must have proof. Original sketches? Something to just knock the air out of this."

Riley had been so consumed with the accusation that she hadn't even planned out a way to prove that she was the original designer.

"I have them. They're in my desk drawer. And I've faxed a few to a friend," Riley said, thinking of Jade.

"See." Mia nudged Simone. "So tomorrow, get the drawings and call Josh. He's not leaving for the holiday until late Sunday. I'm sure he'll meet you in the morning; then you can put an end to this before it goes any further."

Christmas. Darn it. She had forgotten all about Christmas. She'd been so excited about spending the holidays together, and now—*oh, no*—she had no idea what *now* would hold. "I will. Hopefully that will put an end to it, but I'm so embarrassed. I almost quit this morning."

"Did Josh call you?" Mia asked.

She blinked away the memory of finding him asleep on the couch, so peaceful and handsome. That was before…before she knew what lay within his heart and he broke hers.

"Yeah," she lied.

"Did you tell him it wasn't true?" Simone asked.

"Yeah, but…"

"But he'd already spoken to everyone and knew that no one had seen you doing any designing," Mia said.

"Yup," Riley said, relieved when the waitress brought their drinks. She took a gulp of her drink and closed her eyes as it burned her throat on the way down. "I still can't believe this is all happening. I don't blame you guys for not believing me. You hardly know me. I promise you, though, I didn't steal anyone's design. That wedding dress was my original idea."

"When did you draw the dress, Riley?" Mia asked. Her tone wasn't accusatory, but rather curious.

Riley shrugged. "I don't know. Whenever I could find a few spare minutes. It's not like I kept track. I wish I had started drawing it back home, but I was really just thinking about ideas until I got here. I never thought I'd be in a position of defending myself."

Mia and Simone exchanged another look.

"In this business, covering your behind is one thing you should never forget to do," Simone said. "Have you told your boyfriend yet? This town has eyes and ears everywhere. I wouldn't be surprised if Claudia has already shouted it from the rooftops. Can't you just hear her?" She flung her head back dramatically and put the back of her hand over her forehead. "The wolves have stolen my work. Woe is me. Come to my rescue."

Mia slapped her arm. "Cut it out."

"You don't think she'd really tell anyone outside of JBD, do you?" It was bad enough being humiliated in her coworkers' eyes, but having something like this go public would be too much for her to take. She guzzled her drink in one gulp. "I've gotta go. You guys are freaking me out." She grabbed her purse just as her cell phone vibrated.

"Listen, we're on your side, even without the evidence," Mia said with a friendly smile.

"That's how much we despise Cruella," Simone added.

Mia rolled her eyes.

"What? We do despise her," Simone said.

"Yes, but that's not why we support Riley. We support her because we believe her," Mia explained.

"Of course. Jeez. I thought she knew that already," Simone said.

Riley wasn't listening to them bicker. She threw money on the table and read the text message from Josh.

Can we talk?

Chapter Thirty-Two

THE DISTANCE BETWEEN Josh and Riley was far larger than the two feet that separated them on his living room couch. Riley fidgeted with the edge of the throw that was draped over the back of the couch. She had hardly looked at Josh since she'd arrived, and it was killing him.

"I went into the office today to see what I could find on my own," he said.

"All of my original drawings are in my desk. I know she's accusing me of stealing Max's dress, but it's with the other ideas that I've thought of over the last few weeks. And I forgot to tell you that I had faxed the design of Max's dress and another dress I was thinking of making to Jade a while back," Riley said.

"I went through your desk. There were no drawings."

Her hands froze. He watched her finally lift her disbelieving gaze to meet his.

"No drawings? That's impossible. I kept them all in the bottom right drawer. They were there a few days ago."

He covered her hand with his. "Maybe Claudia took them."

"She had to. Josh, this is awful. How am I going to defend myself if I don't have my drawings?" She stood and paced.

"What about the drawings I saw at your apartment the

night we had dinner with Peter?" Josh asked.

"I drew those the weekend I got to New York, before I even started working there, and they had nothing to do with Max's dress."

"Is there anything else you can think of that would prove that you drew Max's dress? I wish you would have shown me the drawings when you first began sketching them. Why didn't anyone else see you doing it?" The accusatory tone of his words surprised him, and he quickly added, "I'm sorry. I don't mean that the way it sounded."

Riley stared at him, her lips a tight line, her deadpan stare unmoved by his apology.

"Riley, these are serious accusations. I've gone through it all hundreds of times over the last twenty-four hours. I was ready to fire her this morning at the office."

"She was there?" Riley asked.

"When I arrived, she was drawing."

"Of course she was," Riley said with a shake of her head. "She's one step ahead of me, Josh. How can I ever prove myself if she's stolen my drawings? I can't believe it's come to this. I have to prove my innocence? This would never happen in Weston."

He held her stare, wishing he could tell her she didn't have to prove a blasted thing, but he knew that wasn't true. This was a serious issue, and it had to come to some kind of closure.

"You're right, Riley. This would never happen in Weston. But we're in New York. It's where you wanted to be, and with your skills, it's where you *should* be. I'll bring you both into my office and we'll hash this out," he said.

"Hash this out? What does that even mean?" She flopped back onto the couch, shaking her head.

He sat beside her again and lifted her chin. "Babe, this whole thing sucks, but we can't let it ruin us."

A tear slipped down her cheek. He wiped it away with the pad of his thumb.

"How can this not ruin us? How can it not ruin me? Everyone thinks I'm a thief. We can never go public with our relationship now—that would only make things worse, and if we wait, then people will think badly of you for being with me. She's single-handedly ruined my life," Riley said. Before he could answer, she added, "And you hurt me. You don't trust me, Josh." Tears sprang from her eyes. "How can I be with you, knowing you don't trust me?"

"Riley, baby, I will spend the rest of my life making it up to you. I made a mistake, a huge mistake, but my mistake wasn't not trusting you." Josh loved Riley. He trusted her, and he believed with his whole heart that she was telling the truth, but that didn't stop a little nag in the back of his mind from reminding him to be careful. *Your reputation is on the line.* He hated the sickening feel that the nag brought with it, and he did everything within his mental capabilities to squelch that little voice, but the voice would not be silenced. He pushed forth, ignoring that awful voice that conflicted with his heart, and as he tried to convince Riley, he had to wonder if he was also trying to convince himself.

"You have to believe me on this, Riley. My mistake was not coming to you before bringing the staff into it. I was trying to clear your name. I realized my mistake after calling them, but by then it was too late." Words weren't enough to express the sorrow that felt like needles beneath his skin. He reached for her hand and she turned away. "Please don't tell me that in an effort to clear your name I've lost you forever."

What could he do but tell her the truth? He felt her slipping away, and he couldn't stand it. "Riley, please. I reacted. I jumped in thinking I was protecting you. I screwed up. Please forgive me."

She turned and faced him, tears streaming down her cheeks. He wanted to take her in his arms and hold her until all the hurt fell away, but he didn't dare move.

"I swear, Riley, I'll never hurt you again. Not ever. Please, Riley." He'd beg all night if that's what it took. "I messed up, and I regret it more than you could ever imagine."

"It'd be easy for you to walk away. Everyone would forget what happened, and your life could go back to normal. You'd be free of this mess," Riley said.

"Easy? You think it would be *easy* for me to walk away from you? To be free from this mess would mean losing you, and that would be the hardest thing I could ever do. I'd rather lose everything to be with you than go on without you." *Holy cow. I really would.*

Stunned by his own admission, he couldn't move. He and Riley stared at each other, each wrapped in a cloak of pain. He wasn't letting go. Rage brewed within Josh's gut—an unfamiliar, heated, uncontrollable anger. He fisted his hands. There was no way he was going to let Claudia take away what they had together, and there was no way he'd let her ruin the career that Riley deserved. *Claudia.* He clenched his jaw against the thought of her. His pulse raced, and Josh looked away from Riley, trying to calm the mounting, menacing hatred. He'd never felt out of control of his own temper, and he didn't understand what was happening. But he was sure of one thing. There had to be a way to prove Claudia was lying.

His cell phone rang.

"Go ahead. You can get it," Riley said.

"It's okay. I can get it later."

It rang again.

"I'm fine. Please," she said.

He reluctantly got up and picked up his phone from the mantel. *Mia.*

"Yeah?"

"Just got a call from my contact at Page Six asking for a statement," Mia said.

"What the…? A statement?" Josh shot a look at Riley, hoping it wasn't about the designs.

"Claudia must have leaked the issue. They're doing a story on it," Mia answered.

"You've got to be kidding."

"What?" Riley flew to her feet.

He took her hand and held on tight. *I won't let go. Ever.* "Do you know what it's going to say?" he asked Mia. His pulse raced. This was the worst thing that could happen. He had no proof to stand behind Riley.

"No. Just that they're doing the story," Mia said.

"Here's my statement. You got a pen?" Josh fumed. He pulled Riley against him and hoped he was doing the right thing. "We believe the allegations made by Claudia Raven are completely unfounded. An internal investigation is underway."

He hung up the phone without waiting for Mia to respond and wrapped his arms around Riley.

"What's going on?" she asked.

"All hell's broken loose."

Chapter Thirty-Three

THE FIRST CALL Josh made was to Claudia, placing her on administrative leave while he had the matter investigated. She was livid, but he didn't care. The second call he made was to Kelly Treejen, his public relations manager, the third was to his attorney, advising him to hire a private investigator to find out the truth. After the calls, he went into the master bedroom, where Riley was sleeping, and lay beside her. After Mia called, they'd talked for an hour and he'd finally gotten through to her. He didn't know what he'd have done if she didn't take him back; the thought of losing her was too dark to ponder. She stirred beside him, and he wrapped his arm around her.

"You okay?" he asked.

She rolled over and faced him. She was so beautiful, even with the world crashing down around her, the essence of her positivity remained. He brushed her hair from her eyes and kissed her.

"We need to talk," he said.

Riley's body went rigid within his arms. "Don't worry. It's not anything horrible."

She sat up and crossed her arms. "Okay."

"I put Claudia on administrative leave." He searched her

eyes, but knew she had no clue what he was about to say. "And I have to put you on administrative leave, too, just until this thing is dealt with." He expected her to get angry, just as Claudia had. Instead, she nodded.

"Okay, I understand."

"You do?"

"Of course. If you didn't take equal measures then it would look like something was up between us," she said.

"That's the other thing. Riley, I have to hire a private investigator. If you have no way to prove that was your original design, then someone else has to find a way."

She furrowed her brow. "What can they possibly do to prove they were mine?"

"Maybe nothing, but we have to try; otherwise this nightmare will go on forever." He drew in a breath and blew it out slowly. "That means we're going to be exposed. You and me."

"But that'll make things worse," she urged.

"Maybe, but if we're going to clear you, we have to be transparent about everything. Including us." As much as it worried Josh to reveal their relationship alongside being sucked into Claudia's craziness, he was also relieved. In his heart, he knew Riley didn't steal those ideas, and he was tired of pretending that his love for her didn't exist.

"So what happens now?" she asked.

"Page Six is doing some kind of article on the accusations. Who knows what it will say, but you heard my response. It's Christmas week, so, hopefully, this will blow over and come to a resolution before the New Year. I want you to go back home so you're not caught in the crossfire."

"Aren't you coming?" She moved closer to him. "I don't want you to deal with this on your own. Isn't it better if you leave town, too?"

"No. I have to be here to manage things. I'll come home for Christmas, but I want you to leave tomorrow morning. You don't need to see this craziness spread out before you. I'll take care of it, and then I'll join you." *At least I hope to.* Josh recognized that he was putting himself in a vulnerable position. Without proof that Riley didn't steal the design, he might not be able to clear her name, and then not only would JBD be seen as the scandalous design studio, but he'd be seen as the designer who was duped.

One look into Riley's eyes told him that none of that mattered. He had faith that she was telling the truth, and his only regret was not standing behind her that first night. He should have climbed right into bed with her and told her what was going on—and believed every word she said afterward. He knew the message silence and hesitation sent, and he regretted having done both.

He stripped off his clothes, needing to feel Riley's body against him before she left, and climbed beneath the covers. He helped her out of her T-shirt and panties, and pulled her close. Her chest pressed against his, their hearts beating in perfect harmony.

She looked up at him, and he lowered his mouth to hers, taking her in a deep, passionate kiss, wanting to kiss the hurt right out of her heart. Needing to heal the pain that slayed them both.

He took her face between his hands and whispered, "I love you, Riley. You are what matters. You're my life, my love, and I will never again fail you."

Chapter Thirty-Four

"IT'S NOT FAIR to drag you through this mess with me," Riley insisted. It was five o'clock Sunday morning, and she and Josh were getting ready to leave for the airport. They'd just showered, and Riley was pulling on a pair of jeans.

"I'm already in the mud, and there's no one I'd rather be there with," Josh said.

She didn't know how their lives had become so crazy in such a short period of time. Yesterday morning, she'd wanted to run away and never come back. Now, with Josh's declaration of support, she wanted to stand by his side and figure things out—but she also knew it wasn't fair. Josh had a great career, one that had taken years to build, and a reputation that she didn't want to be responsible for soiling.

"But you don't need to go public with our relationship to figure this out. Don't hire a PI. We'll figure out a way. Isn't there a handwriting expert or someone who could validate my work on the drawings I gave Max?"

"That wouldn't prove that they were your original drawings," Josh said. "Look, we were going to eventually have to tell people about us. This just brings it up a little sooner than we had anticipated."

"And attaches it to a scandal," she reminded him.

He pulled her against him as she slipped on her blouse. "Maybe so, but if this whole nightmare has made me realize one thing, it's that there is no doubt that I love you, Riley, and when you love someone, you endure their pain." He kissed her nose. "Come on. We have to go."

"Wait. I really don't want to leave. Can't I just stay with you and we'll deal with it together?" she asked.

"You have no idea what it will be like. Once this mess gets out, we'll both be hounded day and night. It will be a nightmare. You think we have to hide now? When the media hounds get word of a scandal, they'll be all over us. By this time tomorrow, I won't be able to leave my apartment without camera flashes going off from all directions."

"Josh, why stay? Come with me, then. Let's both escape it." She touched his cheek. "Please?"

"I can't run from it. I'll have to hold a press conference, and I want to meet with the PI and have him go through every inch of the office. There's proof somewhere. I'll go through the security tapes, too. Where there's a crime, there's evidence." He picked up her bags and headed for the door.

As they came off the elevators and headed for the front door of the building, Josh's cell phone rang. He answered it as Riley swung the door open and stepped onto the sidewalk.

"Hi, Mia."

Josh looked up as cameras flashed; a mob of reporters circled Riley.

Riley knew she must look like a deer caught in the beam of headlights. She saw Josh's mouth form the word *bastards*. The muscles in his biceps flexed, and his legs shot forward, pushing through the crowd. His eyes darkened as he scanned the unruly mob of reporters. She'd never seen him look so angry, like he'd kill anyone who touched her. He shoved his phone in his pocket, putting his left arm out in front of the photographers— a protective line they could not cross, her bag dangling from his fisted hand.

"Josh!" she yelled.

He encircled her in his arms, shielding her from the press and lifting her bags in front of their faces as they made their way into the waiting car. Jay flew out of the driver's side door and barged in between the photographers and Josh and Riley, his arms outstretched as he shouted at the photographers to back off.

Riley felt Josh's muscles, rock hard and straining around her. His face reddened, as if a surge of rage was driving him forward. He pushed her into the car, then climbed in beside her and locked the door.

Riley blinked away the black splotches left from the camera flashes. She'd never seen anything like the rush of photographers and reporters thrusting microphones in her face and hollering questions one above the next. Her heart slammed within her chest as she tried to catch her breath. She stared at the crowd of photographers outside the tinted windows as they chased the car down the street.

"You okay?" The muscles in Josh's arms and neck pulsated, his hands still fisted, his knuckles white from pressure, as if he were still ready to attack.

She nodded. "What happened?"

"Mia said there's an article on Page Six. That media night-mare is what I was trying to tell you about all along." Josh shot a glance behind them. They'd blended into traffic with no photographers on their tail. He drew in a deep breath, blowing it out slowly. His eyes darted along the streets as they whisked by.

"Are you okay? That was awful," Riley said. She leaned against him. "I've made your life a nightmare. I think I should just go home, and you should just live your life as normal. You don't need this craziness." Her gut ached as she made the suggestion. "I refuse to let Claudia, or those media parasites tear us apart."

She watched his eyes narrow, then close for a breath, and when he opened them again, his jaw relaxed. He rubbed his hands on his pants, then rubbed them together, taking another deep breath. Riley knew he was trying to shake off his anger. When he took her face in his hands, as he'd done the night before, she was drawn into his serious, loving gaze. His breath still held the minty smell of toothpaste; his palms were warm and sure.

"I'm with you. Photographers or no photographers. Scandal or no scandal, Riley Banks. I love you."

She fell against him. "Thank you for not walking away from us." Guilt clenched her heart. "I'm sorry my being here caused all of this."

He kissed her forehead. "This isn't about you, Riley. This is about Claudia. It's her effed-up issue."

His cell phone rang, and she tried to move away. He lifted the phone with one hand, keeping her safely against him, and he pushed the speakerphone button. "Treat," he said.

Treat's concerned voice came through the speaker. "What is going on over there?"

Riley was embarrassed to be listening in on his phone call, and she tried again to pull away, but Josh's grip was too strong. She pointed to the phone and brought her hand to her ear, mouthing, *You can pick it up.*

Josh shook his head and pulled her closer. "A bit of a circus," Josh said.

"What's this about Riley stealing the design for Max's dress?" Treat asked.

Riley couldn't help herself from calling out. "I didn't do it," she said.

"It's Claudia's newest ruse. We're dealing with it," Josh said.

"Dealing with it? Not from what I can see. Have you seen the headlines? *Airing the Dirty Laundry of the Designing World.* This can't be good for your career, or Riley's. It's not exactly what I meant when I said to turn the media on to her design skills."

"Treat," Josh said. "Please, this is stressful enough. No jokes, all right?"

"I'm sorry. What can I do? Want me to make a statement? Say she showed us the dress two months earlier? I assume she's innocent in this mess," Treat said.

"I am, but I don't want you to lie." Riley was astounded by Treat's offer, but she wanted to prove herself honestly.

"We'll handle it," Josh said. "I'm sending her home so she's out of reach of the media. I'm hiring a PI to figure it out."

"Sounds smart," Treat said. "Let me know what I can do. If you want me to come back to New York, I can be there in a few hours. By the way, Riley, where'd they get that picture of you? You definitely looked like a kid with her hand in the candy jar."

"Picture? What picture?" Riley asked.

"Front of Page Six," Treat said.

"We gotta go, Treat. Thanks for calling." Josh pulled out his iPad and pulled up the *New York Post*'s website. Riley's startled face stared back at them above the article beside a photograph of Claudia holding up the drawing of Max's dress.

"Oh my gosh. They took that at the trade show yesterday. That's crazy. I look guilty." This was ten times worse than she'd imagined. How could she ever show her face on the streets of New York again? What would this do to Josh and his reputation? As she stewed over those questions, a concern rose to the forefront of her mind. "Josh, they caught us leaving your apartment together."

"No, they caught us both leaving the apartment building," he corrected her.

"With you carrying my bags and then running to my side to shield me from the cameras. Come on. There's no covering this up. Pictures of us together will be on all the websites in an hour, if they're not already."

"I'm not trying to cover it up. I told you: I'm with you, scandal or no scandal." Josh Googled his name. With a piercing pain in her stomach, Riley read through the first three listings.

Designer Josh Braden's new girlfriend. Is she a thief?

The Braden Scandal: Is he dating a fraud?

UPDATE: Fashion Designer Josh Braden leaves home with accused design thief/lover.

"What are we gonna do now?" Riley could barely get the words from her lungs. She'd come to New York looking for a career, and not only had she lost hers, but she'd ruined Josh's in the process.

Josh's phone rang again. He pushed the speakerphone button again. "I've already seen it," he said to his sister.

"You're sleeping with Riley and I'm the last to know?" Savannah asked. "Do you have me on speaker? I hate that."

"Yes, and Riley's right here," he said.

Wishing she could grow wings and fly away, Riley said, "Hi,

Savannah."

"Hey, Ri."

"Sorry we didn't tell you we're dating. We were trying to keep it quiet," Riley explained.

"Maybe you should have thought about that before leaving Josh's apartment together. What's this cockamamie story about you stealing Cruella's designs?" she asked.

"Even you call her that?" Riley asked.

"Everyone does," Josh answered. "She didn't steal them. This is one of Claudia's tricks. We just have to find a way to prove it."

"I told you to fire her years ago. I never liked her," Savannah said.

If only he'd listened to her.

"Shoulda woulda coulda, I know. I'm over my loyalty to Peter, okay? It took me forever and it sucks, but it is what it is. Listen, Savannah, my attorney is hiring a PI, but do you know anyone who might be good?"

"Know anyone? I've got the best one in New York. Call Reggie Steele. I'll text you his number. And, Josh, are you all right with all this?" she asked.

"I'm fine, but I'm sending Riley home. Where are you?" he asked.

"Heading back home to Colorado. Riley, we'll get together after you're home, okay?" Savannah offered.

"Thanks, Savannah. I'd like that, and I'm sorry if I've embarrassed your family," Riley said.

"Nonsense," Josh whispered to her.

"You can't embarrass a Braden." Savannah laughed. "We've got thicker skin than alligators."

Chapter Thirty-Five

JOSH SENT RILEY a text as Jay drove away from the airport. *Don't worry. We'll get through this. Love you. J.*

He waited for Riley to respond, and when he hadn't received a response ten minutes later, he ignored the unsettled feeling in his stomach and assumed she was going through airport security. He called his attorney, who advised him that he had not yet reached his private investigator, he assumed because of the impending holiday. Josh mentioned Reggie to him, and when his attorney agreed that Reggie was qualified and one of the best, Josh called him. An hour later, he was sitting in Reggie's office.

Reggie Steele's voice was deep and gravelly. He was a burly, dark-haired man in his late thirties, Josh guessed, with slate-blue eyes and an affable personality.

"Savannah called me this morning after speaking to you. I'm sorry to hear about what you're going through. The media can be a bear—but I suppose you already know that," Reggie said. "If the claim is false, this kind of nonsense should be easy to crack."

"I hope so, because I can't find one piece of evidence to discount Claudia's allegations, but my gut tells me she's lied her way onto the front page." Josh's nerves wrenched just thinking of Claudia's smug face—and Riley's sad one.

"I take it that you and the accused are an item?" Reggie leaned back in his chair, steepling his fingers before him.

"We're seeing each other, yes. We were trying to keep it out of our professional lives." Josh now wished that they'd exposed themselves as a couple from the start. It would have been one less issue to deal with. His phone vibrated. *Mia.* He clicked the Ignore button.

"Anything else I should know that could impact this discovery process?" Reggie asked.

"Only that Claudia has come onto me several times, and a few weeks ago, I shut her down pretty harshly. But I can't see how that would affect your investigation one way or another." At least he'd remembered to document those instances in her personnel file, alongside all the rest of the complaints, which he'd never filed formally. Out of loyalty to Peter, he'd wanted to keep her indiscretions under wraps. Now he wished he had canned her the first time she'd come onto him and had just faced Peter with the truth.

"You'd be surprised at what comes up with these types of investigations. You might find out things about other staff members that you don't want to know. And, I hate to say it, but you might find out that you're wrong about your girlfriend, too," Reggie said.

"I appreciate your candor, but I doubt that's going to happen. She's been under Claudia's thumb the past few weeks, and when she hasn't been at work, she's been with me. She didn't have time to steal anything. If anything, we might find out more about Claudia than I'm prepared for." Josh realized the truth of his words and was even more determined to get to the bottom of this garbage.

"Fair enough. Tell me more about Claudia's habits. Does she work later, come in early? Does she work odd days, weekends, through lunch? What kind of access did she have to Riley's work files? And I'll need to know the same about Riley, of course."

Finally, a break. He'd been with Riley every morning and evening. She'd never been in the office alone. "Riley has no access to personal files. She works earlier than some, later than others, but there's always someone here before she arrives and after she leaves. She works from home when she needs to on the weekends, whereas Claudia has been with us for five years. She's often in before anyone else, and on the weekends she's often alone in the office. As the head design assistant, she's the password keeper for the entire design area. She has full access to Riley's files." It all sounded so easy to decipher. Riley had no access. Claudia had full access. Why was it so difficult to find proof of what seemed so obvious?

"Have you gone through security tapes?" Reggie asked.

Josh shook his head. "Not yet, but…"

"Don't sweat it. That's what I'm here for. Do you have separate security files for each area of the office?"

Thank goodness, yes. He felt warmth run up his chest, re-membering the things he and Riley had done in his office. "Yes, I'll give you full access to the design room tapes."

Reggie nodded. He lowered his chin and looked down the bridge of his angular nose. "This is just one woman against the other, right? You don't think any other employees are involved? It's not a case of one trying to get a promotion so she can bring another up riding her tail feathers? Tag team?"

Josh shook his head. "Claudia isn't well liked enough to

have a partner in crime."

"And Riley?" Reggie asked.

Josh's protective urges surged forward. He reminded himself that Reggie was only doing his job—a job he was hiring him to do.

"Not that I'm aware of," he said, meeting Reggie's stare.

"I was planning to take a few days off for R & R before the holiday, but it sounds like this might be a good time to get a jump on investigating while your employees aren't in the office. What's your time frame?"

"Now," Josh answered. "The media's following my every move. I came here directly from the airport, so they have yet to link us together, and I'd rather they didn't get wind of my hiring you."

"I'm very good at being discreet. I'll keep you abreast of critical findings, and until then, I'll need access to your security files, the desks of the employees in question, their personnel files, and of course, access to their computers."

"How long do you expect this will take?"

Reggie shrugged. "I won't know until I get started. We could get lucky and find something in an hour, or it might take weeks."

"I'll go with you to the office," Josh said.

"Don't you want to know my rates?" Reggie asked.

"Savannah says you're the best. I trust my sister's judgment. I'll pay whatever it takes to get this misery over with as fast as possible. Just do something so you don't look so much like a PI." Josh smiled.

Reggie looked down at his jeans and T-shirt and smiled. "Shall I wear an Armani suit?"

"I was kidding," Josh said. "I'm heading to the office now."

Reggie tossed a folder toward Josh. "I'll need you to complete these forms, and I'll be right behind you," Reggie said.

Josh called Claudia from the car.

"Yes, Mr. B.?" she said.

The sound of her too-perky-for-the-situation voice addled his nerves. "I'm sending Jay to pick up your key to the office."

"What? Why?" Claudia snapped.

"Because you're on administrative leave, and all employees on administrative leave lose their free-office privileges. He'll be there within the hour. And, Claudia, I need your password."

She sighed. "Fine. It's *winners take all*, all one word, no caps."

The next call he made was to Riley. When her voicemail picked up, he left a message. "Hey, babe, just wanted to be sure you arrived safely. Call me when you get a second. I've met with the PI and I think we're in good hands." He ended the call and hoped he was making the right choice by hiring the PI—and putting his career on the line by supporting Riley.

When his phone rang, the last person he expected it to be was his youngest brother, Hugh.

"Hey, Hugh, how are you?" Josh asked.

Hugh spent his days racing Ferraris and his nights bedding women.

"I'm great. Working my way down the West Coast at the moment. I hear you've been working your way into a new employee," Hugh joked.

"Hugh."

"Sorry. I saw the crap on Yahoo! News. What's going on? You're sleeping with an old schoolmate and she's a design thief? Fill me in. I don't know Riley very well, but she seems pretty much like the rest of the Weston women. Not exactly the conniving type." Hugh was usually the last to reach out to a family member in crisis, and this time he'd beaten his brothers Rex and Dane to the punch.

"She's not," Josh said flatly. "I'm dealing with it. It's a mess, but we'll figure it out."

"You need anything? Want me to come run someone over?" Hugh laughed.

Yes. Josh smiled at the thought. Hugh looked like a taller, more muscular Patrick Dempsey, and he pictured his brother's wide smile, his eyes alit with laughter. Josh was only a year older than Hugh, but the way Hugh lived his life—like it was one big party—made the age difference seem much greater.

"Nah, I think I can handle it, but I appreciate the offer."

"When are you arriving at Dad's?" Hugh asked.

"Wednesday. You?"

"Tomorrow. I'll see you then, and if you need anything, I'm your guy," Hugh said.

What Josh needed could come only from Riley's innocence. "Thanks, Hugh. Love you, man."

Chapter Thirty-Six

THE SECOND RILEY stepped out of the airport and breathed in the crisp Colorado air, she felt better. She dropped her bags on the pavement, opened her arms wide, and looked up at the sky. Then she closed her eyes and inhaled.

"Have you turned all New Agey on me?"

Riley screamed at the sound of Jade's voice and ran into her arms. "I'm so glad to see you! Thank you for picking me up."

"Who else would do it?" Jade teased.

"Shut up." She hugged her again and retrieved her bags. "It feels so good to be home. I didn't realize how much I missed seeing the grass and the mountains. I didn't realize how much I missed smelling something other than perfume, electric heat, subway steam, and garbage." She laughed.

"Come on. Are you hungry? Want to grab a bite?" Jade wore jeans, cowgirl boots, and a dark T-shirt beneath a flannel shirt, and it made Riley long to wear the same comfortably familiar ensemble.

Riley tugged playfully on Jade's waist-length black hair. "I thought you were going to cut your hair. I see you went with the take-me-hard length so Sexy Rexy could grab hold and tug," she teased.

"Duh. What else would I do? You've seen my man."

"Oh yes, I have," she said, thinking not of Rex, but of Josh. She missed him already. She'd gone over and over their situation, and no matter how she looked at it, she couldn't get around the selfishness of it. She loved him so much her heart ached when she wasn't with him, but did that mean that it was fair of her to drag him through the mud with her? She threw her bags into Jade's car and tried not to let the weight of her situation spoil her time with Jade.

Hunter Hayes was on the radio, and they both hummed along.

"Fingers okay?" Jade asked.

It took a moment of staring at her hands for Riley to realize that Jade was asking if she'd like to go to Fingers Bar and Grill, in Allure, a town just outside of Weston and on their way home.

"Sure, perfect," Riley said.

They rode in silence. Riley laid her head back on the headrest and promptly fell asleep.

RILEY BLINKED AWAKE when Jade pulled into the parking lot of Fingers Bar and Grill. "I'm so sorry. I haven't slept much lately."

Jade wiggled her eyebrows up and down with a wide smile.

"That's not why." Riley swung her arm around Jade as they entered the restaurant. "I missed you," she said.

"I missed you, too," Jade said.

They sat at a corner booth and ordered lunch, and then Jade folded her hands on the table. Her vibrant blue eyes burned a path to Riley.

"What?" Riley asked.

"Nothing," Jade said.

"Liar."

"Okay, I'm waiting for you to spill your guts. When I went online to get my email, I saw all the pictures of you and Josh and the whole awful story. You must be ready to die inside, Ri." She reached across the table and took Riley's hand in her own. "Don't you want to talk about it?"

Riley blinked away the rush of emotions that was becoming all too familiar. "It's all so...wrong. I mean, one minute Josh and I are happy as can be, and the next minute, I'm being accused of stealing Max's wedding dress design and I can't prove it's mine. It's such bull. That woman is evil, truly evil." Riley pursed her lips. "She's...You know I don't hate people easily, but she's really awful, and she made moves on Josh, too."

Jade's eyes opened wide. "No way."

"Way. And now all of my other original designs are gone, too. There's no record of my drawing, and of course, no one ever saw me drawing at work. That's what I get for trying to keep my extracurricular designing a secret, I guess."

The food came, and Riley pushed her salad away. She couldn't eat if she had a gun to her head.

"What about the faxes you sent me?" Jade asked. "That has to prove something."

"Josh said that won't prove they were my original designs. I don't know...I've been thinking about it the whole way home. I'm not sure I should go back. I mean, look at what Josh is being dragged through, and it's all because of me. He was this well-respected, successful designer, at the top of his game, and suddenly I waltz in and he's being seen as a man who's sleeping with the enemy." Hot tears streamed down her cheeks. Riley turned away, swiping at them.

Jade grabbed her hand across the table. "Riley, honey, you're not the enemy."

"I know," Riley cried. "Stupid tears." She wiped her eyes with a napkin. "I just feel like I want to hide in a cave. I don't ever want to go back."

"You don't have to do anything you don't want to do," Jade said.

Riley remained silent. She needed Jade's support. She needed to know she could come home and stay home if she wanted to.

"Cruella can have your drawings. She can even have your man, for that matter. Really, Ri, why do you need Josh Braden anyway?" Jade took a bite of her baguette, her eyes never leaving Riley's.

"I know what you're doing. You pushed me like that in New York. I'm not stupid, Jade."

"Are you sure? Because I know many women who would give their left arm to be loved the way Josh loves you," Jade said.

"How would you know?"

"Rex told me that Treat said he'd never seen Josh fall for a woman at all, much less practically live with one. And Max said that Josh looked at you like Rex looks at me—and you know how Rexy looks at me." She shrugged. "Small town and all that."

"They said that?" Riley knew how much Josh loved her. It showed in everything he did: the way he told her to look at him while they made love, his confession about not having women in his apartment, running all over creation to secretly be with her. Who else would throw their career on the firing line to stand beside her? Then the memory of that awful night when she found him on the couch came searing back, and the hurt of the accusation came right along with it. She reached up and rubbed at the pain in the back of her neck.

"Yes, of course," Jade said.

Riley wished the cave was really an option. It would be so much easier than weeding through her tangle of conflicting emotions.

"Let me ask you something," Riley said. "If you knew that you didn't deserve something, but that if Rex stood up for you it could hurt him, would you let him do it? Or would you extricate yourself from the situation so he wouldn't have to deal with it?"

"Hasn't he already?" Jade answered. "We've both gone up against our parents at the risk of losing them. That was very painful for all of us. It might not have been Yahoo! News painful, but it was every bit as emotionally disabling."

"I guess." Riley sighed.

Riley's phone vibrated, and she ignored it. She'd seen a message from Josh while she was waiting for the plane to take off, and she'd been too conflicted to respond.

"I'm so afraid of hurting him," she admitted to Jade, ignoring her phone's incessant vibrations.

"Riley?"

"What?"

Jade nodded toward Riley's purse. "I know what you're doing. You can't just ignore him. Relationships don't work that way, and you're not that kind of woman. You're a communicator."

Riley sighed. "I'm just not ready to talk to him. I can't help but feel like I've hurt him, and when he first told me what was going on, I swear I hated the look of pity in his eyes. It was like he loved me, but he wasn't sure if he quite believed me at the time, and he felt sorry for me."

"So tell him that. That's what you would tell me to do. Pick up the phone and tell the man. He's going to the ends of the earth to make sure you're taken care of. It's the least you can do."

Riley dug through her purse. "Sometimes I hate you when you're right."

"I know. Luckily, we have a love-hate relationship that can survive any man problem," Jade teased.

She read the messages from Josh. She couldn't deny the love she had for him. She texted back. *I'm here safe and sound. Thank u 4 standing by me. Love you. Ri.*

Then she scrolled to a message from Mia and read it.

Hang in there. Here if u need me. Xox. M.

"Mia texted me." She smiled and texted back. *Thx. U r not mad at me for not telling u? I'm so sorry.*

"And?" Jade asked.

Riley's phone vibrated. *Maybe a little hurt, but I get it. Don't worry. We're cool. Xox.*

"She's supportive." Relief swept through her. *Thank you! Xox.*

She listened to Josh's voicemail and then put her phone away.

"Don't you feel better?" Jade asked.

Riley let out a sigh. "I do, and I'm glad Mia texted. I guess I've made a friend. Thank goodness, because it's been weird not having any girlfriends."

"Hey, what about me?" Jade feigned a frown.

"You'll always be my best friend, but you're here, and sometimes I need someone there, too. Thank you, Jade. I feel much better having read Josh's text and hearing his message. He said he's met with the PI, and he thinks we're in good hands. Knowing how much he loves me does help." *If I could only remember that ten minutes from now.*

"Riley, this stuff will pass. It'll all work out."

"But what if it doesn't? What if we can't clear my name? Josh hasn't said anything, but can she sue me for my own designs? And by now the whole world has heard about it. What must Max think? Oh my gosh, poor Max. I've got to call her."

"She's fine. I talked to her earlier today. She said Treat told her it was all lies."

"I can't believe the way the Bradens go to bat for one another," Riley said. "Before seven o'clock this morning, both Treat and Savannah had already called Josh."

"Let me tell you something. All that family loyalty stuff, it's genuine. I see it on a daily basis with Rex, and not just for his family members. He's just as loyal and protective of me and even my family, which I didn't expect at all, given our family histories."

"Whatever their father did when he was raising them, he did well, I guess." Riley remembered the conversation she'd had with Josh about how different he'd felt from his brothers. She didn't think he was so different after all. He didn't hesitate to go to bat for her once the initial shock had worn off. She picked up her phone and texted him again.

Sorry for everything. Can't wait to see you. Miss you already.

Chapter Thirty-Seven

JOSH WALKED THROUGH JBD's design studio remembering when Rex had first asked him about looking over Riley's portfolio. Never in a million years would he have imagined that Riley was as talented as those sketches had proven her to be. Then again, he never would have imagined himself so in love with the woman he'd spent years crushing on. He assumed that once he'd left Weston, he'd never see her again. Now he stood beside her desk, and sadness slithered around his heart once again. How could she ever feel the same about New York—or JBD—or him, after this?

He reached into his pocket to answer his ringing cell phone.

"Hi, Dad." He tried to muster a smile.

"Son." His father's deep voice stirred the emotions he'd been holding back all morning, causing a fissure in his iron facade. "I hear you're comin' home Wednesday. That right?"

Hal Braden had a special bond with each of his children, and he handled each one different from the next. He didn't pressure them to visit, and he didn't pressure them to do much of anything in particular, but he was the one his children turned to when they were considering life-altering decisions, and at that moment, Josh couldn't have wished for a better ear to bend.

UNRAVELING THE TRUTH ABOUT LOVE

"Yes. Wednesday." He hesitated in spilling his guts to his father, though the little boy in him screamed, *Dad, tell me what to do. Please tell me.* Hal Braden didn't believe in computers and didn't really understand the enormity of the press. Josh hoped his brothers and Savannah wouldn't worry their father with his issues, although by now, he was sure the Weston grapevine was buzzing. He bided his time, waiting to see if his father brought it up.

"Good. You talk to Dane lately?" he asked.

"Not in a while, why?"

"Just thought you might want to. I get a feelin' he's in need of a little time with his family. He's coming home for Christmas, but he could probably do with a call if you can fit it in." He heard the worry in his father's slow drawl.

Josh furrowed his brow and sat down in Riley's chair. "Dad, is something wrong?"

His father sighed. "No, not wrong. I just got a feelin' about him, much like I've got one about you."

Josh and his siblings were used to hearing about their father's *feelings*, or rather, worries that their father claimed came to him through their dead mother. Josh wasn't sure if this was one of those times, but he'd call Dane and make sure he was okay.

"What do you mean about me?" Josh asked, knowing exactly what his father meant. He leaned back in the chair and stretched his legs.

"I hear Riley's back in town," his father said. "And a little bird tells me she's run into a devil of a nightmare out there in the big city."

Josh righted the chair, needing the stability beneath him. "I'm handling it."

"I'm sure you are. Son, I also hear that you and Riley are together. That right?"

Josh had hoped to tell his father in person, to see his eyes and read his expression when he told him, but he'd never lie to him. "Yes, sir. We are."

"Well, then, you make sure you nip this nonsense in the bud. Don't let those highfalutin city folk shame our good name, you hear?"

If only it were that easy. "Dad?"

"Yeah?"

"I'm standing behind Riley on this, and my gut tells me I'm right, but what if…?" He couldn't force the words to come. They made him weak, selfish, and saying them out loud again felt akin to disrespecting Riley.

"What if she's not the woman you believe her to be?" His father cleared his throat. "Son, there's no easy way around that question, and I can't tell you what you should or shouldn't do, but I can tell you what your mother would have said in this very situation."

"Please." Josh heard the urgency in his own voice.

"Your mama was a heart-driven woman, but she was the smartest woman I ever met. Stubborn, too. Once her heart made a decision, she'd chew on it for a bit, mull over the ins and outs of the sanity of it, and she'd come away with a big smack-eatin' grin and she'd have her answer. She'd look me in the eye and say, 'This one just might bite me in the arse, but darn it, my heart cannot survive without it.' Ask yourself, son. Can your heart live without her? Once you figure that out, you'll have your answer."

Josh shook his head. "But Mom's decisions wouldn't tank her career." Josh clenched his fists and he had to force them to relax.

"Don't you go down that line with me, Josh Braden." His father's stern tone caught him off guard. Before Josh could answer, his father continued. "Your mother's life was every bit as important as yours. Her *career* was her family, this ranch, me, you, and every one of your siblings. When she made decisions, she had seven other people's lives relying on it. She held your life in her hands."

"I'm sorry, Dad. I'm just confused. I've worked hard to get where I am."

"Yes, you have, and your mother worked her rear off to get our family to be who we are. You think that was easy? You think it didn't come with her own understanding that one mistake could turn the Braden name into a laughingstock? Heck, in this small town, one wrong move could shut down a ranch. Josh, I'm not angry at you, but darn it son, gain a bit of perspective. People matter. Family matters. The rest of that garbage—fame, cars, high-rise apartments—it'll all mean nothing without a full heart."

AFTER THE ABRUPTNESS of his father's words sank in, Josh took one final look at Riley's desk, then headed into the security room to check on Reggie.

"How's it going?" Josh asked.

Reggie stopped the video he was watching and leaned his large body back in the chair, crossing his right ankle over his left knee. Then he clasped his hands behind his head. A wide grin spread across his lips.

"Well, if the videos I've watched are any indication of

what's to come, I'd say your hunch is right, and we'll probably come up with something soon."

"Really? What have you found?" Hope swelled in his chest.

"Not much. Just little things. Body language, the way Claudia watches the others like a hawk." He shrugged. "Could be that she's just a nosy woman, but I've got a feeling there's more to it. She's really focused on Riley. Lookie here." He rewound the video and pressed play.

Josh watched Claudia eyeing Riley as she walked away, her eyes running up and down the length of Riley's body. She narrowed her eyes, and a sneer curled her thin lips.

Reggie turned it off again and sat back. "Might be nothing, but I've seen women look that way before, and trust me, it's never a good thing."

"You must really have a solid grip on people by now, huh?" Josh asked. "What's your take on Riley?"

"With all due respect, Josh, until we have a definite answer, I think I'll reserve my right to pass judgment."

Pass judgment? On Riley? That flash of anger that had surprised Josh over the last few days rose within him again. He crossed his arms to keep it reined in. Did he think Riley was up to no good? Did he see something in her Josh did not?

"Don't get yourself all riled up," Reggie said. "She's your other half at the moment. I don't want to say anything until I'm certain."

At the moment? "Okay, fair enough," Josh said.

"I'd like to work through the evening if you don't mind, since the holiday's coming up so fast. I've got their passwords to get into their files. You can leave me here if you have plans. Is there a security guard who can lock up?"

Josh scrubbed his face with his hand. "I'll stick around."

"Suit yourself. Oh, and your sister said to tell you, 'Don't even think about not coming home on Wednesday.'" Reggie turned back to the computer.

"Oh, I plan on it, unless this mess explodes in our faces."

Chapter Thirty-Eight

DANE ANSWERED THE phone on the fourth ring, just as Josh was about to hang up.

"Josh! How's my little brother?" Even though Josh stood eye to eye to his six-foot-three brother, Dane never failed to throw "little" at him as often as he could.

"Hanging in there. How about you? Where are you?" Josh asked.

"Heading home, actually. Making my way to the airport now."

"Dad said I should check in with you. Anything going on that I should know about?" Josh clicked on his computer and opened his email.

"Dad." Dane laughed. "How does that old man always know when something's up? There's no great shakes happening in my life."

Josh noted an emptiness in Dane's response. "You sure? What am I hearing in your voice?"

"Nothing, Josh. Really." Dane blew out a loud breath. "Nothing like the mess that's going on in yours, thank goodness." He laughed again.

"Great. Take pleasure in my pain. That's a supportive

brother for you."

"Sorry. It makes me realize how lucky I have it. No ties that bind."

Josh heard another twinge of something...loneliness maybe, in Dane's voice. "You sure there's nothing you want to talk about?"

"Not at this juncture, but it's good to know you're there. I appreciate it. Anything I can do to ease your situation?" Dane asked. "I feel for Riley. I mean it's hard enough going from Weston to New York. A whole new world. And the poor thing is attacked by the wolves. You don't think she did it, do you?"

Josh hated the voice running through his head, *I don't think so, but how can I be sure?* "You know Riley. You think she'd ever do something like that? Jeopardize a career she just began?" The words felt wrong tumbling from his lips.

"Or her relationship with the boss?" Dane tossed in.

"Right, there is that."

"No, I don't, but we never really know someone until the muck comes up the pipes, right?" Dane said something to someone in the background. "I gotta go. My flight's boarding. See you at home. Love ya, bro."

Satisfied that his father's radar must have been off and Dane was just fine, Josh ended the call and turned to his emails, clicking on one from Peter Stafford.

Josh,

I'm in Switzerland with limited access while I'm with the family. We've scheduled a meeting on January 4, and I intend to make it. I've got a new venture I'd like to discuss. I've reviewed Riley Banks's portfolio, and you were correct. Her talent is unmatched. Please be sure to include her in our meeting, as agreed. I'd like to get her input on the spring lineup for our girls. I believe you have a winner on your hands.

Best,
Peter

Josh closed his email and pushed away from his desk, wishing Reggie hadn't left him so conflicted about Riley's innocence. His father's words ran through his head. *Can your heart live without her? It'll all mean nothing without a full heart. Man...* He wanted her input on the spring lineup? Josh really needed to get some answers and clear her name.

"MR. B, YOU here?" Mia sailed into his office carrying a cardboard coffee tray in one hand and a paper bag in the other.

Josh reached for the drinks. "You're supposed to be going home to spend the holidays with your family," he said, though he was glad to see her. His nerves were coiled like a snake. He needed a distraction.

"So are you," she said. "I knew you'd be here, so I brought you dinner."

"You didn't have to do that."

"No, I didn't, but that's what the world's best assistant does. She plans ahead, fixes problems before they occur, and..." She looked up as she set the sandwiches down on his desk. "Oh darn, I don't know what else, but I didn't come here to prove how great I am. I came here to make sure you weren't falling apart. You didn't answer your phone messages from me, or the text I sent."

"It's been quite a day," Josh admitted.

"I bet. How's Riley holding up?"

"I haven't spoken—" He remembered that their relationship was front-page news and added, "I haven't spoken to her since she got to Colorado, but she texted, and she seems to be okay. Rattled."

Mia nodded, and guilt swallowed Josh. Mia had been a loyal and dedicated employee, and he valued her friendship. He should have told her that he was seeing Riley, even if under the veil of confidence.

"I'm sorry for not telling you about me and Riley, Mia. She didn't want to come under scrutiny and gossip."

Mia smiled and sipped her coffee. "Yes, you should have, so I could have protected her. Remember, part of the world's greatest assistant's job is to fix problems before they occur."

"You would have protected her?" He lifted his drink. "Of course you would have. I'm sorry. It was shortsighted of me. But you know you couldn't have stopped Claudia."

"No, but I could have watched her more closely and maybe caught her in the act so things didn't escalate so fast or so far." She sipped her coffee. "So, this is it? She's the one you've been hoping for all these years?"

Taken aback by the directness of her inquiry, he answered, "I haven't exactly been waiting around," Josh said.

"Right. Out of the last eighteen dates, you have returned phone calls for exactly two, and of those two, you have seen one of the women one more time, and that was to take her to an event. She went right home afterward, and you had me end it after that. As I recall, you had me send her an outfit and tell her thank you on the phone, but no thank-you card. I think you were waiting around, even if you didn't know it."

"You kept track of my dates?" Josh already knew the answer. Mia kept track of his entire life. It was Mia who'd called him before six a.m. to warn him about the media, and it was Mia who brought him dinner when he didn't ask. "Okay, you win, Mia. Maybe I have been waiting around, or hoping, for Riley to appear. But even still, it took me by surprise."

She kicked back in her chair and crossed her arms and legs. "I've been thinking about this whole thing. Claudia's really clever. If she stole all of Riley's original drawings, then Riley doesn't have a leg to stand on. What can she possibly do or say that would substantiate that she was the original designer of that dress? Then I started thinking. If Claudia really did do this, then she had to do it here, right?" Her eyes grew wide. "You know where I'm going with this, right? Security cameras. We have them all over the place. Even if we didn't see anything, it would be recorded. Mr. B., I think Riley might just catch a break."

"I'm one step ahead of you. Come with me." He led her to the security room, where Reggie stared at a blank screen, his face a block of stone. "Reggie, this is my assistant, Mia. She's aware of the situation."

Reggie spun around and pushed to his feet. "I think you have a very wise thief on your hands." His eyes darted to Mia, and he extended a hand, his sharp stare softened to an appreciative gaze. "Pleasure to meet you," he said.

Mia shook his hand. The attraction that sparked between them practically burned Josh. He cleared his throat.

"Wise?" Josh said.

"Wise, yes." Reggie pulled his attention back to Josh, his eyes darting to Mia with every few words he spoke. "The security camera schedules have been tampered with. Over the past four weeks, the cameras have been set to roll until eleven thirty in the morning. Then they're off until after nine in the evening. Weekends are off altogether. Whoever is doing this has access to the schedules."

Josh shot a look at Mia.

"That would be anyone with a master key, as opposed to a front-door key. The cleaning people, me, you." She nodded at Josh. "Claudia, and I think Clay has one. I think that's it. But we check the videos daily to see that they're running. I personally check them every morning at eight." She closed her eyes and sighed. "Of course they are. They're turned off later in the morning."

Josh swallowed hard. He'd given Riley a master key as well, and he'd failed to report it to Mia.

"Well, that nails it, right? It's got to be Claudia," Mia said.

"That's circumstantial at best. This could be a completely separate issue from the design theft." Reggie crossed his thick arms over his chest and planted his legs in a determined stance. "I've seen it a dozen times. We find a secondary issue while searching for the primary. I'm going to look into the files on their computers. We'll see what else we can turn up."

Josh bristled at his use of the word *their* and the implication that Reggie still thought Riley might be part of this whole scheme. No matter how much he loved her, he remained true to his ethical and moral standards and reluctantly admitted what he'd done. "I gave Riley a key. The only spare I had was a master." He shrugged.

Mia arched a brow.

"It was the one from the safe," Josh said.

"Why didn't you tell me?" Mia asked.

"I forgot, and she's never used it." Josh saw the disappointment in her eyes, and knew he deserved every bit of it.

Mia arched a brow.

"I'm with her, Mia, morning and evening. She's never here alone."

"A run of the electronic keys will tell us when specific employees entered the building. You do have a list of the employees and their key codes, right?"

Mia nodded.

"Does this door stay locked?" Reggie asked.

"Yes," Mia answered.

"Then unless the key records have been tampered with, we should have a few more answers. And key records are ten times harder to falsify than cameras. Josh, I'll need you to complete that paperwork I gave you so we can request it all on your behalf."

"No problem. I'll get it done now." Josh answered without thinking, his mind still stuck on the fact that Riley had a master key.

"Depending on what we find, we may need to consider that other employees could be involved with these security tapes. I'll let you know when we wrap up this end of the investigation," Reggie said.

"I'll take you over to their desks," Mia offered. She turned on her heel and walked away.

Josh's legs were rooted to the floor. Could Riley have done this? He sank into the chair Reggie had just vacated and covered his face with his hands. He had phone calls to make. Another round of inquiries to the people he trusted. Clay, the cleaning woman, Wella…and Riley.

Chapter Thirty-Nine

THE EVENING BREEZE blew across the front porch of Riley's parents' single-story home. Riley watched the sun dip behind the trees and hunkered down in her thick sweater, anticipating the chill it would bring. She heard the front door creak open and turned to see her mother joining her on the porch. Her once dark brown hair now laced with plentiful threads of silver hung just above her shoulders in thick waves. She wore a barn coat over her sweater and carried a bottle of wine and two glasses, which she set down as she seated herself in the rocking chair next to Riley.

"How's my girl?" her mother asked.

Riley considered herself lucky to have always enjoyed a strong relationship with her mother, Arlene. Her mother had always used a tender tone, even when Riley knew she'd deserved a strong reprimand, and because of that, she'd always felt comfortable seeking her advice.

"I'm okay, Mom. It's good to be home." Riley had been thinking of Josh all afternoon. She wondered what he was facing back in New York. Was the media hounding him? Had he found any further evidence of Claudia's guilt? Was he having doubts about her? About them? She was still wrestling with the harsh reality that by being linked to her, Josh's reputation would be tarnished.

"We've missed you, but we all knew that one day your time would come. You're too talented to be wasted at Macy's," her mother said.

"Thanks."

"Do you enjoy the work as much as you'd hoped you would?"

She knew her mother was dancing around the subject of Claudia's accusations, but she, too, was not ready to jump in and discuss it. "I'm only doing assistant work right now, but yeah. I do like it, and I like New York in general—or at least I did." The porch boards creaked beneath her rocker's rhythmic motion.

"That's good," her mother said. "You've always been able to adapt to change easily. Even when you were a little girl, when we'd travel to see Aunt Betty or to go on a summer trip, you never had trouble sleeping in new beds or adjusting to new schedules."

"I remember." Riley smiled at the memory of her aunt's gingerbread cookies. She always had a batch ready when Riley arrived.

"There's not much you can't handle, Riley."

Her mother looked at her then, her hidden meaning exposed in the glint in her eyes and the nod of her head.

"I'm not so sure," Riley admitted. "Mom, how did you know Dad was everything you'd ever want?"

"I didn't," she admitted. "I'm not sure he is now, either."

Oh no. Please don't tell me any more bad news. She fixed her stare on a knot in the railing and set her rocker into motion.

"I love your father. He's a remarkable, caring man who

would do anything for you or me. But, honey, we never know today what we'll want tomorrow, or why."

Riley met her mother's gaze.

"How can you know in your thirties what you'll want in your forties? You haven't been there yet. Love is a powerful thing, but desire is, too, and one without the other can be deadly to even the strongest relationship." Her mother paused to pull her jacket tighter across her chest. "I didn't know when I married your father if I'd still want to be with him in two years, much less thirty, and I knew that despite how much he professed his love for me, there was no way he could possibly know either." She looked out over the mountains. "I took a leap of faith, and I hoped for the best. I knew that I loved him, and I knew that I desired him. The rest"—she shrugged—"I figured I'd deal with along the way."

"And?" Riley pushed.

"And desire and love wax and wane in relationships. Even the strongest of them. I'll let you in on a little secret that my mother shared with me."

Riley leaned forward, ready to hear her grandmother's secret.

"I'm not so sure that the powers that be knew what he was doing when he gave us the idea of living together, even after being married. Men and women are just wired differently. We think differently. We have different wants and needs, and that alone can drive a couple apart pretty quickly."

So I was right; you don't have a loving relationship with Dad?

Her mother smiled up at the starlit sky. "So I had a heads-up going into my marriage, and I knew that we'd probably come across some frustrating times when I'd feel like I hated something your father did or wished he'd do something I knew he never would. I think my mother saved our marriage by sharing that with me, because when those times came, I was prepared. I saw them for what they were. Tiny bumps in a very long road. I didn't give up, and I didn't walk away. And when desire seemed very far away, we both worked to reel it back in."

How could I have been so wrong? "So?" Riley asked.

"So, you might never really know what the future holds, and you have to go on what your heart tells you when you believe you've found your forever love. You'll know when it's time to take that giant leap of faith."

Riley let out a breath. "A giant leap of faith."

Her mother picked up the bottle of wine and poured each of them a glass. "And a little wine might help clear your mind."

"Yeah, it just might." Riley sipped the wine, processing what her mother had just revealed.

"Riley, relationships aren't always hot and heavy, and sometimes it's that deeper, more meaningful love that pulls you through. Being held by the person you cherish most, or hearing their voice at the end of a particularly grueling day, those can be far more powerful than the initial hot and hectic passion of new love."

Riley felt her cheeks flush. "I didn't mean…"

"No, but you wondered. Every woman wonders about what will happen when that wears off, and that's where your leap of faith comes in, and your strength and courage to bring yourself and your partner back to the place where you both are happiest."

Riley nodded.

"You and Josh. Do you want to talk about it?" her mother asked.

"I don't know, Mom. I miss him already, you know. That's

crazy, and I know that. I just saw him this morning, but every time I think of him, I see his face. And seeing his face brings goose bumps to my arms." She held out her arm, and her mother ran her hand over the bumps. "But there's so much more." Riley continued. "He's so different than I thought he'd be. When we were growing up, I was crazy about him, but he was a Braden. A good-looking, confident guy who was wildly out of my reach."

"Don't pull the wool over your eyes, Riley Roo," her mother said. "You steered clear of Josh because of that silly feud between the Bradens and the Johnsons. If that nonsense hadn't been going on, I'm not sure we could have kept you two apart."

Her mother hadn't called her by her childhood nickname since she went away to college, and that should have made her feel warm and safe, but Riley was too hung up on the fact that her mother knew she'd had a major crush on Josh—and that he had one on her. Before she could respond, her mother continued.

"You could have had any man you wanted—and you still can. Not that you need one, mind you, but you're smart as a whip and pretty as can be, and your personality has always drawn people to you."

Riley let out a laugh under her breath. "Thanks, Mom. You knew about my crush?"

"Honey, everyone knew about your crush."

Embarrassment rushed through her. "Really? Thanks, Mom. Maybe you could have clued me in that I was ogling him too blatantly or something."

"It wouldn't have mattered what I did. You would have continued. You couldn't stop yourself any more than Jade could stop loving Rex."

"Okay, fair enough," Riley said. "Anyway, that's not what I meant. I just meant…I don't even know. I always felt like he'd be more…I don't know…stuck up or something, especially now that he's at the top of his career—or at least he was before I came along." Her smile faded.

"Oh, honey, you know better than that. None of the Bradens are like that. I'm not sure why you had that impression, but they're a very nice family. Very accepting, hard-working. Hal has done well by each of his children."

"I know all of that now. It just took me by surprise, and now I worry that I've brought shame to their family." There. She'd said it aloud, and with the words, a heavy load lifted from her chest.

"Oh, honey, I'm sure that you're overreacting."

"We're on Yahoo! News, Mom."

"Yahoo! News?"

"I forgot you don't use the computer. You really should, you know. Yahoo is a big website that provides email to millions of people and carries the news along with it. My big mug has been spread all over to millions of people, along with an article saying I stole designs that I didn't steal."

For a minute, her mother didn't say anything. She sipped her wine and looked out over the field in front of the house.

Riley wondered what her mother must think of her now.

"Now I can see why you've been walking around here with a heavy heart," her mother said. "Riley, you didn't steal the designs, so how could you have shamed anyone? It's the person accusing you who should be ashamed of herself."

The difference between Weston and New York was staring Riley in the face. If the same accusation were made in Weston, Riley could have confronted the accuser face-to-face, with the community backing her based on her reputation alone.

"It's not that easy," Riley explained. "I don't know if she can place formal charges against me, even though they're my designs. I don't know what impact this will have on Josh's career, or mine, or our relationship. Oh, Mom, it's such a mess."

Her mother nodded. "I don't claim to be very worldly, but I do know that in time things like this blow over. While you're in the thick of it, it might seem like that could never happen, but trust me. Time really does heal all wounds."

"It might heal wounds, Mom, but it won't be able to heal careers. And what if even though Josh loves me, he wakes up one day regretting that he stood by me because a year from now, or six months from now, or in ten years, this whole thing comes up again at some inappropriate time, like a fashion event or something else with a lot of media coverage?"

"What if he does?" her mother asked.

"I don't know," Riley cried. "That's why I asked you. It would suck, I guess."

"Yes, Riley, it would. But what if this whole thing never happened, and you and Josh remained together, or got married, and a few years down the line Josh woke up and said he didn't love you anymore? Would that be any better?"

Riley finished her wine in one gulp. "You're supposed to make me feel better, not worse."

"Don't you see, Riley? All you can be certain of is the here and now. The tangible, the time that you can hold on to and enjoy, one kiss at a time. You can beg for all the answers you want to, but understand that we're all guessing at the tomorrows of the world. You have to take hold of the now and make the most of it. Savor it. Josh's family is a testament to that. Do you think they thought they'd lose Adriana at such a young age?"

"No, but…"

"Don't you think she told Hal a million times how much she loved him and that she'd never leave him? It's all a leap of faith."

Her mother refilled their glasses, then continued. "The way I see it, you should be less worried about the shame you might bring to others and more worried about reclaiming the rights to those designs you no doubt worked long and hard to create."

"Josh is working on it," Riley said.

"Since when do you let other people fight your battles?"

"Kinda harsh, don't you think, Mom?"

"No. I'm being real, Riley. You've always stood up for your-self. You've confronted bigger rivals in your life than some New York woman. Remember in fourth grade when sixth-grader Alex Harper got it in his head that he was going to make fun of Jade every day?"

"Yeah, but we were kids," Riley said.

"Yeah, you were. But that didn't stop you from going right up to him and socking him in the nose." Her mother shook her head. "I still remember his mother shouting at me on the phone, and I was so darn proud of you. I didn't love that you settled the issue with your fists, but I was proud that you had taken charge of a situation that the teachers and principal failed to handle. I have faith in you, Riley. There must be something you're overlooking. Some proof of what you've created."

"Well, if there is, I can't think of it."

Her mother frowned. "Then you're not thinking hard enough, and maybe, just maybe, you've fallen into the victim line and can't find your way out."

Chapter Forty

JOSH STOOD IN the lobby of the Dakota with his shoulders hunched forward and bags under his eyes as the elevator made its slow descent.

"I always knew there was more to you hiring her than just her skills."

Josh spun around at the sound of Claudia's voice. "What are you doing here?" He pushed the elevator button several times, wishing it would move faster so he could escape Claudia.

Wearing a pair of tight-fitting jeans, spike heels, and a GUESS Candide faux-fur jacket, Claudia looked more like she was going on a date than throwing virtual darts at her boss.

"Why? Afraid she'll see us together? According to my sources, your girlfriend is long gone. She ran back home to hide. Oh…" She feigned a long look at her red nails, then planted one hand on her hip and set her eyes on Josh. "I guess you already know that, since you took her to the airport."

Every nerve tightened. Josh fisted his hands, his nostrils flaring as he bit back the impulse to tell her to get out of his sight. The elevator opened and Josh stomped inside. Claudia stepped in beside him, and in the next breath, bright flashes of yellow blurred his vision as a photographer clicked picture after picture of Josh and Claudia.

"What the...?" He covered his face. "Get out, Claudia. You're a sick person."

She sauntered out of the elevator. "You should have taken me up on my offer when you had the chance."

The elevators closed behind her. Josh swore. By the time the doors finally opened on his floor, he was red with fury. He swung his apartment door open and then slammed it shut. He paced, cursing and punching the air. Too angry to speak to anyone, he ignored his ringing cell phone. *Thank goodness Riley isn't here. The last thing she needs is Claudia on her back.* He stomped into the bedroom and took off his dress shirt, throwing it onto the chair in the corner, and caught sight of the photo of him and Riley on the dresser. He picked up the frame with a groan, then set it back down. He was too angry to think, much less feel anything other than the river of hate that Claudia stirred in him.

Ten minutes later, he stepped into a hot shower, letting the scalding water beat the tension from his back and shoulders. He knew he had to make a decision. What if he found no proof and Riley was stuck taking the blame for stealing the designs? What then? How could they move forward? Claudia hadn't taken any steps toward placing formal charges against Riley for supposedly stealing her designs, which only further pushed Josh toward believing that Riley had done no wrong and that this was all some sort of game to Claudia.

Josh stepped from the shower and toweled off his lean, muscular frame. His phone rang again and, still reeling, he let it go to voicemail. It was all becoming clear to him. While he'd been worried about proving Riley's innocence, he'd completely overlooked the bigger issue. *What if she's never cleared of the accusations?* He felt himself teetering between two worlds, and he didn't want to let go of either.

Chapter Forty-One

IT WAS NEARLY midnight when Riley finally got around to emptying her bags. She unzipped the suitcase and pulled the flap open. On top of her clothing was an envelope. *Josh.* She sat down on her childhood bed and brought the envelope to her nose, smelling the scent of him that remained on the fine linen paper. She ran her finger under the flap, withdrew a piece of monogramed stationery, and read the handwritten note.

> *Hey, babe,*
>
> *This stinks, huh? I'm sorry for everything. For not coming to you before talking to the staff and for this whole mess. I believe in you, and I'll do everything I can to get it worked out quickly so that I can come see you. By now you're at your parents and I'm back at my apartment, wishing you were here. Never before has the thought of sleeping alone felt so lonely.*
>
> *We'll figure this out. I love you.*
> *—J*

Riley lay back on the bed, holding the note to her chest. *But will you still love me tomorrow?*

RILEY AWOKE THE next morning to commotion downstairs. She climbed out of bed and took a quick shower in an effort to wake up. She hadn't slept well after falling asleep waiting for Josh to call and convincing herself not to call him. What if he was wavering in his support of her? What if he was having second thoughts about them? She hadn't wanted to hear the difference in his voice then, and now she felt guilty. She'd left him to tackle the situation head-on and alone, while she was in the safety of her parents' house with the support of family and friends. She glanced in the mirror and sighed. The stress of the past two days was evident in the dark rings under her puffy eyes.

She checked her cell phone for messages and read a text from Josh that had come in at four in the morning. *Know I love you today. I can't wait to see you Wednesday.* She loved that he'd thought of her in the middle of the night, then wondered why he would have waited until it was so late to text.

She texted back, *Love you too. Call me later?*

Riley pulled on her skinny jeans and a thick, comfortable sweatshirt, intentionally veering as far away from designer labels as she could. She needed comfort today. This week. *Maybe forever.*

On her way down the stairs, she heard Jade's voice, then Max's, and then Savannah's. *What is going on?* She crept silently to the wall beside the kitchen and listened.

"What she needs is a girls' day out to forget about all this nonsense," Jade said.

"And a girls' night out," Savannah added. "I can't believe that photo. Maybe she won't see it."

What is she doing here? What photo? She had a sinking feeling in the pit of her stomach.

"I still can't believe this is actually happening," Max said. "I mean, one minute I'm in love with my bridal gown, and the next minute it's the center of some scandal. How is Josh handling it all? Treat couldn't reach him last night."

"He's not answering his phone," Savannah answered. "But I spoke to the PI he hired, and it looks like they're working as hard as they can to figure it all out. The photo though...poor Riley."

Riley crept back upstairs and closed her bedroom door. She navigated to Google on her phone and searched Josh's name. Her jaw dropped open when she saw the front page of the *New York Post*. A photo of Josh and Claudia in the elevators at his apartment building stared back at her. She narrowed her eyes, scrutinizing Josh's face, then zoomed in, hoping to see an obvious Photoshop marking or anything to indicate that the picture had been faked. She read the article, which was sketchy, at best, claiming that the two were "seen together" in the lobby of his apartment building.

She checked her text messages, then her voicemails. Nothing from Josh. Was that why he hadn't called last night? She lay back on her bed, wondering what was going on, her pulse kicking up a notch with each passing second. *Frigging Claudia.* Her mother's words came rushing back. *You've confronted bigger rivals in your life than some New York woman.* She sat up and dialed four-one-one.

"Claudia Raven, Manhattan, please."

After calling three wrong numbers, she finally connected with the right one. Riley took a deep breath and held the phone with a trembling hand. Claudia answered on the first ring.

"Hello?"

Her casual tone threw Riley off. "Claudia?"

She didn't respond. Silence filled the airwaves, and just as Riley opened her mouth to speak, Claudia said, "Riley Banks. What on earth might you want? Oh, I saw your boyfriend last night."

The taunting sneer in her voice came through loud and clear and sent Riley's mind careening in ten different directions. She stood in an effort to walk some confidence into her shaking body and spinning mind. When that didn't work, she closed her eyes and blurted out what she'd called to say.

"You stole my drawings. You're dragging me through who knows what kind of muddy nightmare, and you've obviously pulled no punches getting that picture of you and Josh." Riley didn't realize she was yelling until her bedroom door flew open and Jade, Max, and Savannah tumbled in. Her mother stood in the doorway, giving her the courage she needed to continue.

"Well, let me tell you something, Claudia Raven. I might not be a savvy New Yorker, but I'm a Weston woman and Weston women are proud, honest, and strong. If you think your tactics will tear me away from Josh, you've got another thing coming. You could be naked in the pictures, for all I care. I know Josh, and he wouldn't touch the likes of you if his life depended on it." Her eyes jumped from Max's wide eyes to Jade's thumbs-up, then up to Savannah's wide, mischievous smile, and finally landed on her mother's nodding head.

Claudia gasped, fueling Riley's rant.

"It doesn't matter to me if we prove this or not," Riley said. "I know the truth, and so do you, and you're the one who will have to live with the guilt of knowing how low you sank and how many lives you hurt along the way." Riley pushed the End button on the phone.

"You did it, Ri. You really did it." Jade wrapped Riley in her arms.

"Wow, you go, girlfriend!" Savannah laughed, embracing both Jade and Riley.

"I can't believe you did that," Max added.

Riley's mother stood in the doorway with a proud smile that filled her eyes with tears. "Now, that's the girl I raised."

Tears streamed down Riley's cheeks. Her legs trembled. She collapsed into her friends' arms, hoping that she hadn't just done the absolute wrong thing.

Chapter Forty-Two

JOSH STARED AT the photo on the cover of the *New York Post*, his cell phone pressed against his ear. Kelly, his publicist, had been hammering him for ten minutes about not calling her last night when Claudia had showed up.

"I could have jumped them on this, Josh. You know that. Even if I couldn't have stopped the presses, I could have had a rival article written. Now it will look like you're just covering your footsteps with a retaliatory article," Kelly said.

"I realize that. I wasn't thinking."

"Did you tell Riley when it happened at least? Is she prepared?"

"No," he said, realizing his mistake. "I was too pissed, and by the time I settled down from being angry, I wasn't thinking about the newspapers," he admitted. He'd been too wrapped up in figuring out what he'd do about Riley if her name was never cleared. The impact this situation would have on his career had yet to be seen, but if this mess never went away, if Riley was linked in articles and photos as a design thief, how would he overcome that? He wasn't prepared for the rage that ripped through him over the past twelve hours and still held him prisoner. Just seeing the picture of him and Claudia made him want to rip someone's head off and throw it into the East River.

"You have to always—always—be thinking about the newspapers. Especially now. I'm serious, Josh. I'll do what I can, but you'd better get in touch with Riley. If she's seen this, as I'm sure she has—I mean, everyone has—then you've got a lot of explaining to do. I swear it's like you fell in love and lost all your faculties."

I swear it's like you fell in love and lost all your faculties. If that was her impression, then what was everyone else thinking? His mind came back to Riley. It always came back to Riley. He pictured her trusting eyes, her smile when he told her he loved her. He did love her. *I do love her.* But he also loved his career, and his career wouldn't survive if he couldn't contain the rage that kept his fisted hands at the ready.

When his phone rang, he brought it to his ear, distracted by the argument going on between his heart and his mind.

"Hello?" he said.

"What the heck are you doing?" Treat fumed.

"Nothing," Josh snapped.

"Max is over at Riley's right now; so is Savannah. They're trying to clean up this mess so you don't lose your girlfriend."

Josh didn't answer. *My girlfriend.*

"Listen, little brother. I don't know what's going on, but if you want to salvage your relationship with Riley, I don't think hanging out with Claudia is the way to do it."

"Shut up, Treat. Do you really think I'd do that? She showed up and the photographer snapped the photo, and then she was gone. I'm not thrilled about any of this."

"Did you tell Riley when they took the picture?" Treat asked.

Josh closed his eyes. "No," he snapped.

"It's like you want this relationship to fall apart." Treat softened his tone. "Josh, what's going on with you?"

Josh didn't have an answer.

"Open your front door," Treat said.

Josh went to his front door and opened it, watching Treat, in person, lower the phone from his ear and open his arms. Josh felt like a needy kid again as he accepted his brother's strong embrace, and he felt his protective, steely resolve begin to thaw.

"What are you doing here?" Josh asked.

"You're used to the upside of the media circus. I've been on both sides. I figured you might need some support." Treat headed for the kitchen. "I'm starved. You have eggs?"

Leave it to Treat to fall right back into Mom mode. Ever since Josh could remember, when he or his siblings were having a hard time, Treat would swoop in and cook for them and figure out how to fix things—or at least make them feel better. At this point, Josh needed all the help he could get.

"Fridge," Josh answered.

Treat whipped up egg-white omelets and toasted whole-wheat bread while Josh explained what had happened with Claudia and the quandary his mind was now tackling.

"So, let me get this straight," Treat said as he handed Josh a full plate of food. "After two days, you're ready to tell the world about your feelings for Riley; then this crap happens, and now you're questioning if you can stand behind her if she never gets cleared because you're afraid that a year from now, or ten years from now, you might kill someone if they badmouth her? Even though you know she's innocent."

Josh speared a hunk of eggs with his fork and nodded. "I'm a jerk."

Treat shook his head. "Yeah, you are. Riley is dealing with

seeing you and Claudia together and you haven't called her?"

"I was going to…"

"But you wanted to figure out your own stuff first." Treat narrowed his dark eyes, pinning him to his chair. "Don't be surprised if you've already lost her. I thought you were smarter than that, Josh."

Josh threw his fork down on the table. "Damn it, Treat. I don't know what I am. I love her. I *adore* her. Every ounce of me wants to be with her. But what if someone says something about her and I lose it? Then we're right back in this nightmare again, with Riley going through it all as the innocent party. And what if that means losing what I've created? I'm not like you. I can't give up what I've built. I love my work. I love my business, and trust me, I know just how much of a self-centered jerk that makes me."

"It does," Treat said with a nod.

"I *know*."

"Why do you see this as all or nothing? You know how these things go. It's a setback, Josh. So what if you fall back a year or two while this thing blows over? You climbed that ladder once; you'll climb it again. And as far as losing it goes, or hitting someone, you're a Braden. Your first line of defense isn't your fists. You might feel like it's going to be, but your mind will always override that physical side."

Josh ran his hand through his hair. "I want an assurance that I'm not going to kill someone, and…" He pushed past his embarrassment and admitted what he'd been thinking for the last twenty-four hours. "I want to be like you and be ready and willing to give it all up for the woman I love. I know that would make me so much more of a man, but—"

"Yeah, *right*," Treat said with another glare. "Being a man has nothing to do with giving up anything. I built my business to prove something to myself and to my family. That was it. There was no *love* built into that. I love negotiating, but I could have done that in any business. I could have built a business on resorts, sailboats, or freaking playground equipment, for all I care. You built your business based on something you *love*, and you wouldn't love doing any other work the way you love designing. We've known that since you were six years old." Treat shook his head.

"What are you getting at?" Josh asked.

Treat sighed. "What makes a man isn't what he'll give up, Josh. It's the grace in which he lives his life. The level of honesty and the moral code he lives by. The ethics of being aboveboard, and…" Treat looked away.

"And?"

Treat drew his eyes back to Josh, and when he spoke, his voice was tender. "And the value he places on those he loves combined with the efforts he takes to protect them. Those are the qualities that make a man. What I did wasn't manly. What I did was sort of cowardly." Treat laughed. "I would have walked through a field of dinosaurs to be with Max. Nothing else mattered to me. Doling out my responsibilities for work to enable me to be by her side was weak. It was the easy way out, but it made me happy, and I'm okay with that. I could have fought for her to bend to my lifestyle, and she probably would have. No, she definitely would have. But I can tell you this. Working on Dad's ranch and running my businesses remotely was worth it. I've never been happier than when I'm with Max."

"It wasn't weak. It was chivalrous," Josh said.

"Hardly," Treat said. "Okay, maybe to some people. But, Josh, we all have our own paths to happiness. Yours doesn't have to include giving up your career. You just need to figure out if you can live with the world around you seeing Riley one way when you know her to be another."

"That's just half of what I've been wrestling with," Josh admitted.

"And what have you come up with?" Treat asked.

"I can't imagine my life without her. I've spent my career worried about doing the right thing, dating the right women, dressing appropriately, attending all the right events, and for the first time in my life, when I'm with Riley, I feel free from that. But it's more than that." Josh took a deep breath, hoping his brother wouldn't think less of him for what he was about to say. "It's like there's another person controlling my emotions. The anger..." Josh looked away.

"Go on," Treat urged.

"Treat, man, if someone were to say something derogatory about Riley in my presence, I don't know what I'd do. When those media hounds were all over her, I felt something I had never felt before. I swear my blood was on fire. It was all I could do not to rip them to shreds, and that's not who I am. I had to stop myself from getting physical. I mean, really stop myself. Tell myself, 'This isn't you.' You know me. I'm not a fighter, never have been." Josh watched a smile spread across Treat's face.

"You're also a man in love, little brother, and that's something you've never been before either. It takes you by surprise, doesn't it?"

"Like you wouldn't believe," Josh said.

"All those protective urges that you always thought were reserved for your family members suddenly apply to someone else in a bigger, more powerful way, and it scares you. That's natural. It *should* scare you," Treat said.

"Scared the life out of me. It still does." Josh sighed, feeling the tension in his shoulders ease. Treat understood. He wasn't losing his mind after all.

"Your rational mind will always override the physical," Treat assured him.

"I keep going over and over this in my head. As scary as all this is—and believe me, lately it feels like the Incredible Hulk is trying to break through my body—it's not half as scary as losing Riley. I know I messed up. I should have fired Claudia ages ago, before Riley ever came to work there. Claudia's been an issue for a long time, but she was so good at her job, and she's Peter Stafford's niece, so there's the whole ridiculous loyalty thing. I never thought…"

Treat leaned back and crossed his legs. "You're a good person, Josh. You see the best in people and want to believe no one is as slippery as they are. You've been that way your whole life. Remember when Hugh used to do stupid things, you'd try and take the blame for him so that he didn't get in trouble. Dad would turn his back and chuckle."

"If he didn't believe I did those things, why did he allow me to take the heat?" Josh remembered a handful of times he'd taken Hugh's punishments, usually for Hugh being selfish toward others. Josh had never wanted to believe that his little brother could be selfish and self-centered. He'd learned a lot about Hugh over the years, and he'd come to accept that the youngest Braden was, in fact, exactly that. Although, Hugh's recent call had him questioning if the assessment was still accurate.

"Because Dad was teaching you a lesson just as he taught the rest of us. If you're going to step in to take the heat, you're going to get it. It was a good lesson, at least for me. You learn to pick and choose your battles. You do realize, Josh, that if you move forward with Riley, nothing in your life will ever be the same."

"You've convinced me. No one could ever make me believe Riley stole anything, and I feel better knowing you understand the anger that's been eating away at my gut. I'll trust your experience, Treat, that I won't hit someone," Josh said.

"What are you saying?" Treat asked.

"I'm picking this battle." Josh nodded as he stood from his chair.

"And what if you're wrong and she stole the design? You can't have a life with a woman you can't trust," Treat said.

"Maybe I really am a jerk, because now I want to hit you," Josh said.

Treat shook his head. "Seriously, Josh."

"It's Riley. She's worth it, and I'm not wrong. She didn't steal the drawing, and even if we can't prove it, I'm ready to take the heat."

Chapter Forty-Three

RILEY, JADE, MAX, and Savannah sat in a café in the village of Allure. They'd spent the morning walking through shops and talking about how crazy Claudia was, Max's wedding, and the house Jade and Rex were having built. Riley tried to add to the conversations, but as each hour passed, the fissures in her heart deepened. She hadn't heard from Josh since the text he'd sent at four in the morning, and she couldn't get the photo out of her head.

"What does my brother have to say about the latest?" Savannah asked. She looked chic in her jeans, long-sleeved white shirt, and suede blazer.

Riley drew in a breath, trying to formulate an answer that didn't sound whiny or clingy. The best she could come up with was "Not much."

"Do you think he's all right? Gosh, maybe he needs one of us down there with him." Savannah pulled out her cell phone.

"Treat's with him," Max said.

"What?" Savannah and Riley asked in unison.

"He chartered a plane in the middle of the night. He said he was worried about Josh. Apparently, he had tried to call him several times, and he said Josh had a tendency to pull into himself and block out the world when things went awry." Max sipped her iced tea and then continued. "He's with him now. He texted me about half an hour ago."

Treat texted you? Why didn't Josh text me?

"What did he say? Is Josh okay?" Savannah asked.

Riley was dying to know the same thing. She was relieved Savannah had stepped in to ask.

"He said he's having a hard time, but they're going to meet with the PI and get this figured out today," Max explained. "He sounded pretty firm, like neither of them was going to let this nonsense continue." She touched Riley's arm. "Treat said Josh was worried about Riley but that he was in no shape to call and that they were rushing around taking care of things."

"No shape to call? What does that even mean?" Riley asked.

"I guess he's really angry about everything, but, Riley, he's also probably in that befuddled stage that guys go through, where they don't know up from down when they're first in love. Imagine being newly in love and thrown in a blender with your lover's nemesis."

"I'm living that nightmare, remember?" Riley said.

Jade touched her arm. "Oh, I know that befuddled stage," Jade said. "Remember, Ri, when Rex was all tied in knots? He was so cute and so passionate."

Riley knew Jade was trying to sidetrack her from her hurt over Josh not calling.

"Please." Savannah pretended to cover her ears.

"No, I mean he was protective and loving." She winked at Riley. "And passionate that way, too."

Savannah swatted her arm. "Ew! That's my brother, okay. Let me think of him as a brother, please. Gross."

Jade laughed.

"Well, Josh isn't that way. He's loving, but he's not passionate like Rex is. He's very in control when it comes to his protective urges. I can't even imagine him getting that mad at anyone," Riley said.

"Not even Claudia?" Max asked.

"Well." Riley reconsidered. "Mad, yes, but viscerally angry, I doubt it."

"Don't underestimate my little brother, Riley. I bet this situation is making him see all sides of himself that he's not used to." Savannah leaned closer to Riley and whispered, "And please, when he does, don't use the words *passionate* and *Josh* in the same sentence. He's still very pure in my eyes," she teased.

Riley couldn't take it anymore. Why hadn't he called her? Why hadn't he warned her about Claudia? What was she missing?

"Savannah, you said Josh pulls into himself. What did you mean?" Riley finally asked.

"Josh is the most passive of my brothers. When something goes wrong, he tends to close himself off until he has a way to deal with it." Savannah narrowed her eyes. "Riley, is he doing that to you? Shutting you out?"

"No." The word shot from Riley's lips.

"Oh no, honey. Haven't you talked to him since you saw that picture? Oh goodness, you've been with us the whole time. We've been monopolizing your time. We're such idiots." She looked around the table. "Call him, Riley. It'll make you feel a lot better."

Everyone stared at her. She didn't want to call Josh in front of everyone. What if he hadn't called because he wasn't sure about them anymore? What if he didn't tell her about Claudia because he was on her side now?

"Call him," Savannah said.

Riley pressed speed dial and put the phone to her ear. *Don't pick up. Don't pick up.*

"Riley," he said in a rushed whisper. "You okay?"

Hearing his voice made her want to climb through the phone and crawl into his lap. "Josh? Yes. You?" Too many questions cluttered her mind.

"Yeah, fine. I'm in the middle of something. I'm sorry about the *Post* and about not calling. I can explain."

"I don't care about the *Post*." *Yes, I do. Explain, please!* "Why are you whispering?"

"I'm in the middle of a meeting. I love you. I'll call you later. Promise. 'Kay, babe?"

Riley ended the call feeling more confused than she was before. "He says he's okay and that he can explain about the *Post*."

"Of course he can. Jeez, if there's one thing about my brothers, none of them are cheats. My father would have whooped their butts if he thought he raised cheaters," Savannah said.

"I'd never have pegged Josh as a cheater, but I have to admit, I do feel better having heard him say he can explain," Riley admitted.

"What are you going to do, Ri?" Jade asked. "Have you thought any more about what happens if they don't clear your name?"

"That's all I can think about, and if it's fair to Josh to stay with him. I mean he's a great guy, but he could do so much better than a woman with an accusation like *design thief* on her résumé." Riley averted her eyes from Savannah's dark stare.

"Are you telling me that you would break up with him…to

protect him from being—what?—connected to you if they don't clear your name?" Savannah pushed her chair back and crossed her arms.

"I don't think she's saying that," Jade said.

"I'm so confused, Savannah. What would you do?" Riley needed answers, and since she hadn't come up with any, she sure hoped someone else had them.

"Any man that would stick with me through thick and thin would be making his own choice." Savannah clenched her jaw. "If you plan on hurting Josh—"

"No, that's not my intent," Riley said. *Great. Now his sister hates me.* "I'm saying that…" *Don't cry. Please don't cry.* Her eyes betrayed her and filled with tears. "I just don't know what to do." Her voice cracked as warm tears spilled down her cheeks. "I love him, Savannah. I don't ever want to be without him, but what if being with him hurts him? He loves his career. I could kill his reputation."

Jade was by her side in a heartbeat, her arms wrapped around her. "Shh. It's gonna be okay. We'll figure this out," Jade said.

"I went through this with Treat," Max added. "I'm not sure if you knew about this, Savannah, but I didn't want Treat to give up his work for me. I knew how much he loved the traveling, the negotiations, the fast-paced lifestyle, but in the end, I realized that I could only control what I did, not what he did. These are men, not boys, Riley. They make their own decisions, and from what I've experienced with Treat, I can honestly say that he's never regretted his decision."

Riley wiped her eyes. "So you think I shouldn't worry that he'll change his mind?"

"No way," Max said. "If Josh says he loves you, he will stand by you. How can you or anyone else dispute what comes from his heart? They're his feelings, Riley, not yours or anyone else's. Just Josh's."

Riley looked at Savannah, who was watching her like a lion on the prowl—one wrong word about her brother and she'd pounce.

"Savannah, I need to know. Do you think if Josh decided to stay with me he wouldn't turn around and regret it a month, a year, or even ten years later?" Riley held her breath, waiting for Savannah to answer.

Savannah opened her mouth to speak, then closed it again. She took a drink; then she put one hand on Riley's hand and the other on her heart. "I'm not Josh, but cross my heart, this is what I believe. If Josh makes a commitment, it's a commitment that he won't break unless you force him to." She pulled Riley into a hug and whispered against her ear, "If you hurt him, I'll kill you, so decide before he gets here."

Riley pulled away with her eyes wide, her heart racing.

"Kidding," Savannah said in a high-pitched voice. Something in her voice told Riley she wasn't.

Chapter Forty-Four

"YOU'RE ONE HUNDRED percent sure about this?" Treat asked.

Josh tucked the package he'd just purchased into his pocket as he and Treat climbed into the waiting car.

"Definitely." Josh hadn't ever felt more certain of anything in his life. "You assured me that this desire to hammer anyone who hurts Riley is normal. All I can do is believe you. You have more experience with that than I do. But if I land in jail, you've got to bail me out."

"I'll bail you out, and then our other brothers and I will stand by your side while Rex pummels the bastard again."

Josh laughed. "Then he'll end up in jail."

"Family honor. Sometimes it's a vicious cycle," Treat said with a nod.

"Let's get this over with. I want to get back to Riley. I've wasted enough time on this garbage."

"Did you get ahold of Savannah?" Treat asked.

"Yeah, she knows just what to do. By the way, Savannah apparently told Riley that if she hurts me, she'll kill her. Did she do that to Max?"

"Savannah's pretty protective. I'm sure she said it to Max, to

Jade, and whoever the women are who Dane and Hugh fall for will be in for the same threat."

JOSH'S HEART SLAMMED against his chest. He and Treat had just come from his attorney's office after finally taking care of filing a formal sexual harassment suit against Claudia—one he should have filed long ago. Thankfully, his attorney was well connected and had expedited the process. He should have taken the appropriate measures long ago, but he couldn't change the past. All he could do was concentrate on doing all the right things to ensure his and Riley's future, and filing that suit made him feel a thousand times better. He had a flash of worry about what doing this would do to his relationship with Peter, but he bit back the worry. He'd deal with that later. He was taking strides in the right direction, and he had to maintain his focus. As he climbed the narrow apartment stairs, the nerves across his shoulders pulled tight once again. He looked over his shoulder at Treat, stealing confidence from his brother's determination. He needed a witness. He needed his brother.

Josh threw his shoulders back, straightened his perfectly pressed, white dress shirt, lifted his chin, and knocked on the door of apartment 213. He'd never been in this particular Greenwich Village apartment building, and he hoped he'd never have cause to go there again. He lifted his hand to knock again as the door swung open.

Claudia stood before him in a red silk kimono. He recognized his own design and cringed. She ran her index finger down the open cleavage of the short robe.

"You've finally come to your senses?" The right corner of

Claudia's lips lifted. "I was just relaxing. Come in, please." She stepped to the side, making way for Josh to pass.

Treat stepped behind Josh. The three inches he had on Josh allowed him to look over his head and meet Claudia's eyes with a harsh glare.

"Oh, you brought Treat." She smirked. "Long time no see. I didn't know you were into threesomes."

Josh fisted his left hand, clenching an envelope in his right, and bit back the inflammatory words that vied for release. Instead he let loose the speech he'd practiced for months and had never found the courage to say.

"Claudia, you have come onto me one too many times. You've been rude and manipulative toward other employees and made JBD a tension-filled environment. As of this moment, you are no longer an employee of JBD. Details of your termination are in this letter." He handed her the letter and stepped to the side as she whipped it from his hands.

"You can't fire me. My attorney will have a field day with this. I'll file charges against you and Riley Banks," she spat.

Treat handed her another envelope, and with a calm, measured voice, he said, "You aren't going to do any such thing, because Josh's investigator has proof of you stealing the designs. You were clever to cut off the security cameras, but, Claudia, did you forget that those were just the company's security cameras?"

Claudia's jaw dropped.

"That's right, my dear," Treat continued. "The building has its own cameras, and what Josh's PI found will put you away for years to come. You might want to read this before calling your attorney."

She took the envelope with shaking hands.

"You've been served," Treat said with a wide grin. He turned and grabbed Josh by the upper arm, guiding him toward the stairs.

Josh moved robotically beside his brother. As soon as their feet hit the pavement, he pulled from Treat's grip. "What the…? None of that is true."

Treat opened the door to the waiting car and shoved Josh in, then slid in beside him. "You sure you don't want to make a quick stop at Reggie's before we take off? He might have the answers you need," Treat offered.

"No way. I just want to get home." *And into Riley's arms.* "Reggie will call when he knows something. Mia's given him access to the building and anything else he needs."

Treat leaned forward. "Jay, Teterboro Airport, please." He turned to Josh. "I chartered a flight to avoid any further media hassles. Listen. We don't know if what I said is true or not, but when you reach Reggie, you can find out. None of that matters, though. She's been fired. She's been served, and if you're sure Riley is innocent, then I'm one-hundred-percent sure that between the sexual harassment suit and what I told her, she's not stupid enough to take her to court."

"What a mess," Josh said. "And what a relief." Laughter bubbled out of him. He threw his head back and scrubbed his face with his hands. "I always knew it would feel good to be rid of her, but never did I imagine it would feel *this* good."

"You're not rid of her yet. As your attorney said, filing the sexual harassment charges against her will probably keep her from taking any of this public, and the security tapes from your office will validate the harassment claims, but she still needs to save face with her accusations about Riley. There'll be something that comes back at you. This isn't anywhere near the end of it." Treat narrowed his eyes, grabbing Josh by the shoulders. "Even though you're confident about all of this, there's still the chance that Riley is in the wrong. You still have no proof."

Josh couldn't ease the smile on his lips. The freedom that releasing Claudia from JBD brought felt like a noose had been removed from around his neck, and if he'd learned one thing from the past few days, it was that his father had been right. After feeling what he'd felt for Riley, his life *would* never mean anything if his heart wasn't full.

Josh nodded. "I have all the proof I need." He covered his heart with his hand.

Josh and Treat pulled their cell phones from their pockets at the same time.

"Who are you calling?" Treat asked.

"Texting Savannah. I need another favor." He texted her, then began typing another message.

"Who else?" Treat asked, reading the response from Max.

"Riley."

"Why? I thought you weren't going to tell her yet."

Josh smiled. "Because I miss her."

Chapter Forty-Five

THE LAST THING Riley felt like doing after spending the day with her friends was going out to dinner with her parents, and to Christos of all places, the most expensive restaurant within sixty miles. She stood before her closet in her pink lace bra and matching thong, freshly showered, her hair dried, makeup on, and a frown on her face as she flipped through her dresses with a loud sigh. She hadn't heard from Josh since that strange whispering phone call. The nerves in her stomach pinched so tight, she knew she wouldn't be able to eat a thing, much less feign pleasantries. Riley eyed her sweats, the desire to curl up in them with a big bottle of wine and a thick blanket in front of a sappy movie so she could wallow in her worries and drink away the ache of missing Josh was so strong that she considered doing just that.

"Fifteen minutes, sunshine," her father said from behind her closed door.

"Okay," she called. She wished Josh would call. It had been hours since they'd spoken. What could he possibly be doing? She picked up her cell phone and checked her messages.

"Thank goodness," she said, scrolling to Josh's text.

My heart + your heart = happiness. Xo J.

"That's the corniest thing I've ever read," she said aloud. *I love him. I trust him. I miss him. Gosh, I miss him so much.* Instead of wrestling with the unfairness of the situation and thinking about how Josh shouldn't be dragged through the mud with her, or how he didn't deserve the web she was stuck in, she took a giant leap of faith and texted back, *You're a romantic fool. I love you. Thank u 4 sticking by my side. Please come home 2 me.*

The room looked brighter, and Riley knew her mother and Max were right. She could spend her whole life worried about what might happen next, or she could believe. She could trust. She could love. Riley chose love.

With her attitude adjusted, she went back to leafing through her clothes. She'd worn every outfit a hundred times. She scrutinized herself in the full-length mirror that hung beside her closet. She turned to one side, then the other. Riley didn't believe in scales. She didn't care what she weighed as long as she felt good about how she looked and felt healthy, and as she ran her hands along her sides and down her hips, she swore something had changed, though she didn't feel any physical difference.

She moved tentatively toward the back of her closet, reaching behind the winter coats in the back and retrieving a dress she'd made while she was in college. She had no idea if it would still fit, but it was one of her favorite designs. She ran her fingers along the red silk, thinking about what she told the customers in Macy's. *Ninety-nine percent of feeling good is looking good. If you dress in sweats, you'll feel sluggish, but throw on the right outfit, and you'll immediately get a new boost of energy.* She pulled the dress from the rack. Riley slipped the cowl-neck dress over her body, shimmying against the silken fabric, then belted it with the matching silk tie. Admiring the elegantly finished cuffed sleeves, she turned to face the mirror and slammed her eyes shut, silently praying she looked at least passable.

A knock on her bedroom door brought her eyes open. She gasped at the image in the mirror. The combination of the hint of cleavage exposed by the low gather of the cowl and the mid-thigh hem were pretty, but it was what she felt inside, the illumination of her heart, the explosive love she felt for Josh and accepted more and more with each passing second, that made her feel breathtakingly stunning.

"Wow," she said to the empty room.

"Honey."

"Yeah, coming, Mom." She slipped her feet into a pair of nude heels and pulled open the door.

"My word." Her mother's eyes ran down her body.

"Too much?" Riley asked, covering her waist with her arm.

"Goodness, no. You are a vision, Riley. You look like you've just walked out of a fashion magazine." Her mother thrust a package into her arms. "We have to leave, but this just came for you." She called over her shoulder, "Sweetheart, come here and see your little girl."

A moment later, her father stood behind her mother, one hand on her mother's shoulder and the other on his slim hip. "Sunshine, you are gorgeous." He whistled. "Beauty and brains, you're a dangerous combination. No wonder that woman is accusing you of horrible things. She must be jealous."

Riley felt her cheeks warm. "Daddy."

He wrapped his arms around Riley. "I love you, sunshine."

"I'll be down in a sec, okay?" Riley watched her parents descend the stairs; then she went to work opening the package. Her pulse kicked up a notch when she withdrew a box of gingerbread cookies, along with a note—not in Josh's handwriting—*Comfort food.* She dug deeper and found a compact disc of Hunter Hayes, featuring her favorite song, "Wanted." She brought it to her chest and closed her eyes. *Josh.* She tossed aside the packing and withdrew the last item from the box. A photograph of a bouquet of peach roses, with a note taped to the back.

> *Josh asked me to get these for you, but finding them at a moment's notice was impossible. I'm so sorry, and I know he'll kill me, but this is the best I can do. Love, Savannah.*

Savannah? Riley flipped open her laptop and Googled the meaning of peach roses. Within seconds, she had her answer.

Peach roses—closing the deal; let's get together; gratitude.

Her heart swelled, and she knew she'd made the right decision. When she leapt, Josh would be there to catch her.

Chapter Forty-Six

JOSH BARRELED INTO his father's house after the four-hour flight, during which he'd come to realize just how much Riley meant to him, how much the few short weeks had changed his outlook and his heart, which was bubbling over with love. Even the anger he felt toward Claudia had subsided, as if he'd left it behind when the airplane had taken off.

Hugh grabbed Josh's arm as he came through the door. "Josh, is it true?" A few days' worth of stubble peppered his chin and cheeks, and the gray button-down shirt he wore was a refreshing change from his typical T-shirt and racing jacket.

Josh beamed. "Absofrigginglutely. I need to shower. Where's Dad?"

Treat embraced Hugh. "Good to see you."

"Dad? How about me?" Dane called from the next room. He appeared in the hall and pulled Josh into a hug. "Get over here. I'm happy for you, bro."

"Thanks, but it's not a done deal yet."

The heavy hand on his shoulder nearly brought tears to Josh's eyes. "Dad," he whispered as he turned to the man who had always been there for him. Hal Braden stood three inches taller than Josh, and as Josh walked into his arms, he took comfort in the strength of his father's embrace. He feared the day that strength would diminish and his age would erase his father's commanding presence. His dark hair was now streaked with gray and not quite as thick as it once had been.

"I hear this is a big night for you," his father said.

"I hope so," Josh said. He looked around the house where he'd spent his formative years, where he'd learned most of life's hard lessons, and where he'd lost his mother. He swallowed past the lump in his throat and forced a smile. "Still talking to Mom?" he asked.

His father clenched his jaw and flexed his biceps, a habit he and Rex shared. "Son, I'll never stop talking to your mother," he said in a serious tone.

"Good, Dad. Good. Where's Rex?" Josh asked.

"He and Jade are meeting us at the restaurant. Savannah and Max are already there." Hal looked at his watch. "Seems to me you have about ten minutes before we need to walk out the door. You about ready?"

"Quick shower and shave." Josh headed down the hall toward his childhood bedroom.

THERE WAS A war going on in Josh's gut as he stepped from Treat's Lexus SUV and stood before the restaurant.

Treat came to his side and swung an arm across his shoulder. "Second thoughts?"

"No, just nervous as all get out," Josh admitted. He was done hemming and hawing. Riley was the woman he wanted to spend his life with, and he was ready to tell her. He knew she might not want to return to New York after the mess she'd already gone through, but his heart drove him to her, and he wasn't going to turn away—no matter what was going on in his gut.

"That's good. If you weren't nervous, there would be something wrong with you," Treat said.

"What if she says no?" Josh asked.

Treat shrugged. "Then you try again and again until she says yes."

Josh handed Treat the package they'd bought earlier that morning. "You'll make sure Rex knows what to do? And Savannah?"

"Sure will," Treat said.

"She won't say no, Josh," Hugh said. "You're every girl's dream. You're wealthy, handsome, and quite a catch with your social status."

"None of that matters to her," Josh shot back.

"But the thing that does matter is too obvious to mention. You're a good man." Hugh patted him on the back and took a few steps forward, allowing Dane to come to Josh's side.

Josh wouldn't have believed those words came from Hugh's mouth if he hadn't heard them himself. *My baby brother is growing up.* "That means the world to me, Hugh. Thank you."

"You're crazy, you know that? You sure you really want to tie yourself down? Take yourself out of circulation? Get that old ball and chain?" Dane grinned.

"Get outta here," Treat said.

"Uh oh, you just spent time with Mr. Lovesick? No wonder you're doing this," Dane teased. "No, really, Josh, I'm happy for you. I've got your back. You need anything, I'm here."

"Thanks, Dane." Josh looked over at each of his brothers, feeling the absence of Rex and Savannah like missing limbs.

He'd see them inside, but he wished he had a private moment with each and he wondered if they felt the same. Treat, Dane, and Hugh stood before him. Josh felt support coming off of them in waves.

"Boys?" their father said. "May I have a word with Josh?"

"Of course," Treat said.

Dane's phone vibrated, reminding Josh to get rid of his. Josh took his phone from his pocket and handed it to Treat.

"Can you hold on to this? I don't want it vibrating, and I'm too nervous to mess with the buttons right now."

"Yeah." Treat looked at it. "There's a missed call from Reggie. You might have your answers."

"I've already made up my mind, and I'm doing this no matter what the answers are," Josh said. He watched Treat and the others head toward the restaurant.

Hal wore a pair of dark slacks, a cream-colored dress shirt, and a dark tie. Set against his ever-present tan, massive height, and dark, emotional eyes, he looked like an aging movie star.

"Son, I wish your mother were still alive to see this night. She's proud of you."

Josh didn't miss the present tense his father used when speaking of his mother. "Thanks, Dad. I wish she were here, too, and I can only hope she'd have been proud." Josh felt the lump return to his throat.

"She's here with you." He touched his jaw, as if he were thinking, and then he put his hands on Josh's shoulders in the same manner Treat had in the car on the way to the airport. "Son, I assume you know what you're doing with Riley Banks. She's a nice girl and she comes from a respectable family. And I assume you know what you're doing with regard to all that nonsense that's going on back in that big city you live in. You're an intelligent man, and you make good decisions, always have."

"Thanks, Dad," Josh said. His father's eyes searched his, and his grip on Josh's shoulders hadn't eased. "Was there something else you wanted to say?"

"Yes, there is. Come with me."

Josh followed his father to the edge of the woods at the far end of the parking lot.

"Dad, we don't have much time. I want to get in there before Riley notices the family."

"Rex is holding them in the lobby. Relax. Make time for your dear old dad. Listen, son. Look in there and tell me what you see." He pointed to the woods.

Josh could barely think straight. Anxiety prickled his nerves, and his pulse hadn't calmed since they'd stepped off the plane.

"I don't know. Trees, dirt, rocks."

"Okay, that's pretty good. What else?" his father urged.

He stared into the woods, trying to think like his father. Like a rancher. He came up empty. He shifted his focus, much like he did when he was designing. If inspiration didn't come from one presentation, he took it apart and started again, looking from many different angles. He began at the treetops, following the bare branches down to where they met the ground. Dead leaves layered the earth, interrupted by large rocks and fallen branches. Nothing came to mind, so he shifted his focus and began anew. He set his eyes on the ground. The earth. The foundation. Like a streak of lightning, inspiration set in.

"I see a solid foundation upon which life has grown," Josh said.

"Better. I'm not going to torture you over semantics. Son, that foundation is all those trees have. It's what gives them nourishment. It accepts their roots, thorns and all, and it accepts the leaves as they fall, covering its beauty. The rocks that are embedded into that foundation probably caused hurt at first, burrowing into the depth of it, or sinking in fast and hard—either way, that foundation had to move and shift to accept them. It had to give. And as you can see by that enormous boulder to your right, sometimes it had to give a lot."

He looked directly into Josh's eyes and laid his hand over his own heart. "The heart of the foundation has to be open enough, and secure enough, to allow that change to happen and to accept it even when it hurts or when it makes the appearance of the foundation not quite as attractive."

Josh's throat tightened.

"Son, I'm proud of you. It takes the strongest of men to endure what you have and to deal with what's ahead of you. It would have been a heck of a lot easier to back away. There are a million women in the world. You've always been empathetic, loving, and strong. Seeing you put your love for Riley ahead of everything else proves you're with the woman you were fated to be with." He took Josh in his arms and whispered in his ear, "Your darn mother made me say the whole woods thing. I would have just given it to you straight, but she thinks that a designer is all about presentation and layering."

"Dad," Josh managed. Man, how he loved him.

"And Treat told me about you feeling like you could rip someone apart. That's a good thing, son. Family knows no boundaries."

Chapter Forty-Seven

THE DIMLY LIT restaurant smelled of warmed olive oil and spices. A roaring fire burned in the fireplace across from where Riley and her family sat. Classical music filtered through the air. Riley felt at peace for the first time in days. She sipped a glass of wine and listened intently as her parents filled her in on the lives of neighbors and friends.

The waiter appeared by her side and placed a single red rose wrapped in pink paper across Riley's plate.

"Thank you." She looked at him. "Is this something you do for all the women?"

"No, ma'am." He walked away without an explanation.

Riley leaned forward with a laugh. "What was that all about?" she whispered.

Her parents shrugged.

She smelled the rose and unwrapped the paper. Inside was a handwritten note, and she recognized Josh's handwriting.

Hi, beautiful. Turn around. J.

Riley's breath caught in her throat as she spun around in her chair. Josh, dressed in a dark suit and holding a bouquet of white and red roses, stood before her.

"Josh?" she managed.

She pushed to her feet as Josh approached. She caught sight of each of Josh's siblings, and his father, standing behind him, their hands clasped in front of them.

He kissed her lightly on the lips.

"What are you doing here? What's going on?" She eyed his family, then shot a glance at her mother, whose eyes were suspiciously damp.

"Sorry it took me so long," Josh said, and handed her the bouquet of roses. "Red and white. For unity."

"Oh, Josh, they're beautiful, but you didn't have to." *You're here. You're actually here.* Riley could barely think past the sound of her heart beating way too fast.

"I'm done doing what I have to do, Ri. I'm doing what I want to do." He reached behind him, and Savannah picked up a bouquet of yellow roses from a nearby table and handed it to him.

Riley's eyes burned with tears.

"Yellow roses, the promise of a new beginning. Babe, I want to share my life with you. We'll get through all the garbage, and then we'll put it behind us." He handed her the flowers.

Riley's arms wouldn't move. A tear dripped down her cheek. Riley felt her knees weaken. She reached for the back of her chair. "I want that, too."

Her mother appeared beside her and took the bouquet from Josh, then set it on the table behind Riley.

Josh dropped to one knee. The tears Riley had been fighting slipped down her cheeks.

"Josh?" Unable to hold her trembling body erect any longer, Riley sank into the chair.

"Riley June Banks, I love you more than I've ever loved anyone in my life."

Ohmygoshohmygoshohmygosh. She couldn't take her eyes off of him. He was really there, before her, sticking by her. He was catching her. He looked at her like she was the only one in the room, like he wanted to wrap her in his arms and keep her safe forever—and, oh yes—she wanted that too, so much that her booming heart ached, but...

"But what about work? The allegations?" The words tumbled out before she could stop them.

"I'm not asking you to work for me," he explained.

You're firing me? On one knee? I thought...

"I want you to be my wife, my partner in every aspect of my life, including my business. You won't work for me. You'll work with me. Partners. No hiding in any aspect of our lives."

She couldn't breathe. Riley feared she might pass out. Could this really be happening? She gripped the sides of the chair. The hope in his eyes mirrored the hope in her racing heart. "You don't have to do this," she said.

"If you accept my proposal, it's done. I never want to hide again. Partners in love and life. Forever. That's what I want, and it's what I'm offering you. Side by side, you and me, out in the open."

Riley leaned forward and practically fell out of her chair. Josh caught her in his arms.

"Is that a yes, or were you trying to run away?" Josh teased.

"Yes," she said through her tears. "Yes. Oh, Josh. Yes!"

They rose to their feet and Josh kissed her like he'd been waiting for her his whole life. Riley came away trembling even more than she had been before.

Rex stepped forward and handed Josh a Tiffany's jewelry box.

"Here you go, little brother," Rex said.

Riley covered her mouth; her eyes flew open wide. "Josh," she whispered.

He opened the box and slipped the ring on her finger. "I wasn't sure what you liked, and we can have one designed eventually. It's a cushion-cut yellow diamond with, well, you can see, surrounded by white diamonds."

Riley had never seen anything so beautiful in all of her life.

"I love it, Josh, and I love you." Riley wrapped her arms around his neck and kissed him again. When they parted, his brothers were beside them, reaching out to them, embracing Josh, and her mother was crying as hard as Riley was.

Riley looked up, and in that second she saw Jade, her cheeks streaked with tears, too.

Jade mouthed, *I'm so happy for you*, which only made Riley's tears come faster.

Jade jumped into Riley's arms with a squeal. "You got engaged before I did!"

Riley was still in shock, moving on autopilot. "You knew?" she asked Jade.

"Of course I did, and it was painful not telling you."

Hal Braden extended his arms to Riley. "Looks like we've got two weddings to plan."

Plan? Riley could barely think past her next breath. She folded herself into his arms. "Thank you, Mr. Braden. I promise to make him happy."

"Oh honey, you can't *make* anyone happy. That's not how happiness works. Being part of his life will feed his happiness, and he'll feed yours. We're honored to have you as part of the family."

Riley watched Josh from across the room. Treat had his arm around his shoulder. Hugh and Dane said something that caused Josh to bend over in fits of laughter. His back was to Riley, and he must have felt her eyes on him, because he turned and instantly found her eyes and smiled.

Riley couldn't take her eyes off of him as he crossed the room toward her. She saw the gallant man he'd always been and couldn't believe he was going to be her husband. *Husband!* She blinked away tears of joy as he approached. His dark eyes washed over her body, lingering on her breasts, then lowering to her hips, and finally drawing back up to her eyes as he closed in on her.

He wrapped his hands on either side of her waist and whispered, his cheek against hers, his breath hot on her ear, "I cannot go another night without touching you."

A shiver ran up Riley's back. She scanned the immediate area, making sure no one was within earshot. Josh slid his hands down to the curve of her hips.

"You're wearing Gucci Première, just like our first night together," he said.

"You remembered," she whispered.

He pressed his hips in to hers and embraced her. "I'll always remember. I want to feel you close to me."

Riley felt his desire swell against her. "Josh," she whispered. "Kiss me."

He took her face between his warm palms in the way he had so many times before, the way that made her knees weak and her heart sing, and he kissed her, hesitant at first, she assumed because of their families in the room. Their tongues touched lightly; then, as if they were both too entranced to control their body's demands, more aggressively, their tongues colliding. Riley felt her body giving in to him. Her hands wandered down his legs. *Oops. Restaurant.* Riley's eyes flew open.

She pulled back. "Josh." His name came out in one long breath.

He looked around and she saw reality coming back to him, too. "Come with me." He took her hand, and they hurried past the groups of family members, who were too busy talking to notice as they escaped.

Josh pulled her toward the front of the restaurant. She giggled.

"Where are we going?" she asked.

"Shh." Josh looked around when they neared the entrance.

"No. Someone will see us," she protested.

Without a word, Josh lowered his mouth to hers and kissed her again, until she had no breath left to breathe and her legs threatened to dissolve beneath her. He guided her down a hall toward the bathrooms, stopping short at a closed door. Her eyes scanned the plaque, COATROOM. He opened the door, and in the space of a breath, they disappeared into the dark room.

"Josh." She reached for him in the dark. Her eyes tried to adjust, but there wasn't an ounce of light.

He brought her hands to his waist and cupped her cheeks again. *Oh, how I love that.* He was so tall, so muscular beneath her hands as they moved up his chest and then down his back.

"You deserve more than a coatroom quickie, but I have to love you, Riley. Now. Not later, not tomorrow, not when we get to New York. Now."

She stood on her tippy-toes and met his lips, sinking to her heels with the weight of him as he deepened the kiss. Dizziness reminded her that she needed to breathe. She stole air from his lungs, unwilling to part. *Please, please, kiss me forever.*

Chapter Forty-Eight

LATER THAT EVENING, when Josh's dad and Riley's parents had turned in for the night, the Braden living room was alive with conversation. Riley sat on the couch beneath the curve of Josh's arm, Jade's legs stretched across her lap. Jade's head rested in Rex's lap at the other end of the couch. He stroked her long dark hair. Hugh and Dane occupied the leather recliners, and Savannah sat on the floor, her back leaning against the bottom half of Hugh's chair. Treat and Max shared an oversized chair beside the warm fire. Dane's phone vibrated, which reminded Josh that he needed to check his own messages. He pushed the thought away, not wanting to break the closeness he was enjoying with Riley.

Josh had spent most of the evening watching Riley stare at her ring, then look at him with disbelief in her beautiful eyes. He pulled her tighter against him and whispered, "I love you."

"I love you, too, but you didn't have to do all of this," she said, looking up at him from beneath the fringe of her bangs.

"I know. I wanted to."

"I want every bit of this night to last forever," she said.

"Me too," Josh said.

Dane's phone vibrated again. He pulled it out, read the text, smiled, then typed a message into the phone.

"Did you ever listen to Reggie's message?" Treat asked.

There was still the chance that Reggie would have news about Riley that Josh wasn't prepared for. He pushed away the thought.

"I forgot," Josh said.

"Please, listen to the message. The sooner this is behind us, the better," Riley said. "I still can't believe you fired Claudia." She reached down and tickled Jade's feet.

"Cut it out," Jade said with a laugh.

Dane's phone buzzed again.

"I should have done it ages ago," Josh said.

Rex leaned down and kissed Jade's lips. "If you're going to put your feet there, then you have no say in the torture she imposes."

"Oh, really?" Jade poked Rex's ribs.

He bent over, and in one swift move, pulled her up onto his lap and began tickling her. Jade squealed.

"Get a room," Max said.

Dane's phone vibrated once again.

"Jeez, Dane, who are you talking to?" Savannah asked.

"Please check the message," Riley urged Josh again.

"Lacy," Dane answered.

"Ri, it can wait." *I want to enjoy this happiness for a while.*

"Please?" she urged again.

"Fine." He pulled out his phone and dialed voicemail, half listening to the others as the electronic voice answered.

"Lacy Snow? Really? This has gone on a long time," Treat said to Dane.

"Yeah, it sure has," Dane said. "Do you mind if she comes to your wedding?"

"Lacy? Really? Oh, Dane, I was going to invite her anyway. Of course she can come," Max said.

After listening to messages from Reggie and Peter, Josh left the room and returned Peter's call. Ten minutes later he reentered the room. Josh hung up the phone and spun Riley around to face him. "You, my dear, are brilliant. If I ever forget that, please slap me."

"What did I do?" she asked.

"Reggie said the portfolio you sent to Peter Stafford included the drawings that Claudia claimed as her own, and—and here's the kicker—he said Claudia's drawing of Max's wedding dress has a later date than when you sent the package to Peter. Peter's been in Switzerland. I got a message from him, too, but let me tell you what else Reggie found first. He looked at the building's security tapes—not JBD, but the actual building's tapes, the ones Claudia didn't realize existed—and he found footage of Claudia not only going through your desk and your trash, but your HR files, too, which means she had seen your portfolio before you even came on board. She was ready for this. She must have seen the quality of your drawings and felt threatened, or overlooked, or whatever." Josh punched the air with his fist. "I knew my girl would never do those things."

Riley rose to her feet. "I forgot about those drawings. I had included a few sketches of that dress, but they were so rough, and in my mind it wasn't really going to be Max's wedding dress. I drew them after lunch at your dad's a few weeks ago and put them in the portfolio because Peter had said he was interested in any new designs I was playing with. I didn't make the connection. Does this mean…?"

He pulled her to him. "It means Claudia's full of it."

"You called it, Josh," Treat said.

"I also had a message from Peter, and when I called him back, he apologized for being so far out of the loop since he'd been in Switzerland. He said he would have brought the portfolio to my attention earlier had he heard about the issues with Claudia, and more important, he wasn't upset with me about firing Claudia. Once I explained the games she'd been playing, he said I should have come to him a long time ago."

"That's great news," Riley said.

"There's more," Josh said. "Apparently, Peter's interested in backing a new line, a partnership of sorts, and after seeing Riley's portfolio, he wants her included in the process." Josh turned to Riley.

There was a collective cheer from all but Dane, who was typing on his phone.

"Dude." Treat tapped Dane on the shoulder.

"Yeah, what? Sorry." Dane stood. "Riley's in the clear?"

Savannah swiped the phone from his hand and ran across the room with it as she read his messages.

"Oh." She laughed. "Gosh, blush, blush."

Dane chased her. "Give me that, Savannah." His voice boomed across the room.

"Goodness, who knew you were so into Lacy? Those Snow sisters must be something else. Blake fell just as hard." She turned her back to Dane as he swooped in and retrieved the phone.

"How long have you been dating her?" Savannah asked Dane.

"We're not exactly dating," Dane answered.

"Don't tell me you're...sexting a girl you've never actually taken out," Savannah said with a *tsk*.

"I'm not sexting. Our schedules haven't come together yet,

but she's coming to Treat's wedding," Dane explained.

"Do you even know how to read a calendar? Are you telling me that she's going to wait for you for the next three months?" Savannah shook her head and flopped into the now vacant couch.

"I'd wait for Dane," Jade joked.

Rex pulled her close. "Oh no, you wouldn't."

"We talk all the time," Dane explained. "You know how crazy my schedule is."

"That's hogwash, Dane. Make her a priority or set her free," Treat said.

"What makes you such an expert? Lacy understands my schedule," Dane said.

"Then I need to have a talk with her," Treat said. "No woman deserves to be treated that way. It's been, what? A year? Inexcusable. Push a button or get off the elevator. Women are different. You may have other women filling your nights, but I'd put money on the fact that Lacy Snow isn't dating anyone else. I met her, Dane. She's not that kind of girl."

Dane let out a breath. "Look, I'm not trying to hurt her. I really like her. Maybe too much."

"You haven't even dated her yet," Savannah reminded him.

"I'm well aware of that fact," Dane said.

"Okay, listen, guys, this is supposed to be a happy time for us," Josh said. "Can we just break out the champagne and let Dane worry about his love life? I can't wait to meet her, and if it's at Treat and Max's wedding, then it is. Whatever. Let's just keep the good mojo rolling."

"You're right; sorry," Savannah said. "Dane, I'm really good at dating advice, and I'm here." She stretched her arms out to the sides.

Dane rolled his eyes. "Yeah, haven't you and Connor Dean been off and on again forever?"

Savannah looked away.

"Sorry, man," Dane said to Josh.

"No worries." Josh headed for the kitchen. "I'm breaking out the bubbly."

Dane followed him. "I'm really sorry for all that. Congratulations, Josh. I'm happy for you." Dane leaned against the refrigerator, watching Josh uncork the champagne. "Can I ask you something?"

"Of course."

"For years, we've had no idea if you're dating, much less who you're dating, and then, all of a sudden, you're getting married. How does that happen?" Dane asked.

Josh spun around, ready to defend his relationship with Riley.

"I don't mean that in a judgmental way. I guess I mean, how did you know?" Dane added.

Josh poured them each a glass of champagne. "One day nothing in your life makes sense except for the happiness you feel when you're with that other person. And you get the sense that this meaningful life is floating around your head, just waiting for you to grab hold. That's the best way I can explain it. There's no secret message written in the wind or any of that nonsense. It just…is." He shrugged.

"When that day comes, Dane, you'll have all sorts of craziness going on in your head. But, man…" He watched Riley walk into the kitchen, her long legs bare below her short red dress, her smile adding light to the expansive kitchen, and her eyes locked on his in a way that made Josh feel like he was the only thing that mattered.

He reached for her and kissed her forehead. Then he turned back to Dane. "When it happens, you'll thank your lucky stars that you were there to catch it."

Chapter Forty-Nine

AFTER SPENDING CHRISTMAS with their families, Josh and Riley had come back to New York to prepare for the annual JBD New Year's Eve party and to wrap up the loose ends regarding Claudia. Her attorney had been in touch with Josh's attorney, and Josh had agreed to drop the sexual harassment charges in exchange for a public statement from Claudia stating that all allegations against Riley were unfounded. In addition, he demanded that she personally apologize to Riley, which she reluctantly had done. Now, as Riley stood beside the bed in their apartment, watching Josh secure his cuff links in place, her stomach was doing acrobatics for a different reason. Josh was going to announce their engagement tonight at the JBD New Year's party. Riley had yet to see anyone other than Mia since returning to the city, and she had no idea how the others might react. Thankfully, Mia was genuinely happy for them.

"Nervous?" Josh asked as he slipped his arms into his tuxedo coat.

"Very," she admitted.

"Don't be." He crossed the room and touched her cheek with his palm.

Riley leaned in to the familiar caress.

"I'm not going anywhere. Not everyone is as cutthroat as you know who, and if anyone makes a remark about you sleeping your way to the top, you just smile and hold your head high," Josh said.

"That's easy for you to say," Riley said. She smoothed her long black gown along her waist.

"Babe, do I embarrass you?" Josh asked.

Riley spun around and ran her eyes down every inch of his six-foot-three frame, lingering over his arms, chest, and the naughty place at the juncture of his thighs. She drew her eyes back up to his freshly shaven cheeks and took a step closer. She placed her hands on his cheeks, her engagement ring sparkling in the light. She ran her hand through the side of his hair, loving the feel of him.

"Never," she said, then pulled him in to a deep kiss and pressed her body against his.

"We're not missing this," he said with a smile. "You can seduce me all you want, but we're going. We're doing this, Ri."

"Sheesh, how can you know me so well?" She slipped her feet into her heels, secured the diamond earrings Josh had given her for Christmas in place, and feigned annoyance. "Shall we go?"

Josh wrapped his arms around her from behind and nibbled her ear. "We can make time…before…if you want."

Riley playfully pushed him away. "You canned my strategy to dodge the party. Now you'll have to wait."

MIA MET THEM at the front door, wearing a form-fitting navy gown with a plunging neckline and long, arm-hugging sleeves. "Everyone's talking about you two; I just want to warn you." She hugged Riley. "You look gorgeous. I knew that would be the perfect dress. Josh, wow, you clean up real nice," she teased.

"Thanks, Mia," Josh said.

"I'm a wreck. Are they saying horrible things about me?" Riley was so nervous she thought she might be sick. She clung to Josh's hand with a vice grip.

"They'd better not," Josh said.

She felt his arm tense.

"No, no," Mia said. "All anyone knows is that you two are dating, so they're still in the have-you-heard-the-news stage of gossiping and trying to figure out what they missed over the holiday."

Riley let out a long breath. "Okay, I guess we need to get this over with."

Josh put his arm around her. "I'm right here. Besides, Savannah's coming, so you'll have even more support."

"She is?" Riley asked.

"Yeah. She's all bark, you know. She loves you," Josh said.

They headed into the ballroom, which was alive with festive music and the employees mingling among themselves.

All eyes turned toward them when they entered the room. Riley tried to swallow past the lump that was pressing on her windpipe. She clung to Josh's hand and felt a hand slip around her waist.

"You are gorgeous," Savannah whispered in her ear.

"I'm so glad you're here," Riley said, remembering Savannah's semithreat. "Savannah, I'm not going to hurt Josh," she said.

"I know. But if you ever are tempted to, you'll hear my

voice in your ear," Savannah said with a wide smile.

Josh and Riley made their way around the room hand in hand. Simone and K.T. were drinking champagne together when they approached. Riley felt the heat of Simone's stare, wishing Mia were there to play interference. She and Simone had gotten close before the holiday, but Simone had an edge, and by the look in Simone's eyes, Riley was on the wrong side of it at the moment.

"Simone, K.T., I hope you're having a nice evening," Josh said.

"Oh yes, Mr. B.," K.T. said. "Riley, you look smashing. No Juicy for you tonight, huh? JBD all the way."

Riley bristled. *Is he making fun of me?* She looked down at her JBD gown, then forced herself to smile. "Thanks, K.T., you look great, too," she said. "I love your dress, Simone."

"Thanks," Simone said.

Her answer came with a wave of icy wind. *Here it goes.* "I know I should have told you and Mia, but I didn't know how to handle it. I'm sorry," Riley said.

Simone worked her jaw from side to side. She looked into her glass and shrugged.

"Simone," Josh said.

"It's okay," Riley said. "I would be upset, too. Simone, I'm not a conniving, devious woman. I love Josh and I've loved him since we were kids. I just tried to ignore it and pushed it all away. I know you and I were getting close, and I should have trusted you and told you, but I was so scared. I didn't want to be known as the girl who slept her way to the top, and it was—" She looked away as tears filled her eyes.

"Babe, you don't have to do this," Josh said. He cast a stern look at Simone.

"Yes, I do," Riley whispered. "I'm fine."

Savannah sidled between Riley and Simone in her long green dress and tossed her fiery hair over her shoulder. "Simone? Hi, I'm Savannah, Josh's sister. I don't think we've met."

"Hi." Simone eyed Savannah.

"This whole stink-eye thing that's going on? That's not going to continue," Savannah said. "It wasn't easy for Josh and Riley to make the decision to keep their relationship private, but they had to because of scrutiny just like you're showing right now."

Josh stepped in between the two women. "Savannah, that's enough."

"No, Josh, it's not. That look she gave Riley is exactly why Riley was afraid to let people know about you two," Savannah said. "Riley's going to be my sister-in-law, and if you think I'll sit back and let anyone hurt her, you're dead wrong."

"I'm sorry," Simone said. "I'm not upset about you two seeing each other. I'm only upset because I thought Riley and I were getting close, and friends share things like this." Simone crossed her slim arms over her chest.

Great. Now I've lost a friend, too.

"Simone, honey," K.T. said. "Calm down."

"No, this is garbage," Simone said. Every muscle in her lean legs was taut and clearly visible beneath her short black dress. She motioned toward the other staff members as she spoke. "Yeah, Riley, everyone thinks you've slept your way to the top, so what?"

"Simone, that's enough," Josh demanded.

Riley took a step backward as the room went silent, save for Simone's rant.

"So what?" Simone continued. "You're happy. Mr. B.'s

happy. Who cares what anyone thinks? What I care about are friendships." Simone looked from Riley to Josh, the sharp ends of her hair whipping against her cheek.

"I said that's enough, Simone," Josh said. He took a step forward.

"Simone!" Mia ran to her side. "What are you doing?"

"Talking to Riley," Simone snapped. Her black eyeglass frames slid down her nose. She pushed them up with her index finger and lifted her chin.

"Sometimes I wish you had an electric collar so I could zap you when you went off the deep end." Mia dragged her a few feet away and said to Josh and Riley, "I'm sorry. You know how she can get when her feelings are hurt."

"It's okay. Simone, get ahold of yourself," Josh said.

Riley pulled her hand free from Josh's and went to Simone. "I'm a really good friend. I am. You may not believe it, but you could ask Jade, my best friend…if she were here…which she's not." *Yikes, where was I going with this?* "I didn't mean to hurt you. I'm not very thick-skinned. What my coworkers think *is* a big deal to me, and I wanted nothing more than to spill my guts to you and Mia, but I was so freaking scared. Even now, standing in the middle of this room with everyone looking at me, it's my worst nightmare. So let me just say this, to every-one…" She turned and faced the other employees.

"Riley." Josh reached for her.

She twisted away and raised her voice. "I'm sorry, okay?" she said to the others. "I fell in love with Josh and we kept it a secret, but it wasn't meant to hurt anyone, and I didn't sleep with him because he's my boss." She looked at Josh and lowered her voice as she took his hand. "I've known Josh all my life, and I spent years trying to push away the feelings I had for him and feeling like he was too good for me, and you know what? *That's* what's bull. Josh is the kindest, most generous person I know, and I'm proud to be with him. I'm not going to hide anymore, or feel bad because any of y'all think I did something wrong." *Oh no, y'all.* She turned back to Simone. "And I'll never hurt my friends if I can help it. I'm sorry, Simone."

"Okay, well, nothing like a grand entrance," Josh said.

A muffled laugh rose from the group.

Josh addressed them. "Look, this is pretty simple. We're in love. We're getting married, and JBD is going to be JRBD very soon. I value each of you, and I have a speech ready that outlines exactly what I value about each one of you, but none of that matters at this juncture." He went to Riley's side and took her hands in his.

Riley tried to steady her trembling limbs.

Josh let go of one of her hands and turned back to the staff. "The bottom line is that whether it's JBD or JRBD, we're the same designing family we were before. We just have one more family member, and an important one. Y'all know I'm not one for ultimatums, but tonight I'm making one, so please listen carefully. Riley is going to be my wife, which means she's more important to me than anything else. If you cannot see yourself working in our offices with Riley and me as equal partners in the business, or if you feel that you'll cast sneers in her direction, or you cannot refrain from gossiping about her, or us, then please take this time to walk out those doors forever, because I will not tolerate snide looks, nasty comments, or any type of innuendos."

"Y'all?" Riley whispered.

"Sometimes I slip," he said with a wink.

"Sorry I gave you the stink eye," Simone said to Riley.

"Sorry I didn't tell you about me and Josh." Riley embraced Simone.

HUSHED WHISPERS ROSE from the crowd. Savannah and Mia appeared by Josh's side.

"That's what you should have done ages ago," Savannah said.

"I'm just learning about this relationship stuff," Josh admitted.

"Mr. B., look." Mia turned toward Riley, who was now surrounded by the other staff members. "I think things are going to be okay," Mia said.

Josh let out a breath as he watched his fiancée with the employees he trusted, and he realized that the protective instincts he'd felt for Riley were never going to change. Riley looked over, catching him watching her.

Riley came to his side and touched his hand as she said, "Thanks for standing up for me. I hope I didn't embarrass you too much."

"Nothing you do could ever embarrass me." He pulled her against him and said, "I'm just going to have to get used to the Incredible Hulk rearing his powerful head and taking my body over every once in a while."

"Mm. Incredible Hulk? Powerful head? Now, *that's* something we should explore."

"Get a room," Savannah teased.

"You know, that's not a bad idea." Josh kissed Riley, and then he said, "Mia, can you handle the rest of this?"

"I've got this," Mia reassured him.

"You have to make your speech," Riley reminded him as he pulled her toward the door.

"I think I just did. Come on. Let's go find some his-and-her edible underwear."

Ready for more Bradens?

Fall in love with Dane and Lacy in *The Art of Loving Lacy*

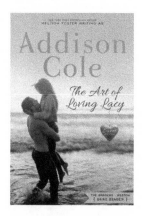

Chapter One

LACY SNOW SAT between Kaylie Crew and Danica Carter, literally surrounded by her half sisters. In the year and a half since she'd met them, they'd become her closest friends, her coconspirators, and the women she most looked up to. She'd known they existed her whole life, but as the child of their father's mistress of more than twenty years, she couldn't exactly knock on their front door and introduce herself.

Kaylie reached for her hand and squeezed, flashing a sisterly smile. She and Lacy shared the same robin's-egg-blue eyes and buttery blond hair, though Kaylie's was shiny with a natural wave and Lacy's was a mass of spiral curls, like Danica's, save for the color. Danica took after their father with dark hair and olive skin.

"This place is gorgeous," Kaylie said.

"It was built in a similar fashion to the original Chequesset Inn, which perished during an ice storm in the 1930s," Lacy said.

Max and Treat had fallen in love in Wellfleet, Massachusetts, and it was only fitting that they wed at the Wellfleet Inn. The two-story inn overlooked the bay. Treat owned resorts all over the world, so it came as no surprise when he purchased the inn and added it to his collection.

"You're such a *fact* girl," Kaylie whispered, looking at the altar. "Excited?"

Nervous, Lacy mouthed. She'd waited more than a year to see Dane Braden, Treat's younger brother, in-person again. More than a year of sharing emails, texts, intimate phone calls, sexy video chats, and too many unfulfilled fantasies to count. Months of working twelve-hour days seven days a week, vying for a promotion at her job, and long nights spent dreaming of Dane. She reached for Danica's hand and—deep in conversation with her husband, Blake—Danica took Lacy's hand like it was the most natural thing in the world. She'd met Danica and Kaylie just before their double wedding, in a Nassau resort owned by Treat Braden, the six-foot-six, darkly handsome man now standing at the altar, gazing into their friend Max Armstrong's eyes. Max's dark hair fell in gentle waves over the spaghetti straps and soft lines of the beachy wedding gown that Riley Banks, Treat's brother Josh's fiancée, designed for her. Weddings had a way of making the beautiful even more glamorous. Max and Treat were a striking couple, and they should have held Lacy's attention as Treat held Max's hand and looked lovingly into her eyes, promising her a lifetime of adoration, but Lacy's gaze shifted to his right. To the line of Treat's four striking brothers, proudly standing as his grooms-men, each one more handsome than the next. Each brother's dark eyes were trained on their eldest brother as he vowed to love, honor, and cherish his soon-to-be wife—each one except Dane. Dane's smoldering dark eyes stared hungrily at Lacy, sending a shock of heat right through her. *Oh gosh! He's so sexy.* Lacy couldn't blink. She couldn't look away. She couldn't even breathe.

"Careful," Kaylie whispered, "you'll drool on that pretty dress of yours."

Lacy felt her face flush, but she still couldn't tear her gaze away. Each of the Braden brothers had thick dark hair, and while Treat and Josh wore their hair short and Rex wore his cowboy-long, covering his collar, Dane's hair fell somewhere in between, as if he'd missed his last trim; it brushed the tops of his ears, with sides that looked like he'd just run his hands through them. *No.* Lacy narrowed her eyes. *That's not it at all.* As she watched Dane's lips lift into a smile, she bit her lower lip and thought, *He looks like he could have just come from the bedroom—or, like he's ready for it.*

He winked, and Lacy caught her breath.

"Behave," Kaylie warned.

"Oh my," Lacy whispered, drawing her eyes to her lap. "He's so…"

"Sexy? Gorgeous? Hot?" Kaylie offered, arching a brow.

"Shh." Danica shot a harsh stare at them.

Lacy and Kaylie drew their blond heads together with a silent giggle. Danica shook her head, and though Lacy couldn't see her face, she knew that her eldest sister was rolling her eyes at them with her lips pinched in a tight line.

"Ladies and gentlemen, I give you, Mr. and Mrs. Treat Braden."

The announcement sent a shiver of nervous energy through her stomach. Everyone stood as Max and Treat walked down the aisle hand in hand. Max's smile lit up her eyes, and Treat walked with his shoulders back, his eyes on Max, beaming with pride. Kaylie's blond hair tumbled down her back as she reached her sinewy arms around her husband Chaz's neck and kissed him. Lacy watched Danica smile lovingly at Blake; then he took her chin in his hand and kissed her. Lacy turned away, thinking about Dane.

As Treat and Max approached, Lacy and her sisters tossed rose petals.

"Congratulations!" Lacy shouted, but her eyes had already left Treat and Max and had settled on Dane once again. She hadn't remembered how broad his chest was, and the wanton look in his eyes hadn't seemed quite as strong over Skype and FaceTime. Her pulse ratcheted up a notch.

"You're so beautiful!" Danica said to Max.

The groomsmen made their way down the aisle next, and Kaylie squeezed Lacy's hand so hard that Lacy winced.

"There he is," Kaylie said.

"Stop," Lacy said under her breath. "I'm nervous enough."

Dane walked toward her, his perfect pearly white teeth visible through his wide smile. His broad shoulders swayed slightly, and those dark eyes of his never wavered from hers. Her legs turned to Jell-O, and she gripped the back of the chair for stability. The man in the aisle in front of hers reached for Dane.

"Hey, buddy. I haven't seen you in months. Good to see

you," the older man said.

Dane embraced the tall, thin man, his eyes still pinning Lacy in place. "You, too, Smitty. We'll catch up at the reception." Dane took a step closer to Lacy's row. He embraced his cousin. "Blake, great to see you." Then he pulled Danica into a soft hug and kissed her cheek. "You look as gorgeous as ever," he said. He reached for Kaylie next.

Lacy's heart slammed against her chest as Blake and Danica moved into the aisle, following the rest of the guests into the reception room. She had forgotten how tall he felt when he was near, and as she watched him wrap his arms around Kaylie, she realized that she'd also forgotten how large his hands were. *Big hands, big—Stop it!*

"We need to call our sitter before the reception. Good to see you," Kaylie said. She gave Dane a quick hug and pulled Chaz behind her, leaving Lacy alone with Dane.

IT HAD BEEN four hundred and fifty-seven days since Dane had seen Lacy in person. *Too long.* He reached for her hands and then drew her close, placing one soft kiss on each cheek and inhaling the sweet smell that he remembered: a combination of citrus and floral with an underlying hint of musk. To anyone else, it was Chanel Coco Noir. To Dane, it was the smell of Lacy that he remembered from the day they'd met, and their only afternoon together, the day before her sisters' double wedding in Nassau. The smell he'd dreamed of, which had carried him through those long afternoons out at sea when they were tagging sharks miles from shore.

"Lacy."

Her slim fingers trembled against his palms. A shy smile lifted her supple lips and sent Dane's pulse into overdrive.

"Hi," she said softly.

Her blond curls fell in thick spiral ropes across her tanned, lean shoulders. She wore a royal-blue halter dress that fell to the middle of her thighs, revealing her long, toned legs. It just barely covered the edge of the scar Dane knew held the worst of her fears. Dane lowered his lips to one of her slender hands and pressed a soft kiss to it. All those months of emails, phone calls, and video chats came rushing back. They had never been enough, but his demanding travel schedule as founder of the Brave Foundation made it almost impossible to steal away for a weekend, and Lacy was working day and night in hopes of obtaining a promotion, so even if he had found the time, she probably wouldn't have been able to break away. Brave's mission was to use education and innovative advocacy programs to protect sharks, and in a broader sense, the world's oceans. Dane's passion for saving and educating had begun right after college and had only grown since. He'd created a life around doing what he loved, and now he lived on a boat on the coast of Florida, where Brave's headquarters were located. He had a small administrative staff and was well connected enough to have temporary staff and volunteers in the areas where he worked. When he wasn't in the water, he could be found running the foundation, which required heavy travel, a busy social calendar, and a boatload of butt-kissing. Unfortunately, over those months, his and Lacy's schedules hadn't come together.

"Are you going to introduce me, or just block the aisle?" Dane's younger brother Rex pushed in between them.

Dane shook his head to clear his thoughts. Rex was a year

and a half younger than him and had worked their family ranch for years, which was apparent in his brawny cowboy build. Dane turned to face his brother with a joking sneer.

"Isn't Jade around here somewhere?" Dane asked.

A year earlier, Rex had fallen in love with Jade Johnson, and their love had brought a long-standing family feud to a head—and then to a long-overdue end. Dane had never seen his brother so happy. Rex and Jade had bought the property in between the two families' ranches in Weston, Colorado, and had recently built a house there.

As he stared into Rex's dark eyes, he had a momentary flash of unease. His height matched Rex's six-foot-three inches, but his brother's arms were as thick as tree trunks, and the way his tux stretched tightly over his massive chest would turn on any woman. He knew his brother's ever-present five-o'clock shadow and longish hair gave him a bad-boy quality that had sent even the strongest women into a state of rapture. But Dane also knew that there was no need for a silent warning, or even a hint of possessiveness where Lacy was concerned. Rex had eyes only for Jade, and he was all too aware that Lacy wasn't his to possess.

"Step aside." Rex pushed his massive forearm across Dane's chest and held out a hand to Lacy. "I'm Rex, Dane's brother. You must be Lacy."

Lacy blushed. "Yes, hi," she said. Her eyes darted to Dane, and the surprise in them was blatant. "He's mentioned me?"

Rex laughed. "Oh, he might have mentioned you once or twice." He cracked a crooked smile at Dane. "Pleasure to meet you, Lacy. No wonder Dane was so distracted during the ceremony. Well"—he let out a dramatic sigh—"you two kids have fun. If you'll excuse me, I need to find my girlfriend."

"Bastard," Dane whispered as Rex passed with a sly grin and

gave Dane a playful shove. The room emptied quickly as the guests moved toward the reception hall. Dane turned his attention back to Lacy.

"I'm glad you're here."

"Me too." Lacy smiled. "Your brother seems nice."

"Yeah, he is," Dane said. The image of Lacy wearing the tiny bikini she'd worn in Nassau came rushing back to him. He swallowed hard to repress the memory before it could excite him the way it had over recent nights, when he knew he'd be seeing her again.

"Save me a dance?" The anticipation of seeing Lacy had been mounting for weeks, but he hadn't expected his nerves to be strewn so tight, or the desire to kiss her to be so strong. He stood so close to her that all it would take was the slightest dip of his head to settle his lips over hers, to tangle his hands in her hair and pull her against him.

"Sure," she answered, and he'd almost forgotten that he'd asked her a question.

"Dane."

His father's deep voice pulled him from his thoughts.

Hal Braden took a couple steps toward them. He stood a few inches taller than Dane. His skin was a deep bronze, rivaling Dane's rich tan. Fine lines snaked out from his father's eyes and mouth, and a deep vee hunkered between his thick brows. "Excuse me. I'm sorry for interrupting." He held his hand out to Lacy. "Hal Braden, Dane's father."

Lacy shook his hand. "I'm Lacy."

"Dad, this is Lacy Snow." Dane watched his father's dark eyes change from serious to warm.

"Lacy Snow. Related to Blake's wife, Danica?" he asked.

"Yes, I'm her half...her youngest sister." She flushed again.

Dane had an urge to put his arm around her and comfort the nerves he heard in her voice.

Hal nodded. "Well, any sister of Danica's is a friend of ours. It's a pleasure to meet you. They're taking pictures, Dane. Don't be too long."

"I'll be right in, Dad," Dane said. He watched his father walk away and felt pride swell in his heart. He'd always had a good relationship with his father, and now, in his midthirties, he found himself seeing his father in a different way. Dane's mother had passed away when he was only nine years old, and his father had raised him, his four brothers, and their sister. And to this day, when he spoke of their mother, the love he exuded hadn't dimmed. Dane hadn't thought of marriage very often, but lately he wondered—no, he hoped—that one day he'd find whatever it was that his parents had found together. He wanted to experience that love.

"You'd better go in," Lacy said. She blinked her long lashes several times and fidgeted with her hands.

She's so cute when she's nervous. Dane wondered if she could tell that he was just as nervous as she was. The last thing he wanted to do was leave her side, but the sooner he got those pictures over with, the sooner he could be with her again. "Yeah. I'd better. Remember our dance, okay?"

"I look forward to it."

To continue reading, please buy
THE ART OF LOVING LACY

More Books By Addison Cole

Sweet with Heat Big-Family Romance Collection

Sweet with Heat: Weston Bradens

A Love So Sweet
Our Sweet Destiny
Unraveling the Truth About Love
The Art of Loving Lacy
Promise of a New Beginning
And Then There Was Us

Sweet with Heat: Seaside Summers

Read, Write, Love at Seaside
Dreaming at Seaside
Hearts at Seaside
Sunsets at Seaside
Secrets at Seaside
Nights at Seaside
Embraced at Seaside
Seized by Love at Seaside
Lovers at Seaside
Whispers at Seaside

Sweet with Heat: Bayside Summers
(Includes future publications)

Sweet Love at Bayside
Sweet Passions at Bayside
Sweet Heat at Bayside
Sweet Escape at Bayside

Stand Alone Women's Fiction Novels
by Melissa Foster (Addison Cole's steamy alter ego)

Chasing Amanda (mystery/suspense)
Come Back to Me (mystery/suspense)
Have No Shame (historical fiction/romance)
Megan's Way (literary fiction)
Traces of Kara (psychological thriller)
Where Petals Fall (suspense)

Acknowledgments

As always, there are communities of people whom I'd like to thank for helping me during my writing journey. A huge thank-you to my readers, who have emailed and sent me messages on social media sites, asking me to write faster and to bring you the Braden siblings' stories faster. You inspire me on a daily basis, and I appreciate each and every one of you. Please keep the letters coming. I do write faster when I know you're waiting.

I must extend an extra virtual hug to Bonnie Trachtenberg and Kristen Weber, who fielded all of my questions regarding New York and the surrounding area. You have the patience of saints, and I appreciate your time and energy.

A hearty thank-you to the community of bloggers, readers, authors, and friends who support me and cheer me on through social media and email. Thank you for believing in me. Gratitude and hugs to my girlfriends Kathie, Stacy, Amy, Tasha, Marlene, Juliette, and, of course, my mother. Thank you for being there in good times and bad.

My characters would be peaking when they should be peeking and doing other things that would make no sense at all if it weren't for my editorial team. These women deserve buckets of chocolate: Kristen Weber, Penina Lopez, Lynn Mullan, Juliette Hill, Elaini Caruso, Marlene Engel, and Justinn Harrison.

To Les and my youngest boys, thanks for being my biggest fans and most patient supporters. I love you.

www.AddisonCole.com

Addison Cole is the sweet-romance pen name of *New York Times* and *USA Today* bestselling and award-winning author Melissa Foster. She enjoys writing humorous, and deeply emotional, contemporary romance without explicit sex scenes or harsh language. Addison spends her summers on Cape Cod, where she dreams up wonderful love stories in her house overlooking Cape Cod Bay.

Visit Addison on her website or chat with her on social media. Addison enjoys discussing her books with book clubs and reader groups and welcomes an invitation to your event.

Addison's books are available in paperback, digital, and audio formats.

CPSIA information can be obtained
at www.ICGtesting.com
Printed in the USA
LVHW010040260619
622381LV00001BA/145